THE POLITICOS

THE POLITICOS

KEN CHAMPION

First published May 2019

ISBN 978-1-913144-05-0

PENNILESS PRESS PUBLICATIONS
Website :www.pennilesspress.co.uk/books

Also by the same author:

Fiction

Urban Narratives
The Dramaturgical Metaphor
The Beat Years
Keefie
Noir
Thrust

Poetry

Of Course, The Yellow Cab
But Black & White is better
Cameo Metro
Cameo Poly
African Time

Urban Narratives

'I thank him for gracing us with his literature. His realism is enriched
with imagination, the most real of all qualities.'

Meredith Sue Willis, Hamilton Stone Review, USA

The Dramaturgical Metaphor

'An existential thriller which sees psychoanalyst James Kent embark on
a disturbing European journey, capturing a sense of time and place that
transport us to his host locations whilst also slightly dislocating our
commonsensical assumptions. Think Jean Paul Sartre reimagining
Alastair Maclean.'

Chris Connelley, Hastings Independent

The Beat Years

'I found some beautiful writing here.'

Susie Reynolds, Chimera

Keefie

'This is a splendid novel of the London Blitz that captures life mostly through the eyes of a bright and creative working class boy whose knowledge of what is happening is limited, but whose experience leads us deep into a time and place – and the lives of ordinary people – with more power than any history book can convey.'

Meredith Sue Willis, Books For Readers, USA

'I really enjoyed Ken Champion's latest novel and am still thinking about its characters. It is an absorbing read. This is a writer who pays intense attention to the extraordinary details of ordinary life.'
Joanna Ezekiel

Noir

'This is probably Ken Champion's best novel to date, a book of great depth, tightly written and with a surprise - and so much life - on almost every page. It's an unusual, gripping book.'

Meredith Sue Willis, Books For Readers, USA

'These are vast, topical themes, edging Champion closer to explicitly political discussion than in any of his previous work, ensuring NOIR enjoys deep currency in a year that has seen alienation and anger on the part of disconnected publics generate upset on both the domestic and international stage.'
Chris Connelley, Hastings Independent

Thrust

'This is Champion's best novel to date. It carries acute observations of people struggling to find ways of urban living where forces, at times beyond their control, bend and strain their lives.'
Phil Ruthen, Waterloo Press

'In this expansive novel, at times angry, funny, touching and tender, the author confidently strides the world's stage posing huge questions that need to be answered. It is a compelling read.'
Chris Connelley, Hastings Independent

CHAPTER ONE

He could almost hear the kids in his long-ago street with their jibes of 'Them big words won't getcha nowhere, Kearnsy.' and the 'Wot, swallowed a bleedin' dictionary?' The latter also often uttered` by his father.

Sitting in a London café sipping a latte only marginally hotter than the sun-cooked pavement outside, he recalled his first philosophy lecture at a university he'd attended as a mature student some years previously. He'd heard the original quote before, something like 'There are more things in Heaven and earth, Horatio, than are dreamt of in *your* philosophy.'

He'd not known who'd said it or its motivation, but the twist put on it, delivered with a smile and an arched eyebrow by the lecturer, of 'There are more things in philosophy than are dreamt of in *your* Heaven and earth.' began an almost love affair with the subject.

A philosophical and political awareness had, a little vaguely, been growing from his teens; his father, a victim of the very system he seemed to embrace, once telling him that he didn't want a communist in his house; the house in question being rented and neither of them really knowing what a communist was. Entering his late twenties, naively unaware that although presently having few qualifications he could obtain some and actually get to university, and hearing the comment delivered rather affectedly there on his first day, seemed to light some sort of vapour long lying fallow in his intellect.

Aristotle, Plato and the like, he decided, weren't for him, nor moral philosophy - as morals were largely culturally determined and thus variable, what could count as evidence of some sort of absolute morality? And an 'is' couldn't be derived from an 'ought,' anyway.

The cafe was a change from his local greasy spoon, though its owner, from Stepney was, like himself, also familiar with the cockney argot of 'airship on a cloud' and 'babies on a raft' for sausage and mash and beans on toast.

He continued his remembering. At the time, he'd never heard of positivism but knew that he wished to know what was *in* the world - seeing himself with determined lips and deep frown when thinking it. He knew it begged the question of what was meant by 'to know' and what it was that was doing the knowing. He learnt also of the ultimate tautology: What is in the world is determined by how we *know* what is in the world, and how we know what is in the world is determined by what is *in* the world. He couldn't quite remember what this one was called.

And then there was the idea that we all have our own reality based on previous experience and see the world through its filter, thus strongly implying that there's no absolute one - an absolute denying an absolute. Perhaps philosophy, he briefly thought, would eventually disappear up its own arse, but reality *had* to be based on the senses. What else? And god, of course, like any suprahuman deity, could only be inferred.

Looking around him he saw obese women living in solipsistic bubbles loading dipped fries into their mouths and licking their fingers though surrounded by chrome boxes of napkins. He was probably on the side of Raymond Blanc who thought the English hated food and 'lived in a very dark country where they go into revolting cafés and eat something disgusting to endorse their working class status.' He'd blamed it on Empire. Ralph Kearns preferred the idea that cafes were offering succour, a gulping at the nipple.

He'd just finished wandering around an arts fair not far from his childhood streets with toys, china, a few clothes and other bric-a-brac - though rarely books - outside front gates or front doors with invariably a price on the tat. This was a characteristic shared with the upper class, who, in his limited experience of this stratum, rarely gave stuff away for free, often claiming the need to flog stuff to offset the relative poverty caused by the maintenance costs of their creaking old properties and the crippling effects of school fees.

He doubted whether he could afford to live in these turnings - he could hear himself automatically use the old East End word for street - where, since almost his earliest memories, he'd wanted to escape from.

He tried not to think about privilege. People who began life with it had no other salient frame of reference, their insularity, their taken-for-granted *weltanschauung* just... there; the way the world was and, for them, should be. Not so for the people he had grown up amongst.

'Money don't bring yer 'appiness.' 'It's not where yer live, but 'ow yer live.' 'As long as you've got yer 'ealf.' and other long-ago and regularly heard solace-giving aphorisms came to mind.

Before looking around he'd been to his local clinic, a place where even at half-past seven on a winter's morning were queues of twenty or more people waiting for its dead-on-time eight o'clock opening. He'd often felt as if he was being left to drown in the entrails of an undernourished NHS or in a refugee camp run by *Medecins San Frontieres*.

Afterwards, in a nearby chemist to pick up a prescription, he'd seen Mike Green who he hadn't seen since canvassing for him as the local Labour MP some years before but, with a face whose eyes and thin-lipped mouth were almost lost in fleshy jowls wider than his forehead, was instantly recognisable.

'Getting something to recover from an all-night sitting?' Ralph asked lightly.

The man frowned. 'Do I know you?'

'No, but I did some canvassing for you when you first stood about a hundred years ago.'

He laughed. 'It actually feels like that sometimes. Look, I have to go, but, er, thanks for the canvassing.'

He did a quick victory sign and left.

Ralph hadn't heard much about him, he was still a stalwart backbencher who said little in the House and was, seemingly, assured of a safe seat for ever. When Ralph had first heard of him he'd called himself a 'communications operative.' He'd been a postman.

It reminded him of another political aspirant he had attempted to help; a man recently standing in the north of the borough. He was a little younger than Ralph, keen and enthusiastically articulate; but, especially when crowing about his party's ambition to abolish inequality and create a meritocracy, seemingly lacking an awareness of the deterministic strength of the economic system he lived in. To counter this, Ralph had invited him to come to an evening class he was teaching at a local college for part-time degree students.

The timing had been appropriate, he had just begun the sociology of education and would liked to have impressed upon him - no, drilled into him and all politicians - that as capitalism *means* a systematic economic and social inequality, a meritocracy was impossible.

Inequality, he wanted to tell him, is determined by values and as dominant values are maintained and reinforced by powerful social groups and that, as groups, we were differentially exposed to dominant values, then the value-clash between the cultural characteristics of the working classes and formal education *must* mean that we cannot have equal educational opportunities. The would-be Member had been too busy with his own door-to-door selling to attend.

Finishing his coffee he switched off from his internal lecturing mode and, thinking of his new job, went home to prepare for a seminar the next day.

His previous employment, commencing several years after finishing his degree when he had begun lecturing at various colleges in and around east London, was in Havering, Essex, where he had a one year full-time contract which included a Friday evening class for mature students. Most of the people sitting in the classroom - he saw it proprietarily as his - were indigenous working class pupils and recently arrived Africans and East Europeans all wanting to get into Higher Education.

Towards the end of the first term he was finishing the subject's founding theories when a student at the back raised her hand, self-consciously lowering it as he looked at her.

She hesitated before asking why he disliked theories like Functionalism so much. Was it because he was a Marxist?

'I'm partly against it because it has no predictive power, and its organic analogy, that institutions are like the major organs of the human body all working for the good of the whole, is patently untrue. Do you object to Marxism then, er… '

'Doreen.'

It was probably only the third time he'd spoken to her in class. She was rather mournful looking, sad, tall, with a model's shoulders and something quietly deliberate about her.

'My guardian is a Marxist,' she said more firmly, though still looking a little awkward and shy.

There was a slight pause in the class and he continued in his often proselytising manner.

When they'd finished he briefly answered someone's question about an essay he had set then left the room. Doreen was in the corridor just in front of him, awkwardly putting on her coat. On impulse he pulled the collar up at the back for her. She smiled a little shyly and said thanks. He guessed she was about thirty five, A little younger than him.

'It's going pretty well isn't it,' she said

'The evening class?'

'Yes.'

'Do you come far?'

'About eight miles or so. I live just down the road really, but I'm staying with a friend tonight.'

They walked in silence through the main doors.

'I tell him what you're teaching. He's suspicious.'

'What of?'

'Well, being a Marxist, he - '

'Your guardian?' He smiled at her. They began walking through the car park.

'Yes. He'll be happy about your demolition job on post modernism, though.'

It was her quiet, friendly awkwardness - and her wide smile with those slightly protruding front teeth - that tipped the words out.

'Maybe I could meet him sometime.'

He was now walking through the car park with her.

'Maybe,' she said, and as she got into her car added, 'Oh, did you know that Annie, the dark-haired lady who sits next to me, is a niece of Gramsci?'

She smiled, got into her car and drove out of the college grounds.

He'd mentioned the uncle in class, but nothing more than the name, aware of how little historical knowledge he had of Italian political activists.

She didn't turn up the next week, but the week after as they reached her car at the far end of the car park he asked her if she fancied a drink one evening.

'Yes,' she said simply, as if she'd been expecting him to ask.

They met in a pub near the college the next evening. She was little different from her student role as if the ability to express herself was dulled by a reluctantly enforced stoicism. She told him she had a ten -year-old son whose father had left them both years ago.

They then talked generally, her saying that the class had gelled well, had a good camaraderie and that she was enjoying the subject, but wouldn't tell him why she had become someone's ward, though she did inform him that it had occurred when she was sixteen and that Frank, her guardian, was now in his eighties. Ralph calculated that he was about sixty-something when he entered her life. He was a 'well known communist' she said with seeming indifference but a quiet pride.

'His elder brother left Oxford half way through his degree to join a merchant ship that was gun-running for the Republicans in the Spanish Civil War. He was eventually torpedoed. Frank really loved him.'

This, again, was uttered with a matter-of-fact casualness as if, somehow, everything that she'd experienced had happened *to* her, unavoidable, outside of her own volition, and that she looked out at a world she expected would treat her dispassionately and a little unkindly.

A month later they slept together at her flat on the top floor of a converted ex-council house near the college. For a month or so they went to cinemas, to alternative comedy venues - mostly small rooms above pubs - the occasional restaurant, a play, and then, after the last evening class of term, she suggested they pay a quick visit to the farmhouse.

'Just to meet Frank, we won't stay.'

He sat silently next to her while she drove, a little unsure of how he should feel, as if he was about to meet the father of his 'intended,' about to ask his permission for her hand, to seek his approval of him, of his abilities as a teacher, what he knew of and, perhaps, even his commitment to Marx or Marxism and to test his knowledge of political history; a sort of box-ticking exercise. Would he, Ralph wondered, want to know what he knew of the Second Spanish Republic, whether he favoured anarchism or Trotsky, what knowledge he had of the Basques, Colonel Borlegui, of the Siege Of Madrid? The generic answer would have been very little.

He wasn't in love with Frank's 'daughter,' though there was a quiet practicality and honesty about her that he liked. She was pale, leggy, with a gauche artlessness he enjoyed and was, he felt, beginning to fall in love with him. He didn't want to hurt her, but sensed she knew this.

They walked towards the house - he not knowing it would be a farmhouse - through a small, lit, apple orchard, the lights under the symmetrically planted trees making them look like enchanted fans, the dark bulk of the building looming in the background. There was a porch lamp above the narrow door at the side of a black-painted, weather-boarded, barn-like house. She put her key in the lock - reminding him of the neighbours in his childhood terrace who would 'let themselves in,' nearly all, it seemed, having keys to each others houses.

He'd felt Frank was some sort of absolute certainty in Doreen's life; there was a shut-off implacability, a fatalistic acceptance when he thought of her in relation to Frank, as if he was a symbol of some authoritative, atheistic deity.

As they entered, a man was looking down at them from a balcony. He was tall with long grey hair, slim and appearing markedly young for his age and leaning slightly forward, fingers casually curled on the wooden handrail in front of him. He looked from Ralph to Doreen, nodded, turned and walked towards the top of the narrow staircase.

Ralph looked quickly around him: pale grey walls, high pitched cream ceiling with oak joists, the doors of the rooms off the balcony in the same dark, polished wood as the handrail all the way around the four-sided gallery, beneath which weren't turned spindles or metal rods, but wooden carvings from the Karma Sutra of women being penetrated by men in a variety of acquiescent positions. One of these figures was a female with puffed cheeks kneeling behind a priapic male and holding one end of a straw to her lips, the other just behind his testicles. He wondered if this was the origin of 'blow job.'

Frank came off the last step and walked towards him, deep-set eyes, hair swept back from a lined, tanned face, a full, trimmed moustache and dressed in dark grey almost completely. An ideologue, and a seemingly rich one, it seemed.

They shook hands, a tiny smile in Frank's eyes, a casual but almost formal grip.

'Come through,' he said.

Ralph followed him into a large kitchen, noting the eclectic array of the new and old: small windows with leaded panes, a slatted blind, long kitchen range, oak table, modern blender and coffee grinder, copper kettle and an incongruous Thirties cloud-back chair.

'Do you want a drink?'

It was spoken in a rather curt tone. There was the sound of a flushing cistern, quick, light feet, and a boy with blue eyes and wide, thin-lipped mouth was looking up at him. Doreen, who was filling the kettle, said, without looking round,

'Alistair, this is Ralph, my friend.'

Alistair nodded at him then threw his arms around Frank's thigh and squeezed. Frank lightly touched the child's hair.

'Doreen tells me she's enjoying her subject and the class are too, it would appear.'

'They do appear keen, though it's a little difficult to get one or two away from god and to politicise them. I shouldn't be doing that, of course, but detachment's difficult.'

Frank smiled. 'It wouldn't matter much if you rammed Marx down their throats would it? The system can take it, can it not? It's just accommodation by the Bourgeoisie.'

Ralph was feeling challenged, though knew what had been said was correct. He told Frank that he was more interested in Marx's analysis of class society than revolution.

Frank frowned slightly, forced a grin and asked again if he wanted a drink. Ralph told him that he was driving and Frank then, with surprising nimbleness, picked Alistair up, dropped him over a shoulder and said, 'Well, I'm gonna put this little toe rag to bed and then I have things to do. Hope to see you again.'

He said this without looking at anyone and went out of the room.

Ralph expected Doreen to follow him so she could say good night to her son, but she handed Ralph a coffee and after a few silent minutes beckoned him to follow her as she started walking back through the apple trees as if, somehow, she wasn't allowed to tuck Alistair in when Frank was putting him to bed. She drove them back in silence to the college car park.

'That was... interesting,' Ralph said. 'You going back there now?'

'No, the flat.' She drove away.

They returned a few weeks later, again in the evening, for Doreen to pick something up. Frank was at a council meeting. Ralph hadn't known he was a councillor. While she was upstairs he wandered around, looked in the large through-lounge with its oriental rugs, Sixties three-piece suite, Deco cocktail cabinet and coffee table, a half-drunk cup of coffee and a hardback copy of Debord's 'Society as Spectacle' on the latter.

But he was taken by the paintings. There were vividly coloured scenes of street markets, fountains on a Madrid boulevard and a stark black-and-white photo of a vertical half of a *pensione,* the other half just chunks of rubble. There was also a crayon sketch hung in the centre of a wall of a girl in her late teens with large, dark eyes, impish grin, and an energy in her that made the rest of the room seem almost lifeless.

He walked up the stairs, along the balcony and stopped at an open door. Doreen was putting what looked like a skirt into a bag. She gave a hesitant smile as she came out of the room and closed the door, but not before he'd seen a four-poster bed complete with canopy and a nightshirt hanging from the dark headboard.

As they went out he asked her if it was a painting that he could see the back of against a wall of the open garage.

'I think it's a Braque. I don't know much about art.'

He went in and turned it round. He knew little of the artist's work, but recognised the style immediately.

'It's an original,' she said. 'Can we go, I'm getting cold.'

It was this almost dismissive casualness, a gentle flippancy that both simultaneously intrigued him and pushed him away.

One night at her flat, he asked who the face in the sketch belonged to. She became immediately animated.

'Oh, that was Mariela. She was lovely. Frank met her when he was in Spain, she was about twenty then. His brother had known her mother and had gone there for a holiday to see her again, taking Frank with him. Her husband had been a Republican and had been shot. It was the *asesinatos* he called them, executions, both sides were doing it. They came after Mariela's mother too, but Frank's brother hid her. He and a group of others lived in the hills and she stayed with them. Afterwards she used to come over and stay at the farm sometimes and he would go to her in Spain.

'Mariela came here a couple of times. She died last year. Frank was very upset and so was I. She loved Alistair. She used to get so excited around him. She would grip his hands and swing him around, and shout, *Alistair, 'eres un chico encantador y tu papa es magnifico!'* She was lovely.'

He asked what it meant.

'Doesn't matter,' she said. 'I miss her.'

Towards the end of the academic year - they'd seen much less of each other, though he wasn't sure why, but she was an ever-present in class - a full-time job came up at the college. The evening class was the only sociology teaching he had, the rest of his timetable consisting of English literature. This job entailed mostly his subject.

The opening had arisen because a lecturer had been sacked. He, Allen, was short, stocky, ginger-haired, quietly intense and though Ralph didn't know him that well, for he was relatively new there, he liked him. He always seemed to be surrounded by young females both in class and in the staff room. They were obviously fond of him.

The word was that he politicized his students, was an 'anarchist,' a 'trouble maker,' and that management had got rid of him by sending a lackey to keep tabs on him. He was seen going into his class five minutes late. That, apparently, was all that was needed.

Whilst feeling sorry for him and disliking management - in particular and in general - Ralph needed the job and applied for it. Three of his fellow lecturers said they would see the Vice Principal and suggest strongly that they wanted him on the staff.

He was surprised and disappointed when told he wouldn't be short-listed. He had a meeting with the Vice Principal and asked him why.

'I do not,' he was answered patronisingly, 'want a communist cell in the college.' Ralph felt he was the sort of man who thought a communist meant someone who shopped at the Co-op. He was rendered inarticulate, all he could think of saying was an almost choked, 'But, that's ridiculous.' before the Principal entered the room on 'urgent business' and he had to leave.

He told Doreen. She seemed surprised. The next day she showed him a letter she had written to the Head of the college in which she talked of the difficulty of the subject, the teacher making it such a pleasure for the class and her amazement that a competent teacher of such an important discipline wouldn't be at the college next year.

'I do not look forward,' she wrote, 'to having a teacher perhaps unqualified in sociological understanding and am thus thinking twice about continuing my studies at your establishment.'

It was gratifying, but Ralph wanted her to continue. She'd been working as a temp at an IT recruitment firm for the last year and had an ambition to do a social work degree.

A few days afterwards she showed him a copy of the letter Frank had sent to the borough's Education Officer in his role as shadow chairman on Further Education.

'Whilst I must stress that your selection standards are nothing of my business, apart from their bearing on my daughter's education, I must state that I am disagreeably surprised to find her progress threatened.'

It was signed Frank Gibson, and had the Lower Melsham, East Orley address.

Ralph didn't see her over the two-week Whitsun period - 'I have things to do at Frank's' - but was in a local library preparing a letter to circulate around colleges and to see what teaching jobs, if any, were being offered, when he thought of the charcoal drawing. He wasn't far from the language section and took a book of Spanish-English back to his table.

For someone whose knowledge of Spanish began and ended with *dos decaffeinado con leche por favor,* it took him a while to find and interpret what Mariela supposedly and ritualistically had said to Alistair whenever she'd seen him.

He could imagine her, then about seventy or so he supposed, but still vivacious and strong, swirling around the boy, dancing with him. It seemed obvious suddenly that she had been Frank's lover for many years. Ralph didn't know why he had remembered her words related by Doreen, but he had. Apparently in English it was 'You are a lovely boy and your daddy is magnificent!'

And this was something else so obvious he'd missed. It reminded him of when he'd stood on the observation floor of the Empire State at night a few years before and, looking at the Chrysler, the Woolworth building and Times Square, had wondered for a second why he couldn't see the Empire State. Alistair's father, though his mother had given herself the surname of Fenton, was Frank.

He sat there thinking of him; someone who had pushed his beliefs as a councillor, whose brother had risked his life for something he believed in, had saved lives, been, perhaps, responsible for taking them. The nearest Ralph had got to any sort of cause was walking around the centre of a university town with a belated

CND banner, and once, as an apprentice signwriter, had been part of a building site go-slow, and quite recently, along with half-a-dozen other lecturers wearing t-shirts proclaiming '0% - is this all we're worth?' being photographed for the local paper after their college had turned down a pay-rise request.

He felt admiration, respect, but then remembered what Doreen had said to him one evening a few weeks before; something else he had pushed away, deflected, sidelined. Lying on her bed she'd said casually, as he got dressed to go home, 'Frank wants us to do it in front of him because he can't any more.'

He hadn't replied.

And there was a memory of a glimpse of a crumpled nightshirt dropped in the corner of her bedroom when she'd first invited him into it. Was Frank, he thought, still sleeping with her, here and at the farm?

He'd grown fond of Doreen, but realised he'd felt somewhat dispirited when with her. Experiences were, occasionally, some-how blunted; any sharing, of humour, of situations, of giving emotionally, became jaded and diluted. He tried to categorize his time with her as an interesting but disappointing episode; for he knew he wouldn't be seeing her again and intuitively felt she knew this, too.

The only stimulus, other than in her bed, had been the teaching. He could give something to her then; she was intelligent, though carefully, methodically so, as if her intellect was in abeyance and her identity, the sixteen-year-old self, had no real expression except through or with Frank.

He wanted to teach, encourage, preach; he had a picture of Frank nodding in approval as he thought this. Ralph had met him just once, but could feel how Doreen had been influenced, taken over by him.

He had applied for more social science lecturing, wanting to deal with the empirical, *a posteriori* synthetic truths, people as Durkheimian 'things,' to escape into a more understandable world.

He didn't see Doreen again, but did hear her voice. He'd just got back to his flat from a class at a college where he was working part-time when the phone rang. It was Doreen telling him that Frank had died in Spain. He remembered what she said almost verbatim.

'He hadn't been back there for quite a few years and wanted to meet up with Mariela's younger brother who his brother had helped to get to Catalonia. Apparently he was away on holiday, so Frank went on his own to the hills in Miranda de Ebro, near a monastery by the river, 'Our Lady of the Wheel' it's called; I re-member these places because he often told stories he'd heard from his brother about them. Alistair used to be fascinated. It was where he'd hid Mariela's mother... ' She stopped speaking.

'Doreen?'

'It's okay. It seems he was walking around the bottom of a hill; a couple from the village were picnicking there and saw him. He kept stopping to look up, probably trying to find the caves his brother had hidden in.'

In answer to his unspoken question she said, 'I was his next of kin, so a policeman rang me from Madrid and told me all this. Frank was wearing his brother's black cap he used to call his 'comrades cap.' They found it near his body. He was climbing up a slope. Perhaps he didn't know the caves had been filled in. He slipped and slid down. Not far, but both his legs were broken.' A silence again. 'He was nearly ninety you know.'

He heard a whimper and could feel the effort it took for her to repress it.

He asked her when the funeral would be.

'Oh, it's gone. I didn't know what to do. I even thought he might want to be buried over there; how silly. I was almost con-fusing him with his brother, they seemed to be so close, as if somehow his late brother would have wanted to be buried near Mariela's mother.'

There was a silence. Then she said, 'It's all over now though, I bought him back and he's in the churchyard near the farm now.'

'Why didn't you... '

He was about to ask, in a moment of immature arrogance, why she hadn't told him before and perhaps asked him to go to the funeral with her.

He told her he was sorry about Frank and, as he said it, felt regret at only seeing him the once, at not making efforts to get to know him, to see if he could have pierced that teak-like exterior, the toughness he seemed to carry with him. He asked her what she was going to do.

'I'm going to sell the farm.'

At least she had that, he thought.

'I shall move somewhere, I suppose.'

He wanted to say, 'Find something for yourself, Doreen, find what *you* want, convince yourself you can, you're *allowed* to.' Instead, he asked about Alistair.

'He's okay. He's sad, but he's alright.'

She asked what he was doing, was he teaching. He mumbled something.

'Well, all the best then, Ralph,' he heard. She then hung up.

Next day, not teaching till the afternoon, he took a detour off the A13 to drive past the farm house which he hadn't seen for a year. The orchard was no longer there, most of it now a paved area with barbecue equipment scattered about, and where all the latticed windows had been were PVC mock Georgian glazing bars. The subtle carriage lamp on the side door had turned into a crass mock-up of an early Victorian lamp, and though the outside was still in East Anglian black, it had now been glossed. It looked rather cheap. The chimney stack, in its crumbling authenticity, was still there.

He didn't stop. He had to get to work - finish off Marx's theory of economic determinism. He felt that Frank, in a narrow-eyed, cautious way, would be quite happy with that, even if conditionally.

As he drove back to the college he felt empty, dull. He missed Frank. He couldn't understand this. He knew *of* him rather than knew him. Perhaps he had become, unknowingly, a talisman, perhaps a figure to be emulated, someone mature, solid; complete. He wasn't sure, but knew he had to be himself or become whoever he was going to be. He drove a little faster, wanting to get back to the students, to the beginning.

CHAPTER TWO

Outside, a Jamaican traffic warden walked expressionlessly towards a car with a penalty notice in his hand, on the side of a house opposite was a satellite dish that looked as if it could pick up signals from Mars, then a long road of Edwardian houses, PVC windows, undernourished pavement trees and the inevitable mattress leaning against a wall. All this was seen through the plate-glass window of a restaurant where one of the staff with an English vocabulary of twelve words was tidying chairs, the scraping of metal on the marble floor screeching into Jordan Wilde's ears.

It was a bit of a backwater he'd been posted to, he'd have much rather been back in the City office of his family firm with the people he had virtually grown up amongst, but it had been decided he be farmed out for a while to help run the outpost - as he internally referred to it - and learn different, maybe new things for his own, and eventually, the firm's good. He also, surprisingly, missed the traders; most of them it seemed, originating from points east of Romford.

He missed Henry. He hadn't seen his older mentor for years. He'd been friends with his daughter. She'd fallen for some sort of entertainer, a rapper, he'd heard - rap is crap, it ruins rhythm, murders melody, he'd mused - and he'd seen neither of them since. It was the absence of Henry that seemed to hold the deeper emptiness.

An age of Henry swelled in his mind. He'd been lecturing at Cambridge where Jordan had done his degree in economics. He was an excellent speaker; fellow lecturers and students from other disciplines would come to the hall to listen to him - he'd given a lecture at Columbia University in New York to a packed hall that, Jordan was told, had ended with a standing ovation.

He had first seen him at an introductory session in the lecture theatre where he'd strolled about the stage pointing up at and singing the names of members of the faculty staff to the tune of

'Welcome to Cabaret,' replacing the last word of the title with 'lots of pay.' He'd felt an immediate sense of belonging.

During the three-year course he saw him occasionally at lectures and seminars; though rarely speaking other than about the work that was required of him. Halfway through Finals, Henry had told him, with mild but genuine concern, he was doing badly. He made a little more effort and eventually got the obligatory 2.1.

He saw him next at a business conference. Henry recognised him and seemed interested in how he was faring. At the next conference he gave him an invite to his office. Rather bizarrely, his father had owned a farm where he'd grown a large acreage of carrots. Henry inherited, sold it and moved to London where he'd advised investors and continued lecturing freelance, currently at a university annexe in Marylebone. He had a house in Chelsea, It wasn't a large place, but had a considered opulence.

As well as introducing Jordan to his daughter, he encouraged, advised and occasionally bullied him into working harder to establish himself at his firm as somebody other than a family member.

Soon after arriving home from the restaurant, Jordan decided to ring him.

The voice was just as gruff and seemingly disinterested as ever. Jordan asked him how he was. There was a short, huffing sound.

'I'm glad you rang. I suppose I should have rung you, really. You're better at social norms than me. But, sod those, I'm glad you rang. Let's meet.'

They met at a restaurant near Henry's office. He seemed to Jordan to have changed little; burly, broad-shouldered, a thick bush of grey hair and a voice as tough and rumbling as always. He seemed, in his sometimes rather off-hand way, to be as pleased to see Jordan as the latter was him. They ordered, Henry insisting that this was on him.

'I want to get this out of the way, Jordan,' Henry began, 'I thought, guessed, that you were falling in love with Lesley without realising it and I knew, though she doesn't tell her father everything, she wasn't with you. She's never been in love, but is now. I know you were her close friend, *our* close friend, but she does seem rather happy now.'

He sounded almost apologetic, or as near as he could get to it.

This didn't hurt Jordan as much as he thought it would, unless the bruise came later.

'And of course, it makes me happy,' he continued.

'Yes, I can see. I understand, it's - '

'But I do feel guilty, as if somehow it was me that - '

'Transference,' said Jordan. They both laughed.

'Of a rather incestuous sort I suppose. Let's have our meal first, interests and text books later. We'll talk business, though I'd rather chat about behavioural economics, it's become a bit of a hobby of mine.'

'Hardly a hobby. If I remember, you were interested in it from way back, you used to bring it into the seminars; you gave a lecture on it once.'

'Sometimes I wish I'd done psychology.'

'More money in what you're doing, though.'

'Of course.'

Jordan hadn't eaten grilled salmon for a while; he felt the taste gradually stimulate him. They talked shop as they both knew they would, Jordan telling of his work, the debentures, issued share capitals, scrip dividends, the codes and concepts, the work practices, attitudes, the sometimes grinding pressure of it, while Henry casually mentioned a client list of well-known people, some of whom were on Forbes rich list, and three, a DJ, a fashion model and an actress, even Jordan had heard of.

Henry was silent for a few seconds then looked at Jordan.

'I know that I advise people to maximise their money, to invest successfully et cetera, but I'm rather tiring of it. It's partly the sort of people I seem to be getting. Working for a firm I shouldn't think you meet many of its clients; what's it called, customer-facing? But it's not that. In a wider sense, academically, I'm moving away increasingly now from the usual, rather predictable syllabus economics, even from my Keynes, towards a more Marxist view, a more political critique; his criticism of capitalism, incidentally, forming an economic and philosophical treatise, he never really expounded blood on the streets.

'We've never really discussed politics have we, but with your background I assume that unless you've had a *volte-face* even bigger than mine, you're on the side of the status quo of course. But there you are, that's me nowadays.'

Jordan was surprised by Henry's revelation, if that's what it was, but had no wish to argue, he'd never thought at all that there'd be any ideological differences between them, it was just good to be with his old teacher again.

Henry seemed to sense this and changed the topic by telling him of a thought he'd recently had, but hadn't pursued.

'I was thinking about what sort of society would fit an unso-cialized human nature in order to optimise that nature, to fulfil itself. But of course, given the power of the id, the force of the instincts, there couldn't *be* a super-ego, no social values counter-ing the id's expression; in short, there could be only a war of all against all.'

'If that's the case how did we form society in the first place?'

'Another chicken-and-egg dilemma.'

'The psychology boys say that our subject's too generalizing, but, for them, isn't each individual a particular case of general law?'

Henry grinned wryly.

'Yes, it is so, the oedipal, paranoia, they do generalize, but not as much as... '

He stopped. They both laughed again. This was typical of their old conversations; there were few people Jordan knew now who he could have them with. He felt somehow replete; the meal and... Henry. It was good.

After their discussion of the financial strengths and weakness-es of the western world - Henry contributing appreciably more - the older man then casually told Jordan that he had a client who wanted to make even more money than he seemed to have al-ready and had only latterly become interested in finance and in-vestment.

'I think his family have money from land ownership and he doesn't want to put what he has in tried and trusted stock, he's more interested in start-ups, IT, technology, he uses the word 'en-trepreneur' a lot. Remember when Dubya' said the French didn't have a word for entrepreneur? He's about your age, uses a jargon language that I'm not completely au fait with - it takes an effort to dispense with what we're comfortable with, learned when younger. Plus, I don't think I like him a lot. But you may be able to handle him, you'd earn pretty well from him. By that, I mean for you to take him on as a personal client, not your firm's; he seems to have your sort of background.'

'What sort of background is that then?'

'Well, only a little like my own grammar school one, but I would think pretty much like his other than the landed gentry bit and Eton, though you did go to a decent public school. He's a bit of a dilettante, and seems to have problems, gets pretty restless at times. But he wants to make money, sometimes I feel just for the sake of it. If you want him he's yours, unless he's found someone else.'

He then interrupted himself by beginning a quasi-argument about contemporary economists; convinced their influence was overestimated, and suggested he text Jordan's number to the man later that evening.

Knowing Henry had intended mixing business with pleasure, Jordan was a little hurt, though a pragmatic part of him was glad to have the chance of a client. He'd occasionally given a little advice to acquaintances, but rarely a paying customer outside of the firm.

His friend looked at his watch, signalled to the waiter and raised himself from his chair. He put his arm around Jordan's shoulder as they walked out. And there, standing in front of them and a little breathless; was Lesley.

'I wanted to see you, but couldn't get through and the new housekeeper said that... ' Her eyes widened. 'Hello, Jordan.'

She smiled and held out her hand. Jordan shook it. It was instantly strange, the brief action feeling stilted. She looked exactly as he'd last seen her, when she'd told him, unsuccessfully hiding her excitement, that although she wouldn't mind them continuing as friends, there was now someone else. But there was a maturity to her now. As Jordan looked at her, he still couldn't quite understand why he'd not told her what he felt for her. He could never do so now.

He was now feeling the odd one out, a reminder that when the three of them were together he often had. With a forced smile he told Henry that he would leave them alone and that he was going back and would keep in touch. He thanked him for the meal, turned to Lesley and said goodbye, feeling stiff and formal. She gave a rather over-executed grin, put her arm quickly in her father's and they turned away.

Jordan was in a grey, morose mood on the way home. It lasted till he went to sleep.

His potential client called him three days later wanting to know immediately whether his listener thought he'd 'get on' with him. Jordan told him that he was here to advise him financially, although he hoped they would have an amicable relationship.

When he saw him, in a restaurant the day after, he was roughly as Jordan imagined from his Hollywood construct of a name, Luke Kenyon; tall, good shoulders, long, fair hair, lightly tanned face, confident, estimating blue eyes, and clothes that were bought to convey an academic personae: soft, un-ironed shirt, creased linen jacket, faded jeans, suede sneakers. There was a foppish, contrived air about him.

'Hi,' he said easily, hand outstretched then almost dangling it as if offered for the respondent to lightly stroke. 'How are you?'

There was a covertly patronising feel to him which Jordan guessed was feigned.

He was asked to sit. He raised his arms a little as if to ask 'What else?'

Jordan began by informing him of what he thought he may do for him. Using the institutionalised argot he gave him a prepared list of entities he felt he could profitably invest in.

He looked at it for a while before saying, 'Only one of these was mentioned by your colleague, I guess he's a little old-fashioned. 'Safe and solid, eh?'

'I don't think so, but - '

'Aren't you going to ask me why I didn't get on with your colleague?'

'I wasn't aware you hadn't.'

'He was kind of hard ... almost rough, cold.'

'Maybe he can appear like that, but did you want sympathy? You were with him to make money, were you not? That's also why you're here, or have I missed something.'

'Well, I tried to talk to him about things other than investments. I don't talk to many people, certainly not about personal matters; they don't seem to want to talk of things like that.'

'Things like what? What do you want to tell them then,' Jordan asked, feeling immediately that if he listened there would be more chance of his business.

'I know a problem's only a problem if it's defined as such, but... I'm not happy, I get annoyed, frustrated so easily. I'm angry much of the time. I don't know why.'

He looked at Jordan, for a second seemingly sincere, without affectation.

'Do you mind me talking to you like this?'

'Not at all.'

'Silly word, happiness, but I've looked at the usual things preventing it; you know; boarding school and my parents splitting up not long after I left the place. Lived with dad mostly; often in the south of France, occasionally with my mother in Wiltshire.'

'You say 'my mother,' yet for your father it's 'dad.' Any significance there?'

He thought of his own childhood, he couldn't remember ever calling his parent 'mummy', as far as he could recall it had been 'mother' always, perhaps entrenched by his prep school experience.

Ignoring the question, the man continued.

'It's text book stuff for the rich kid isn't it. I was also taken in hand, literally, by an older woman when young; the maid, actually. It's all so corny isn't it.' He looked at Jordan defensively. 'Money does bring its own problems you know, or don't you like the 'poor rich' line?'

He leant back. 'Anyway, I've just trod the boards for a little theatre company,' he said, flicking his forehead as if he had a forelock to tidy back.

'People seemed to like my little performances.'

He gave a mock-modest smile then looked satisfyingly around him again. Finding nothing else he wished to comment on he looked at his watch.

'I don't want to go, but... You'll send me these share recommendations and other bits of financial advice of course. And you should be the one to call me, should you not?'

He smiled, gave a hint of a mock - almost mocking - bow before departing, leaving his host to pay the bill.

After he'd gone, Jordan felt that the short time he'd been with him had been an airy, affected whirl of his client's effete, fair-haired charm; he was a barmaid's dream of a gentleman. The analysis of his psyche would perhaps be better left to Henry; pity he hadn't felt able to talk to him. He would send him some more investment options to choose from and, If not receiving a reply, contact him. Maybe he would see him again.

On the train he sat looking out of the windows at gasometers, overhead cables, the edge of the Olympic Stadium silhouetted against a lowering sun and briefly wondered why Henry hadn't seemed to have bothered with the man, refusing a chance to practice his psychological interests and knowledge - at least in theory - on him. Perhaps Kenyon's' background, his money, his quiet flamboyance, had irritated him, added to by the man seemingly having, despite what he'd said, the emotional capacity of a teaspoon.

Jordan had looked up to his mentor and advisor for years, but guessed that he wasn't so happy with the dog-eat-dog realism of the financial universe, being more comfortable in his academic milieu. If this was so and he'd trusted Jordan with Luke Kenyon then this act of respect from him was a kind of honour, but seemed to be outweighed by Jordan's slight feeling of loss, of something rather rock-like he may have been part clinging to in his professional life shifting away slightly.

He felt that Henry appeared, somehow, to be changing, he wasn't the same Henry, the amiable, almost tweedy figure; if he'd smoked a pipe he would have fitted an avuncular stereotype. Weren't people supposed to become more conservative when they aged? He was kind of switching sides, it seemed. He felt a little disappointed with him. For the first time since he had known him, he wondered whether he really cared whether he saw him again, and if he did he would, frustratingly, be reminded of Lesley.

They slowed, a goods train thudded by; Maersk... Sealand... P & O... Lesley... He played a little game where he stepped off the train and looked quickly along the platform to see whether his was the first foot that touched. He often did it, knew it was utterly childlike, but didn't care. If he wished he could run up the station stairs three at a time, tango with an imaginary partner on the forecourt, skip along the pavement or play hopscotch.

He felt dissatisfied, institutionalised, he wasn't really sure now whether he really wanted to make money for people. He was working inside a symbolic arena of a mathematically, algorithmically-based form of bingo, the FTSE being a giant Ladbrokes or Paddy Power; money from money, neither producing nor created by anything tangible, anything solid. Money was supposed to be a means of exchange; it had become a quarry to be chased, harried then abused; an end in itself for itself. He wasn't completely opposed to the latter, but wanted... needed, something else, something more.

He wanted power, power to make decisions that affected people; affected... something. The idea that seemed to have come to him suddenly, had, he was aware, been there for a while. Politics. He smiled at himself. If he was to go into politics he would have to practice his speaking, phrasing, perhaps be a little more solidly articulate in espousing his thinking.

He needed to be more determined, perhaps a little tougher. He needed a first step. The jokes he didn't really care about; he'd made up a few himself: I think, therefore I am not an MP. Politicians are like nappies, they should be changed regularly and for the same reason, et cetera. He decided he was now feeling serious about it. He would do something. Who did he know?

CHAPTER THREE

'Why is it that when people talk about someone being a wanker they put the tip of their thumb on top of their middle finger to make a circle and make up and down motions with their hand, yet never put two fingers together, the others neatly tucked in, and move *them* up and down?'

'You mean like a woman masturbating?'

'Yeah, you'd think that feminists would see the first one as yet another sign of male dominance.'

'Perhaps they'd sooner have that than be associated with wanking.'

'As if they don't do it.'

'Or not perceived to do so.'

Paul was starting another 'Why?' conversation with Ralph, this time while they were passing through Stratford market and hearing two men selling fruit and veg on a stall and, between their 'apples a puhnd pears,' one saying to the other three times in one sentence, 'Well , I mean… '

'Why,' asked Paul, stopping and not being able to help himself, 'do you say, 'I mean'? It implies that if you don't preamble your next sentence with the same, then you may not mean it.'

The man, a bowlful of pears in hand and not understanding what had been said, continued talking to his mate.

'Yeh, but I mean, if a company don't make profits then yer get no jobs, then where will yer be? We gotta work ain't we.'

Another shallow accepter of the powerful doctrine of the inevitability and 'naturalness' of the economic system, Ralph thought, this inability to break into the next tier of comprehension and to see that the people others worked for would have no income without those who worked for them.

They, somehow, didn't seem to know that the system wasn't 'natural,' but ideological, an ideology disseminated by a powerful ruling class. And, he said to himself as if he was in a classroom, before you cry 'conspiracy theory,' the powerful usually have similar educational and social backgrounds, thus sharing a similar world view and, importantly, know their position in the world, thus not needing any overt conspiracy.

He wondered what he would do without a pedagogic theatre for himself, as small as it was; knock on people's doors and harangue them? Take a megaphone to a football match? As a student had good-naturedly said to him recently, he was an 'autodidactic secular preacher.' He'd had a few worse things said of him.

Walking into a park after leaving the market was another annoyance, as a dog owner, pulling the barking creature back from a child it was lunging towards, said 'Oh, it's alright, 'e wont' 'u rt yuh.' How would the child know?

'D'you ever wonder,' Paul was asking, 'what the connection is between character and face shape; a receding chin suggesting weakness, a jutting one, strength? How could there possibly be a link between the shapes and rates of bone growth and... '

He'd known Paul since their early twenties. He'd changed hardly at all in his iconoclasm, insights, analysis, his contempt for people's lazy thinking, their stereotypes, their jumping on linguistic bandwagons, their inability to recognise how much of the world their views, opinions were a projection of themselves. But then, if they weren't, would that mean there wasn't a self, could there be a complete detachment with no projection from an ego? An ego, a self is largely culturally determined anyway. If there were, perhaps we wouldn't be human; be robots, automatons.

He was being Paul-like, in fact being himself he supposed; they'd virtually grown up together; 'Like two peas in a pod,' his mother would say when she came into the front room with cups of tea, where they were gesticulating, debating, arguing. They did the same walking around the local streets, the parks, sitting in cafes talking into the night, feeling there should be people flocking around them with silver pens glinting in the street lights writing down everything they said. Neither knew at the time that nothing they'd said was new. But it didn't matter.

Ralph had recently found his mother's old watch. It had triggered a memory he'd buried for years; the moment he'd been told she'd died. He'd been in a local pie-and-mash shop he hadn't visited for some time, about to enjoy the thick, liquor-splashed mashed potatoes and the charred, but soft pastry of the minced meat pies, when his mobile rang and his bully-boy cousin's voice was demanding he get his 'arse over here' because his mother was dead.

When he'd arrived she was in the living room jammed awkwardly between skirting board and table, her eyes still and staring, with a smear of jam on her chin and a small plate neatly covering her dressing-gowned breast. He'd asked to be left alone and knelt beside her, thumb and index finger gently closing her eyes. He had an image of her being held up in front of the cooker by his father, feet tapping a tottering staccato as her angina had taken command.

Another memory: of his father when he'd owned greyhounds; and once, in a cafe as a trainee signwriter with the decorators, pressing and squint-eyed after telling them one of his dad's dogs was running at White City that evening, hearing 'Gotta chance 'as it? gonna win?' and 'Gets out the traps quick, does it?' and Wag sailing in, fists pumping, ''it that lid six, go on my son.' He could hear Johnny sit down next to him and ask if it would finish in front.

He remembered Sykesey saying ''ope it runs faster than you can paint them letters,' accompanied by guffaws, heads back, snared teeth and spittle. He could hear 'Be of some fuckin' use then, tell us.' then the foreman rising. 'Let's do some; it's a big ceilin', long run till tea.' Leaving the café they'd squeezed past him and, two strides back, face into his, one of them saying with a snarl, 'Better not cross that line in front if we ain't on it.'

It was something else that was, somehow, his father's fault, as when he'd taken him as a child to a door at the side of a shop selling musical instruments which clearly said 'Dentist' above it. He'd spoken the word aloud. His parent was surprised.

'Didn't know you knew yer alphabet, son.'

He and Paul went out of the park and down a side street towards a café for one of its occasional music evenings amongst the rather second-rate artists' work on its walls. As they passed a terrace house, Paul stopped and asked two builders in the small front garden whether they knew that the angled pointing was to help the rain run off the bricks. They looked up, both frowning.

'It's called 'weather-cut fret,' said Paul.

They frowned some more then one said '*tai,*' the other, '*aciu.*' Paul knew the second; the Lithuanian 'Thank you.'

'You're such a geek, Paul,' said Ralph as they walked on.

'I chat to café waitresses a lot. I pick it up.'

'You're still a geek.'

Blue Sash was a Victorian workshop that was now a studio-cafe with almost obligatory eclectic and paint-splashed furniture along with a metre high plaster Buddha on top of a piano, a man sitting behind a table piled with speakers playing some Sixties pop and rock, and a small space where folk singers would some-times entertain by singing through their nose by ear. It was opti-mistically called the East Edge Artistic Community. A little bit of Hoxton-Shoreditch in Newham.

They sat there for a while, Paul using some of the eight-inch square scrabble board letters on the tables to make the name 'Karl Heinrich Marx', having to use an upside-down 'w' for the 'm,' raising a fist and looking half-triumphantly around him at the few people present. There was no response. As Ralph watched the woman who ran the place pour tea into Paul's out-size mug, Ralph tried to think of the declared aims of the Com-munist Party, or rather the English one. He'd once learnt them off by heart. Something like:

'To achieve a socialist Britain in which the means of produc-tion, distribution and exchange will be socially owned and uti-lised in a planned way for the benefit of all. This necessitates a revolutionary transformation of society, ending the existing capi-talist system of exploitation and replacing it with a socialist soci-ety in which each will contribute according to ability and receive according to work done. A Socialist society creates the condi-tions for advance to a fully Communist form of society in which each will receive according to need.'

It was unquestioned by him when he'd first heard it and a year afterwards had joined the party, not keeping his membership sub-scription up for long. He thought of it now, and that the methodo-logical problem with all ideologies, doctrines and grand theories was the annoyingly intrusive fact of the individual. What if someone enjoyed their job, pay, who they worked for? How could that be exploitation? What, and whose, criteria is used to determine what work is functionally more important than any other? And the 'according to need' bit. Who or what defines this? He was aware he was academicizing it, stepping back from it, but in terms of what he felt, he was for it, of course he was.

There were plates cutlery, shelves, light shades, flooring in the café, some of which he knew came from other countries accepted welcomingly, in the name of globalized capitalism - a euphemism for political, economic and social exploitation by unregulated multinational corporations.

It was all so obvious. Why could so many not see it? And If someone said to him yet again, 'Well, if it wasn't for the governors making money we wouldn't get no jobs.' he felt he would punch him.

Paul, he could see, was making a sketch in the note pad he perpetually carried of their immediate surroundings: an outline of the two people nearest them and the piano and the DJ, and knew that once he started filling it in, the detail would become more detailed, obsessively so, and he'd lose himself in what he was doing, possibly for the rest of the day. He had an eye for buildings too, often drawing them, sometimes showing virtually each brick.

Paul often saw buildings, houses as somehow mystical, even mythical, like trees, especially period buildings like Edwardian, Georgian and Thirties homes; thinking, he'd told his friend, that the latter Came from his first experience of a world, other than a Victorian terrace, when as a child he'd visited an aunt living in east London suburbia.

Ralph had had a similar experience at an uncle's home. He'd remembered it clearly: the sunray gate, garden steps, a rockery either side, the front door's leaded glass yacht, the zigzag wallpaper, swallowing dry cake from a Clarice Cliff plate, and a 'Don't ask don't get' nudge from mum.

Even now when walking the city with Paul and seeing curved bays, herringbone bricks, Court foyers and chrome, chevrons and pantiles, he could still see Auntie Joyce and her bright lipstick, tilted hat, dislike the people who lived in the houses he admired. He would, on occasions, touch the back of Ralph's hand saying,

'Look at that', and pointing at an attic window, a chimney or Georgian front door. Then someone would come out of the house and Paul would stiffen, as if the person was an alien intruding on his psychological ownership of the place; unless, perhaps, he could imagine that they were wearing a lounge suit and a bowler, or a broad hat if it was an Edwardian home, or tweed suit or a car coat if it was a Thirties suntrap.

Ralph wondered whether his friend's autism - he saw it as that - was somehow the result of pushing away a memory or memories from when very young or maybe later. Ralph had - a relatively rare occurrence - challenged him about his near-obsession with some of his activities: cleaning whatever it was having to be perfectly cleansed, his sketches and paintings having to be as perfect as he could make them, and sometimes when with people, saying nothing except spasmodic observations on the colour of someone's eyes or a fine thread hanging from a jacket sleeve.

Looking across the table at him now, his friend pencilling away, probably unaware that Ralph was even with him, he tried to recall some details - though there had been relatively few - of a narrative Paul had related.

He'd been seventeen and his mother, apparently increasingly despairing about her son's obvious depressions, had virtually ordered him to see a therapist. He tried to imagine the scenes and the conversations.

He would be offered a couch or armchair. Choosing the latter, sitting uncomfortably still, looking across at the therapist's knee-caps, he would say quietly, 'I'm sort of... lost.'

'Try to describe what you feel,' he'd be asked.

'I can't.'

'Anything to do with your parents?'

No answer.

'Do you hate them?'

He'd look bewildered, frightened.

'Don't know.'

'If you do, it's okay.'

He'd look down, nod slowly, lips quivering, obviously wanting to cry.

'I've got Ronnie, though,' he says, looking up.

'Friend?'

'I've known him since we were kids, infants really, we played together, you know, we... ' His voice trails. He looks down again.

'Has anything happened?'

He doesn't respond for a while, then, 'He's got a motor bike, he goes out with his... with his new friend sometimes.' It's almost a stutter.

'Are you jealous of his friend? It's alright, you can say it.'

Still looking at the floor, he nods again.

'You don't want a motor bike, too?'

'I'm too young, anyway.'

''Anyway?' Do they frighten you? The noise?'

'Yes.'

'So you decided that your fear of motor bikes outweighs your feelings of jealousy about your mate's friend? I don't mean it was a clear cut, logical decision, but in effect?'

There's no answer.

'Have you found a job?'

'I started as an order clerk for Jameson's, but I can draw, I should have gone to Art College.'

'Why didn't you?'

Again, no answer.

'Do you enjoy art?'

'Yes, I've always done it; I'm good at it I suppose.'

He doesn't smile, there's no sign of any satisfaction.

'Does it please you, this ability?'

A shrug.

'Do you really *feel* it, Paul, this expertise, this talent you say you've virtually always had or is it a little fantasy world you go into when you draw. I suspect it's not very real, is it.'

He looks alarmed. There's a long pause.

'No,' he says quietly.

'That's all you've got, isn't it? You and Ronnie, that is.'

'Yes.'

He is barely audible. He puts his head deep between his knees.

'Have you always felt this dreadful, this insecure?'

After a while Paul nods a reply.

'Your parents. Do they - ?'

'Mum. There's just her. Always has been, really; well, seems to have been. She's so fuckin' distant, so... I'm sorry, I don't really swear. Anyway, I've got Ronnie,' he says again, clenching his teeth and hands. 'We do things, always together; make up crosswords, go everywhere together, go to the movies a lot, we joined a film club, see French films, Japanese classics.'

'Your mother?'

'My mum works at Waterloo station, don't know what she does, manual job I think. We haven't always lived around here; we used to live in Mile End, the Bow end.'

The man allows him to talk of the area, the streets, the shops, the boys he used to know, the bunking into the pictures, playing over the park.

'That's all for now. When you come to see me next week maybe well talk about your father and other things, eh?'

Paul leaves, more animated than when he arrived.

The next time they meet, he immediately waves away questions about his father and talks articulately of art and his crossword-compiling.

'Your crosswords are not such an easy escape as drawing, but a visualisation of the words would still provide you with an aesthetic satisfaction to compensate for your morbid fears of the real world I think. Would they not?'

The question isn't answered.

'Shall we talk of motor bikes?'

Paul looks apprehensive. 'What about them?'

'Have you thought about asking Ronnie if you could ride pillion? Why not suggest it? You'd be together.'

His client is silent.

'What frightens you the most; the bike, or being refused the ride?'

Paul looks distressed and says nothing for minutes.

'Jealousy's okay you know, its part of being what we are. It can be horrible, I know, but it means that you - '

'I might. I've been thinking about it for a while now. Perhaps I should. But, I'm sorry Mister Judd, I can't keep here long, honest, I'm going to see a film with Ronnie tonight.'

'Call me Phillip.'

Reluctantly encouraging him in his deflection, the analyst lets him talk about a drawing he's just finished, a movie he and his friend have recently seen and the one they're going to watch that evening.

'I'd like to see you in less than a week, but it wouldn't be fair on my mother.'

'If you don't like her, does it matter? You're saying it out of principle. I'll waive the cost of this one.'

They arrange a time for five days hence. The patient doesn't show up. Mister Judd isn't unduly concerned and resists the impulse to ring the mother. He leaves the call for two days then rings twice during the next week. There's no answer, nor any provision for leaving a message.

Days afterwards Paul's mother has rung to tell him what had happened to her son's close friend. There had been a road accident involving a lorry. He had died. Her son was okay. He had been on a pillion. For a brief moment Mister Judd would, perhaps, feel as if he were part of a bereaved family, an 'affectual social entity' as he professionally called it, which had lost one of its members.

Ralph sat there, thinking of their horror as they saw the vehicle coming at them, an absolute fear diluted minutely by the optic nerve's fascination with a large object coming straight at the eye. He saw the tip of a foot support gouging the road, sparks spattering.

Watching Paul now, wearing down his pencil on the paper, he wondered whether he had been aware of what was going to happen. With his head bent, he may not have seen anything. Ralph could almost see his friend's arms clasped around the body in front of him, so relieved, happy; wanted. Perhaps Mister Judd had wondered how much a part he himself had played in it. It had been his suggestion that…

He finished his coffee and looked across at Paul again, still drawing intensely, cross-hatching a shadow of what looked like a vase of flowers, and tried to understand what the effect of the loss of such a large part of his frail, vulnerable ego had had on him.

Then he heard: 'Haven't seen you for a time. How are things?'

It was Liz, the Polish lady who ran the place.

'Like show business, no business,' Ralph said, knowing she wouldn't understand the quip. But then, it wasn't funny; it was about as funny as a teenager being a participant observer in his best friend's obliteration.

He watched Paul once more; the intense expression, the slick, accurate lines on the page.

He gently said, 'Paul, want to finish that later? There's nothing going on here, I don't particularly want to stay.'

His friend looked at him, gazed down at his work again, put his pencil and pad away and they left.

They took a train back, Paul quiet and occasionally taking out his pad and looking at it, while Ralph thought about when Paul had gone to a Communist Party meeting. He had gone along in his late teens with a couple of friends for a kind of dare more than anything. It had been rather formal and stiff - 'no razzma-tazz,' he'd said - with few people present; and they'd left early singing what they knew of The Red Flag.

Ralph knew that you needed to be a little older, a little more mature to listen to and join in with some pertinent comments or, even, to go again. Maybe both of them should be a little more active now, do something constructive, spread the word, help make something, however minor, happen.

He preached ideology within, and without, his syllabus, telling his proteges to question everything - a student had recently asked if that included him. 'Especially me,' he'd answered - and if he was sowing some seeds of an informed cynicism, that was fine, but he could, perhaps should, do more.

CHAPTER FOUR

It had to be a committee of course. Truisms like 'a camel is a horse designed by a committee,' and 'a group of the unlikely chosen by the unfit to do the unnecessary,' came to Jordan's mind as he stood before a rather long mahogany table supporting the elbows of six earnest-looking people and feeling like an auditioning Billy Elliot. It was in the hall of a Victorian building in a High Street next to a dilapidated public library. The connection to his presence here had begun three weeks before when he'd been invited to a party in north London.

It seemed a pleasant enough place; a Georgian house with Ikea interior - the blond leading the bland over the edge of beige - its owner, a maths lecturer with a fashion designer wife who Jordan had known slightly at Cambridge, greeting him with a smile as he entered. It had an interior full of plants, large painted butterflies, a wall mural of two geisha girls, and he could see through an open doorway, past the many people there, the French windows to the garden: a large green space with a rockery, pond, small waterfall, fountain and a table and canvas chairs. It had a dated Hampstead feel of plants inside the house and furniture on the lawn.

Though Jordan had known him only a little, his host always seemed an affable man, possessing an easy manner originating from his position in a salubrious, self-recruiting ship-owning family. His standard attractive wife also came forward and shook his hand.

'Welcome. Peter tells me he knew you at Cambridge - don't you just *abhor* the 'uni' abbreviation? - but I'll let you both catch up, do have a drink.'

She beckoned to a large table with lots of bottles - he glimpsed a good Pinot Noir and a Syrah - smiled at him again and rejoined the main throng.

His host asked him what he wished to drink, went to the table, had a little banter with some guests and returned with his request.

'Cheers, good choice,' he said, raising his glass. 'It's been rather a while hasn't it. Difficult really to catch up, as they say, in a short time, but glad I saw your name in the City mag, thought it was probably you.'

'I'll precis it for you if you like. Kept in touch with Henry Bishop, you probably didn't know him, he taught economics while you studied Eng Lit - guess you wanted to do what you fancied knowing you were going into the Firm anyway, like myself of course - learnt the ropes, did some managing and... here I am today. And you?'

'As you say; the Company. Father was the CEO - the position had a different name at the time - and recently my uncle, his brother, became the big man and I'm hoping to follow in his footsteps. Bit of a cliché, eh? It's a living. Been there for ever now, what else can I do? Are you married?'

'No.'

'Let's go in.'

He ushered his guest through to the party. There was no music, perhaps the hum and swirl of conversation were the only rhythms needed.

Jordan was attempting to squeeze past a casually-dressed couple and while trapped for a few seconds heard 'And did you hear what that awful football manager said to a reporter off-camera, that he was 'tempted to punch her even though she was a woman'? How sexist.'

He wondered what they were offended about; that a man would even think of hitting a woman - after all, the fair sex, the age of chivalry et cetera - or was it because the scrambled, muddled push for a nebulous entity called 'equality' meant that a female, being treated the same as a male, *should* be open to being slapped? What did they want? Another inherent contradiction of liberalism.

He briefly mused on why he'd heard no moans about the women's national football team being referred to as 'Lionesses' when guns are almost loaded if a woman is called an 'actress.' But of course, one can choose what to be offended by. He felt that if he gave his views on the current, repressive state of political correctness the people surrounding him would have wondered why he had been let in.

While he was being introduced to a clean-shaven man in an expensive jacket and designer jeans who had Finance written all over him, he saw the couple smile briefly at the hosts, mutter something and leave. Peter briefly nodded to them and mouthed, with a slight sneer, 'Neighbours.'

For a brief while there appeared to be a hiatus in the conversational sound and then a man a little older than himself and wearing a rather retro navy blue blazer and indigo tie nudged his arm and said, 'I saw the way you looked at that couple. Get on your tits did they?'

'They did.'

'Right ROs they were.'

'ROs?'

'Right-Ons.' Self-congratulation disguised as humanitarianism, eh?'

'Indeed.'

The man held his hand out.

'Mike Archer. I'm a neighbour too, but fortunately not living near those two. Another thing that gets on my mammary glands - or is that sexist - is this buzzword 'discrimination.' We discriminate every second of the day. Me putting this jacket on discriminates against me wearing any other jacket, the fact that I'm drinking red wine means I've discriminated against the white, et cetera.'

'Quite.'

'One time, having discrimination was seen as a good thing, a touch of class. What do you call a thousand liberals at the bottom of the ocean? Well, it's a start.'

'Like it.'

'I don't know your name. What do you do, anyway?'

Archer asked the question with, Jordan felt, a mild aggressiveness, though that could be his everyday personality. He was medium height, stocky, with small eyes and thick lips; someone who could perhaps fight his way out of most corners. Jordan told him what he wanted to know.

'Good money, huh? Nice for some, but I'm not complaining. Want another drink?'

Jordan hadn't finished the one he was holding. He asked the man what he did.

'Interesting, in the US the first question they ask at parties is, 'How much d'ya earn?' Here it's, 'What do you do?' Guess it's the class thing, eh, still alive and well.'

'Need the rich to help the poor. I don't mean charity of course, but there has to be profits, people wouldn't be employed otherwise.'

'Spoken like a true Conservative.'

'I am if what we wish to conserve is the status quo. It's successful.'

'For some.'

'Yes,' but think of something else, another system.'

'I can't . Wouldn't want to.'

'Like most people, fortunately. After the crash there wasn't any sign of revolution; people wanted the same, only better. I occasionally criticise the money bubble I work in, though I wouldn't want it any other way, but - '

'There must be something more?'

'Quite. And you haven't answered my question.'

'A political agent. It's difficult to define, but I give advice, do some PR, help choose candidates, that sort of thing.'

'Local MPs?'

'Not necessarily local, I have contacts all over the country. For example, there'll almost certainly be by-elections in Norwich and Wansford fairly soon, there certainly won't be one in this borough any time soon. Why? Considering it?'

Jordan smiled. 'Well… yes, I suppose so.'

'You don't seem that sure.'

'The question's rather sudden, new to me. But, yes.'

Archer looked at him, narrowing his eyes, head slightly to one side.

'You know, you could be right. You have to have the requisite personality; it's more about personalities these days than policies. What are you like at public speaking? Pretty good I should imagine.'

'I speak to the board sometimes; occasionally address the workers, that is have tribal get-togethers to urge them to work harder. The last time I spoke politically with any seriousness, I suppose, was as captain of a debating team for Cambridge against Oxford.'

It doesn't surprise me you're an Oxbridge man; but no overt political involvement, eh?'

'Well, politics isn't just about elections and coups and so forth is it. Arguably, everything's political. It's about any individual or group that has power over any other individual or group. A father telling his teenage daughter to be home before midnight is a political act.'

'Yeah, but we're talking of politics with a capital P, the big picture.'

He looked at Jordan's glass, it was empty. He took it from him.

'I'll get you another.'

He made his way, rather brusquely brushing past people, to the wine and vol-au-vent table and returned with a drink.

'What more than the 'bubble' do you want then? Do some good for the economy, for people? Something like that?'

'I could do things.'

'Pretty vague at the moment, eh?'

'Yes, but I think I'm getting to the point of sharpening it, perhaps not quite crystallizing it, or having a target. But yes. The big picture.'

Archer looked sideways at him.

'This Wansford thing. Between you and I, I'm not that happy with the line-up they seem to have; it's one staid councillor, a raging feminist, and a very ordinary true-blue who seems never to have left the doorstep of his Buckinghamshire farmhouse.'

He turned to Jordan again, face a little nearer.

'Fancy it?'

'A candidate?'

It was sudden, too sudden, but he didn't dwell on his answer. It felt good when he stated it.

Mike Archer raised his drink.

'I'll give you the where and when before we leave. Cheers.'

He did so, and before leaving Jordan thanked his host - he couldn't see his wife - and left, realising he'd spoken to only three of the people present in the last two hours, one of them seemingly far more significant than the others.

'What do you think is the most important concern facing this country today?'

Jordan, mildly pleased that the ubiquitous 'issue' hadn't been used, said, 'Europe. It has to be, skilled workers in the financial sector for example, if we lose them it's not good.'

'And unskilled workers?' the thin man with a rather annoying pencil moustache asked.

'Need them for profits, quite frankly. There's not going to be any investment from other countries if large margins are not perceived as obtainable, and favourable trade deals will have to be made internationally of course.' He looked quickly along the table. 'I'm stating the obvious I'm afraid.'

A particularly corpulent man with the end of his tie flopped on the table, who Jordan guessed would be the constituency chairman, asked, 'Ever been a councillor?'

'No, it hasn't interested me.'

'Too small-time?' asked another with large horn-rimmed glasses and a trace of sarcasm.

'I suppose so.'

'Entrepreneurs, businessmen good, trade unions bad?'

'I wonder why you ask that.' He took a chance, and grinned, he hoped winningly. 'I assume this *is* a Tory Party selection committee?'

'Indeed,' said the first man who'd spoken. 'You know the financial world, the most influential of all, of course, but politics needs an emotional dimension that goes beyond spread sheets. You - '

'What would you say to the people, the electorate?' the woman at the end of the table asked. 'They don't really want to hear about investment and profits; they're interested in *their* income. We know they're tied together, but how would you address that?'

'You need to angle it,' said the fat man.

'Spin it.'

'Of course.'

Jordan had intermittently been imagining a spiel at a hustings somewhere. He took another chance and, remembering it as best he could, stood, took a step back, looked around at the committee and began:

'I want to revitalise a rather tired phrase, the 'Caring Conservatives.' We *do* care. We care enough to tax the often unjustified salaries of the highest earners, No, we are not in their pockets, we can do it. Care enough not to burden the middle-income earners and to help those with lower incomes. Care enough for an excellent education system, a good living, a good life for all, not just for the few. It can happen, not overnight, but during the time of the next Parliament, a Conservative Parliament.

'Yes, the centre ground. Centre: the middle of everything, the core, the crux of it all in which every one of us can be what we want to be. All that we want to be. But a vision is nothing without will. No vision ever clothed a family or fed a hungry child. No vision ever built a business by itself. No vision ever changed a society on its own. Change can be a great thing, change outside of Europe and into the world. This party, this next government will be a turning point for this country, this nation. For all of us. And a last word: immigration. It *can* be controlled.'

As Jordan sat again there was a silence from his listeners, then, as if orchestrated, the two people who hadn't yet spoken said in unison, 'Very good.' one of them adding 'A little over-ambitious, though.' and after a quick glance at the other, said, 'You have the right tone, though there was a little too much 'Leader of the Party' stuff there for a local candidate I think, but the right feel, you speak well.'

The fat man leaned back on his chair and said, 'Yes' I think I can say,' he bent forward and glanced at the others either side of him, 'that the consensus is that it was quite impressive, though it's not just about the applause you get at a Party Conference. However, we do have other candidates to see, Mister Wilde, so thanks for coming and we will let you know.'

After some murmured 'Well dones' and 'Thank yous' from the rest, Jordan left.

As he opened the door of his Abarth Spider, which he'd managed to park directly outside, the woman in the committee appeared behind him.

'Just to say, I think you may well get it. I was quite impressed, especially as you don't seem to have much of an active political background. Most promising.'

He turned and thanked her. As he started his car he noticed how shapely her calves were as she re-entered the building. But other things looked good, too: the pavement plane trees in a side street, two children excitedly pulling their mother along the pavement outside an M&S store and an elderly, bearded man with large white teeth, his head back, laughing with a companion.

He was feeling fine. As he drove, the stimulus from what had happened at the meeting drifted away a little and he mused on whether he really did want power to do good things for others or whether it was just... power. No, it was the former. if chosen he would, as he Americans say, go for it.

'Another thing that pisses me off is when they confuse sex with gender. The former refers to the biological differences between males and females, men and women, the latter alludes to behaviour such as masculine and feminine which are largely culturally determined and defined, thus variable.'

'Indeed.' Ralph was aware that Paul knew he would agree with him.

'They talk of 'women' and 'men' - notice I placed women first - in terms of gender inequality yet talk of sexism which, according to their confusion, should be 'genderism.''

'I know these things, Paul; I try not to let them get to me, though not always successfully.'

They were sitting in another café, this time on the side of the Thames near Ham.

'It's eroding democracy, mate, destroying irony. Somebody referred the other day to Kipling's 'indefensible gender-specific punchline that, if you meet the required conditions, 'you'll be a Man, my son.' The poem's not *talking* of women; It *is* sex specific - it would also be if it was 'You are a woman, my daughter.' What was he *supposed* to write then? 'You are an adult, my child'?' Great punchline.'

'That'll be ageist wouldn't it? Discriminating against teenagers.'

They'd found the café after halting in their walk along the Thames Path and moving inland a little to look at a mound of stained rocks rising from a pool atop of which were two rearing stone horses, a chariot between their spread wings. It was driven by a female, her hair held high between her fingers, whilst lower, in the pool, a maid stretched out an arm in worship, while nearby a kneeling nymph helped up a friend, their arms clasped around each other.

Another girl, delicately carved, sat in a shell, where, between her finger and thumb, she held a nut for a horse, or it could have been a pearl for the charioteer. Arms wide, a girl bent backwards as if suddenly aware of the animals above, and near her a lass leant over the water looking surprised at her reflection. As the tide rose, Ralph could see weeds wash up to an ankle then behind a knee to the palm of a hand.

He realised that, on the other bank, those who looked across would probably see, above the trees, only a tip of stone, a curl, a tress, not thinking there could be figures here larger than life; elegant, playful, drowning... Another dimension of this city he liked: the sculptured, architectural surprises.

Paul was, it seemed to his friend, beginning a kind of emotional convalescence having recently lost a job in a branch of a High Street bank for disagreeing vehemently and constantly with an authoritarian manager who supposedly couldn't understand the level of conceptualising and the processing of information his underling was consistently capable of.

He knew he probably wouldn't see his friend again for a while after this walk. It had happened before when he'd got fired; the time he'd dabbled in advertising. Apparently, once he'd learnt the ropes - and he had inevitably done so quickly - he'd argued for a push away from the current cheapskate use of animations and cheap visual tricks back to the days when people valued TV commercials as being as entertaining, if not more so, than the programmes they were interrupting.

One that typified what he'd meant, he'd argued, was a commercial that had featured a helicopter carrying, swinging above the Grand Canyon, what looked like an unopened tin of sardines which, gazed at implacably by the lizard in the foreground, opened to reveal a well-known brand of cigarettes. He had read somewhere that at an annual ASA awards there had been a standing ovation when it was shown.

Paul had the knack of casually knowing these things as if from inside knowledge and experience in the field. The instant rejection of his idea was met by an arrogant response which meant another few weeks unemployed and more time on benefits.

Ralph knew that during that time his friend was busying himself reading, researching, writing - though never coming to published fruition - and generally walking around the borough and, sometimes, further afield. The times Ralph had seen him, he'd report back to him in some detail on the places he'd been.

A few days later, Ralph performed a teaching observation in an ancient school near London Bridge for the teaching course at his college, invariably telling student teachers that though officially he was supposed to watch them for an hour he would leave after a quarter of that time - knowing a good practitioner almost immediately. He observed two: the first ineptly taught by a cognitive therapist, the second by an engineer who translated his experience and knowledge casually and effectively.

Afterwards, he sat for a while in a room that was grandly called a refectory. A woman carrying a tray passed his table, stopped and turned towards him.

'You sat in on a class earlier, didn't you? I was in it. I also teach.'

He wasn't sure how to answer.

'Er, really. What do you teach?'

'French.' Frowning, she pointed to the seat next to his. 'This seems to be the only seat available at the moment. Do you mind? I shan't be here long.'

'Sure.'

She sat. She had dark eyes, brown hair and told him she used to teach history in a nearby school and was now doing the counselling course. At first he didn't recognize the accent then noted the slight glottal stress on the 'r' and occasionally the 'i' as she told him a little more about what she was doing there.

He took a chance.

'Why do the French eat snails? Because they don't like fast food.'

The frown again. 'Can't you do better?'

'I can. To be a historian you need a poor memory and a good imagination.'

She grinned slightly and began to eat her small meal.

'I guess you're at least bilingual, so here is my excuse for being no good at French. It has up to seventeen vowels depending on the dialect, and most of them are nasal. Many words sound exactly the same, but mean completely different things and everything has a gender. It can take days of examining your relationship to someone before you figure out if it's more polite to call them *tu* or *vous*. Am I right?'

'Have you finished?'

'I think so.'

'At least you were honest in giving the reasons why you're *merde* at it.'

He asked her when she'd first come to the UK.

'When I was fifteen. My father didn't stay long, he went back. He's a factory worker, union organiser outside Paris.' She gave him a grin. 'I know I've only just sat down, but...'

She shrugged and, standing up, said, 'Nice to meet you.' and went across to sit at a suddenly vacated table on the other side of the room, except for a girl with a leg across a seat. It was a waitress from the café next door, who he'd aimlessly chatted to before his class observation. He guessed she, too, was a student here and earning a little part-time cash.

Instead of going to the cramped staff room he began writing a report on the lecturers he'd just seen while his impressions were still fresh. He looked over to the table. Students were getting up and others taking their place, their chatter bright and fast as they picked up bags and books and turned towards the door, reminding him of the excitement and camaraderie of his own university experience.

After another observation next day and looking at his notes sitting in the same cafe, he saw the girl from the college clearing a table.

He could see she recognised him. He told her why he was at the school and asked how long she'd been waitressing.

'Not long, a few weeks. I saw you in class yesterday. What were you there for?'

'Observing. Your lecturer should have told you.'

'I've just started. Therapy interests me. I'm sure the practice is different from all the theory though.'

'I believe it is.'

He asked what she liked about the subject, not bothering to use his own subject's perspectives to comment on the theories she was learning.

She went off to serve someone, he watching her; the purposeful stride, the slightly plump rear.

He saw the woman from the refectory the following day as he stood at the back of a full classroom. She was standing by the inside of the door and frowning at the lecturer who was looking around at her students and smiling as if projecting a healing beam onto them. She delivered her lesson quietly, its content as thin as her voice. He was tempted to wait until the students had left and tell her what he thought, but his brief was merely to note it for the college, and he didn't want to hurt her by showing his annoyance.

The refectory woman was leaning against the corridor wall waiting for him as he left. She shook her head.

'As you may guess, I learnt little in there. We could compare notes about her somnambulistic performance, but... ' She shrugged. 'I'm merely a student here.'

She and the situation suddenly attracted him; her mature playfulness, the walking away from a classroom with a woman carrying books under her arm as if he was an undergraduate again.

'They say that when god realised he'd made France so beautiful, to stop the rest of the world getting jealous he filled it with French people.'

'Perhaps you really can't do better.'

'Okay. Fake definitions. Avocado: cry of the Italian croupier.'

'That's better. How about... Falsetto: Italian dentures.'

'I can't beat that. Look, forget this. Let's have a coffee or something. I don't even know your name.'

She considered the offer for a while.

'It'll have to be tomorrow. And it's Claudia.'

He told her where he'd like to meet her, he'd been there only once but it seemed appropriate. She moved quickly down the stairs and out of sight. He went to the staffroom and looked out the window. Down below he could see her and the waitress crossing the road, animated and laughing.

When he entered the incongruously named Café Paris, she was already there, leaning back on her chair with a slightly mocking smile.

'Have I smashed a stereotype? I even worked out where the south side of the High Street was.'

'A slight crack. And there are reasons why females are no good at spatial concepts,' he said casually, joining her. 'That's why I rarely ask women for directions'

'I know where this is going and you'll lose, but I'm hungry.'

They ordered. He asked her why she liked history.

'Because I was good at it.'

'All second-rate opinion, conjecture, distorted fifth-hand anecdotal evidence and research often clouded by what historians *want* the result to be. Not so dissimilar to science, maybe.'

'I still like it, and it wasn't like that for me. And you haven't as yet come across very winningly, have you.'

'I'll try harder. What about what you're doing now?'

'Okay so far, but - '

'Not precise enough maybe? I think that's as it should be, even more so when you get to people like Freud.'

Their food was brought. They ate, studied the menu for dessert.

He asked about her parents. They'd met in Paris. It was just her mother now, but her father came over to see her sometimes. When the waiter brought their drinks she said, *'Je vous remercie.'*

'Je comprend pas, je ne parle pas francais, je suis desole,' said Ralph. 'That's parrot- fashion. I know no more, sorry.'

As they drank, he noticed the way her short hair swung a little at its end and the grin widening her lips.

He walked with her to a bus stop. As she boarded a bus she turned to him with one of her frowns and said, 'Surprisingly, I enjoyed that.' and gave the grin once more.

He saw her again two days later at the college where he was finishing the last of his pedagogic observations. She wore a tight-fitting skirt, looking attractively at odds with the other mostly younger, jean-wearing, students. He felt no pressure to impress and there was little probing, just gentle questioning. After his 'Logarithm: contraceptive method used by lumberjacks' and her 'Radish: like a radiator,' they agreed to stop giggling and showing off and to be adult. She asked him if he liked the theatre, she'd had two tickets given to her for that evening.

They went. It was a Pinteresque play, she watching him between the silences turning his head aggressively towards someone unwrapping sweet wrappers, and another slurping a drink.

On the way out he asked her if people thought, 'I feel hungry, let's go to the pictures or the theatre and have a nosh.' They talked about the performances as he travelled on the Tube with her to her station where his offer to walk home with her was graciously refused.

She wasn't free the following day, but was the one after. He hadn't intended going to the college, but after having only one seminar group to attend at his own place of work, he did anyway. They saw each other for a few minutes before her class and then afterwards went to a local bar. It was late when they left. Together they walked back to her flat near the college.

After she let him in he leaned against the hall wall. She closed the door and turned around. He wanted to pull her towards him, kiss her. She hesitated for a moment then went into a living room where he followed her into a kitchen where she made them coffee. She seemed somehow rigid, as if whatever he was feeling or thinking was pointless, she wouldn't yield.

He didn't stay long. The Frenchness of the place: the books, a copy of *La Tribune,* on a table and something she seemed to have been writing; he could understand nothing. It felt a little alien. They talked for a while, she telling him about some sort of test at college next day. He finished his coffee and went home feeling dissatisfied, a little rejected.

There was an observation for him to do the following afternoon and, in the cafe, while immersed in writing his notes, his table shook slightly. He looked up at Claudia's laughing mouth saying:

'I got an A for the test *and* my essay.'

'You've woken me up. What was the question?'

'How far can human motivation be said to be social?'

'What, this early? You did well.'

'Want to celebrate with me?'

'Of course. When? Where?'

'Tomorrow, the Cuckoo Club. You'll find it.'

She got up, gave him a quick kiss on his cheek and left; Ralph, as always, suspecting that when a woman did this to him it was implying something platonic because she wanted nothing else. He pushed the thought away. It was replaced by mild surprise at her being in the café.

Ralph didn't go to the venue. Neither did Claudia. She rang him as he was crossing the road towards it. She sounded more French on the phone, partly because she was anxious and speaking rapidly. Her father, due to give a series of union talks at workers' rallies back home, had been taken ill; it was a family friend who had contacted her. She needed to go; she was on the way now. It was all she said. He was disappointed.

He was busy for the next few days, though doing one more observation where he found himself surreptitiously glancing around for her. She rang him again. There was some desperation in her voice; her father wasn't any better. Despite her situation he was glad she'd called him.

He thought of her sporadically then more consistently over the following days; thought of her in Paris and of his last visit there; of the sting of sun at Orly and an aeroplane droning over the city with a *Votez Pour Liberte* banner floating behind it above the Theatre du Chatelet, where the bourgeoisie clapped themselves for being there. Perhaps, one day, they could be there together. The thought excited him.

She rang him late one evening, frenetically using words from her first language. He caught *pere,* thought he understood *bonne nouvelle* and *une belle chose*. She was so thrilled; *Genial! Genial!* It seemed that her father was out of danger.

'I will tell you more when I am back. It will be good. I miss you. *Au'voir.'*

He liked the idea that she missed him.

He fretted. He wanted to call her, but hadn't saved her number and, knowing it would be difficult to get it from the college, had decided to ask one of the students, perhaps the waitress. Then she called him.

'He is well and coming home soon. I really have something to celebrate now, haven't I. *La vie est belle!'*

'When are you coming - '

'I am back. Do you want to come to the place I mentioned before? Do you remember?'

Of course he did and of course he remembered. He realised how much he wanted to see her again. It seemed such a long while since he had.

It was a club off Goodge Street. He was early. He'd been to a club only once before, it was called a disco then and he didn't want to be inside that lung-shaking sound again. But this was quieter, with low, melodic music, a horseshoe bar and a dance space at the end of the long room. Getting himself a drink he leaned against the counter and looked around him.

There was something a little... odd. He wasn't sure what. A few couples danced quietly under a glitter ball, but they weren't the expected sort of couples. They were, with the exception of two men moving slowly with each other, all women. They reminded him of his teenage dances at the local Palais where, under their flashy bravado, lads would look nervously at the girls dancing with each other, bored with waiting for pimpled youths to clumsily invite them. .

He'd recently found a sepia photo of two young girls in an East End street, one being bent acutely backwards by the other, her arm around the small of the girl's back, kissing her chin, pretending to be grown up. This, for Ralph, was what these women should be doing, just chatting, playing about. But they weren't; two of the couples were holding each other tightly - 'romantically' was the word that came to mind before realising how inappropriate it was. One of the twosomes consisted of a woman kissing her younger partner ardently on her mouth. It was Claudia and the waitress.

They moved away from each other, laughing. Claudia gripped her friend's hand and, still laughing, pulled her towards the bar. She looked up and saw him. She grinned broadly.

'Bonsoir.'

He didn't move.

'You look lost. I believe you know Jeannie?'

She pushed her forward.

'Hello, Mister Kearns.'

Her plump, blue-eyed face was flushed. Ralph nodded; he wasn't sure what else to do.

'Come back to our table,' urged Claudia, pulling the younger girl after her. 'Get some more vodkas for us, would you, Ralphy?' she shouted.

He did, then stood at the bar still not quite feeling anything. He took their drinks to their table, heard Jeannie saying, 'Yeah, he's got this psychiatric hotline; you know, 'If you're schizophrenic listen carefully and a little voice inside will tell you what number to press.' 'If you're...' She stopped, laughing almost hysterically.

He stood there, still holding the glasses.

'Come on, sit down Mister Kearns,' said Jeannie.

'Yes, Mister Kearns,' mimicked Claudia, 'but not on *my* lap.' Again, the giggling.

'Sorry, we're like a couple of kids, aren't we. I expect you thought it would be just you and me celebrating.'

'Claudia, can you let go of my hand?' Jeannie said with mock seriousness.

Ralph broke his inertia. He put their drinks down.

'Could we go somewhere else for a while?' He looked down at the girl. 'She won't be long... Jeannie.'

He walked firmly towards the exit, Claudia following. Outside it was raining slightly. She went to step inside again. He grabbed her arm.

'What's going on?'

She frowned, 'Well it's pretty obvious isn't it. Yes, I should have told you. You're a nice man, Ralph, but you're - '

'The wrong sex?'

She didn't answer.

'You don't seem sure. And why meet here, should I have known about this place? Were you trying to tell me something?'

'I thought you were more liberated than this.'

'Are you showing her off?'

'I'm sorry. I met her on the course and - '

'And?' He could feel his anger growing.

She pulled away from him.

'You'll be giving me the usual male response next,' she said, voice rising. "What do you *do*?' and 'Can I watch?' Okay, I should have told you. But I didn't.'

She was silent for a moment.

'I enjoy being with you, you know that, but - '

'I was falling for you. I thought; I was hoping… Does that mean anything? Is the phrasing un-cool?'

She turned quickly and went inside and closed the door. It immediately opened again. He couldn't tell whether she was angry or disappointed.

'Every time you're with me, it seems as if… I have no idea what you're really like. I feel that underneath the humour, the intelligence, you're acting; there's a detachment. The very thing that attracts women to you pushes them away.'

'What women?'

'The students here. They see you sitting in classes; they see you talking to me.'

'I'm not interested in other - '

'But *I* am, Ralph. I want something else.' There was a pause, then 'Look at your face, like a little boy. *Pleurez vous, allez pisser moins.*'

She grabbed the door and slammed it behind her. He stared at it again and reverting to a familiar defensive cynicism, said quietly, 'No chance of a shag then.' and walked away.

He caught a bus, got off at St. Paul's and walked towards Bishopsgate thinking of her, of them; anima, animus… He automatically went to enter Paulo's but decided he didn't feel like going to another café, ever. He caught a packed train home.

Next day was a clear, warm, autumnal one, one of those where, if having no teaching, he would go to a favourite London spot and walk. He felt he had none. He randomly chose Highgate. From there he walked to Crouch End, trying unsuccessfully to march her out of him. He was hungry and almost reluctantly went into a café. He sat there thinking of her; of causes, reasons, and decided that she needed a surrogate mother, but then, what about Jeannie? He pushed the simplistic equations away.

He had an urge to understand what had occurred during the last few weeks. It had happened quickly. It was a new experience; he'd known very few people who were overtly homosexual. He was a man who'd been rejected for another woman and at this moment felt irrelevant.

As he was leaving he heard the Eastern European accent of a girl behind the counter. With his usual reflexive curiosity he asked her where she was from. She looked at him and shook her head, implying that she wasn't going to tell him. A second woman behind the counter said pointedly,

'If she doesn't want to tell you where she is from, then she doesn't want to tell you where she is from.'

Two women again; he felt ganged up on.

'Why? This is *your* prejudice, not mine; don't project it onto me.'

He pushed through the door, barging into someone entering and nearly knocking them over. He knew he had to take hold of himself. He wished to be in a world where human beings would be just intellects, no wanting, no prejudices, just... detached, detached.

Later, unusually, he told Paul of what had happened with Claudia - he hadn't mentioned her, and very little of Doreen, before. Paul, his psyche partially recouped after being forced to find work, of any variety, had insisted, because he knew a little French, that his friend tell him exactly what it was that the woman had shouted at him. Ralph attempted to pronounce what he remembered as accurately as he could. It was, according to Paul, apparently, 'Go on, cry; you'll piss less.'

She had told him little more of her father than that of his membership of the *Paris Communiste Francais* and his support of the Left Front. He seemed to be another man who stood firm for his politics, his principles, someone else who, in their name, battled for others. He'd been reminded again that he, also, should do something like this; something of some worth.

CHAPTER SIX

With an air of frankness, and a little amusement flickering around his lips, he began:

'Right, let's try to get an obstacle out of the way. It's one of attitude, perceptions, stereotyping which exists in virtually all companies, namely, the demarcation between, as it were, the work force - you, the traders - and the investment people, the advisers, the salesmen. That is, you think that people like me who could apparently sell ice to Eskimos, but probably perceived by you as wankers, see people like you as being merely cogs in a noisy machine.'

Jordan wanted, or rather it had been suggested by the top man, that he inform the traders of what he and a few others in the upper echelon did. He couldn't see the point; they were where they were because they, well, deserved to be, and the traders - still seeing them collectively as 'Essex Man' - were, he sometimes thought, rather lucky to be doing what they were, they could have been on building sites or serving in shops.

'Let's compromise; let me help you to understand more about what I sell, and you help me learn more about your connection with the product, the nitty-gritty, the communicating.'

Gritting his teeth he ploughed on as if walking through porridge. He finished what he intended to say then listened reluctantly to his listeners' views, who not really caring about 'that side' of the game, were almost as glad to leave the conference room as he.

His effort, really, had been to get some speaking practice for a second selection speech, this time with a different audience. Mike Archer would be there, not having been to the first one because of a 'bit of a crisis call,' as he'd called it, from an ex-MP client preparing to stand again in Norwich. One of the selection panel who had heard Jordan before, had called him to say that he merely wanted him to confirm his interest and determination by speaking to some more people and perhaps answering a few questions.

He drove to an ordinary-looking house on the edge of the ward he was intending to fight, its ordinariness betrayed by posters in its upper and lower windows with his photo squarely in the centre of them. It was the campaign house, or Headquarters as his agent termed it.

A middle-aged woman opened the door.

'I know who you are. Welcome. We're still setting the place up. I was just looking at the map to work out the best places for you to begin.'

'Campaigning.'

'Of course,' she smiled. 'Mister Archer was supposed to be here.'

'I know.'

He was offered tea and after a few sips looked around the large front room which had more Conservative posters but with no pictures of himself. There were a few quotes from his own speeches referring to caring and innovation, and others which, to him, now felt rather staid. There were, apparently, two other volunteers that wee usually there, one with quite a few years experience. He felt he should be visiting this place occasionally to add a personal touch.

Archer then rang him, apologised for his absence and suggested a pub not too far away. He thanked the woman and asked her to also express his gratitude to the absent others and left.

A half-hour afterwards he met his agent in a pub in Wansford where Archer insisted the drinks were on him. After a quickly scoffed pint and looking even more pugnacious than Jordan remembered, he said, 'Yeah, I got me boy back, but she told the social worker she had parental responsibility. What a liar, the court had given it to me. But they believed her. Your drink okay is it?'

'Fine. Who's 'she'?'

'The missus, well, ex, know what I mean? And this bloke she was living with then, Billy, my boy, said he was always sniffin.' Well, he would be wouldn't he; he was on cocaine like she was. Sorry if this shocks you. Anyway, this bloke Bert, turns out bits of him were found in a lake. It was in the papers, 'Guardian' and that. They arrested a bloke next day. He'd chopped his arms off and put 'em in a garage in a Tesco bag. They haven't found the rest of him yet. He said it wasn't him, but they found a receipt for reward points in the bag, so it must have been.'

Jordan felt a vague sense of the surreal in the combination of severed limbs and supermarket points.

'Suppose I shouldn't have told you. The boy's okay. Guess it's been on my mind again and you were here in the firing line. I won't mention it, or her, again.'

Jordan assumed that he'd reverted, after a drink or two, to his primary accent having reconstructed himself a while back. Class, thought Jordan, was tattooed on the tongue.

His companion bought himself another drink, put it on their table and rubbed his hands.

'So, where were we? Tomorrow. From what I've heard, there doesn't seem much point in asking you to do it again, the job's yours. There'll be some questions though this time, usually friendly; the people who go to these things will be on your side.'

'You sure?'

'Maybe it'll be good for you if they're not, the cut-and-thrust of political debate and all that.'

'I can imagine you've done a bit of that, perhaps literally. Sorry, kidding. It's just that you strike me as - '

'Tough? Seasoned? Guess I am, but you're the one who wants a seat in our cherished Parliament. As a constituency agent I'm here to help you.'

His phone rang. He moved away saying, 'Excuse me.' and took the call. He nodded into his phone rather than spoke and, looking at Jordan, said, 'Sorry. See you tomorrow, you've got the address.' and left.

Jordan was quite looking forward to this encounter; hopefully, it would be a more-or-less pleasant exchange of ideas, a chat amongst the like-minded.

Less than twenty four hours later he turned into a tree-lined avenue north of Wansford Station and stopped outside a large, double-bayed, mullion-windowed house and was let in by a man he felt vaguely he knew and, as he introduced himself, Jordan recognised as a rather prominent backbencher. Behind him was Archer. They both led him downstairs to a large basement with

Tory posters dating back to Pitt the Younger, with Disraeli, Churchill and Thatcher prominent.

There were no more than twenty five people there, a third of them standing with drinks in hand talking, some quite passionately, others sitting on rows of canvas chairs facing a lectern with a whiteboard behind it.

The man who'd opened the door to him beckoned him to the lectern and introduced him as, 'The man who will contest our by-election.'

Jordan realised then that they'd made their mind up; it was going to be him.

'A man whose family have been in, and helped make, the City's financial world for decades, and thus knows how important that part of the universe really is for the country.'

There was some clapping and a cheer or two.

Jordan faced his audience, smiled and said confidently, 'Capitalism: the greatest agent of collective human progress ever.' He paused. 'We are talking of a free market across the world. Globalization. If you want to sell more, drop the price, if you can't drop it far enough then give up that activity and do something else where you can be competitive. If everyone does that, nations will come to specialise in what they do best and the world will be a more efficient place.'

As he finished his opening, a tallish figure with designer stubble and greying sideburns, said, 'The free market idea's been around for at least two hundred years, but it hasn't worked, Mister... sorry, I didn't catch your name. You make it sound as if the move from one activity to another is seamless, instant and painless; it also assumes nobody will cheat. I'm aware that if history teaches us anything it's that history teaches us nothing, but years of poverty, waste and dislocation means that this market doesn't and really cannot work.'

'I have a feeling that you're going to propose some sort of nationalisation. Am I correct?' Jordan asked.

The speaker stood and looked around him.

'I don't want to teach grandmothers to suck eggs, but with State ownership all profit is ploughed back - the farming analogy is a good one, the earth being, in the end, the people - but it has to fight the most entrenched taken-for-natural value on that earth: the inescapable norm of profit.'

'You almost said 'surplus value' instead of 'profit' then didn't you. Yes, we can see where *you're* coming from,' said Jordan.

'Going to give us a chorus of The *Internationale,* are you?' asked someone from the back of the room. There were a few chuckles.

'Nationalisation,' said Jordan - lines from rehearsals and practice now gone - 'is an ideologically extreme rejection of a successful system. It lands up with the enslavement of the individual by the State. I'm for the system we have. It means - '

'That we all get the benefit through osmosis? It's crumbs from the rich man's table again isn't it,' countered the previous speaker.

'What we want, and certainly what a Conservative government will continue to do, is to *support* our system, to carefully create and maintain checks and balances and, let me assure you, for the good of the whole. For all of us.'

There was a round of rather loud clapping and 'Hear, hears.'

'Does 'carefully' mean a fear of attempting to collect corporation tax from large multinationals?' the initial questioner asked.

'Of course we'll see that - '

''Good of the whole' implies an equal distribution.' The man, now standing, glanced around him again. 'The system is so ingrained now it could well have become part of the western world's genetic make-up.'

'Why bother to fight it then? asked Jordan. 'Our system *is* us.' We can't fight what we are.'

'We *feel* it's natural because it's been around a while, but - '

'I think we're getting too academic here, don't you?'

It was Archer's voice. He was 'standing in a corner at the rear of the room.

'Any questions from the floor? Other than the man who, I think, has had his fair share of time.'

A woman asked Jordan if he was married.

'No. Why do you ask?'

'Just that I always think that people feel it's better if an MP is married, it seems more conventional, more... '

'Safe?'

'Yes.'

'I can understand that, but the implication is that if one hasn't 'settled down' he's going to maybe do erratic things, wild things.'

'Jordan Wilde things?'

She looked around her, her expression oozing an expectation of acknowledgement for her wordplay. There were one or two grins.

'Any more pertinent questions?' Jordan asked.

An elderly man, slowly and with some difficulty, stood.

'I just wanted to ask what you think the Russian Revolution achieved; you know, in nineteen seventeen. Think it changed the world at all?'

'To be honest with you, I don't know a great deal about it, but if you think maybe it was ultimately a triumph of people power, my impression is that it was no more than a political *coup d' etat* that replaced the existing feudal nation of supposed aristocratic excess with nothing more than, I suppose, a sort of blood-soaked totalitarianism. But then, that's communism for you.'

The first speaker, remaining seated this time, said, 'There's never been the utopian communism envisaged by Marx, and there doesn't have to be authoritarianism, a counter ideology doesn't *have* to land up with an ideologue. There could - '

'Thank you,' replied Jordan, you had your say a little while ago, as was noted. Are there any more questions?'

Another senior citizen asked whether the government was going to do anything about the unions, followed by a woman concerned with the shortage of teachers, suggesting that immigrants were totally to blame for oversubscribed classes. The last questioner was a man who wanted to know what Jordan would do about his right-of-way being transgressed by an annoying neighbour

Jordan handled these competently enough, reminding the questioners that more money had been promised for education by the existing government. Then, after answering more questions, the man who had introduced him appeared by his side and thanked the audience for attending and Jordan for speaking. He told the former that there was no immediate hurry to leave and, if they wished, could finish their tea and biscuits. The clapping this time was a little hurried as people returned to their refreshments.

Having no-one coming up to speak to him, and spotting Archer, Jordan went to him and told him he could do with a drink.

'Sure, there's The Albert round the corner, come on.'

Before leaving they thanked the backbencher in charge, who told Jordan that he liked his direct, no-frills style, the agent replying that maybe they'd found the mythical creature everyone wanted, the honest politician.

On the way to the pub Jordan asked his companion how he thought he'd fared.

'Let's talk about it over a drink; I didn't fancy the wine there or the biscuits.'

They sat down comfortably in a typical London gastro-pub: fascia and windows painted in grey matt, anaglypta ceiling paper in the same colour, potted plants by the entrance and inside, plaster-stripped Victorian bricks and a terra cotta dining area.

Archer began. 'Right, I liked the way you treated Mister Big Words - okay, so it wasn't that friendly - but not the 'checks and balances' bit you spouted, It's too tame, it implies a lack of power, People want authority, a government that can do things, they feel - '

'Safe? It is true though, no party can really do more in day-to-day life than interfere, really, to implement things to a greater or lesser degree.'

'What's truth got to do with it? Look, there's some political growing-up to do, eh? And you weren't exactly tactful with the marriage question were you. You could have told her you were trying to but nobody would have you, or something, turned it into a little joke. You could, maybe, have been a little kinder to other questioners.'

His listener was silent.

'Granted, old Big Words does fall into my dislike category. He's smart, you don't want too many of him on the campaign trail. You also, incidentally, need to learn very quickly how to say something without saying anything of any consequence. However, generally... Yeah, the boy did good.'

He raised his glass.

'Here's to the next successful candidate for Wansford East. Cheers.'

He knew it would be difficult telling two dozen African females and six males from the same continent that god didn't create us, we created god. And it had been. After a break he had
gone back to the class, walked in, closed the door and almost
shouted, 'Ideas, family, State, religion, all *socially* constructed.
We're talking positivism, determinism; sense-data.'

He'd begun to strut then crouched and spun back to the empty
board, his marker slashing across it, using it as a tabula rasa analogy of man. As a late student slid in he rolled his eyes, grabbed
the register and demanded his name.

'Adam,' the youth had stuttered. But he needed an Acheam-
pong, Kojali, Abegonde or Okoti, not a Christianised forename of
ubiquitous Catholicism.

The latecomer had walked to the back of the room and sat next
to a girl with an apple on her desk. The others had looked down,
hiding their grins.

He had to smile himself as he recounted the lesson to Paul
while they were sitting in a café near the college. It was a new
class. He'd wanted to drain the religion from them so they'd have
space to absorb the concept of detached observation - even if it
was impossible to achieve - to look at the world, be apart from it
for a while, observe it, analyse it, see social facts as things.

It was Paul who had tried to persuade Ralph to go to a political
meeting in the next borough the evening before.

'You told me you'd once canvassed for an MP,' he'd said.
'Come on, let's go, let's see if the stereotypes have some validity.'

'Such as?'

'The Eton thing; Eden, Macmillan etcetera'

'A bygone age.'

'But they'll be white and male, Right and The Mail.'

'That was laboured. What do you want to go for? It's a Tory
thing.'

'Let's go anyway.'

On the way, passing a group of football fans, Paul had said, 'Whatever happens you're never gonna get a revolution while there's football; that and the telly, the opiate of the masses.'

As they had neared the large suburban house, Ralph had halted and said, 'You go. I can't.'

'Chickening out?'

'Partly, but I've also got some stuff to mark; just realised it's for tomorrow. Sorry.'

Paul was telling Ralph how un-enjoyable it had been, except for some of the questions asked.

'You ask any?'

'No.'

Knowing that his friend could, on public occasions, lose his articulacy when frustrated or irate, which led to more frustration, more exasperation, Ralph wasn't surprised.

'There was no picture of Blair, either. There should've been, he was Thatcher's greatest political creation. I posted a job application letter just now, and thought of you and your complaint letters. Perhaps they give you more satisfaction than having a go at authority face-to-face. Perhaps they sink in deeper.'

'I get some vexation out either way; what a dated word.'

'Remember the ones you wrote to the mayor a few years ago? You know, the graffiti one, the cycle lane one. I liked the graffiti one. I remember the beginning: 'The 'Showcase London to the World' Olympics has an ugly crack in the glass: graffiti, the aesthetic of indulgent infantilism."

'Yeah, I remember.'

'And mentioning when we were in New York for a few days and walked thirty miles around the five boroughs and saw just six pieces of graffiti, and a cab driver telling us that the city had been cleaned up and that he'd been to London, and saying 'Wow! What's happened to dat place? dere's fuckin' graffiti everywhere."

'Out of the mouths of babes and taxi drivers.'

'And the other one: 'London,' you wrote, 'is a city in the northern hemisphere, it is not the capital of a Mediterranean country, neither is it in Florida. Bright blue doesn't suit it, it is alien, especially when it's a five-foot wide strip painted on its main roads and with double yellow lines looking like a renegade promotion leading to a circus.'

'Your memory, man.'

'I liked the bit about seeing it from outer space. 'I suspect that, when completed, it will be possible to see these luminous strips from space; the Great Wall of China and Barclays Bank forming a famous duo. Welcome to Barclays London City!''

'You brought yourself to write one too, you renegade, you.'

'Yeah, New York again, on the subway. I mentioned that transatlantic accent announcing, 'No eating, littering or smoking is allowed on this train, and those of you with cell phones or other electronic devices please have consideration for other passengers.'

'Civilised.'

'We're da Moan bruvvahs, blud.'

'Wha'evah.'

Paul looked about him again looking like the original cockney sparrow, head and eyes darting around like an over-excited *flaneur*, this time it was the women walking by. Putting on his best cockney, Paul nodded his head towards one of them and said, 'Look at the arse on that.'

He got up and went out of the cafe to look. He turned then walked backwards, craning his head, still looking, and rejoined his friend.

'You're like a child.'

'Since when have children looked at arses?'

'How's job-hunting?'

'I was at the benefits place yesterday and I met somebody in the line who used to work for the Department of Employment and he said the worse thing about it is that when you get sacked you still have to show up the next day.'

'At least it wasn't a political joke.'

'I don't approve of political jokes; I've seen too many get elected. I wonder if the bloke I listened to yesterday will get in.'

'Sure to. Over the past eighty years this area has produced a Tory PM, a Foreign Secretary and a load of other mutual ineffectives.'

Looking at the café clock, Paul told Ralph that he should have been at the Benefits Agency half an hour previously, and left, knowing his friend would pay the bill.

The latter looked at a Lempicka-like picture on the wall of two women leaning a little apart against a bar counter, one holding a wine glass, and looking at each other with a hint of sensuousness, or was it his projection? He nodded to the grey moustached patron with a menu in one hand and worry beads crunching in the other. Was it a habit learned from his culture or was he playing with them for a specific reason? Three hundred-pound smart phones were the contemporary worry beads, he mused.

He went out. Unusually, he had a free day except till the evening when he had a class. Sometimes, depending on his own mood and the intelligence and responsiveness, and occasionally the combativeness of the students, he would be stimulated enough for it to delay his getting to sleep afterwards.

As he walked along a short terraced road whose houses were built straight from pavements, he looked at yellow stock bricks, cannon-head chimneys, slate roofs and wondered what affect the first row houses, as they were initially named just after the 1666 fire, had had on their residents.

He imagined, as he strolled, that in the first strangeness of them, a new resident, assuming opposing walls as his, chances upon the architect's blueprints showing forty one parallel lines demarcating forty homes and, realizing the deceit of psychological ownership, knocks at his neighbour's door to tell him that one of his walls isn't his, is arbitrarily owned, then, vexed, returns to angrily punch a dividing one.

Ralph sees plaster crumbling and distemper flaking, leaving the neighbour suddenly insecure. He, in turn, flails his fists against friezes and wainscots, their movements almost synchronised as if they could see each other; then both are running along the road carrying the word that the ownership of walls is in doubt.

Then all are attacking walls with hammers, picks, pokers and boots. Lathes are torn away, bricks dislodged, and the first hole is knocked into a parlour, a bloodied hand showing through. Ceilings start sagging, glass explodes, roves split and fall, leaving them all in a dust-fogged streetscape, in a rubbled wasteland.

Perhaps, he thought, there's some sort of analogy there for impromptu revolution; people getting together, beginning to change things. But wouldn't this context work against the idea of all property being theft? And anyway, all analogies break down because they're... analogies.

He then saw someone coming towards him, head down, forefinger stroking his phone. Ralph halted, half turning his shoulder just before the man knocked into him and looked up, frowning.

'People with their nose in their phone,' Ralph said slowly, 'are, in effect, using them to outsource the task of avoiding a collision.'

The man's frown deepened then lifted.

'I know you. Christ, it's Ralph from Suffolk.'

For a few seconds Ralph couldn't remember him; then did. It was Terry Binns from their old university.

'Good old Suffolk, eh?'

Terry held his hand out. Ralph shook it.

'It's been a while. Where you going?'

'At the moment I'm going nowhere really, just perambulating.'

The man looked at his watch.

'I'm supposed to be somewhere in two hours. Fancy a drink, or food or something? And sorry about bumping into you, literally, though you could have made the contact easier.'

'Guess I was a little rude. Sorry.'

The entrance to a City of London cemetery was on the other side of the road.

'We could go in the cafe there, it'll be pretty empty.'

Terry agreed and they walked under an imposing Victorian mock Tudor entrance and went into the cemetery's eatery. They sat and ordered.

'The Communist Party of Britain, eh?' said Ralph. 'Remember that? A bit new, then.'

'Yes, seven years old and breaking away from Eurocommunism and the old Gramscians,' said the man Ralph had literally bumped into.'

'Betcha not still in it.'

'I go to the occasional meeting. Not the same place of course.'

'What d'you do now?'

'After a few years of teaching, mostly kids, I now do some copywriting. You?'

Ralph briefly recounted his life since Suffolk before Binns said, 'You know, it's been about fifteen years, yet we recognised each other almost immediately.'

'Well, with your blue eyes, fair hair, flashing white teeth and still desperately trying, and succeeding, in looking like a young Kirk Douglas... '

'Thanks, and you haven't changed that much either.'

'It's hard to associate Bolsheviks, Lenin, revolution et cetera with someone's front room - well, it was like someone's front room - in a rural hamlet in the Home Counties.'

'I enjoyed it though, didn't you?'

'Sometimes. As it was our last year my mind was on Finals, though I did pick up some stuff for the political questions, especially from Spencer, remember him? A rabble-rouser without the rabble, really. I guess most rural people see the bosses as, somehow, being bred to take charge, landed gentry and all that, ordained almost. There were a few savvy regulars, though it was sometimes hard to take their country accents proclaiming people power seriously.'

'That was our own urban conditioning. I liked the way old firebrand would thump his fist on that table to push home the idea that what appears in western society as traditional cultural phenomena like capitalism are relatively recent developments that help justify and maintain hierarchy and exploitation.'

'Indeed, people tend to accept the divine right of tradition. They won't challenge it. 'Well,' they say, 'it's always been like that,' or 'done that way."

Their food was placed in front of them, neither seeming aware of it being so.

'I remember what he thumped on about more than some of the lectures I sat through.'

'Me too,' said Ralph.'

'He was certainly committed. Guess he got the old barbs flung at him, like 'There must be something wrong with him,' 'He's inadequate, jealous, neglected as a child.' You know the sort of things.'

'Psychological reductionism as an attack on someone's opinion that doesn't agree with your own.'

'"The politics of envy,' all that stuff. Done much politics since then?'

'Proselytize to students, not much else.'

'I thought you would have done. The few times we did go I went along for interest really, but you seemed more committed.'

'Think of ham and eggs; the chicken's involved, the pig's committed. You're right, I should have done.'

'You still could.'

Ralph said nothing for a while, then, 'What got to me from that time was when I lived in Easton during the first year because the new campus residences weren't yet ready and the local accommodation had been used up, so quite a few of us had to go out further. It wasn't that convenient at times.

'It was a coastal town with no industry as such, though fishing still went on, but it centred round a small number of extended families, and even the thought of toiling in the traditional trades was alien for a segment of the white locals.'

'Guess their default position was benefit dependency.'

'It was. To be a 'benefits family' was almost a kind of badge of pride, rather than a reflection of illness, redundancy or short-term ill-fortune. It was a way of saying, 'We don't work, and don't expect to.'

'They had little self-belief, and were given, and accepted, shite services.'

'Quite. Fatalism and acceptance as mutually reinforcing attitudes, eh?'

'It's probably the same now. They could plant magic money trees in their barren orchard, but... '

They finished their savoury, ordered and consumed their dessert saying little.

'That was nice,' said Terry, finishing a microwaved crumble. 'I always think that the two main parties are like divorced parents who care more about getting the kids to hate the other one than in their welfare. You married now? I am.'

'Nope.'

'I remember in philosophy the 'two premises and a conclusion' bit, and you said it was like marriage; 'two promises and a confusion.''

'Me trying to be clever.'

Terry then had a glance at his watch and said, 'Gotta go, got this meeting thing, advertising stuff.'

He stood, handed Ralph a business card and told him it had been nice seeing him again.

'Let's meet up.'

Ralph quickly wrote down a phone number and handed it to him before Binns left.

He looked at the card; it had a Facebook address on it, something Ralph had never bothered with. He wasn't interested in a friend of a friend of a friend, who he probably wouldn't like anyway, informing him of what he'd had for breakfast or how many times he'd pissed the previous day. But it was good to see his old party member companion again, though neither of them had made any positive contribution to it.

He vacated the place soon afterwards, having to circumnavigate bollards to eventually get onto a pavement; a phone company digging holes in the road whilst the pavement opposite was being re-laid behind protective plastic barriers, narrowing the road to a single lane. There were, he knew, more than a hundred-and-fifty separate firms that were allowed go dig up London's streets, some, involving small excavations, merely having to pay a small fee to do so. Another argument, he murmured to himself, for the state ownership of utilities, along with some joined-up thinking.

The same went for basic public necessities. What, he thought, could be more of a natural monopoly than water? There were no coal mines left to nationalise, as a reformist government did over sixty years ago, and there was no more Attlee and Bevan to push things through, though the latter's well-known loathing of the Tory Party seemed to resonate with what he himself sometimes felt. Though recognising when he did that it was perhaps simplistic and rather cheap and that hate wasn't much use in politics - hate never built a new school - he didn't care; the ex-Minister of

Health's sentiment was like a flashing neon sign behind his own perceptions of various events and moments which seemed to be increasingly plentiful. It lit up a kind of repression, and he knew it wasn't healthy to let these annoyances, frustrations and indecisions lie there, trapped.

On the Tube, glancing through the food, fashion, celeb, and property porn of the Evening Standard, he saw an item about a proposed protest against female genital mutilation or, as his African students called it, 'infibulation.' He had felt sorry for the African women in his classes when they'd spoken of it, but wasn't particularly bothered by the matter at the time.

Some of the students would occasionally research the topic, he sometimes helping them with their phrasing, and he knew that it had happened to them or a member of their family. He would also encourage them to research things they felt strongly about that had happened within their culture - in their home country or in this. It was often abuse in many forms.

Thinking of it now, he felt a little more keenly about the protest, it was a justifiable cause. He had two classes the next morning. He would go there afterwards.

CHAPTER EIGHT

It was a pleasant-looking house: frilly net curtains, fish scale tiles, a lack of plantation shutters, and a hanging flower basket in the porch made it more so. Not having canvassed before, for himself or others, he initially thought that he might go for the less-affluent pockets of the neighbourhood, not expecting them to be Conservative voters, as a sort of test. But travelling along The Drive with those large windows, pitched roofs, verdant front gardens and the park and the lake opposite, decided to take the easier option. Archer was supposed to have met him nearby but had called to tell him he would be late, so he thought he'd try it on his own for a while.

'Hello, I'm Jordan Wilde your local Conservative candidate for the up-coming by-election, you should have our leaflet. Can I count on your vote?' he cheerily said to the middle-aged woman looking like a bit-player in a Forties drama who opened her front door to him.

'When is it?'

He told her the day and date.

'I might vote for you If you can do something about the traffic in this road, it's getting worse, and all the run-ins people are having done, they look out their front windows at cars' bums. They're ruining the street.'

'Well, er... '

'If you're not interested in doing anything about it then I'm not going to vote for you.' She shut the door.

Jordan was disappointed. It seemed so... small, parochial; apolitical.

His knock on the next door wasn't answered. The next was. A large man appeared and said, 'Yes?'

Jordan began telling him his name when the man said, 'You're not from them Liberals are you?'

Stating who he represented, Jordan asked if he could count on the householders' vote.

'As long as you're not a Lib. We'll be like Nazi Germany soon; people accepted what was happening, not realizing the danger. It's getting the same here; the snowflakes getting annoyed at ridiculous things like saying the transgender community, probably only about point-nought-five of one percent of the population, would be offended if we call pregnant women 'mothers.' If someone's pregnant then they must have a womb, therefore they're a woman, a soon-to-be mother. End of.'

'Agree totally, and - '

'It's easy to laugh at it, it's ludicrous, but it's dangerous as well. It creates fear, and people in power allow themselves to be frightened. They make the wrong decisions. It can cost lives. The whole movement's dangerous.'

'Yes, but it doesn't have to stand in the way of our city, our country becoming stronger, richer, nurturing the economy - '

'Heard it all before, mate. It's one thing agreeing with me, another trying doing something about it. Good afternoon.'

The door closed.

Turning away towards the garden gate, Jordan felt rather lost. He agreed about the liberal overkill, but surely, *the* important thing was the economy, in the end it would benefit everyone. The man must surely be interested in that?

'Couldn't wait?'

It was Archer. 'Sorry I was late. Some prat of a labour councillor having a go at me, I must be getting well known. But you shouldn't have started on your own. Dunno what you've been saying, but you probably shouldn't have. I've brought some stuff for us to give out. It's pretty focused and forensic these days, it's about data capture.'

He showed Jordan a form with some questions:

'If there was an election tomorrow how would you vote? (Canvassers show the punter a list of options). Can you remember how you voted last time? What are the issues that matter most to you? 'What do you like most about X (the party you are canvassing for). Will you vote for this party at this election? Is there anything we can help with today? (If it is a 'Yes' vote).'

'Get the point? Gone are the days when we made it up as we went along.'

'But this is a by-election.

'Never mind, we can use it anyway.'

'What about a little human contact, doesn't it help?'

'Very rarely. Come on, I'll introduce you. Where you up to?'

'I was going here, next one.'

They walked up a garden path, both noticing the pile of books on the brick pillar holding the gate, and rang a doorbell. A woman appeared immediately.

'Sorry if I startled you, I was picking up some mail.'

She was slim with dark brown hair and, under an attractive smile, Jordan felt, a firmness; an opinionated but informed personality.

'Good morning,' greeted Archer, 'This is Jordan Wilde, your Conservative candidate.' He gestured briefly to his companion.

'He's not my candidate; I don't wish to own him in any way.'

Ignoring this, Archer handed her the form and a pen.

'Could you quickly fill this in for us?'

'I could, but I shan't.'

'Let's see if we can persuade you to.'

'I shan't be voting for you, Mister Wilde,' she said, looking directly at him. 'Nothing personal.'

She began closing the door.

Jordan felt a little hurt, despite the 'non-personal' claim.

'Let's talk about it.'

'I don't wish to waste my energy.'

'D'you want to talk facts, principles; what?'

'Alright.'

She stepped forward and folded her arms.

The stereotype of a folded-arm woman, for Jordan, was a battle axe, a mother-in-law, perhaps a turbaned, domestic matriarch from World War 2; certainly not in this case, her arms merely lifted her neatly-shaped breasts a little higher.

'The economy,' she said, a little challengingly.

'Just up my street.'

'Though it's often a hazy euphemism for profits being made by a relative few; and are you aware that multinationals operating in this country owe six billion pounds in unpaid tax?'

'I can assure you that when we resume governing, HMRC will have even more powers to claim this money.'

'No, they're treating the symptoms, not the disease. We need an international agreement including tax haven countries, but it's not going to happen.'

For a second he wasn't sure how to respond; the women he had known wouldn't have said what he'd just heard.

'Er, Mrs… '

"Mrs? An assumption. You really are Jurassic, aren't you.'

'I was surprised at the cogency of what you said. But we can make a difference here. This party is strong enough to make a big one. The money will be gathered in from these companies and in the end this country will be fairer and - '

'Don't say 'more equal,' it implies there's already some equality. Are you aware that o.06 percent of the population own half of all rural land in England and Wales? A third of this land is still owned by rural gentry and aristocrats; the eighth biggest land-owner has 240,000 acres. The top ten British land owners own 6 million acres between them in a country of 60 million acres. This is pointless. Good day, Mister Wilde.'

She closed the door firmly. He stood there for a few seconds.

Archer, who hadn't spoken a word throughout, said, 'That went well didn't it. You've got to be prepared for all sorts; you weren't. Shall we try the next one? I'll introduce you. I'm not putting you off am I? Let's see what the next one has to say.'

There was no response from the next two abodes, while the third had its door opened by a stooping, lank-haired, grey-stubbled man with rather faded eyes, who Jordan imagined to be a life-long Conservative voter who, perhaps, had done so out of an unthinking ritual.

Immediately after Archer again introduced his protégé, the man looked steadily at the former and said, as if by rote, 'Social mobility is in decline while wealth is concentrated in the hands of those in privileged positions and is disproportionately so in property.' He then switched his gaze to Jordan. 'Furthermore, the Bank of England, through low interest rates, has boosted the asset-rich which is fuelling inequality.'

'But there has to be investment, there has to be the wealthy, how would the majority get the money, anyway? How would they receive an income?'

The man, still stooping, stepped backwards and with a quietly-spoken, 'Oh dear.' another door was closed.

'What is this expectation they have of some sort of perfect equality?' asked Jordan, turning to his agent. 'What's equality anyway? In what form? I've heard this before: the posing of an absolute ideal. It's so... '

'Naive? Impossible? Perhaps it's something to do with this side of the road. Maybe Islingtonites have discovered this place and from this side of the street they can see the dawn sun confirming their place in a glorious utopian future.'

'Or maybe they've been listening to that lady too much.'

'I didn't like her, but I'd like to give her one. A hotbed of revolution in suburbia, eh? Difficult, isn't it. You've had to do all the listening and it's you who's supposed to talk, to tell them how you're going to solve their problems. Let's cross over.'

They went across the street and again began knocking on doors and ringing bells. Most of the people they spoke to - lifting Archer's mood - seemed long-established Tories; no comments on men who were 'too old and too white' to run the country in these leaf-surrounded semi-detacheds.

They trawled a few more streets, Jordan learning quickly when to and when not to have his say; his smiling but politically pragmatic answers to often unspoken questions. One householder, worried about his son's recent redundancy, was veering closer to the subject of nationalisation when Jordan reassured him that the government would willingly intervene if the market allowed some areas to stagnate or left workers feeling exploited.

'Otherwise,' he said with a smile, 'it would be a loss of faith in free markets and risk a return of the failed ideologies of the past.'

He continued in this manner in other doorstep conversations with 'need to keep markets stable,' 'competition's good,' 'freedom of choice.' and other platitudes, some suggested by Archer, between their calls.

As they turned the corner of the next road, Jordan implied that what he had been saying seemed a little trite and predictable.

'That's what they want. You've been speaking largely to the converted, they wanna hear it all again, gives 'em a sense of security if you like; a sort of 'it always was, it is now and it's always gonna be.' It won't be like this on every patch, as you've sussed by the Leftie loonies in The Drive.'

'A bit strong.'

'Why not use The Sun's and The Mail's perceptions? It suits The Telegraph readers, too; stereotypes, mate, it gives 'em a known world and people's places in it, and they want more of it. I like the way you haven't, so far, promised the earth. If you arouse hopes and expectations, when they're not realised the more disappointed people will be, and that'll be expressed at the next election. Anyway, you're getting there; you're doin' okay, geez.'

'How many more streets?'

'Let's do one more.'

They worked a slightly less affluent road, though the majority of people they spoke to said they would probably vote for Jordan. After this, the agent suggested they have a drink. His car was parked behind the nearby George And Dragon.

They walked to it with Archer discussing some more upcoming hustings and where and when they would be held; Jordan feeling excited and nervous about them in equal measures.

Sitting at a table, Archer asked him if he was on Facebook or Twitter, emphasising, when he'd received an affirmative reply, that opinion-forming was increasingly residing in social media.

'Increase your Facebook friends; certainly grow your twitter contacts. Okay, so one couldn't imagine the Right Hon. Harold McMillan using them even if they were around then, but don't overlook it. You don't have to get down with the kids, those kids have grown up now, to an extent anyway, and they can bring joy or pain to a politician. And that's what you're gonna be. Help make it happen.'

'Facebook use: adolescent, narcissistic hubris rooted in insecurity. I'm also wary.'

'Why?'

'Well, though it's created, in some countries certainly, a kind of political populism, that populism could turn lurid and swing Far-right and Far-left, whatever. I'll use it, sparingly, but as you say, trolling et cetera can get into the press and… it's not worth it.'

'Christ, it's looney lass,' said Archer, giving a little smirk.

Jordan glanced in the direction Archer's head was indicating. It was the intransigent woman from The Drive.

'She's on her own,' said Archer.

'Women can do that these days.'

'Sitting there, drinking.'

'Are you going to say that she's looking for someone to pick her up?'

''Course not; I'm not that much of a dodo.'

Jordan wanted to speak to her again. He got up and walked across to the wide bay window where she was sitting.

'Hello again.'

She looked up questioningly.

'I thought I'd seen the last of you.'

'You haven't. Would you say,' he asked her quietly, 'that nationalisation is an ideological rejection of a successful system?'

'Successful for whom?'

'Some more than others of course, but the others are doing okay.'

'Relative to what? And you're not going to give me the past as a reference point are you? The 'You've never had it so good' syndrome?'

'I wasn't; no.' He sat down opposite her. 'Tempting as it is, I wouldn't use the 'Ordinary people of this country are better off now than at any time in the past.''

'Not unless you're really desperate. You can select any comparison that suits your argument.'

'Of course, it's the political game.'

'Is politics a game to you then?'

'Well, there are rules, it's competitive and has accepted ways of behaving.'

'Like football? That's rule-bound. In fact, it reflects the norms and laws of society, it reinforces society's rules.'

'Interesting. But as far as I know, and I'm not a fan, it was initially an early twentieth-century industrial phenomenon which, if you like, is now for classless consumers of entertainment.'

'It's gone from a weekend outlet for the working class to a twenty-four-seven money machine and a proxy showcase for rival petrodollar economies.'

'No more the mirage of after-work, eh?'

'It's just an outlet; it gives those who don't own productive property, own little or nothing, the psychological ownership of 'their' team. They have an emotional stake in it, and if it wins then *they've* won, for a few days anyway. Rugger man are you?'

'Of course.'

'What do you do when you're not attempting to be a politician?'

'Finance, Investment.'

She smiled. 'It figures.'

She took a quick gulp from her glass, quickly wiped her lips with the back of a hand - the action seeming oddly, intriguingly, sexual to him - and stood.

'Must go. Excuse me.'

He stood. 'Look. '

'Yes?'

'On a scale of North Korea to America, how free are you this week?'

'Are you serious?'

'I'd like to see if I can change your mind.'

'My political position? You're not serious then.'

'I am.'

'I admire your nerve.'

'Yes, then?'

She thought for a while, her smile narrowing a little; then nodded.

'Okay then. You won't change me and I doubt if a Tory's mind *can* be changed.'

She paused, looked down then up again.

'This is ridiculous,' she said, shaking her head. 'Where then?

'Here on Saturday, about eight.'

She shook her head again, but with not so much emphasis. As she began to walk away she turned.

'Have you noticed that in movies when two people arrange a date, sorry, meeting, the time's never mentioned?'

'It's too real.'

'Don't you like real?'

'Do you?'

'Always.' She went out.

When he went back to his table, Archer informed him that he, also, was leaving.

'I'm going to sort out some meetings and things. I'll ring you soon.'

He briefly shook Jordan's hand. 'Yeah, she's attractive isn't she.'

Picking up his folder with the questionnaires, he put it under his arm and said, 'What are you doing, Jonathan Wilde, eh?' and left the pub.

Jordan sat there for a while thinking of the last few hours, but mostly of the girl. He then walked a few streets to his car, passing in the High Road a small pub with a scrawled sign outside welcoming open mic comics with the proviso that they, 'Must not engage in racism/sexism/homophobia/transphobia/ disabilism... '

He couldn't be bothered to read the rest. Didn't they know that there's a difference between what a comic thinks and what he thinks is funny?

He could think about this another time. He didn't want annoyance to get in the way of thinking about her.

CHAPTER NINE

It had started outside the town hall, he was late for it but after a couple of enquiries soon caught them up. It was as he'd assumed; mostly white women with a few African females walking with them. It interested him that the history of women's subjugation in the world's second largest continent had been internalized by its inhabitants so strongly. There was a smattering of white males but, of course, no Negroid men. It wasn't a large gathering, only sixty or so people.

Ralph stepped off the pavement and tagged along behind them. He knew only a little of the history of what they were protesting about; that it was initiated and carried out from days after birth to puberty and beyond, usually by women who saw it as a service of honour and that their failing to cut their children would mean social exclusion for their daughters. There were also notions of beauty, honesty and purity in the mix.

He was considering speaking to some of the men, but wasn't sure how passionately they felt about it, if at all, or how involved they were with the self-righteousness that comes with marching along the moral high ground.

He recognised the profile of someone towards the front, an ex-student, Perpetua; he'd never attempted to pronounce her surname. Only a week previously he had found amongst his folders a copy of her project and remembered some of its Rationale. It had begun:

'Being a woman who grew up in a country where they were regarded as men's property, I always thought that women who faced domestic violence from their partners deserved it, it was the way things were meant to be.'

He had pointed out to her at the time that they were classic characteristics of a belief in a traditional fate.

'Several times in my professional life when working with male colleagues they have expected me as a woman to serve them. After spending the whole day working together, we go home and as a woman you are expected to cook, fetch water to wash their hands and after finishing eating they want you to wash the dishes while they just sit.

'Most of them believe your purpose is to service them sexually and if one refuses their advances they say you are 'Westernised.' I've heard men at work saying they would never marry a black, educated woman because hey have 'lost their culture.''

How insecure men are, he thought, how frightened of losing a woman; in some cultures they are paid for, in others they are dressed in garments which hide their face. He wondered what the banners held by the people at the front would be saying, he hadn't noticed. He was glad she was here, publicly protesting.

He recalled her saying to him, when he called students up to discuss their work, sitting with him at his desk in class: 'I got married to a Zimbabwean man who is of mixed race and because of my culture I have faced domestic violence from this man for the past four years I have been married to him. When my husband demands sex from me and I tell him that I am tired he will beat me up and tell me that he has paid for it. In Zimbabwe culture there is what they call 'lobola, it is what men pay to the woman's parents if they want to marry their daughter; it is like selling the woman to her future husband and that is why men take women as their property.'

He'd once noticed a bruise on the side of her face when she'd come into the classroom. He could see, close up, that it was fresh. Aware that he was looking at it she'd said, 'I don't deserve this do I.' She'd been the youngest in a class of thirty.

He decided to go to her, and began to move between those in front of him. Moving forward he inadvertently pushed into a woman at the side of him. He mumbled a 'Sorry' and briefly mentioned there was someone towards the front he wanted to speak to.

"Sister Anna will carry the banner.' 'But she's in the family way.' 'She's in everybody's friggin' way," she said quietly.

'Can't beat the old ones can you. Actually, she's not carrying the banner.'

'One of the African girls?'

'I used to teach her.'

'Will she recognise you?' She asked it with a gentle grin and a slightly raised eyebrow.

'Should do. I had many students, they had few teachers. I suspect you remember yours more than you remember most of your school friends. Excuse me.'

He moved between other marchers and got near to the girl. He was about to tap her on the shoulder when she turned.

'Hello, Ralph,' she said, strangely matter-of-factly as if expecting him to be there.

She looked towards the front again. Her eyes seemed dull, as if she wasn't really caring about the protest, as if she was doing it because it was expected of her. Perhaps she'd been on other demonstrations about the same thing and felt they were getting nowhere, or maybe she was expecting her husband to appear at any moment and drag her away, reclaim his property.

He stepped aside and stood for a few seconds till they'd passed him and he was at the rear again

'That didn't take long.'

It was the woman again.

'Er, no.'

'Are you going to join us?'

He began walking with her once more.

She looked at him enquiringly; again the quizzical half-smile.

'Didn't go well? Sorry, it's nothing to do with me'. She looked ahead. 'It's good that there are a few men on this march, more a stroll really, but the African women have to fight stigma and shame to do this.'

'Fear, too.'

'Husbands?'

'Those as well.'

'Doing your bit for equality of educational opportunity?'

'A cliché for the equal opportunity to be unequal.'

'Quite. Social mobility's actually declining, and it's not just about money is it.'

'No. The expectational norm of the middle class child is H.E. for the unskilled it's still, possibly, 'Get a trade in yer 'ands, son.''

'Son?'

'Am I being sexist? Sorry, but the notion that we now have some sort of classless society - '

''Cloth cap politics is dead'? It gets on my tits too.'

He laughed. 'I've never heard a woman say that before.'

'Strange that men use it when it's us that has them.'

He glanced at her, behind the large eyes there was something... He couldn't quite tell. A depth, certainly. He mused for a second on the idea that eyes were expressionless; it was the muscles around them, what was being said, experienced, the context; many things that make us feel that they are expressive. He pushed the dulling thought away. He'd also noticed how long her legs were. She was quite tall.

She turned her head and grinned at him

'I'm wondering what you're thinking, whether you want to continue in this vein or talk - '

'About tits?'

'Not really.'

The march was now turning a corner and he asked her where they were going.

'To the other town hall, along this road. It's not a long march, and when we arrive there'll be a few speeches, I suppose.'

'You know more than I do. What d'you intend to do when it stops?'

'Not stay around.'

'Nor me. Have a coffee?'

'I suppose we could stop short of the end and leave.'

'Let's do that.'

They walked in silence for a while until she beckoned him to follow her onto the pavement. He did and went with her into a café.

Telling him she was a vegetarian she ordered a cheese toastie with a large salad, and he, scampi. He asked her if she minded him continuing what he'd been saying. She told him to go ahead.

'There was a pic in the paper recently showing fifty black students outside an Oxford college and stating that there should be more and that Oxbridge were letting down working class and black students. This rather pisses me off, as if whites are class-divided yet blacks and ethnics are somehow a homogenous whole. There's little doubt that the majority of the blacks in the photo, if not all, had at least a middle class background.'

'What about the workers, eh?'

'Quite. White *and* black. I often think that LGBTQ Plus and the feminist outcry is, in the end, a Right wing-backed covert conspiracy to take attention away from *the* significant divide.'

'More of a class ceiling than a glass one?'

'Precisely. Again, power. It could be argued that the symbols of the ruling class are embedded in the education system: essay writing skills, abstract thinking - '

'Classical music.'

'Yeah, these are alien to the less affluent and the poor who are judged on the same skills. Their skills haven't the same status, head knowledge always having a greater worth than hand knowledge. Even their restricted codes have more status.'

'Poetry?'

'That's one of them, certainly a higher rating than The Sun, Eastenders and patterned net curtains. There's a kind of clash of values between the classes and as middle class values are nearer to those of the upper class than the lower classes are... ' He shrugged.

'Those that rule are powerful enough to have their culture accepted as the *only* meaningful one?' she suggested.

'Quite. Sorry if I sound as if I'm lecturing.'

'You could say, I suppose, that a working class child, in order to succeed, has to leave his own culture at the school gates, so to speak.'

'Quite.'

'The perennial political promise of equality through education is dead in the water then.'

'Education can't change the structure of society, anyway. What did Marx say? 'In every age the ruling ideas - '

'Are the ideas of the ruling class.'

He was a little surprised she knew that. And pleased.

A waitress put their food in front of them and returned to the counter.

'I hope you don't feel rescued by the salad,' he asked.

'I don't need rescuing.'

He watched her eat, something he rarely liked doing with other people even when eating himself. It was partly her rather old-fashioned, ergonomically maximised knife and fork correctness, and partly her full lips. She wore no make-up, she had little need to.

She looked up. 'It's a change to sit with someone who doesn't put their phone on the table.'

'It's a change to be with a woman who I can talk to as if - '

'She was a man?'

'I didn't say that. Anyway, I don't always carry mine, but it seems to be the reality of our everyday digital lives that we're increasingly wrapped in a perpetual electronic and virtual present that's turning people into incommunicative idiots incapable of little more than a tweet.'

'Sometimes I think Facebook is like an escaped dog who, when retuning home, says to another dog, 'You know what; I've smelt three hundred strange arseholes today.'

If any other woman had said it he wouldn't have liked it, but it was different with this one. He was aware he perhaps had a rather dated normative perception of a woman's behaviour, but it didn't seem to matter now.

'What do you do?' he asked her.

'Work for a charity, do my bit for things like this little march. Oh, and I did a degree in history.'

'History is a way of organising our ignorance of the past.'

'Perhaps. I had he chance of doing a local TV thing a few years ago presenting a historical look at... what was it called? 'The History of the Mob,' but it didn't work out.'

'Perhaps you didn't throw your arms around enough; you're not a proper historian unless you do that.'

'Not a stereotype by any chance?'

'A TV inspired one, yes, but we all think in stereotypes. We search for order, we're also lazy; they give us a reason not to bother to think. They can be de-emphasised of course, get enough black men playing lawyers in films and people will begin to feel that - '

'All black men are lawyers?'

'No, but it will weaken the initial stereotype.'

'Which is?

'Well, when African-Caribbeans first came here in the Fifties there were a lot of jibes about coming from jungles, swinging from trees, etcetera. As abhorrent as that is, they were the un-thinking stereotypes: black equals jungle equals primitive. 'Oil slicks,' was a favourite term. The same with ethnics, my grand-dad would call someone a 'dirty Arab', it was a derogatory term.'

She looked at him for a while, studying him, slightly frowning, but not enough to cover up the almost invisible half-smile.

'I feel you don't get enough stimulation at work, you need it outside also. Am I right?'

'S'ppose so.'

'Ditto.'

'Let me give you some.'

'You are. Did you notice the cops keeping an eye on our little protest, carrying out their primary function to protect the property class's interests from attacks by the property-less masses?'

'Quite, but they seem to be thinking twice about exercising some of their powers; liberalism has a strange hold.'

'The fear of disapproval.'

'But why so much fear? The primary principle of our justice system, innocent until proven guilty, is seemingly becoming re-versed; people targeted by liberals are now guilty until proven innocent.'

'You've got it bad haven't you.'

'Does that invalidate what I say then?

''Course not, I don't play that game.'

'Political correctness, as minor and laughable as it's made out to be, has distorted truth. Truth has become an insult.'

She looked at him steadily. 'Perhaps it represents for you a denial of what is, a disbelief. You hate it because it's saying truth *isn't*, therefore you are *not*. Too strong?'

'I can't think of that here, I will when I'm on my own. Have you done any psychology?'

'That wasn't psychology, that's a number-crunching game.'

A loud scraping of metal on ersatz marble interrupted them as a waitress tidied chairs under tables while another went outside to bring them in.

'Time to go,' said Ralph's companion, picking up her hand-bag.

He paid at the counter, commenting as they left that it was nice to see a handbag again, his mother used rarely to be without one.

She quietly hummed, 'I'm Just An Old-fashioned Girl… '

He asked whether she'd had to travel far.

'I'll get a bus back.'

'I'll walk to the stop with you.'

He looked casually at the houses while they walked, she looking straight ahead.

'You know, more people can be fitted into terraces like these than in high-rises. What's happening now is we make individual buildings which get bigger and bigger. We used to make places, now we make places with the space that's left over in between buildings.'

'The notion of human scale starting to disappear, eh?'

'Indeed.'

'Look, my stop's around this corner.'

'Maybe I'll see you - '

'Thanks for the meal. Bye, bye.'

She walked away and gave the briefest of turns and smiled. She disappeared around the corner.

He crossed the road and walked back a short distance and entered a small park, a rather too heat and tidy one, too few leaves on the paths, too tightly-pruned bushes, too municipal; even fallen petals seemed to have been cleared away.

He'd enjoyed the last few hours. He hadn't felt quite like this for a while, the adrenalin was pumping. He'd tripped and fallen on a pavement a few days previously, the sort of trip where, in slow motion, arms start to flail and you know you're going to hit the ground. But, getting up immediately, the adrenalin was there and he felt better.

Perhaps, he thought, with somewhat adolescent humour, that he should see her every other day and on the days he didn't, throw himself to the ground to ensure a regular supply of that chemical. He didn't know her name, though.

CHAPTER TEN

'Somebody said to me the other day that being extreme, Right or Left, is now the norm. It isn't. Yes, there are increasing divisions; politically, religiously, socially as well, but it isn't extreme. But let's assume, though, that the country is either under State ownership or everything is owned by, and managed for, the corporations and the rich.'

'It is.' someone shouted.

'It's Centrist. It has to be. The centre: steady, organised - '

'Organised for whom?' It was the same voice.

'Solid, stable, a recognised pattern, the status quo, and I don't mean the old pop group.' Jordan smiled; he'd rehearsed it to lighten things up a little.

'What we want and what you'll get when you vote Conservative are social and economic arrangements as they are, but *better*. We need a new sense of what it means to be British today, we need to find some common ground that people can sign up to, that might renew a sense of shared identity. Otherwise - and this is where I go back to the beginning - it's easy for extremists to poison the political debate.'

'How can we have a sense of sharing if the gap between rich and poor has never been wider?' A different voice.

'And I want to say this; a word that rhymes with sharing: caring. There *can* be more money for our health system; there can be more help for affordable homes.'

'What does that mean?' The first questioner this time. 'A slight reduction in the astronomical cost of the other homes?'

Jordan was in a Sixties-built hall off Wansford's High Street used mostly by a local cinema club and the W.I. It was well attended and at the start, as this was his first formal address on his campaign trail, he'd felt a little nervous, but for only a short while.

'Watcha gonna do for us locals then?' somebody asked.

'Well, for one example; as you may know, the Night Tube has now come to east London and I'm sure there are plans afoot to bring it to Wansford. I will certainly help that effort to boost the local economy most enthusiastically.'

'What is this 'economy,' Mister Wilde? Is it turnover or does it mean, again, profit for the relative few?' A familiar voice by now.

'What this will be doing is connecting with audiences, creative people, businesses and the local communities it serves, and which I will certainly serve if elected.'

'The Night Tube's just for hipsters, mate,' said an elderly man from the front seats. 'We're getting 'em here.'

'It's a bit sad,' opined a woman seated next to him, 'when an area's supposed to be on the up because you've got young people with beards and tight trousers arriving in it.'

'Yeah, and Rodgers, a store that's been here for eighty years, is closing down. What's it gonna become, a cereal café?'

'More likely a high-rise full of concrete balconies and nought-point-one percent affordable flats.' One familiar, and one new voice.

''Stunning apartments.'' someone corrected him.

'Let's take some sensible questions.'

'Is a Tory Government ever going to care about the NHS?' asked one of the previous questioners.

'Of course it cares.'

'Why privatization then?'

''Parts of our health service have to have private support.'

'You make it sound as if the private sector is actually giving money to it.'

'If the service was wholly funded by public revenue then the government, *any* government, would have to borrow. We're still paying for the crash over ten years ago.'

'If corporate taxes were - '

'I've already covered that.'

'What about the Green Belt?' asked someone from the back. 'Will it be built on?'

'There's enough urban sites, enough old buildings that are not usefully occupied that could be rejuvenated not to have to do that, but It could well happen if the Labour Party ever come to power again. Wasn't it Prescott who said that as a Labour Government was responsible for creating it, it could be responsible for building on it?'

There came a string of questions: inflation, defence and police cuts, immigration, HS2 and inevitably Brexit, which he thought he handled quite well, though having to bluff on some topics, reminding himself to step up his research. He assumed one or two people would come to him afterwards with a few more queries, but nobody did.

Archer, again at the back watching thin but this time seated, came to him and said, 'Not bad my boy, nothing sensational, but pretty safe. It appealed to the conservative natures of most of 'em. Too much one way or the other, especially Left, and it's not good, as you pointed out at the beginning, of course. Come on, it's pub time and I know a nice little one round the corner.'

'There's a surprise.'

'You were okay, you've slipped into role pretty quickly, but it felt at times that you could, under that urbane exterior, get a little scratchy, and show it. Not good to do that in public; people want a kind of stable stereotype. They may like politicians to be real people, often saying that those we've got are out of touch with ordinary Joes, but part of them doesn't really, it desires something solid, dependable, at least an image of such. Agree?

'Anyhow, betcha prefer this to pushing leaflets through doors and begging for approval, not that you've done much begging, yet. Dunno whether you've started the phone calls, I should have chased you up on 'em, but I've given out your email address, the party one I told you I'd fixed you up with. I should have done it before. Once the abuse comes in you'll probably wished I hadn't. Didya see crazy gal last week? Just as looney, or not?'

'Tell you in the pub.'

Over drinks he told him little, just that she was bright and attractive and quite challenging.

'Tell me something I don't know.' was Archer's reply, though Jordan's tone seemed to have satisfied his agent.

They talked of Spurs, wine, pizzas, Archer's bespoke brogue shoes, other MPs and would-be ones he'd helped in other constituencies, and an indirect mention of his wife. The beer was pretty good, but he had to get off to somewhere again. He gave his client a friendly squeeze on his bicep and left.

He'd been surprised that she was there before him. Sitting at a table away from the main throng, she was wearing a black pencil-slim skirt and tailored jacket, making the theory that because black absorbs light, women using it to look slimmer actually appear bulkier, seem utterly erroneous. He was about to try a little humour with his 'You don't know me but I'm Mister Right,' but decided not to. As he sat down opposite her she closed her book.

'Hello,' he said. 'Oh dear.'

'Why did you say that?'

'Your book. 'Das Kapital.' 'The capitalist class becomes unfit to rule because it is incompetent to assure an existence of its slave within his slavery.' That's all I remember, and I don't know where I picked it up from. Though, as an aside, it can assure his existence, most people do okay. Alright, so it's relative. Guess you can recite whole paras of it. D'you want another drink?'

'No thanks.'

He got up to get himself one and returned to the table.

"To possess possessions,' she said casually, "a man wills himself to have what another has but it never dawns on him that the more he earns the less he keeps of himself.' It's another quote.'

'But couldn't you argue the self is made from outside sources, that he, she, is made by the society they live in, so whatever he does will be, if you like, what they ought to do.'

'What a cop out. Okay, what *should* an existence be then? What is a non-exploited State?'

'I've never really thought much about these things, but since capitalism surely the majority of people are better off, and that's not just a cliché; it's true. Could there be any other system to do this?'

'Capital turns wants into needs. We do have things, and these things have a built-in obsolescence, fashion for example: What we wore last year is suddenly so last week - and people don't set fashions, brands do with the help of peer pressure - so you buy something more cool which equals more sales, more profits et cetera. It's all so obvious.'

'Why say it then?'

'In case you missed it. I could go on.'

'We're not going to though are we.' He looked at her steadily. 'Hello, how are you? What have you been doing since I last saw you?'

'Why d'you want to know?'

Why are you so... scornful?'

'Why are you so accepting? Because you're doing okay, you have money?'

When she said this, she seemed to him to be a little more ordinary, somehow, even vulnerable, perhaps.

'Look, I don't want to just... associate you with politics.'

'Why not?

'I like your dress, any colour would suit you, I think.'

Even as he said it he thought it was an irrelevance, though wasn't sure what relevant would be. She said nothing.

'You're not making this very easy'

'Making what easy?'

'A date.'

She laughed. 'Why are you knocking on people's doors and asking them to vote for you, anyway?'

'There has to be more than what I'm doing.'

'Well spotted.'

'I guess it's rather a closed world, most of the people I know in it are, I suppose, rather - '

'Unaware?'

'That may be the right word.'

'They don't look outside their symbolic universe of futures, exotic derivatives, asset class, T-bills, whatever they are, at other worlds, at other avenues of existence: the physical world, the making of it, of car-wash workers, of farm labourers, unless they can make out of it. Perhaps you also.

'What gets me is that people buy shares in something that produces something that people want or need and people like you make money out of guessing whether the value of the producer will rise or fall and you'll sell that algorithm-based guess to someone else and they in turn also do; yet Joe Bloggs on the factory or office floor hasn't altered his productive output one iota, nothing's changed. However complex or clever, what you do is essentially parasitic. It's like an infinite continuum of money-making.'

'But without investment - '

'The State could provide that.'

'Seen any good movies lately?'

She looked down and shook her head, grinning.

'I guess that's preferable to 'Weak retail market footfall is creating negatively impacted exposure in trading positions.''

He told her he'd recently watched some musicals from Hollywood's golden age.

'You know, Charisse, Kelly, Astaire, Eleanor Powell, Hayworth. Doubt if you'd like those.'

'Why wouldn't I?'

'I can imagine you religiously watching 'Battleship Potemkin,' 'The Fall of the Romanov Dynasty' and 'October' every six months or so rather than Hollywood products.'

'I'm surprised you know those. But I do like the old musicals.'

'Light relief?'

'Possibly.'

'Let's talk about things we go out to see; entertainment.'

They did, ranging from theatre and film, to an interest in Rugby Union then interrupting it with the political again.

'Have you thought,' she asked, 'about social media? I assume you use it.'

'Tweets?'

'Yes.'

'Why?'

'Well, a kind of generational dislocation is pretty ignorable isn't it in its electoral impact?'

'How long is a 'generation?''

'I know that's a lazy word, but you have to utilise the digital.'

'Wouldn't there be a danger of the kids saying that I was appropriating their music?'

'But they could say, 'He thinks like me, I didn't know we had things in common.''

'I suppose you can get angrier on social media.'

'Well, as someone said, 'If you're not angry you're not paying attention.'

'Maybe I'll bring it up with Archer, he's my agent. He told me once that for most people, politics is a desert of the imagination, a specialist pursuit of the committed.'

'Or plain odd.' She paused. 'Why am I helping you here? You're on the other side. I don't want your party representing the area I live in.'

'I have gathered that. You're not going to let politics get in our way though, are you?'

'Our?'

'Do you wish to tell me about you, at least your background, childhood?'

'Not really.'

'But you will though.'

'Okay. Surrey, and yes, dad was a stockbroker, and if you want to argue that my political conversion was a reaction against all that, you'll be wasting your time. Moved to London, went to St. Paul's - '

'The All-Girls school?'

'Yep, and frightened the life out of a few teachers. Us lascivious, sex-thirsty girls would stuff knickers in a teacher's desk drawer or tie together a string of 'em and drape them over his chair and watch his face as he came into the classroom. We probably terrified them.'

'No complaints about sexual harassment though, eh?'

'Hope not.'

'If it were youths laying their y-fronts over a schoolmistress's desk, what then?'

'Indeed. University, a few economicky jobs, nothing like yours, then did some 'do good unto others' et cetera. Talking of which, I have a presentation for tomorrow which I need to finish.' She rose from her chair.

'There will be another time then?'

'Did I give myself away?'

'When are you free?'

'I'll let you know.'

'You don't have my number.'

'I'll find it.'

She picked up her book, placed it in her bag and stood.

'Goodbye then, Mister Wilde.'

She held her hand out.

'I don't want to shake your hand, it's too formal.'

She grinned, nodded slowly and turned away.

He watched her walk purposely to the door and when it closed regretted not asking her if he could walk back with her. He sat down again, wondering what it was about her that prevented him asking her name or, perhaps, not so much stopping him, but causing him to forget to.

There was another spiel coming up soon, and taking out his pen and a notepad tried to think of a few basics to rehearse. 'Make Britain great again,' 'In it for the long haul,' 'We'll make 'growth' a vibrant word'… No. He couldn't concentrate anyway.

CHAPTER ELEVEN

'It's hard to believe that Facebook took someone's Christmas card down because it mentioned a robin redbreast, saying that 'breast' had 'sexual connotations.' I thought it was a send-up, some silly bit of satire.'

'Leg, shoulder, bottom, foot - not feet, that's ugly, foot singular is pretty - ankle, all contain a sexuality. How did we get here without it?'

'Evolution; though it's a tautology: we're told of the survival of the fittest and when asked how they know they're the fittest, the answer is 'Because they've survived.' And these stamp duty reductions and help-to-buy gimmicks merely inflate house prices and boost the profits and shares of property developers. Only practical solution is to lift the cap on local government house-building.'

'We know that, Paul, it's obvious.'

Ralph was used to his friend's irrelevant randomness and should have been in a more accommodating mood. They were going to a local meeting of the Communist Party which they'd both agreed they wanted to join. Maybe it was his cynicism about ever being able to change the system. Was capitalism a 'natural' outcome of man's nature? Humans as inherently individualistic, hedonistic, competitive, egotistic, self-seeking, or made that way by the system?

He didn't really want to think about models of human nature, and found some sort of escapist satisfaction in walking through the rain; the colours of streets and buildings washed away as a steady drizzle dropped flimsy layers of cool wind and a fine, blurred greyness around people hurrying along in their momentary self-sufficient worlds.

'At least we're not going to a meeting of the Liberal Party,' said Paul, 'a sponge soaking up all opinion and therefore unable to have any formal ideological policy itself. This must be the place.'

They stopped outside a neglected Victorian building, climbed steps under an arch, through scuffed double doors, along a corridor, past a Ladies and into a hall with rose-patterned wallpaper on an end wall and old music hall posters peppering a side one. There was a bar in a corner with a dozen or so men around it and a large hammer and sickle flag attached to the wall above it.

There were about twenty people there, most of them gathered around the bar. The image was that of an old working men's club, other than the flag there was little hint of a brave new world.

A large man walked across to them with a smile, guessing who they were for Ralph had phoned the place the previous week.

'Hello, my name's Eaton. Welcome.' Raising his voice and looking back at the others, he said, 'I think we should start. Take your seats.'

There were half-a-dozen rows of chairs. The two of them sat at the back, the others, leaving their drinks on what seemed allotted spaces on the bar counter, sat down to listen.

'We're welcoming two potential new members this evening.'

Eaton gestured towards them, a few of the other members turning their heads and briefly nodding to them. 'Edward wants to begin, I believe.'

A medium-height, slim man, younger than Ralph, stood and went to the front while Eaton sat in the front row.

'Okay, so take a deep breath fellow comrades, brothers et al. Right, so we are part of the philosophical, social, political and economic ideology and movement whose ultimate goal is the establishment of a communist society, a socioeconomic order structured upon the common ownership of the means of production and the absence of social class and the State, blah, blah, blah.'

'What's new, Eddie?' said someone.

'Not much, but wait. Again as you know, there have been several instances of communist States.'

'That's a term used by western historians, mate, it doesn't mean - '

'Of course, and contrary to this, these States do not describe themselves as 'communist,' they see themselves more as socialist States, workers States et cetera that are in the process of constructing socialism.'

He reminded Ralph of old Spencer when he went to a few of the party's meetings with Binns, but seemed more of a friendly communicator than the old firebrand, less mature but, so far, more casual, but there was a fizz about him.

'Examples are, of course, The People's Republic of China, Cuba, Lao People's Democratic Republic and Vietnam, all of which are Party States in which institutions of the State are intertwined.'

'The State certainly hasn't withered with that lot,' said the same man. 'It just annoys me that the right wing press - '

'All press is right wing, it has to be.'

'Except our own paper.'

'It's such an easy option for them, including the so-called 'quality' papers, and there's not much to gain in me writing to any of 'em to point this out even in simple language 'cos it won't get in. There's not much more I want to say, just wanted to point out what I guess most of you know anyway. Sorry it's a damp squib.'

He momentarily raised a fist and said, 'Fight the good fight brothers, support all strikes.' and walked around the side of the rows of chairs to sit a couple of seats at the side of Paul.

Eaton then stood and said, 'I want to talk about subscriptions. It's that time of the year. Let's get it out of the way. We'll go over to the table near the bar, the details and relevant stuff's there.'

He walked towards it, some of the others getting up and following him.

'Is that it then? No more tonight?' asked Edward.

'Oh, there'll probably be a discussion later,' said Eaton, turning to him. We're getting a guest speaker next time.' He looked at Ralph and Paul 'Are you joining then?'

'Guess so.' Ralph introduced himself and Paul to the man who, taking a step towards them to shake their hands, said, 'I assumed who you were. Welcome, again.'

As Eaton went to the table and busied himself with subscriptions, Edward, saying a welcome to the two newcomers, asked

Ralph whether he thought there could be a classless society. 'I tend to ask most new members this one for some reason.'

'You're seeing class as a status position based on an individual's location in the process of production, yes?'

'Yeah. A study a few years ago in an Israeli kibbutz showed that when they gave doctors, lawyers, plumbers and labourers the same wages in an effort to be classless, the professionals were accorded far more status than the manual workers.'

'If it was a society genuinely attempting the equalising then, gradually, over time, hand and head skills could, I suppose, have a similar status, though I doubt it. How long have you been in the party?'

'Quite a few years now.'

'We don't want to sign up to a Trotskyist party or a Stalinist cult, though,' said Paul.

'You won't have to; there are only a few extremists here; sometimes I'm amongst them. Been members before?'

'He has,' said Paul, nodding towards Ralph.

'A while ago now.'

'I have a feeing that you're kind of committed socialists; a strength of communitarian values, eh?'

'As a contrast to narrow individualism, yes,' said Ralph, though... '

Edward looked at both of them. 'Want more action?'

Just then a woman came in. It was a peripheral glimpse by Ralph initially, but her entrance made a difference immediately for the atmosphere had been blatantly men only.

Her cheekbones seemed more prominent than when Ralph had first seen her and with her loosely permed brown hair and dark schoolgirl-type jumper she reminded him of a figure in a Forties war poster. It was the woman he'd met on the demonstration.

She smiled at Eaton, who had gone over to her as she entered and kissed her cheek. To Ralph it seemed, for a second, to be ridiculously intimate; he childishly felt he didn't want anyone kissing her, anywhere. Arbitrarily, and almost subliminally, his mind harked back to little Peggy who lived opposite his childhood home and her skinny legs hop-scotching on the pavement and, spinning round, showing a glimpse of knickers. He remembered their colour.

She briefly looked around her, nodded to the man next to Paul then glanced at Ralph whom she awarded a little frown.

'Hi, Claire,' said Edward, 'how's the revolution?'

'Working on it.'

'Speak to you later; think boss man wants me; money and things.' He looked at the new members. 'Come with me.'

Paul gestured to Ralph. 'Coming?'

'In a minute.'

As Edward and Paul went over to the trestle table, she stood looking at Ralph.

'You seem surprised.'

'You didn't tell me you were a member.'

'Should I have? I haven't seen you here before.'

'First time. I like your name.'

'Thanks.'

'But it kind of surprises me. It's too... innocent, girlish, if you like.'

'I am a girl. What d'you think it should be?'

'Maybe Zelda, Marta, perhaps.'

'Not Cassandra then? Sadie? Lucrezia?'

She walked across to Eaton taking to people at the trestle table. He grinned up at her.

'Your dues are overdue, Claire Cluckrose, pay them now or you'll be cast forever into the wilderness.'

She said something to him.

'I agree,' he said, laughing. 'A net-curtained semi-detached in Tunbridge Wells may be marginally more of one than the Sahara, but...'

Ralph, looking at her back, felt that even if he'd never seen this woman's face, there was something about the way she stood, leaning slightly forward, that had a presence, a casual authority. He glanced at Paul. He was earnestly listening to Edward talking of strikes and unemployment; with Paul nodding eagerly and occasionally making it a duologue. As she moved away from Eaton, Ralph took her place, confirming that he and his friend would join and, giving him their relevant details, paid both their dues.

Eaton looked at the wall clock and said, 'This is about it I think, though do stay for a drink, and there's a few sandwiches left; most of 'em won't want to stay long, there's a Euro game on tonight I believe.'

'There'll never be a revolution,' said Paul from nearby. 'Can't man the barricades tonight Charlie, Spurs are at home to the Gunners, you know how it is. Another time maybe. Cheers.''

'You have a point. Sorry it's been short. Occasionally it's more like a social club, but they're good lads, they know the score. Come next time, we're having a guest speaker. It'll be at the hut, our usual place.'

He went towards Ralph and shook his hand again. He turned towards Edward.

'Cheerio, Edward.'

As Paul continued listening to Edward, Ralph saw the girl walking towards the exit behind Eaton. He moved quickly to her.

'Time for a coffee? Drink?'

She turned and gazed at him as if she was quickly checking him through a hastily conjured list of 'goods' and 'bads.''

'Okay then. There's a little place around the corner, should be open.'

'Come here often?

'I've been known to.'

'You were the only woman.'

'I believe that's the case.'

'How long have you - '

'A while, and yes, the usual thing: started at university, debating society, some of us fed up with the greed, materialism et cetera; became a communist sympathiser though never joined the party. Have now.'

Ralph looked towards Paul. 'See you,' he mouthed silently.

They reached the café, saying nothing on the short walk - it had ceased raining - entered and seated themselves.

'D'you think your interest could have been a reaction against your, if you like, privileged upbringing? I dunno, maybe you saw struggle, harshness, poverty somewhere or other and realised that some people had it rough; or is that too corny an analysis?'

'You mean not all Alfa-Romeos, nannies and Cote d' Azur holidays?'

'Something like that.'

'Partly, but it all seemed so irrational, based on what's good for human beings. The sheer wretchedness of some people's lives, the dog-eat-dog essence of it all.'

'Pick it up from your dad? I don't mean he was like that, that he embodied the system, but - '

'Why not? He had to imbibe the ethos of the financial galaxy he worked in. Difficult to move out of even if you become aware that perhaps you want to.'

'All this and we haven't got our coffee yet.'

She looked to the counter, held up two fingers like a victory sign, turned back to Ralph again and raised an eyebrow as if she was expecting him to say something, tangential maybe. He did.

'This coffee.'

'What about it?'

'Look at the bags of it at the back of the counter, from Brazil, Africa, from five continents, yet we don't think of it as ours till we're drinking it. It made me think of Marx.'

'Drink a lot of it did he?'

'Dunno, but he reckoned that private poverty was so stupid that an object is only ours when we have it - when it exists for us as capital, when it's directly possessed, eaten, drunk, worn, inhabited et cetera; in short, when it's used by us. We're alienated from the sense of *having.*'

'All property is theft, eh?'

Ralph looked briefly around him, gesticulating.

'I mean, a park, a bus, food, a shop, a... Imagine seeing these things and knowing that although you don't own them, they're not legally your possessions, you can use them, enter them, consume, ride, investigate, travel, be healed, pleasured, edified, satisfied by them as if they *were* yours, which indeed they would be in - '

'Utopian communism?'

'Yes, and not just yours, your neighbours, everybody's.'

'Would that include me?'

'Of course, you're part of everybody, too.'

'No, I mean one of the things you can use without actually owning.'

'You're kidding. Am I right?'

'There's a psychological ownership you're talking about with these things you've mentioned. What of people? Wouldn't that be true here also? 'Free love' as it used to be called?

'It's all I could afford.'

The coffee was brought.

'So, what was it like at home?' he asked her.

'Dad was a quiet man, smiled at me when I talked about things other than the usual topics of the parish, trying, I suppose, to break the insularity. He rarely mentioned pokitics; the elites were in charge, as they should be.'

'Not so different from Mexican peasants and the English working class with their idea that the upper class were born to rule.'

'I used to try to goad him, in my adolescent zeal, I shouldn't have maybe, but he never threatened to throw me out.'

'Mine did, kind of; didn't want a Red in his house, he said. It was rented anyway. Neither of us knew a communist from a cockroach.'

'Seems we have rather different backgrounds.'

'Let's not let it bother us.'

'Us?'

'Alright. You and me.

'Still sounds like 'us.''

'We're trapped in language.'

'Can't get outside of it.'

'Like society.'

'What shall we do when we leave this café?'

'At least you said 'we' then. Some progress.'

'Towards what?'

'If I ask you to see a film with me you'll say no, right?'

'Guess so.'

She took a pack of cigarettes from her bag and lit one.

'That surprises me.'

'I rarely do it, and there's only you ad I here.'

'The way you hold it, slowly blow the smoke out; it's like a Noir film: palms, fedoras, Mulholland Drive, wise guys ... '

'And when the heroes slapped their women there was seemingly something deserved and satisfying about it. Yes?'

He wasn't interested in answering, he was watching the smoke from her cigarette drifting slowly upwards like a helix and imagining the foreground hero with his trench coat and turned-up collar gazing at her as she strolled a highway, headlights stroking her back before she vanished into the night.

She pressed her cigarette out in a saucer and stood.

'That was interesting, but I'm rather tired.'

'I'll walk to your stop with you.'

'It's not far. You stay here, the food's good, especially the snacks. Bye bye.'

Sitting there, the place seemed large and empty in her absence.

He made his way back to the building he'd left Paul and the others in, but there were only two people there, at the bar, quietly chatting. Perhaps his friend had gone off with Edward somewhere, probably a pub, to continue the debating.

For the next few days, in between, and occasionally in his classes, he kept thinking of her, so much so that it began to annoy him. He knew he had a proneness to seductive images that were, often, meaningless pictures; filmic, theatrical, transient, but this time he kept seeing her face, cheekbones, especially the eyes; they didn't seem to blink much.

It had been nice to talk to somebody other than Paul in the way he had. He could almost... be himself. He couldn't remember the last time he'd felt this with a woman. Irrelevantly he briefly wondered what Edward had meant when asking if he had wanted 'more action.'

CHAPTER TWELVE

'Ever been injured, geez?'

'Of course.'

'Think of a time,' asked Archer, 'maybe when you were young.'

'Er... was on holiday, might have been St. Lucia, on a beach making sand castles when a local boy purposely trod on the bucket and I lost half an inch of finger. My father was nearby with his head plunged into the FT.'

'What happened to the bit of digit?'

'Don't know,' said Jordan.

They were sitting in a pub in Hoxton near the agent's office, with chic industrial lighting, sanded floorboards, and eclectic furniture the result of forays into junk shops for Victoriana and bargain Fifties; its pots of ferns almost outnumbering the drinkers. Outside, they'd walked through milling hipsters with Jesus beards, skinny jeans and Fifties-style winkle pickers making them look like court jesters.

'Anything else?'

'I ran across a main road to a bus stop, I didn't drive then, and a removal van skidded to avoid me and broadsided into my back as I turned away, knocking me face down on the road. There were three people in the cab, no-one got out, but they did offer me a lift somewhere if I was going their way. They took me to the station; I walked into it and collapsed.'

'Hospitals involved?'

'Yes, why d'you ask?'

'Queen Mary's A & E has been earmarked for closure. It's in your electoral ward and my bet is that they'll turn it into a private wing.'

'The area's affluent enough to provide it with plenty of customers I should think.'

'What would have happened to you without emergency provisions?'

'Okay, your point is?'

'A campaign's been started against the closure, I think you should join it, make a fuss, it'll get you known.'

'What's the party-line on this?'

'Doesn't matter, it's a local issue and in the area you're representing. Do I have to spell it out?'

'No, you're right.'

'I'll send you the email address of the bloke that started it, I advise you to contact him.'

He left Archer to return to the office, knowing it was good advice and that he should have thought of it himself and probably would have had he known about the intended closure. He promised himself to keep more in touch with local issues and events in the area he hoped to be the parliamentary representative for.

After emailing the address next day he received a reply some hours later saying that although, theoretically, the more the merrier, if he was using the protest in the hope of getting more votes in the upcoming by-election then it advised him not to join.

He replied by saying the cynicism wasn't deserved and that he genuinely wanted to help. The response was: 'Cynicism is an unpleasant way of telling the truth.' But it then went on to say that it would help if he spread the issue around on whatever social media he used, maybe he could even persuade any standing MPs he may know and his 'pals in the City' - if they had a conscience - to help. He wondered how 'johnsmith@bmail.com' knew he worked in the Square Mile.

The following day he received an email informing him that there was a meeting on the first floor of a local pub in a few days to discuss the closure. He saw that he was one of quite a few to receive it.

After a particularly unsatisfying day of trying to persuade some wayward clients away from risky gambles in emerging market stock investments and into high grade government bonds, he went to the meeting.

Although a suburban drinking house, it looked a typical contemporary London one: cleaned-up bricks, fascia and windows painted dark grey and potted ferns by the entrance. Upstairs, in a long room with coloured, leaded glass windows, flock wallpaper, match-boarded dado and a bar were sixty or so people. He'd arrived a little late and as he took a seat a woman walked to the front of the room and began speaking.

'You all know me, or should by now. Incidentally, I'm seen as the chief organiser of this campaign, but am really one of many who are working for it. Our east London population is growing and ageing, demand for NHS services continues to increase and we face ever-mounting challenges to our healthcare system.'

He was glancing around him and thus recognised the voice a second before seeing the face. She had a larger audience than Archer and himself on her doorstep this time, and he promised himself he would know her name before the evening was out.

She continued. 'We need to consider more options for the way both Queen Mary's and Waltham Hospital deliver urgent and emergency services across our communities in north east London to enable us to provide care in the best way for all patients. East London Health and Care Partnership should be doing this. We need to prod them to find out what this government's plan is, if they have one, for a decommissioned Accident and Emergency building.'

She then looked at Jordan. 'There's a man at the back who I'm a little surprised to see here, but nonetheless he is the Conservative candidate for the upcoming by-election, and perhaps would like to speak. The floor is yours, Mister Wilde.'

As she sat down at the front he felt a little trapped, and walked rather awkwardly, to where she had been standing. He had nothing rehearsed, doing only a little impromptu research the day before, uncertain now how much of it he could remember. He knew he should have done more.

'Well, unlike the previous speaker, only some of you may recognise me, but I hope there'll be a lot more of you know me in the near future. This campaign is important, and I speak as a caring Conservative, and quite obviously it isn't just an Opposition Party's concern, this is a cross-party one. I should like to work with your leader,' he gestured to the opening speaker now sitting on a nearby chair, 'and do all I can to keep the hospital's emergency services open.

'We do, however, have to look at this in the context of increasing pressure on health care. Recently, even Royal London, a 650-

bed hospital, ran out of intensive care beds and at the same time, four of London's hospital trusts ran out of general and acute beds.' He'd somehow remembered the figures. 'Thank you.'

As he sat again, at the rear, he was a little surprised to hear some clapping.

There were a few more speakers, asking for volunteers to send emails, to use Twitter and Facebook and any other form of social communication they could to involve more people; and to do more research into what could happen were the emergency facilities to be no more. She came on again at the end, thanked them and said she would arrange a date for the next meeting.

The people left, chattering amongst themselves; most, he assumed, having drinks downstairs. He stayed, watching her pick up a few leaflets from the chairs and quickly sorting through some of her own papers which she tucked away in a satchel. She came towards his row, which was empty other than him, and stood at the end of it.

'You want to work with me for the sake of the campaign or is it about self-interest?'

'Politically? No, I - '

'I wasn't referring to your political career.'

'Obviously I'd like to get to know you more, but I'd also like to help save the hospital.'

'Wouldn't your party rather see some money-making private medicine going on there?'

'Let's talk about it.'

'Over a drink?'

'Something like that, but not downstairs.'

'Around the corner, Mister Wilde.'

They left the building swiftly, he feeling rather silly having, initially, to hurry to catch up with her.

It was an ordinary-looking restaurant. They sat.

'I really would like to help save that hospital,' he began.

'Altruism?'

'Is there such a thing? If you put someone before yourself and get a good feeling doing so, isn't that self-gain?'

'What about love?'

'What about it?'

'I'm guessing the only emotion akin to it that you would feel would involve your job and a strong egotistic urge to make your mark in the political game.'

'Unfair. And what's yours? To destroy the world-wide system of profits? How are non-profiteers going to get money then, by osmosis?'

'You mentioned a coffee. Decaf please.'

He brought them back. She'd removed her jacket showing an expensive roll-neck jumper. Sipping her drink she asked him when he was going to speak publicly again.

'Soon, my agent will fix something.'

'Do you need a heckler?'

'No, but if it's you, that'll be fine.'

'Be rather counter-productive wouldn't it if you wish to be seen as supporting my campaign against the hospital closure?'

'Maybe.'

'D'you always do what he tells you?'

'He's savvy, I'm a novice.'

'And one who seems to be picking it up pretty quickly.'

'Thanks.'

'DOn't let it go to your head.'

'Incidentally, capitalism isn't new, there's a long tradition of financial investments. For example, the code of Hammorabi around seventeen hundred BC provided a legal framework for investment, establishing a means for the pledge of collateral by codifying debt and creditor rights in regard to pledged land. That's just one aspect of the - '

'Does it make it right?'

'It seems to make it natural.'

'So, because something exists for a relatively long while it's therefore natural?'

'I didn't say that.'

'You obviously imply it. But then, anything goes if every-thing's natural. Depends on how big a part of nature sapiens are. It raises the question: Do we have a capitalist personality, in that we are grasping individuals, because of evolution, of nature, or are we made that way by the system?'

'That was constructed by humans. I've thought of that before. Chicken and egg, I guess.'

'Have you ever noticed that whatever colour your underwear, the fluff in your navel is always blue-grey?'

'Don't know what to say to that.'

'And that people who say, 'Oh, you must come round for a meal,' will never ask you? Think of one yourself.'

'Er... there's a brief moment as you just miss your train when you can't believe you actually have.'

'The squealing toilet door in pubs, cafes and department stores will never be oiled.'

'Um... we continue sending Christmas cards to people we don't really wish to see again.'

'You don't know anyone who knows Plato's first name.'

He was beginning to enjoy himself; the slight tenseness when with her was disappearing, she seemed more... it was inappropriate to say 'humane,' but there was a slight difference, though the intelligence and the hint of wariness, even suspicion, under the permanent self-confidence was behind her eyes still. He thought of another observation.

'When someone asks you to 'Keep in touch,' they have no intention of doing so themselves.'

'When you dial a wrong number it's never engaged.'

'I Can't beat that one.'

'Is it a competition then?'

Just then his mobile rang.

'I don't want to get this, but if you'll excuse me. '

He walked away from her for a few yards. It was Archer.

'Got the town hall for yer to spout your gilded words, at least they'll seem like it compared with some MPs who sound like ghosts gibbering in some corner. And after that there'll be a Q and A somewhere with your Labour rival and maybe a couple of others. The town hall one's next Tuesday. It is, as you should know, a Tory-controlled council and you'll be welcomed. Should be a good turn-out I think. Okay?'

'Sure. Thanks.'

'Part of the job. Incidentally, your opponent was involved in some trouble or other at one time, apparently. Rumour or not, I'll have a word in a few shell-likes, it could help you, though he's probably so shiny you could skate on him.'

'I suppose I should say at this point that I want to play fair and square; principles and all that, but I shan't.'

'Since when have politicians acted on their principles instead of their appetites? Be in touch.'

Jordan returned to the table.

'Sorry about that, it was just - '

'It's alright. I'm afraid I shall leave you now.'

'Already?

'Indeed.'

She put her jacket on. 'And it's okay, I don't live far away, as you know. I like walking on my own.'

'You'll tell me your name this time of course?'

'Claire.'

She left the restaurant, leaving him to order a meal, for he was feeling hungry and a little happier. At least he knew her name, though he wondered why she'd used 'johnsmith' as her email address.

CHAPTER THIRTEEN

'Did you understand any of that? I didn't.'

The questioner was sitting next to Ralph in a crowded train slowing into a local station. The unintelligible noise was another corruption of sound that passed for a public announcement - Ralph picking out two 'wivs' and a 'frew' as estuary and Jamaican pidgin skewed the linguistic geometry into shapes previously the habitué of the London working class and Detroit African-Americans. The resident glottal stoppages, the 'bruvahs,' 'whatevahs,' and the 'So I was like's' drilled loudly through his head.'

Alighting then walking half a mile, he came to the venue of a party meeting in a large Nissen hut with a faded 'Royal British Legion' painted on a wooden sign above a metal door. Inside was the hammer and sickle flag from the previous place pinned to cream, hardboard walls. There were brown skirting boards, crittall windows, Forties-looking lightshades, and some tables and a few rows of chairs sitting on a wooden floor. While most people were sitting or standing around a makeshift bar, Paul was sitting in the back row talking to Edward. He could hear him.

'A 'snowflake,' he was saying, 'is a liberal who is offended by those who are not offended by the things *he* is offended by.'

Ralph couldn't resist. He went over to them, bent his head slightly down between them and said, 'It's more serious than that. As we're becoming more secular it's emerged as a religion. Its opinions, conjectures, selective self-congratulatory accusations, its convoluted, illogical, irrational quasi-mandates are becoming the new moral leadership.'

'Yow. And in whose interest is it?' Edward asked, looking up.

'Ah, the age-old Marxian question.'

'Anyway, we're all equal now, aren't we?' asked Edward sarcastically. 'Aren't we? Diverse and vibrant and harmonious.'

'It's not 'diverse' now, it's 'people with protected characteristics,'' said Paul.

'A liberal is just a conservative who hasn't been mugged yet,' said Ralph.'

'So you got here then?' asked Paul.

'Well, I'm not a hologram.'

'Was just gonna say, I actually heard someone say the other day,' said Edward, 'that tax-dodging can be a good thing as it makes the rich richer and their money trickles down to the rest of us.'

'What, by magic?'

'People,' interrupted Paul, 'see magic as something 'other', like fate or some deity, but it's little different from science really.'

'How come?' Edward asked,

'Well, they're all self-contained conceptual systems that cannot, of themselves, be wrong.'

More people were coming into the hut and after some of them had got their drinks, Eaton, who had been talking to a man as broad and tall as himself, went to the front, asked them all to sit and called for quiet for the evening's guest speaker.

'Lawrence Moorcroft,' he began, 'has been a member of the party - unfortunately not this branch - for some years and has helped the cause at various places in Europe; indeed, he was introduced as a teenager to Cohn-Bendit in Paris in the student riots. He was, incidentally, rather well known as 'Larry the Left' by certain right-wing tabloids.'

The man rose from his chair, walked to the space his host had just vacated, held his hands up, palms outwards to curtail the clapping, and in his rich baritone, and briefly stroking his thick, grey hair, began speaking.

'It's not my intention to give you a history lesson, but a reminder. I did, incidentally, meet Jacques Sauvageot as well in the '68 business in the French capital. I also had some fun in New York and San Fran during the so-called 'contra- revolution' around that time.

'The Communist Party of Great Britain existed for over seventy years and was founded by the merger of several Marxist parties, socialist organisations and workers committees, including miners; indeed, two party MPs won seats in the '45 election and up to the mid-Fifties we were at our height of influence. We lost it after the Hungarian Revolution and later with the dissolution of the Soviet Union, as you know.

'The CPGB dissolved itself in '91 - you probably know this, as you may know the rest of the stuff I've mentioned - so now the Communist Party of Britain, us, is the sole representative of the International Meeting of Communists and Workers Parties.

'It may have dissolved itself, but we're certainly not going to dissolve *our*selves or *be* dissolved, not by the acid rain from a capitalist universe that's being showered down upon us. Though the 'C' word is still seen as a bad 'un, there is a media growing in which, perhaps, it's not so bad: I call it the millennials media. We must encourage it, use it. We want younger blood to join us. Do all you can to capture it, enlist it.'

As he paused, Ralph could almost hear Paul thinking, with his sometimes stereotype slant, 'Don't try to get down with the kids at your age, chummy, it won't work.' But this was sensible, rational, stuff and perhaps needed. He was starting to like this speaker. He wondered briefly if Claudia's father had known him.

He continued, and Ralph sensed rather than saw or heard the door quietly open and Claire enter. She was casually dressed, but everything was of a piece and fitted her so well, a kind of easy, posh casual, her dark, near-auburn hair still having that confident, almost old-fashioned wave in it. She sat down in the back row.

'The main thing I really want to draw attention to is all the current rubbish about education and social mobility, which, while the rich get more prosperous and the poor, poorer - one billion people live on less than a dollar a day - the current government's much publicised urge to improve it has become a popular ploy.

'Of course, corporations, conglomerates need a skilled work force, but they don't want skilled artisans and general labourers to even *strive* upwards, the owners of production need manual workers.

'There's a view that states that with the growth of automation, robotics and A.I. there'll soon be little need for manual labour. If that does come it will be, if at all, quite a while in the future. Then, presumably, a different technological transformation of the physical world would throw up different class cultures, but values wouldn't be reversed. Imagine a society where such skills as bricklaying, window cleaning, street-sweeping and serving at McDonalds were endowed with the status of 'superior' knowledge in which, maybe, a City & Guilds could get you into university to do a BA in plastering, and Fine Arts would be confined to Constrution Colleges. Things would be turned on their heads.

'This is of course, in essence, so much trivial irrelevancy; a society like this cannot come about and just to formulate it merely highlights, like most attempts at satire, the entrenchment of the status quo.'

His audience were obviously interested, some absorbed; the concept of social class was a concrete kernel of thought and feeling for them, a primary trigger.

The speaker continued: 'Let us just say that there *cannot* be, in the world of our experience, a society of equals. To be sure, equality before the law - but not after it? - equal suffrage and other equalities are not only possible but in some countries an apparent reality. But, the idea of a society in which all distinctions of rank are abolished seems to transcend what is socially possible and, perhaps, has a place only in the sphere of poetic imagination.'

Moorcroft paused at this point and said, 'incidentally, I'm not putting a damper on our cause. We need to fight, where we can.' He scanned the members. 'I've purposely kept this short so I could take questions from the floor. I'm using that, of course, as shorthand for a preference for any discussion to commence and continue at the bar. Thank you.'

The clapping, led by Eaton, was enthusiastic; the speaker seemed to be a well-known and popular figure. Ralph, seeing Edward look in the direction of the back row and hearing him say to Paul, 'Ah, there she is, I wondered if she'd be here,' went to the bar along with most of the other people. He bought drinks for Paul and Edward and returned to tell Moorcroft, who was talking to Eaton, that it was an interesting speech he'd given.

'You sounded like me in a classroom, the value-conflict part especially. And we could extend your imaginary world couldn't we, and have the WC manipulating their own cultural symbols as part of a core curriculum: page three of The Sun, African-

American cockney speak, Wetherspoons, pies and mash et cetera, though jellied eels would be a bit dated, I think, as weapons in the class war.'

'Indeed. Your name is?'

Ralph told him. This was immediately followed by Claire, who had suddenly appeared beside them, her eyes fixed on Moorcroft, saying, 'It could be argued that equality of educational opportunity is possible in a society without stratification. From an orthodox Marxian view this would mean, would it not, the communal ownership of the forces of production. Without stratification, it's said, a common culture would emerge.'

'But stratification remains in socialist societies '

'But just how socialist *are* they?'

Ralph, noting the sparkle in Claire's eyes when looking at Moorcroft, began to tell him of the analogy he used for cultural capital when teaching, but stopped after Moorcroft merely glanced at him then listened to Claire while she continued their discussion. Ralph felt left out, momentarily excluded.

'In short,' said Claire, 'it's the value-difference again, and the powerful will, with the help of dissemination by the media, which is largely owned by them anyway, carry on spreading theirs.'

'Thus maintaining their position.'

'And increasing their domination.'

Ralph tried again. 'In every age the ruling ideas are the ideas of the ruling class.'

'Indeed,' said Moorcroft, 'Karl Heinrich again. I'm going to talk with these scoundrels now milling around me. But,' he looked warmly at Claire, 'I hope to talk to you later.'

He moved towards the end of the bar where most of the members were and began chatting with them. Ralph spotted Paul and Edward there also. He and the girl suddenly seemed to have their end of the bar to themselves.

He turned to her. 'Hello again, then.'

She gave a brief smile.

'Guess he's well-known, eh?'

'He is. Not exactly a hero, but he's been around.'

'The mature, travelled, experienced man, eh?'

'Jealous?'

'You're quick.'

'And correct?'

'I like your leather boots, the buttons are - '

'Old-fashioned?'

'You look like an upmarket 'Bisto kid,' he said, assuming she'd know the dated reference.

She took a step back, raised a leg and kicked out.

'What am I now, a chorus girl?'

Her action surprised him a little, there was also a quick, adolescent excitement which he knew immediately came from watching the high-kicking, fishnet-clad stockings of the chorus lines at the pantos his father had taken him to as a boy.

Pushing the image away, he said, 'Anyway, the education system's not going to equalise anything.'

'Could *any* nationally-based system?'

'Well, any dominant group will tend to serve its own interests. Ascendancy by cultural reproduction is an expectational norm that virtually *cannot* be escaped. The middle class reproduces itself.'

'I'm not sure whether you really want to carry on with this or you're maybe running away from yourself a bit. I'm happy to continue, though.'

He was surprised by this also. He was silent. She spoke:

'Logically, there doesn't have to be dominant groups do there? though historically they have perhaps always existed, but then you could say that, logically, there doesn't have to be dominant values, that a society could exist without sanctions.'

'But what would an industrial society without such groups be like? What would it *have* to be like?'

He suddenly didn't want to think about social stratification any more. Not at this moment, not with her.

'It's been found,' Ralph said, 'that certain good-looking women have been so shackled by stereotyping that they feel they must hide their brainpower under a kind of dizzy-blonde disguise. A pretty girl will tend to shield her intellect out of fear that it will outshine her physical beauty. You obviously have no problems there.'

'D'you want to play observations with me?'

'What's that?'

'I'll give you an example. If you travel more than two stations on any train you will hear someone say, 'I'm on a train.' into their mobile phone.'

'Another?

'Every poet writes an anti-war poem and a poem about a photograph.'

'Why are we doing this?'

'We're not, *I* am. I thought you may want to give your brain a rest.'

'I just want us to talk.'

'We are.'

They looked at each other, both hearing Edward, whose voice was a little louder than the rest of them gathered around Moorcroft, saying, 'But wasn't Cohn-Bendit an anarchist? And didn't someone denounce some student protesters as "Sons of the upper bourgeoisie who will quickly forget their revolutionary flame in order to manage daddy's firm and exploit the workers there'?"

'Bang on,' said Moorcroft, 'it was the French Party leader Georges Marchais. Excuse me.'

Ralph saw Moorcroft come towards them or, rather, Claire.

'I'm going pretty soon. Maybe we'll meet again somewhere.'

'Why not here?' she asked.

'I could come back, I suppose. There are a few more party groups I'm talking to over the next few weeks, maybe I'll return. Pleasure to have met you.'

Ralph thought for a moment that he was going to kiss her hand, but he made do with a slight lowering of his groomed, grey head.

'I do hope so.' was her response.

He awarded Ralph with a brief nod and rejoined the others to bid a farewell before walking over to Eaton who had been giving attention to his mobile for some time. They talked for a short while, shook hands and Moorcroft left.

Ralph turned to her. 'I do have a name.'

'Really.'

He told her.

'I know, but you've never told me it. I heard you tell the speaker man. Hello, Ralph.'

'Hello, Claire.'

'What happens now?'

'Talk to me. Tell me about you.'

'When men say that, they're usually frightened of revealing themselves.' She looked at him steadily. 'Déclassé?'

'Does it show?'

'The middle class hate being accused of being middle class.'

'Perhaps. Okay, born in east London; went to university late, now lecture. You?

'Guess.'

'Home Counties, but can see you living in East Sheen, some-how.'

'Lived there with a friend while I was at uni, am now working for a charity.'

'Running it?'

'Not yet.'

Just then Paul and Edward came over to them.

'What are you two doing?' asked the latter. Hello, Red Claire.'

She frowned at him.

'Well, that's what Eaton used to call you, with affection I might add. A kind of nickname. I was just kidding, I admire you, actually.'

'Don't see the point of that last word being in the language, but thanks.'

'What I think we should be doing,' suggested Paul, 'is attempting to convince the workers that they have a false consciousness; they don't know the extent of their exploitation. Make them aware of it.'

'How are we going to fight the whole weight of the media?'

'There's another media now, a tech media, Edward, arguably it's a tool for democracy, for revolt.'

'You sound like the converted. Who owns it though? Four of the richest companies in the world.'

Glancing at her watch, Claire said, 'Look,' I'm going to leave you boys, I have work to do.'

'You're always disappearing,' said Ralph.

She walked quickly away.

'See you at the next meeting I suppose,' he called after her.'

She briefly flipped her hand back at them as she opened the exit door.

'Let's sit down,' said Edward, walking towards the rows of chairs. When they had done so he turned to Ralph and said, 'Remember me asking you if you wanted more action?'

'There's been none yet.'

'Well, and this of course includes you, Paul. There's a building at the back of Oxford Street, near the old Marylebone Magistrates Court, that's being refurbished, and there's a builders' strike. It's just started. Don't know what it's about at the moment, just that I remember my dad was a foreman for a subcontractor there way back. He told me that though it had large plate glass windows on the ground floor and a few dressed dummies behind them, it was really an MI5 place, some sort of intelligence agency, anyway.

'I remember him telling me, laughing, that before he and his gang were let in they had to fill in and sign a little bit of paper. The only question on it was, 'Are you or have you ever been a member of the Communist Party?' And that was it. If you answered 'no' you could work there. Thing was, that they were painting the outside windows in boats as he called them, he meant cradles, and they could look in all the windows, only a few had blinds or curtains.

'It all seemed so ... English. 'B picture comedy' he called it. Well, somebody told me that it was still an intelligence agency building. If that's so, I thought we could find out more about it and support, encourage the strike, maybe.'

He looked at both of them. 'Fancy it? It may be just trivial, a nothing, but it also may still be a government building; it's been there for years.'

'I do,' said Paul.

'There's a mid-term holiday in a couple of days. I'm game,' offered Ralph.

'Okay, I'll be in touch. I'm gonna speak with the boss man now then I have to be off. See you.'

Paul flicked a hand at him, and asked Ralph whether he had got enough cash for another drink.

''Course.'

'Let's go and have one then, I wanna talk about a dominant value system being a source of moral authority.'

'Of course it is, by definition. Hope you're going to speak about something more interesting than that.'

'What about the girl then? How interesting do you find *her*?' He raised an eyebrow.

'Let's find the nearest pub shall we.'

They walked out into the night, both thinking of what they would actually do if they got near the building Edward had talked of; one of them again thinking mostly of the woman who had departed the Nissen hut only a short while before.

CHAPTER FOURTEEN

It was his last speech on the campaign trail before the by-election; the one with his Labour rival having been called off for some reason. He'd spoken at the local Tory headquarters and in a hall primarily used for Scouts and Guides, also twice at the local town hall.

She had come to none of them. He'd expected her, wanted her to appear, to challenge him, to try to knock him off the perch that, with Archer's help, he was trying to balance on. But she hadn't.

He was at the Conservative Association again. As he began, he spotted her at the front, almost centre. The pause before he began was a little longer than he'd planned.

'Governments don't really command a country, a nation.'

He looked around at his audience.

'This may surprise some of you, not so much by what I've said, but the fact that I've said it. A specific political and economic system runs nations world-wide, that's why it's called globalization. It is, in times of peace, virtually all-powerful, but in terms of law, order, judiciary, regulations, police, the health service, the public work force et cetera a government, a cabinet, runs a country. That is, unless a dictator does and, surprise, surprise, it often seems to be Far-left movements that give birth to them.

'You could, I suppose, argue that just as doctors are the middlemen between pharmaceutical companies and patients, so a government, effectively or otherwise, acts as the middleman between multinational corporations and the populace.

'A Labour government will, they say, try to swing it all towards the lower paid, and of course they need boosting, perhaps the minimum wage needs more rigidly enforcing, but the middle earners also have needs. This city, this country needs innovators. Let's incentivise them and reduce *their* tax a bit.'

This was followed by a few 'Hear, hears' and some moderate clapping.

'That party will kid you. They'll say that by nationalising the railways - it will take a long while, some private contracts have years to run and don't any of you kid yourselves that the occasional bad service and strikes are anything other than the fault of the unions - will be miraculously and smoothly restored. But restored to what? The outdated, rundown trains that existed during the previous public ownership of the railways?'

While he was speaking he quickly attempted to see her expression. It appeared to be utterly neutral. It wasn't. Remaining seated, she spoke:

'The Tories are against nationalisation yet they're quite happy for State ownership of the railways as long as it's not *our* State,' she said, her voice effortlessly clear and strong.

'State-owned firms from Germany, France, even Beijing have a large share in our rail system. The UK's a capitalist playground. How can it not be with over sixty million consumers packed into these rather tiny islands, the US speaking a version of its language and a Tory government in residence?'

He wanted immediately to argue with her, she was not of his politics, she was the enemy, yet he wanted... he didn't know, but not this. He took a deep breath.

'Any government would prefer to have British companies running our transport systems, and they largely do, but if foreign money makes the bigger bids, the better deals for the country, then we abide by that. As a recent PM would proudly say, 'There are more foreign investors in our country than in any other in Europe.'

'The playground, as said.'

'Of course the Health Service needs more money, but where is it coming from? And yes, high earners, corporations and conglomerates must pay more taxes, but are they to be driven away and unemployment created?'

She continued. 'What do you mean by 'better deals for the country'? You mean, of course, for the companies, especially those that inflict enormously high fares in order to lower those in their own countries. Despite attempts by your party to infantilise the electorate, they aren't all fools, Mister Wilde.'

She then got up, walked to the end 0f the row and purposely, but not hurriedly, walked past the seats to an exit. He wasn't sure what was hurting him the most, her leaving or the impersonal 'Mister Wilde,' again.

He momentarily forgot his prepared talk and improvised with, 'They say politics is showbiz for ugly people, Well, I don't think I'm in the latter category and certainly not in the first. It's far too important.' and began again, talking of doubts about whether a State-owned railway could be afforded without any private investing. He then switched to the importance of local concerns, especially the threatened closure of the local A & E. and told his audience he was working with the campaign leader and that they needed everybody's support.

He finished with, 'Vote for me, and remember you're not voting for my personality, but for a future MP of the only party that can live up to its name. That is, not only innovation, striving, progress, but *conserving,* keeping and growing what we have, and protecting this great country. Thank you.'

He walked off the side of the stage, quite pleased with the volume of applause, and made his way through what his agent, who, for once, wasn't attending, called the 'secret tunnel,' a rather dilapidated and narrow corridor which led to stairs going to the rear of a first floor tea room. It was open, and as he sat, he realised she was sitting on her own three tables from him.

He got up and, once again, sat opposite her.

'What other vested-interest corporate ideology did you offer them?' she asked.

'You could say hello. I told them I was working with you on the closure issue.'

'Wish fulfilment?'

'It's been busy at work and I haven't heard from you, anyway.'

'Expect to? Onus is on you.'

'I know. Let's not talk politics for a while, eh?'

'Why?'

'Sooner talk of other things.'

'Not sure what we'll have to talk about.'

'Why the 'johnsmith' email address?'

'Did it years ago. At the time, unfortunately, the masculine had somewhat more poke in the world of politics and protest.'

'That's alliterative.' He looked around him. 'Do you really want to sit here? We could go to a gourmet place I know that - '

'Your language. Try to see the world in a more proletarian way, eh? Though of course you're hardly, like Jesus, a poor but dishonest carpenter.'

'Let's 'ave a ball and chalk up the frog to Sid's caff then. Better?'

'Perhaps I should apologise for walking out, but it seemed rather predictable Tory-speak.'

'What did you expect? Quotes from Das Capital?'

'I doubt you know any, and I'm alright here. How many more speeches to the converted?'

'Last one.'

'There's another five days to the voting. Going to knock on any more doors?'

'Probably not, but I may, or may not, be on local radio in a couple of days.'

'Anything new?'

'Shouldn't think so. If I do it I'll give a précis version of stuff I've said before.'

'Guess it's comforting for the listeners; safe and stable, dependable.'

'We're still on subject normal.'

'And?'

'Okay, a subject dear to your heart - did that sound potentially sarcastic? Feminism.'

'If you're going to talk about the latest sexual harassment movement, of course I'm for it but I'd criticise it too. My sisters in the cause wouldn't like me saying it but it does seem to be part of a kind of anti-white male racism.'

'I guess extremists, at least temporarily, seem to win in any extreme movement. Moderates tend to be annihilated.'

'Yes, ideology becomes a religion and anyone who doesn't puppet their views is seen as a heretic, or a traitor. But there's a line, not always arbitrary, between sexual harassment and a clumsy kind of flirting, but some men can't seem to pick up non-verbal clues from a woman.'

'Does that mean, 'I'm angry that you can't read my mind?''

'Rather a predictable and shallow answer. You're now going to say that feminism is defined as women always being right.'

'Aren't they? I'm kidding.'

'And being rather silly.'

'It's the effect you have on me.'

'I don't want to affect you.'

'You already have.'

'Tut, tut.'

She stood, looking down at him.

'You're going to go again,' he said.

'Things to do.'

She picked up her handbag.

'Aren't you having anything?'

'I forgot. Like I said, the effect.'

She began walking away.

'When do we meet again?' he asked

'Ne'er the twain,' she said as she reached the door.

This should have hurt him. It didn't. He knew he'd see her again, and had already started looking forward to it.

He was at Archer's place on the third floor of a Fifties block of flats in Stoke Newington, its interior surprisingly pugilistic with black& white framed photos of British boxers from years ago: Bruce Woodcock, Freddy Mills, Randolph Turpin alongside shots of Rita Hayworth and Catherine Deneuve. The rest of the flat was minimalist, the scant furniture, modern. They were drinking beer, and less than half a minute before the by-election result was announced on TV, the phone on the coffee table next to the sofa they were occupying rang. The flat's owner smiled into it almost immediately.

'Thanks Bob, I guessed it. I'll give him your congratulations. See you.'

He stood and, beckoning Jordan to do the same, firmly shook his hand and embraced him.

'That was our constituency chairman. You did it. Well done mate. I've got some champagne for the occasion. He went to the kitchen and returned with two full glasses.

'Cheers. I'm still not sure whether you shoulda gone to the result announcement, but I do agree that if you're the loser - and not for one moment did I think you'd be one - it's a horrible anticlimax; you just fade into invisibility almost immediately. The fact that you're not there adds, I think, a certain, I dunno, mystique. I told 'em, as you suggested, that you had to attend to an important constituency matter; you'd promised to help some people and had to honour it. You're getting savvy, Mister Wilde.'

'Thanks.'

'We'll go to that school hall tomorrow lunch time, anyway, to meet your supporters. The leader and deputy of the local Conservative group'll be there along with a few councillors I'm sure. Guess people will be ringing you any minute now to offer their congrats. I'd switch yer phone off if I was you, but not before ringing headquarters and thanking them for their efforts.'

He did so, speaking to three of the volunteers; they seemed pleased.

'Right then,' continued Archer, 'the nitty-gritty, the practicalities. Other than needing better computers and better security - you won't get them anyway - and a better system of passing on best practice that doesn't rely on random conversations in a Commons coffee bar, you have to make sure all letters sent by your constituents are answered within two weeks. You may, but probably won't, have time to manage that. Also, there is, apparently, not enough room in the Chambers for all the members at the same time, there are no desks in them, and the technology is laughably antiquated.

'A good MP has to be an administrator, office manager, advocate for the poor and powerless, and also a media-savvy communicator, parliamentary operator and be able to understand complex policy questions. Plus, how are you supposed to deal with people who come to your house and, although abusive, it's not enough to call the police? Some people are good at some bits, few are good at all.'

He then, drawing from his experience of other successful clients he had aided and abetted over the years, further discussed the prosaic, mundane and necessary experiences of being an MP before insisting Jordan sleep in the spare bedroom for the few hours remaining till daylight.

Pulling a duvet over him, the new MP's almost subliminal thought was that she would be one of the well-wishers to ring him. He dismissed it.

He had experienced triumphs before, though he only called them that to himself: playing as a substitute in a rugby match when his school beat Marlborough for the first time in a decade and taking part, because somebody had dropped out, in an inter-schools quiz, and winning it for his team as he answered a question on the history of the London Stock Exchange. He'd also helped an uncle pave the way for a takeover deal by befriending, at his behest, the daughter of the CEO of the would-be taken-over company - whom he actually liked, thus not understanding his feting - but none to compare with this.

The turnout hadn't been what he'd expected and the after-vote answers from the tellers by those who had crossed their papers in various halls, entertainment venues, schools and gyms, had promised a greater gap between him and his opponents, but a five-thousand vote win was petty conclusive. Archer seemed to think so as, putting a stocky arm around his client's shoulders in the school hall and briefly squeezing them, he introduced him.

There were others around him, applauding, smiling, a few of them punching the air, while some people standing towards the back gave vent to a few boos then walked out. He couldn't see the point of them having come.

'It's nothing personal mate,' said Archer, still clapping.

'Of course not, they're losers, like the party they so love.'

'They're probably slamming a few doors on their way out moaning that t here's no justice in politics.'

'What's justice anyway? I'm here to win.'

'Which you have. Make your little speech now and use that.'

Jordan held his hands up.

'Thanks to all who voted for me and my party today. I stood for this ward to win. And did. I will try my best. I will endeavour to push through the policies of this grand and good party, this modernising, forward-looking party, and at the next general election I hope there will be more supporters here to cheer another victory. Thank you again.'

He bowed his head very slightly and Archer guided him off the stage past a line of local officials and Tory councillors. As they walked by the chairs to the exit, Jordan said, 'I should have thanked you shouldn't I, publicly I mean. Sorry, I don't know the protocol but my inbred good manners should have informed me.'

'Ne'er mind. Next time.'

Archer had to be off again, leaving Jordan to chat to a few pleased-looking supporters congratulating him, telling him that he would do a good job and were looking forward to reading of his exploits in the press. He excused himself after a while and went home. He looked at his emails, picked up his phone, on which there were quite a few messages, then looked again at the emails. There was nothing from her.

He had never been inside the Houses of Parliament until now, certainly not the Chamber - or, as remembered from his schooldays, 'the Honourable Commons of the United Kingdom of Great Britain and Northern Ireland Parliament assembled' - but had been to the Chapel, noting that its shape, with its configuration of choir stalls, was the model for the Chamber and its benches facing across from each other; an arrangement facilitating the adversarial atmosphere representative of the British parliamentary approach.

He was aware that it was a convention that maiden speeches should be relatively uncontroversial and be more of a general statement of a politician's comment on a current topic rather than a partisan's, also that they should include a tribute to the previous incumbent of the seat. Jordan had actually forgotten the name of the latter, knowing only that she'd stood down for health reasons.

As he stood, briefly looking around him at the benches, the walls, the members, he tried not to be overawed by the feel of history, victories, defeats, of traditions and power.

A script was in his hand but he was confident he would rarely have the need to use it. He'd decided it would be a short address. He began:

'I am pleased to be here as Conservative member for Wansford East. I am a firm believer in what we have in this country, a believer in the political and economic system that rightly rules most of the world - though I'd like us to have a bigger and more innovative share in it - but also in its intervention in terms of the less well-paid of our citizens. As I have often said, caring has to be a genuine tenet of the party, of any party.'

He paused. 'I wish to talk briefly about the Opposition.'

He sensed a slight stirring amongst the listeners, some of whom, he was sure, found first-time speeches both boring and often with the potential to embarrass.

'There is a tension between the role of a populist socialism and the more democratic variety which wants to harness markets for the good of the widest number of people. It is very prevalent in today's Opposition Party. There is an internal split, and long may it continue.'

He looked briefly around him again.

'The parry I am talking of presents its political DNA as a saintly defence of the poor, as being the sole representative of benefit claimants and food-bank users, yet, laudable as it may be, it ends up in a language of pet phrases and cliches. A party serious about government needs to recognise the difference between rhetoric and deliverables.'

He thought he heard a few quiet 'Hear, hears.'

'I will not dwell on how this current Labour Party will attempt to ensure that the State ownership of virtually everything becomes more efficient. It so obviously cannot. And the milk of human kindness sprayed around will inevitably be semi-skimmed. But *this* government can, and is, delivering and will continue to do so, and better. I thank the honourable members of this House.'

He sat again. Somebody said 'Thank you, the honourable member for Wansford East. The honourable member for North Salford will now speak.'

A man got up from a bench and asked the Deputy PM a question about the effects a recent law change had had on his constituents, followed by several more general queries from other parliamentarians.

Some while before the queries and debate had finished, Jordan was becoming rather bored. He wanted to be on his own to enjoy, to reflect on his experience.

He left the Chamber a little quickly, he needed a toilet. Archer had been wise when he'd told him that the first thing he needed to know when entering the place was where the toilets were, they weren't easy to find. Then he was off to meet and mingle with a few other new members in a dingy bar with dated décor and the heavy smell of beer in the air down a dark alley in the underbelly of the Palace of Westminster.

CHAPTER FIFTEEN

As it was a little early to meet Edward and Paul, he got off at a station before his intended one and wandered into Lincoln's Inn Fields. Somehow, the light reminded him of a Seurat painting without the parasols and chimneys. There were young men on the grass; barristers, lawyers perhaps or hoped-to-be ones, playing piggy-in-the-middle with a football, throwing it to each other, the one in the centre galloping in circles, striving to reach it.

They were having an innocent, non-responsible time before the courts' institutionalised game-playing, the big-drinking victories, the kudos, and perhaps leaving a victim frustrated and angry that the person who had made them one had walked out of the court free, or an innocent had become the guilty one solely by the cleverness and trickery of a supposedly impartial professional. He could hear one of them telling - like Irish jokes made up by the Irish to satirise the English - a lawyer joke. 'Did you hear that scientists in laboratories now use lawyers instead of rats? You can get too close to rats and there are some things even rats won't do.'

They laughed, stopped their game and started checking their backpacks - in two piles as if earlier they'd been playing football and the bags had demarcated a goal - perhaps for ties and crisp shirts then, laughing, went off to chancery, the courts and a kind of justice.

He left the square and went into Kingsway, still thinking it had, with its tall pavement tress, a slight feel of the Champs-Elysees, then through to Covent Garden, remembering, in the immediate post-flower market days, the first shop, which sold candles. Then to Leicester Square and north to the Circus where he could hear the intermittent, explosive thumping of pile drivers above the noise of Oxford Street's traffic. After a few minutes he saw that they were operating on a recently-vacant piece of land next to the building he'd come to see. A problem with demolition was that one often forgot what had been there before it. He stood on the pavement opposite.

There was scaffolding covered in the ubiquitous semi-translucent plastic sheeting around the whole font of the building - he guessing that it was being converted into apartments and the outside probably, much to the developers annoyance, listed, so that the exterior had to be saved. The noise seemed to grow louder as he watched the piles being sunk, the two machines surrounded by workers doing little but looking at them.

There were people, most wearing hard hats, some holding placards, on the pavement in front of the building, the line stretching along part of the hoarding in front of the adjacent site. 'Stop Below Minimum Wages.' 'Public - Get Involved.' and a misspelt 'Good Wages For Good Werk.'

He wasn't sure what he'd expected, perhaps more movement, more people.

'I dunno, bleedin' foreigners, come over 'ere, can't spell prop'ly, take our jobs and then want more bloody money!'

He turned his head. It was Paul, beside him was Edward.

'What are you thinking about doing then?' Ralph asked.

'We could stand with them and give our support, encourage them,' said Edward.

'We could start a collection for 'em, I suppose, don't think it'd work though. Even hold their placards for a while, give 'em a rest,' Paul suggested.

'This isn't very positive, is it,' said Edward. 'An idea would be to go to that site,' he gestured to where the pile drivers were, 'and try to persuade that lot to support them.'

'They'd hardly come out in sympathy,' volunteered Ralph.

'I've an idea they're English lads,' said Edward. 'Don't think they'd be that fond of helping out their fellow workers, the construction industry's quite conservative.'

'That lot are mostly East Europeans, anyway,' said Paul.

Ralph asked him how he knew.

'One of them keeps saying, *'Mes norime daugian.'* 'We want more money.' His mate's just said, *'jie nesupranta,'* which, I think, means, 'They won't understand.'

'If you've got this stuff from waitresses, Paul, you must have chatted to a lot of them. Think we should go over and speak with

142

the workers, their English will be a lot better than our Lithuanian, Polish, Albanian, whatever.'

'But don't mention the party,' said Edward. 'If you do that and it gets about, the media, authorities et cetera will say that the strike's been encouraged, even instigated, by 'outside influences,' 'political activists,' thus negating the validity of it. It's an old ploy.'

'The protest's not only theirs,' pointed out Paul, 'there's the question of their bosses maybe not being paid for months by the main contractors, which doesn't actually encourage them to pay good wages to their employees if they can get away with it.'

'Which they seem to be doing.'

'Could be some of 'em are self-employed too, which means they'll have little leverage anyway.'

'Let's go over,' said Ralph.

They crossed the road, Edward leading.

'*Sveiki,*' said Paul to one of the placard holders.

'*Dzien dobry,*' the man said.

'How many of you are striking? *Ile*?'

'There are thirty more of us.'

'You're subcontractors, yes?'

' *Jestesmy,* we are.' We have Albanian boss.'

'You're Polish aren't you; you answered me in that language.'

Just then a dozen or so more workers came noisily through the front doors and joined the others, two of them holding between them a larger board proclaiming 'We Are Being Sexploited.'

'Who put the 'S' in?' asked Edward. 'Who's trying to turn it into a joke?'

'We are building these into flats, you call them,' said the same man.

'We'd like to help. What do you want us to do?'

'Tell more people about us, maybe.'

'Need more than that. Doesn't the noise from next door bother you?'

'Yes, they are loud, those machines, incessant.'

'He is good at English, with words like that,' said a man next to him. 'The labourers get a lot less than we do, you know. This is good country, we come here to work from Poland.'

Ralph asked him where the nearest toilet was and was directed inside the building and told to go down a floor. He went through the foyer then down the stairs, unsure amongst the dust sheets and more scaffolding whether, with the ziggurat mouldings, curved cornices and what looked like genuine metal glazing bars on the windows, it was genuine Thirties or a mock-up,

More work had been done here: plaster stripped to bare brick, wooden lathes from the corridor ceiling lying on the floorboards, and sledgehammers leaning against a wall as if there had been a call to action and the men had just stopped and downed tools.

A rather frail-looking man in blue overalls, somewhat older than the men outside, came out of a room at the side.

'Are you going to try to sack me?' Another East European accent. 'Get me out of the building?'

'Why would I do that? We're here to help you if we can; we're on your side. There's only a few of us.'

'Who are you?

'People who believe that it's wrong to pay so little. That's why you're no longer working isn't it?'

'*Tak*. I am craftsman, I feel like an *ofiara.*'

'What's that?'

'A victim.

'Am I near the toilet?'

He gestured behind him. 'Two doors down. Are you intelligent man?'

'I think so.'

Ralph went to the lavatory. Another worker was using a wrench on a tap.

'Thought you'd stopped working.'

'This for us. We use.'

The corridor was empty when Ralph came out. He began walking to the stairs again when he heard, 'I want to show you something.'

He turned to the overalled figure. He was holding some sort of folder. Ralph could see that it was a rather old one.

'I find this on this floor. Basement. I show you where.'

Ralph followed him to a room at the end of the passage, the door of which had been removed.

The man pointed to a corner where there was an old safe and above it a three-feet-square hole in the wall.

'That was wall safe. Silly things in it: old tea cup, some papers about people I think who worked here, and this.' He held up the folder.

'What is that?'

'I show you,'

He gestured towards a carpenter's stool in another corner.

'You sit'.

He did. He was given the folder.

'Read first one.'

There were four yellowing sheets, the print slightly faded. The first had a number which could have been a date, a '4' preceded by what looked like a backward 's' and was addressed to 'D.' There was no heading.

"This shouldn't have to be sent to you again, you know what is required. Unlike the last message, you must reply to this. You were supposed to inform your Parliament that the Russian Government has evidence of covert western infiltration into their general armaments programme. As emphasised, you must tell your Parliament so as to help ensure an increase in armed preparedness."

There was no signature but a faded number in a bottom corner of the page and some random-looking capital letters.

Ralph quickly looked through some of the other pages but their contents were a meaningless jumble of squiggles, dashes and more numbers and letters. Perhaps the apparent meaninglessness translated into what he'd just read. It appeared to be something from a simplistic and rather unrealistic script.

'Someone said this place was Intelligence place long time ago; it was offices for foreign bank before we came. Apartments now, if we finish them.'

'Who else have you shown it to?'

'Work friends, they not care. No interest.'

'May I borrow this?'

'First page seem only good one. You do something important with it?'

'I don't know. Thanks. Look after yourself.'

'Do not go. Do you know that labourers on this site and those that helped demolish building next to it, are Romanian and they are slave labour? They live in a place in east London that is small place and they are cramped. They were in poverty in Romania but now is worse. They were promised fifty pound a day wage and good place to live. They are cheated.'

'Who else knows of this?'

'Police. They find out; they call it servitude and find boss people who cheat them.'

'You sure of that?'

'Think so. Some good may happen.'

'I hope so. Bye.'

Outside, there were a few more onlookers on the pavement opposite. Edward and Paul were holding the large board with the 'S' now painted over. As Ralph briefly told them what had happened inside the building, the two builders who had originally been holding it, took the board from them, said thanks and continued to hold it aloft.

'The old carpenter,' said one of them to Ralph, is *proto senis,* crazy old man, always finding things, whatever job we do he looks for secrets and things. He is happy though.'

'Let's go somewhere and talk,' suggested Edward.

The worker told them of a nearby café.

Once inside, at a table, Ralph told them of the Romanians and then showed them the page of he'd been given from the file.

Edward began with:

'So, it's lobbying then, the 'quiet word.' They leave their finger prints all over government property, but we never see 'em. And it's not just a few bad apples, the barrel's rotten. Commercial lobbying is a mechanism for corrupting democracy. This one's simple, though: Increase East-West tension, more weapons perceived as needed, more profits for the manufacturers and investors, and bigger bungs for dishonourable members. Bingo.'

'I wonder,' mused Paul, 'whether 'the 'LVFDBS' at the bottom is 'Lockheed Vernon, *Francais Defenseurs,* and British Systems. Some of the biggest firms at that time.'

Ralph asked Edward if he knew much about the Cold War.

'I know a few dates,' Interjected Paul.

'Such as?'

''54, the US launched its first nuke sub, '56, Hungarian revolt and anti-Communist protests in Poland, '57, I think it was, Eisenhower launched a campaign to build fallout shelters and Khruschev challenged the States to a shooting match to prove his boast that the Soviet union had a superiority over the US. Could happen again. History rarely repeats itself exactly, but it often rhymes. That's a quote.'

'I didn't know you were interested in all that.'

'I'm not, I just remember reading it.'

'If so, it turned out they didn't have much need to plant things to create tension,' said Edward, 'it had been done for them and, don't forget, in '48 the party took control of Czechoslovakia.'

'Not the point,' said Paul, 'too early. I mean later than that. The number before the initials could be a date, 1984 I guess. Wonder who D was. An MP I suppose. Thatcher was in charge then.'

'And Gorbachev in Russia,' Edward reminded them. 'Could create a bit of a stink for the current mob couldn't it? Important, even incriminating stuff left in a safe after an intelligence agency vacated their building?'

'Interesting if you like who-dun-its,' murmured Ralph.

'Even more so if it's genuine,' countered Paul.

'I'm convinced,' said Edward, 'that a lot of wars, small ones, are begun by political pressure from arms suppliers and dealers in order to test their weapons. Anyway, we came here to help, didn't we? We've done nought. What would old Moorcroft say, eh? Wonder what he would do.'

'We could send it to a national newspaper,' suggested Paul.

'No, anyone could have written it,' Ralph said.

'Does it really matter? It could be used. No smoke without fire and all that. They could do some sort of forensic test on the paper and the ink, see how old it is, how genuine.'

'Maybe. Doesn't matter, I don't think anything's gonna happen,' said Ralph. 'I guess a local paper'll write something about the strike.'

'It won't last long,' said Edward, 'developer will squash it, lean on the contractors to employ other subbies. Nobody's interested unless it affects them directly.'

He looked out the café window, suddenly a little plaintive.

'Nobody was interested in a little play I wrote about the French students in '68 either.' He turned to them. 'Haven't thought about if for a while. Visited a few fringe theatres with it; no one wanted to know. Eaton tried to help in getting it staged and managed to find someone who read plays for a small theatre company based under a South London railway arch. I sent it and was asked for a writing CV. I didn't have one. I wrote back to 'em: 'The written word is all, surely; no matter who writes something it's *what's* written.' I refused to be a supplicant. It's about power and writers made to feel like Twist with his bowl.'

'Can see why you're so anti-elite,' remarked Paul

'That doesn't make me wrong. Surely you're not gonna go anywhere near the usual critique of Marxists with stuff like 'They've either had a bad childhood or it's the politics of envy.'

''Course not.'

'You can use emotive language to try to invalidate anything that's against the ruling structure. 'Holding the country to ransom' is, of course, a tabloid favourite for strikes, 'infighting' for a trivial disagreement amongst Labour ministers et cetera; all the Lefie pejoratives. All so obvious. You're not saying much, Ralph'.

'Was thinking.' He turned to Edward. 'Assuming you haven't got it, Red Claire's number will be on the party's books won't it?'

'I do have it. I have the numbers of most of the members as a back-up. Boss man can be a little lax with data at times.'

'Like to give it to me?

'Sure. Want to discuss Stalin's formulation of dialectical materialism with her then?'

He fancies her,' said Paul. 'Meanwhile, I'm getting back to fill in some more Kafkaesque forms for the Benefits Agency.'

'I've got to get back to work, and do some party things, too.' He looked at Paul.' You could be right about what Ralph found, you know. See yer.'

Ralph told his pal that he wasn't going straight back, he felt like a wander. Noticing he wasn't too pleased with this, Ralph told him he'd call him in the next couple of days.

When the other two had departed, Ralph rang her.

'How did you get my number?'

He told her. 'Is it a secret then? I should have asked you for it before.'

'What do you want?'

'Fancy a meal or something this evening?'

There was a rather long silence before she said yes. They arranged to meet.

It was her choice; a small place in the local High Street recently taken over by a French chef who planned to change its name to 'La Bakerie' and had as yet not put pictures of the Eiffel Tower and l'Opera on its walls. She was, predictably, wearing casual clothes, her tight jeans accentuating the length of her legs; for him, her femininity seeming, contradictorily, to be increased by her purposeful stride.

He had brief images of her when younger, a teenager perhaps, wearing clothes to suit the colours of her moods: maybe lifting gauzy cottons and twirling in a Home Counties garden, riding a bicycle in pragmatic shorts, hiking in leather shoes, gazing at herself in front of a wardrobe mirror in her first little black dress.

'We meet again then,' she said, as she sat down at his table.

'Order now?

'Not yet'.

'What's a stockbroker belt girl like you doing living in Wansford?'

'I came here once with my parents, and there was just something about the place, it made an impression on me.'

'Part of primary socialization.'

'More secondary really, I wasn't exactly a five-year-old.'

'I probably wasn't much more than that,' said Ralph, 'when I was taken for visits to dad's brother's place not too far from here; curved windows, green pantiles and so forth; it represented a different world, universe even, from mean terraces. Interesting, the strength of early experiences, this was very visual for me.

I have a friend who's almost spiritual about it. Sometimes when we're walking, maybe west London, north, wherever, he gets a feeling of a kind of... magic from buildings, houses, 'shapes against the sky,' as he puts it, and me too, to an extent. It's stronger with him. Sometimes I feel it's more real to him than his relationship with me.'

She looked out along the road and pointed to an Edwardian house with fish-scale hanging tiles and mullioned windows and said, 'Is that more real than me?'

'Could never be.'

She put her head to one side, a gesture he was getting used to, and silently frowned at him. He wondered if, in the way he had said it, he'd expressed more than intended.

'Do you find,' she asked, a little more slowly than her usual conversational pace, 'that it's somehow better talking like this than of the usual things, the abstract, conceptual, political?'

'If you mean more... pleasant, enjoyable. Yes.'

I thought you were maybe going to say 'intimate' then. Do you think that without society there would be a Hobbesian war of all against all?'

'Depends on your model of man. If it's Freudian; yes.'

'Break the spell did it, that question?'

'Society satisfies a primal urge for order, perhaps as a weapon against some sort of irrational fate. The construct of a god gives us order.'

'Would dirt be a disorder?'

'Matter out of place. We have a fear of I, specially when it emanates from our own bodies. But let's not go there. Did you know Freud thought that in pre-history young men who desired their mother killed their fathers and ate them and, in redemption, forced themselves not to want their mothers, therefore not having to kill their fathers? From this, I believe, came the idea of marrying out.'

'Could be true.'

'Yes, the first cultural event leading to civilisation, you might say, though he could have added that the sons were also frightened of being killed by each other.'

She looked at him silently for a while.

'Were you really interested in that well-practised piece of insight or was it a deflection?'

'From what?'

'I think you know.'

He hesitated before answering.

'You mean, from what I could be feeling about you?'

She nodded.

A waitress came over, apologised for taking so long, and asked them what they wished to order. They took their time doing so, and when they had, Ralph forced a grin and said, 'isn't there a by-election soon where you live?'

'Another deflection. Yes, the Tory candidate came a-calling the other day.'

'And?'

'I went to one of his speeches'

I'm surprised.'

'Only to have a go at him.'

'About?'

'Told him not to treat voters like children.'

'They *are* children. Capitalism needs infants, babies. No emotions are new, we've felt them all before as baby and child: jealousy, sorrow, fear, love et cetera.'

'Interesting that you said 'jealousy' first.'

'Capitalism needs all of our 'original' feelings: wishes, desires, comforts, and excitements, our wants - which, through advertising media, we internalise as 'needs.' Emotional security, our need to belong, is used as a tool by advertising media to help us fit in with peer groups. It's an essential prerequisite for us to buy things: the latest phones, cars, techno gadgets et cetera.'

'The trendiest clothes.'

'Fashions are set by brands, rarely by people.'

'Am I like that?'

'Can't imagine you being much influenced by peers, by anyone, really.'

They said little while they ate - their palates were seemingly similar, though his less inclined to strong tastes - and after the savoury, which towards the end she finished quickly, she waved away his suggestion of a dessert with, 'Sorry, I haven't time for any postprandial activity. I did intend to start back earlier than this, really. Once you work for an NPO whose primary objectives are philanthropy and social well-being; you become committed.'

'What are you going to do?'

'Another cunningly contrived presentation to gather more funds. Sorry about this. Do enjoy your pudding. Cheerio.'

She gave what he though, hoped, was a genuine smile of contrition.

Ordering his sweet, he wasn't certain whether he felt slightly deserted by her or that somehow it could be the beginning of something good between them.

CHAPTER SIXTEEN

He wasn't sure whether it was an anticlimax or not. After his first speech, a few members, strictly Tory ones, had briefly welcomed him in the bar - a decoratively fussy and rather aesthetically dispiriting space - but hadn't talked of policies or meetings or of ideologies, or even politics. Whether Arsenal really were on the up, seemed to be the salient topic. Two of them, however, had remarked on his little speech saying it had been rather different than the usual efforts, one of them mentioning that two of the whips had rather liked it.

He went for a walk around the outside of the House, or rather, as he'd been reminded, the New Palace of Westminster. He hadn't done this since a young teenager, reluctantly doing so under parental control. It wasn't a much better experience now, even though he was beginning to accept that he now belonged in it. He decided to join a few tourists and go inside.

The old colour coding - gold in the parts used by monarchs, red for the Lords and green for the Commons, the latter of course now having the power, 'Parliament as sovereign' - reeked with history. Walking through the Lords' Ante-Chamber he noted the Victorian desire to educate and impress the world by its royal portraiture, though a painting of Anne Boleyn as a rather buxom blonde even he knew, though history wasn't his strong suit, she had been a quite slim brunette.

Working in this building, alongside the elected and non-elected members of the formidable institution, was, he reminded himself, now his job, though he was still feeling a little apart from it and really more in tune with the tourists, a few of whom were easing politely past him as he stood there. He was, as yet, not *of* the place, certainly not of its history.

He wasn't certain of his ambitions; he wanted to have his say but wasn't sure what it would take to have power to influence things by what he said. He would have to be patient, a minister's job would take a while to achieve and depended on so many variables; not just his ability but perhaps how good he was at hand-pumping, who of any influence liked him, what favours he could do for them, being loyal, or pretending to be, his media image et cetera.

There were a few well-known backbenchers, however, that seemed to exercise influence and, as Archer said, 'You don't have to be a cabinet member, you're generally better off as a backbencher where you can sit and watch the arteries harden and the ulcers sprout.'

Leaving for home, he caught the Tube to his station, from where he would drive to his house. All so ordinary, commonplace. Perhaps everywhere and everybody was, we were just stimulus-response mechanisms, all eight billion of us. He looked around at his fellow travelers using their phones and wondered, as he had before, if significant human relationships in the future wouldn't be involved so much in the reality of face-to-face confrontation, however meaningful or trivial, but in a world perhaps to be seen as a system of relationships between and among people and their devices. If so, how would this affect formal politics?

Devices would be doing much of the representative work. Even though, arguably, the current political system was more delegatory than representative - politicians couldn't represent everybody anyway, though the word was still bandied about - would it still have its traditional meaning and weight?

Representation would increasingly be in the hands of tech companies, they would grow larger, their global coverage even more persistently and acceptably serving the masses and making more profits. He wondered what would happen to politicians in the future, just how representative they could be, and, if he was still serving, how it would affect him.

He laughed at himself. He had just entered Parliament, spoken a few words of little consequence, had hardly started and was now worrying about his future. He thought again of that building, that institution; how could it have no meaning?

As he sipped a late-night whisky before retiring, as he still liked to call it, he thought he would go in tomorrow and try to get the feel of what was happening, what was supposed to be happening.

He went to the House next day, congratulating himself on his justification for calling it that, and had a brief chat with the honourable member from Merthyr Tydfil who recognised him from a picture taken from Jordan's local paper and put on the commons website. He was tempted to ask him why 'Plaid Cymru' is pronounced 'Plied Kumree,' knowing only the Welsh would know.

Jordan was there to see one of the admin people to sign something or other regarding his constituency office and while there was told not to worry about his surgery, few members did; whatever good he did would get him few votes, anyway. This suited Jordan, he wasn't, he confessed to himself, that interested in the individual. He visited another admin office then went downstairs again for a brief wander from where he had left off the previous day.

There were more tourists gazing around this time, looking more bored than interested. One of them was wearing a wide-brimmed hat with a flower at the front, a bell-shaped skirt and a shoulder-padded top above rather large, wide sleeves. It was Claire Cluckrose. A little girl was with her dressed in a similar style but with more trimmings and lace. He looked again. It *was* her. He went across to them.

'Hello, I thought I'd been transported back in time. What are you doing here? Where's your parasol?'

'Oh, hello. This is almost embarrassing.'

'I can't imagine you being embarrassed.'

'Really?'

'You look - '

'Pretty Amazing?'

'You didn't have to smile. You do.'

She looked down at the girl.

'This is my niece, Isobel.'

'Hello Isobel. Why is your auntie here?'

She shyly turned her head away from him, leaving her carer to answer.

'The husband of a friend of mine is a photographer. He occasionally asks me to model.'

'I bet.'

'I haven't, but this time he's doing something about the suffragettes, so I did. He took some shots outside. I told Izzy about what was going to happen and as she has a day off school insisted on coming too, she likes to dress up. She also wanted to walk around and show it off. Hence, here I am.'

'The centre of attention.'

'I don't wish to be, it's for her.'

'Isn't it a century since you, women, got the vote?'

'Not every woman, only those with property or married to men with property. The rest came later.'

'Trust you to know that. I thought for one mad moment you'd come to see me.'

'That *was* a mad moment. I suppose our cultural norms should prompt me to congratulate you on being duly elected.' She looked around her. 'This could be a place for a history lesson if there was a guide about.'

'Early indoctrination into political life?'

'I want her to know about it, yes.'

He looked at her clothes again. 'Didn't they wear feather plumes in their hats in those days?'

'Yes, and occasionally entire exotic birds that had been stuffed. Most of the plumes came from birds in the Florida Everglades, which were nearly made entirely extinct by overhunting. Millions of birds a year slaughtered for the great god of fashion and profit.'

'I was wondering when the last bit would come in. You know, you'd have made a great suffragette.'

'Suffragist, preferably.'

'Whatever, people would have listened to you.'

'Do you?'

'Yes.'

'Have I changed your mind on anything?

'You want a progress report?'

'If you like.'

'Well, I can... understand, though not empathise with your doctrine.'

'Which is?'

'Ownership of the means of production, distribution and exchange in the hands of the people.'

'A time-honoured way of expressing it, but we know, unfortunately, that it's unlikely to happen, but I'd like something pretty near it.'

'Your niece is looking at you with fascination. Most kids her age would be bored with this.'

'She's not most kids.'

'And you're not most aunties. There's a caféteria place over in the corner. Shall we try it?'

Having asked Isobel whether she wanted something to eat and receiving a positive answer they went for refreshments. Telling the girl to suck her milk shake quietly, Claire asked Jordan how the new boy was doing.

'Made an opening speech. Not really sure what's happening yet. I do have a surgery in a few days, though.'

'You'll learn to make excuses. Been vilified on social media yet?'

'Rarely use it with people I don't know. I should, but… '

'Big data. It's powerful, huge caches of information about every citizen in the world accumulated by the tech giants, and it's probably used covertly to exploit for financial or political gain.'

'Perhaps traditional politics won't be able to keep up with it.'

'Maybe you can make a speech about it, talk about the need to regulate the most dynamic technological revolution in history.'

'But not stop innovation or legitimate expression.'

'Free expression's only notional, anyway.'

'We could, I suppose, eventually have something like a Ministry of Truth.'

'We've probably got something like that now, the merciless court of social media, its bench stuffed with a billion judges.'

'What do you do?' asked Isobel shyly.

'Er, I work here, sometimes.'

'Do you like it?'

'Just started, don't know yet. Want a cake?'

'Yes please.'

She looked up at her aunt who nodded permission. He got it for her.

'Thank you. When I go out with Auntie Claire I'm like 'are you going to get me a cake 'cos - ''

'Don't use 'like' inappropriately. There are only two main definitions of the word, you know this,' Claire admonished.

'Alright, auntie.'

'Rather harsh,' remarked Jordan.

'When you first learn a language the way you speak may stay forever unless it's consciously altered. I'll pay for this,' she said, standing.

'No, I will, of course. We hardly had anything anyway.'

'Thanks. Now I need to get this young lady home. Say goodbye, Isobel.'

'Can't you stay a little longer?'

'You know me. '

'I'm beginning to.'

Her disappearance around the door in a flutter of crinoline and lace confirmed how much he liked like what he knew.

Whilst intermittently thinking of Claire during the next week, he met other MPs at the House, especially those in his own party and listened to the gossip which, he felt, was like sixth formers' banter. The Chief Whip was apparently a monster, the member for Ludford South was gay, but was adamant in his non-ownership of the nomenclature, the PM was a surprisingly clever person, and while the Opposition's leading players were fiercely collective in their world view, it appeared that few were competent enough to organise an orgy in a brothel.

He thought of the subject she'd suggested he make a speech on. He wanted to, and began writing it, though not earnestly because he didn't know when he would be able to give it. He rang her and left a message. As yet she hadn't replied. Then he heard that views were wanted for a debate on social media and the need for regulation of digital technology companies.

It was held a few days later in one of the Chambers in late afternoon and he was asked if he wished to attend. It was only a third full, if that. The speakers preceding him predictably stressed there should be stricter guidelines sent to these organisations so that they could voluntarily regulate themselves. Jordan was happy with this, as long as it didn't reduce profit.

As he hadn't been formally asked to speak he wasn't sure whether he was supposed to, but he'd worked hard at remembering what he wished to say, had even rehearsed it.

Waiting for an appropriate moment, he stood.

'While I am, in essence, all for self-regulation, this debate is part of wider phenomena, it is a large issue.'

He looked around him. There seemed even less people in the room now.

'It's been said before that all mainstream media pander to the bias of its readers and viewers who watch and read what they do because their prejudices are fed. The tech companies, in essence, do a similar thing and they continue to grow and people are caught in the seductive draw of unchecked monopolies.' He paused.

'It could be argued that the immune system of the democratic West may be crashing. There appears to be a collapse of trust in our most basic institutions and it's nurturing a lurid populism weaponised by digital technology. You could also say that they're stoking social unease and division. The impact these West Coast giants have seems little short of seismic.

'The only certainty now seems to be volatility; political prophecy is becoming less credible. If we have uncertainty, suspicion, then authoritarianism will prey on it. This hasn't as yet won the day, but it could do.' He looked around him, coming to his main agenda.

'We have a regime opposing us holding a rigid ideological bias which they may have disguised, reasonably successfully but it's there, and it doesn't really care for people. They have a growing obsession with some sort of skewed, overarching ideal, and their rigid doctrines will, if we let them into power, set the morality of future generations. Let's conserve what we have. This party was built on that. Let's defend it. Let us keep it.'

He sat, realising that he'd turned the topic into a party political broadcast almost. But there it was. After a brief silence, some party members clapped and nodded their heads, a few enthusiastically.

He listened to two other speakers sticking mainly to the nitty-gritty of regulations and what could actually be enforced, after which there was a brief discussion in which he didn't join then they left the Chamber. Though departing in twos and threes, to him it seemed as if they were a solid block and he a lone figure. Then one of t hem turned to him and suggested he come to the bar with them.

It was a time-warp; the Victorian panelling, antiquated light shades, ornate dado rail, high skirting boards, fat architraves and stained oak floor. If the smell of beer, wine, spirits, private dealings, stitch-ups, subtle persuasions, covert but major decisions and hypocrisies could have an odour, this one was all of these things.

There were a few 'Hello, we haven't met. I'm...' and a couple of 'And you represent?' along with some handshakes, then after a pinot grigio someone brought him, he relaxed. He wasn't fully conversant with sentiments such as, 'I see Arthur's kowtowed to the Chief Whip again, though he told me it wasn't that he lacked courage, just that the bastard was a monster,' and, 'No, he's never gonna challenge the leader, he'll be drummed out,' though he did relate to 'And if they *do* get in, woe betide the City, the whole damn country'll go downhill, and fast.'

One of them introduced himself and asked Jordan why he hadn't mentioned the David versus Goliath challenge the BBC had on their hands with the tech corporations.

'You're a Conservative member; why should their woes interest you?'

'It's surely a part of our culture, the values you were just speaking of.'

'The sooner it becomes commercial the better.'

'Are you aware that the tech giants have spent millions on lobbyists to water down US internet regulations?'

'Can you blame them? Power has money.'

'You were against the might of these companies a moment ago.'

'I was speaking of what I thought was true. Is there a bit of projection maybe? Perhaps you don't use social media much.'

'I don't.'

'Neither do I.'

'But this media can contort our view of one another and allow us to live in kind of imagined communities where we only really engage with those who share our views, a kind of echo chamber.'

'As implicitly alluded to earlier, fake news eats away at trust in the media, including the Beeb.'

'Could argue we need a public broadcasting system to help understand ourselves better, remind us of the everyday things we hold in common. These aren't exactly the passions of the West Coast giants.'

'Why would they be?'

'Could argue that…. Let's leave it there. Another time. Nice to talk to you.'

He smiled, put a hand briefly on the new MP's shoulder and went to the other end of the bar. One large occupant of a bar stool then said, 'Okay, it's joke time.'

'It occurred to me,' said one of the group, 'how strange it is that Americans choose from just two people to run for President and fifty for Miss America.'

'Tommy told me that our great leader left orders to be woken at any time in case of a national emergency, even if they're in a cabinet meeting.'

While they were dredging up more attempts at humour, the man who had invited Jordan to have a drink with them, told him he thought he'd made a pretty good contribution to the debate, and introduced himself as Alan Watts, secretary to the Secretary of Finance.

'I heard you made your maiden; I wasn't there. Don't like those, they're a strain to give and to listen to. What did you do before this?'

Jordan told him.

'Ditto for Richards and Pewlett. And you?'

Jordan told him the name of his firm.

'Dealt with them before. I won't ask you why you wanted to be involved in this game; I've never liked that question directed at me.'

'I suppose you'd be a little cynical if I said I wanted to do some good.'

'For the masses? for Joe Bloggs? Who *is* he? The Labour lads are often on about him, at least before they get here. Some come in carrying a sabre, I doubt if they've got more than a blunt dagger now. No matter how radical, even revolutionary they think they are, when they get here they become institutionalised in the ways of the place and quickly adapt to the realisation that there's not a great deal they can do; even if they were in power it would take a long, long time. They just follow their whips. Unless there's blood in the streets nothing's really going to change.'

'I came, I suppose, to help encourage the economy if I could. Sounds rather grand I know, but - '

'Okay, so a few get richer, but the rest do a bit too, yeah?' Watts looked at him for a while, eyes narrowing. 'You know, there just may be something about you - I won't use 'charisma,' dislike the word, it means having he qualities of a prophet, and you're not one - that maybe suggests higher things. Who knows? I could be wrong. Anyway, I have work to do, not of great importance, but I get paid for it. We'll chat again.'

As he passed the others they had come in with, he briefly put a hand on the shoulders of a few of them and left the bar. A little after, Jordan did, also.

What had just been said to him pleased him. He thought of her again. Perhaps she would have been interested in the bar's history, its period decor, but certainly not in the views of most of its present occupants.

CHAPTER SEVENTEEN

Paul had just been to his therapist; the man was generous, occasionally seeing him for free. Ralph had seen him once when he'd dropped his friend off after a five-mile drive and had walked around while waiting for his fifty minutes to finish, strolling past and appreciating the large detached houses in the Victorian estate.

He'd waited in the car for a while, seeing his friend come out and then, briefly, the psychiatrist, a thin man with cropped ginger hair and looking nothing like a stereotype of any analyst anywhere, giving his client a quick wave before closing the door. There had been an almost twenty-year gap since Paul had seen his previous one. His friend had been quiet and tense-looking on the way back and had gone into his flat without a word.

This time, Ralph sat outside the house and thought about what he knew of Paul's condition. He was aware that one of the characteristics of it was that for a long while he couldn't rid himself of an ever-present, analytic detachment that would occasionally destroy his facility to do or feel anything without intellectualising it, 'knowing' it. He couldn't yawn without seeing himself yawning, couldn't speak without hearing himself speaking, and aware that he was aware; a kind of infinite regress of observations.

During the rare moments he discussed such things with Ralph he became almost excited in analysing, even diagnosing himself; it was virtually an internal client-patient relationship.

He would then, as was his wont, comment on something that was utterly irrelevant to what he'd just said, such as asking his friend whether he realised that on a very rigid surface, glass and steel balls bounce higher than rubber ones, or that the Norwegian government had a policy of buying a thousand copies of every Norwegian book and distributing them to the country's libraries.

Ralph would sometimes think of that part of him, the child, baby maybe, as being locked into an alien world by the blocking off of early trauma. Paul had once, and only the once, referred to this, though not revealing what it had been. Ralph guessed that he knew what it was, but the intellectual recognition, undoubtedly helped by the sessions with his analyst, was too painful to be translated into an emotional realisation.

Something had happened to him very early, and part of him had slipped into unreality. Again, the single telling; quickly, almost breathlessly as if he had felt obliged to tell his friend but that if he spoke quickly enough it wouldn't be understood; but it didn't matter, he'd told him.

It seemed that it was a kind of ultimate defence mechanism that had lasted most of his life; was, perhaps, always there. Ralph considered whether the arbitrary thinking, the tangents, irrelevances were, maybe, attempts to stop him feeling its bleak, depressing presence. He also wondered what his first image of the world would have been; his mother as a smiling, loving Madonna or a thing, an inimical object, or had his trauma come later?

Perhaps future pain, virtually any pain, would be magnified and remind the child in him, the child that he was often locked into, of that previous pain. It would be unconscious, perhaps it took him over. Any unfriendly situation or experience would be perceived as hostile and the unreality would cement itself. But the pain of his unreal, acted existence could and probably had now become almost as great as the seminal experience he had pushed away. But Ralph was guessing. He didn't know.

The front door opened and Paul came out of the house and along the garden path hurriedly. He got into the car, where he was talkative, obviously stimulated by his session with the analyst.

'He's a cool bloke. The room's green. Have I told you that? It's the most psychologically restful colour, and he's got water colours on the walls, really peaceful-looking ones. He's got a sepia photo, though, from a mag he was sent by his old college at Cambridge. There are hundreds of male students in boaters outside the college and dozens more looking out of windows and sitting on balconies and above them is an effigy of a woman hanging by her neck from a rope stretched across two buildings. It's dated 1893.

'It's a protest, apparently, against the all-girls Girton College who wanted to be part of the university so they could award degrees. Some are holding a large banner which says 'Get you to Girton, Beatrice, this is no place for your maids.' It's a line from 'As You Like It,' I think, where Beatrice was told she would go to hell and replied that they would tell her to leave and to go to heaven. They've substituted the college name for heaven.'

'What's so special about it?'

'It has a kind of sepia horror, the effigy, hanging there.' He looked at Ralph. 'I wonder why he put it there?'

Then, speaking so quickly he could barely be understood, said, 'He said I was too frightened to leave the womb, and too frightened to stay in it. I was trapped.'

Ralph didn't bother to ask him to repeat it, knowing he wouldn't.

Speaking a little slower so that his listener could catch most of it, he said, 'It reminded him' - Ralph assumed he meant his analyst - 'of an early patient who, recently, had suddenly told him that he was being born and then seemed to try to burrow his way into the couch, to get inside of it, and then screaming for half a minute before he sat, trembling, for the next half an hour. It was horrible, he said.'

'I bet it was.'

Ralph briefly speculated on whether his therapist was hinting that Paul's problems, also, had been forged at his birth.

His friend then moved the window down and put his head out of the car, looking up.

'That could be dangerous.'

'They're the good bits, aren't they,' he said, putting his head back inside. 'You know, the odd castellation on top of a Victorian house, a pediment above Edwardian keystones or the set-back top of a Thirties block. It's almost spiritual: I just saw the sun hitting a chimney cowl then, and I love it on soft bricks. When I went for that job interview - '

'You didn't tell me.'

'I didn't get it anyway, and it was a bit far. I was on the train and this Thirties estate went up-hill away from the track and it was... another world, a past world. I had tears in my eyes. D'you know, according to research, by every measure of educational and professional attainment, manual-working white men are the worst performing group, and that may get worse as the gap between them and the middle class widens.'

'Don't like 'perform,' they're not stage acts, but you've said nothing new.'

'I heard the CEO of a large company on the radio this morning saying that he deeply regretted the pain suffered by investors who've seen shares in the business virtually halve during an *annus horribilis* for his blue chip company which resulted in it being the FTSE 100's worst performer. He forgot to mention that their latest job cuts meant it's got rid of nine thousand staff in nine years.'

'Tell me something that surprises me.'

'Was thinking that with the rise of unqualified celebs and Reality 'stars' - what a devalued word that is - power seems to have moved from a military-industrial complex to a media-entertainment one.'

'Are we supposed to celebrate the semi-literate? What's supposed to surprise me then, you thinking it or the statement itself?'

'That woman, Cluck something, the one at the party meeting. She'd probably say something like I've just said.'

'What do you think of her? You rarely mention the opposite sex.'

'You'll be saying 'the fair sex' next. Don't let a feminist hear you say either.'

'When you think about it, feminism is almost the perfect political issue. It gives the opportunity for vociferous identity politics and volcanic levels of moral certainty.'

'And fourth-form tribalism. D *you* think she's attractive then?'
'Of course.'

'What about the French lady you mentioned?'
'What about her?'

'Well, it's a side you don't share and I wondered if you were gonna, you know, have a relationship with Cluck thingy.'

'Her name's Cluckrose. The answer's 'perhaps.' That okay?'
'Just asking.'

'Perhaps you should get a girlfriend, Paul.'

'You sound like my dad used to. But we wouldn't be so, you know, we couldn't see each other so much.'

'Perhaps not.'

'What d'you think was the most telling thing, the most insightful bit of grand theory Marx said?'

'I'll precis it: Our reality, consciousness, identity, our political, cultural and economic systems are determined by the ways in which we technologically transmute the physical world.'

'Psychology wouldn't be happy with that.'

'Ask your therapy man what he thinks.'

'He'd probably say that Marx was neurotic maybe, but not really disturbed by anything traumatic from his past, not really having to come to terms with any ontological lesions festering since infancy.'

'He doesn't say that of you though, does he.'

'No.'

'You say I don't speak of women, but neither do you talk of what you feel, really.'

'Because I don't always know, but it does come out sometimes.'

'Rarely.'

Paul shrugged

'Any time Paul, any time.'

'I know.'

They were silent for a time then Paul said, 'When I mentioned Mister Myers - '

'Myers?'

'Gordon, therapist.'

'You haven't used his name before.'

'When he told me of the man he thought was going back to his birth, he said he'd been surprised that it had only taken a few years of treatment for him to do so. Usually, he said, it could take a lifetime, or never. He reckoned the man would, the next day, carry on as before, having little or no emotional recollection of the incident.'

'Should he tell you things about his other patients?'

'Think its okay, we've become kinda friends, I suppose.'

'Isn't that unprofessional?'

'Yes, he does remind himself of that occasionally. When I first met him he suggested I view him as an atheistic, confessional priest guided by a code of confidentiality.'

'What else did he say?'

'That it would take a long while; *I* have to do the work. There are no magic wands.'

He looked out the side window for a while.

'He said that his patient had jogged a memory from his training when he'd visited a psychiatric ward at a hospital in Essex. He'd seen a man writhing on his bed, and the doctor he was shadowing - he was walking with him - referred to the two nurses following them, saying 'Noticed the tits on the tall one, Gordon?' He looked only at the patient repeatedly putting his pillow over his face then turning over and placing his face in the pillow till they left the ward.

'He'd had only a second's eye contact, but knew the man would have given almost anything to have cried, to release it all; fear, pain, terror, but knew he wouldn't, couldn't; this only happened in movies. He would need an intellectual recognition initially, then years to become emotionally aware. I don't know why the image of him looking back and the way his mentor talked about the nurse's tits stayed with me.'

'I suppose you could argue that doctors wish to be considered as scientists, who deal with inanimate objects and neurons and such, and thus wish to treat the subjects of their research, humans, also as objects, therefore the man's pain wasn't affecting him. But, to an extent, doctors have to see patients like that. What do they say? If you want to treat a disease become a doctor, if you want to care for a patient, be a nurse.'

'You're clever.'

'Why?'

'All that and driving at the same time.'

'I can chew gum and walk simultaneously, too. It's just that you've never really wanted to drive.'

'Tried once, kept confusing the clutch with the accelerator.'

'I know.'

'He said I wasn't psychologically born yet.'

'Slow it down.'

'At breakfast this morning, I was looking at my piece of toast, close up; there was a low light coming through the French window and the butter was like tiny, glistening hills.'

'Your little images again. For a while you're lost in them aren't you.'

"Nascent schizophrenia,' Gordon says.'

''Gordon' now, is it?'

'When I was coming to you this morning there was a bag of rubbish in a passageway and on the pavement a sofa with clothes dumped on it. I saw a road sweeper walking by, told him about it and he held his phone up and took a picture of it. Thought he might be entering it for the Turner Prize. I wonder why rubbish bothers me so much?'

'Dunno, perhaps it's rule-breaking in general that annoys you, maybe it symbolises somebody getting away with something and you never could as a child.'

'You sound like Myers.'

'Is he helping you?'

'D'you mean, is he understanding me?'

'Yes.'

'You mean, to understand empathetically?'

'If you like.'

'The argument against 'becoming the other' - and you should know it - is similar to the situation of the anthropologist who, not being content to remain 'outside' of a tribe he's studying, turns native, thus moving from being a non-participating observer to a non-observing participant. Myers has been in therapy himself, mainly to learn to separate his own feelings and attitudes from clients so as not to project them.'

'Not always successfully, I assume.'

'Why d'you say that?' Paul asked, raising his voice.

'Just that it doesn't seem possible that anyone could do that all of the time.'

'It sounds as if you're trying to erode my confidence in him.'

'Not at all. You know that.'

'Who have I got other than *him*, Ralph?'

He had turned almost fiercely to his driver.

'Well... you've got me. I don't understand.'

'I'm getting out here. It's not far now, anyway. Can you stop? I'll see you.'

Ralph stopped the car, his friend quickly leaving it and walking quickly away down a side street.

As he drove on, Ralph tried to remember the last time his mate had acted like this. He couldn't recall quite how it had manifested itself or the cause, but it was quite a few years ago. He would see him in a day or so. He would appear calmer and probably wouldn't refer to it again.

Two days afterwards, Ralph was shopping in a local supermarket, watching objects of necessity or mild avarice being plucked off shelves and wondering if it was possible that others disliked the activity as much as himself, when he noticed Claire Cluckrose behind him at the checkout.

Dropping bags back into her trolley she looked a little grim, the first time he'd seen her look uncomfortable with anything. He moved away slightly from the till so that when she went through she nudged into his trolley.

'Oh, it's you.' She didn't look surprised.

'Let's get out first. After you.'

They went to the exit then out to the car park.

'Do you come here often?'

'Is that a chat-up line?'

'No.'

'As little as I can. I buy a lot so I don't have to.'

'Me too. I guess this is the local store for both of us. Do you have to get back right away?'

'Why?'

'Well, just behind my car over there in the corner there's a road with a little café.'

'Why is it men are always asking me to go to cafes with them?'

Again, for a nanosecond, a bump of jealousy.

He put his bags in his car and helped with hers at her nearby vehicle. They walked to the cafe and sat down.

'I should think,' she said, 'that walk took about two minutes and we didn't say a thing.' She grinned at him.

He laughed as easily as the walk had been. He felt relaxed. She wore a beret, tailored jacket, tight skirt, and, unusually, a dark lipstick.

'Let's talk about, I dunno, literature? Movies? I bet you loved Brief Encounter.'

'Of course I did; that surprisingly real script.'

'The hubby was a convenient stereotype though, wasn't he? And with that beret you could have been sitting at a table in the station café.'

She smiled as if he had satisfactorily confirmed the success of her style.

'I just caught an ad for 'Hamlet' with a black actor playing the lead role.' He felt a little like Paul using his tangents. 'I think it's called inclusivity retro-fixing; if Libs don't like a particular fact; that there were, say, no ethnics in the court of Mary Queen of Scots, then when portraying it on film or stage, they'll put some in.'

'Rewriting history'

'And virtue-signalling. A white actor's not allowed to play Othello, and can you imagine twenty white extras playing Negro slaves in eighteenth century Georgia? What the liberal enlightened would say of course is that you shouldn't look at skin colour, but at the actor; it's their performance that counts.'

'Are you testing me? Are you going to say something like, 'So why bother fitting prosthetics to actors to help them look like the characters they're playing, or for them to bother to put on, or lose the pounds, or to have hair dyed or removed or wear wigs et cetera?"

'Exactly. I was testing you. I'll be honest. I thought you were kind of too good to be true politically, but - '

'If something seems too good to be true it probably is.'

'But you're also smart enough to see the convoluted, contradictory mess liberalism is.'

'You have to be smart to see that?'

'Seems so.'

'You and Wilde have something in common then.'

'Oscar?'

'No. Doesn't matter. I'm interested in what is, and the current movement does tend to make what is, isn't, and what isn't, is. I, too, dislike the monoculture of PC.'

'How's charity? Does it really begin at home?'

'It does in mine.'

'Are you going to say that you have another presentation to do and you're leaving me in a minute?'

'Not quite yet, and it's the same one. It's for tomorrow and it'll be finished tonight.'

He asked her what her charity did.

'We kind of service other charities. We could be working in Africa soon, but mostly operate in the Middle East. The Americans are quite strong there.'

'Of course. They're clever; they have teachers pushing American-English in nearly every country in the world.'

'The US is a relatively young nation.'

'Infantile. it's a naive, boiled ice cream, soda-sipping, bubble gum-children populated country, an insular place that probably still thinks Europe - if they know where it is - consists entirely of warring feudal states.'

'Doesn't it? Perhaps you could argue that the 'pioneering' spirit, the gun-owning 'this is mah land' ideology is immature also.'

'Loved the Texas accent, then.'

'Going to imagine me as a cowgirl?'

'And what of the American Dream fallacy?' 'Well, maybe I won't achieve it, but my children will,' says the blue-collar worker. It's this and more that makes the American populace, thirty million of whom don't have health cover, the perfect demography to be fed the 'Hate Commies' routine. Let's give it up for Capitalism, eh? Yeahhhh!'

He looked at her unrevealing expression for a moment. 'I had a quick impulse to hug you and call you 'comrade' then.'

'You may call me 'comrade.'

'We've sat here and ordered nothing yet.'

'I suppose we both forgot, but no matter, my nutrients for the next month are in the boot and I shall now return and finish my work.'

Noticing his frown, she said, 'You may walk with me to my vehicle if you wish.'

He did. This time the silence wasn't so easy, he didn't want her to leave, wanted her just to keep here with him; stay with him, wherever it was.

'I'll ring you,' he said, having virtually to shout as she started her car and gave him an almost imperceptible nod.

It was eight o'clock, the spring dividing line between evening and night; the former a darkened stage set with lights faintly appearing and then suddenly bright against the blackness. As he drove home he wondered how Paul was, he hadn't as yet contacted him.

CHAPTER EIGHTEEN

Jordan was driving to the house where he was to hold a surgery; being neither a doctor nor nurse practitioner he thought it an inappropriate term He hadn't held one yet and wasn't sure what to expect and wondered whether people would be complaining about things he could do nothing about, such as why the local football team didn't put more money into buying decent players and why they should contribute to the cost of the Duchess of Sussex's wardrobe.

He'd been told by the constituency chairman he should do it, followed soon afterwards by Archer telling him it was about time he did one and not to be fooled into thinking they were about personal politics where constituents, if you give them help when they ask for it, become your supporters and vote accordingly.

'Some voters make the rounds of lots of politicians, trying to play one off against the other. Even if you do help 'em there's no certainty they'll vote for you at the next election. They're a mixed blessin', mate. They do have their publicity value, and it's important that voters in the area feel they're getting some attention from you, otherwise they might decide to transfer their votes to a politician who demonstrates greater concern for the area.

'Really, these surgeries are part of the strategy of maximizing a reputation in the local community rather than a means of getting the support of specific individuals. You won't like 'em.'

It was a neat, bay-windowed Thirties house not far from his first canvassing. He was shown to the office by an elderly woman who told him that she lived there and had let this room to the party for years. He thanked her and sat behind a shiny mahogany desk with a bunch of plastic flowers at the side and some A4 sheets and a purple fountain pen in the centre. There was also a carafe of water and some glasses. The room itself was in rather austere beige. Two chairs were facing the desk. He wasn't sure how many people would he attending and could see no names written down.

The first, coming dead on time, was a man who thought the cliche of 'You wait for an hour then three come at once,' was, according to his recent bus stop experiences, actually true.

'Most clichés are born of truth.'

'Well, I want you to do something about this one.'

'I can make an official complaint to TFL I suppose, but they can't control the traffic. I can't see what can be done, really.'

The man wouldn't accept this, but stayed a while longer listing other wrongs: the state of the trees in his local park, the off-license at the bottom of his road rarely being open, the hut someone had put in their front garden to house motor bikes...

Jordan switched off for a short while, wondering when the man would get to the moral wrongness of the currently inclement weather. When he left, he reiterated his main complaint with a reminder to his listener not to forget to do something about it.

The second visitor was a miserable-looking woman in her thirties who seemed to have a justifiable grievance about a magistrate recently letting her husband off with merely a warning as to his future conduct after he had hit her for not complying with his wishes, though she didn't state what they were. Jordan told her that he couldn't interfere with judicial processes, much as he'd like to in her case but, of course, if it did happen again then she must immediately inform the police.

It was obvious to him that her 'victim' existence had been going on for some time, though he wasn't sure if he was being fair to her situation by thinking that she probably perversely enjoyed her role. She then morosely told him about her relatives always taking 'his' side, the cost of clothes and food, the dustmen always leaving bits of rubbish on dustbin day, then left, possibly, he thought, to find someone else to moan to.

The lady of the house then came in to say she'd received a call from someone who was supposed to come but couldn't, and should she show the next person in. He was thrown for a second when Ms Cluckrose entered looking businesslike in a dark-grey jacket with power-padded shoulders and rather long, tight skirt. Her niece was with her, still wearing the period clothes he'd last seen her in. They sat.

'Hello, both of you.'

The girl half hid herself behind her aunt.

'She's rather sweet.'

'Sometimes. Before we came here she was trying some cheese samples we'd been given in Waitrose and she gave me a couple. 'This one's hot,' I said. 'Who?' she asked, looking around her. She thought I meant a man.'

The girl smiled and gave him a subtle wink.

'How old is she?'

'Nearly ten. And would you refer to a boy as 'sweet?' The spectrum of gender is based, like many things, on stereotypes. If a man was to say he 'feels like a woman,' does it mean that he is soft, nurturing, kind, understanding and empathetic? That he's not aggressive, strong, forceful, stoic and brave?'

'Er... perhaps she's cisgender, eh? Whatever that is. Creepy word. What's wrong with being born a woman, or man, and thinking you *are* one?'

'The other day she told me that the world is an island floating in the ocean of the universe.'

'Poetic.'

'She also said that she didn't matter. I told her that she mattered to other people, but she said that that didn't matter because they didn't matter. I was tempted to ask her why she didn't commit suicide then, but she would, of course, have told me that there was no point, because it didn't matter.'

'Pretty young to be a nihilist.'

'You haven't asked me why I'm here.'

'To see me?'

'No, the MP for Wansford East.'

'Pity.'

'There's a Thirties cinema in the High Street, you just may have noticed it, that's in danger of being pulled down.'

'Art Deco fan?'

'That's not the point; it hasn't been a cinema for some time.'

'Bingo hall?'

'At one time, but there's various things going on in there: keep-fit classes, the occasional concert et cetera, it's a community gathering place.'

'Glad you didn't say, 'hub.''

'You're probably not interested, but I want you to do something about it before developers hurl their wrecking ball greed at it.'

'Such as?'

'Make it public, go to the Recorder, I assume you do read the local rag, make it known that you're against its erasing. Incidentally, the A&E seems to have been saved.'

'Good. I didn't know. You did well. I'll contact the paper and tell them I'm behind any protest against destroying the picture house.'

'That's the main reason I came, but I was actually wondering just how political you'd be in the process of helping someone in your constituency whatever their political views. Whether you'd favour those who share yours and not really trying for those who don't.'

'How would I really know other than them wearing a blue tie with an 'I love our Leader' tie-pin or, conversely, holding a board with 'All property is theft' on it and thumping it down on my desk?'

'I think you can pick up on people's politics pretty quickly, there are clues in conversation, attitudes, sometimes dress, really.'

'You mean if they have The Sun stuck in the back pocket of cement-spattered jeans and they're standing in a pub flexing their calves at the counter and ordering a pint of lager?'

'What of Essex Man who put Thatcher in?'

'The manual class who voted Tory in their self-interest and not with their usual deferential vote. I think the name mostly referred to City traders with working class roots.'

'Whatever.'

'Shouldn't she be at school?'

'Yes, but I thought it would further her political education by coming here.'

'I'm flattered.'

'Don't be.'

'I don't think I know enough about the details of government to - '

'Governments: the exploitation of power for improper ends.'

'Going to tell her that?'

'Probably. Also, that elections are just polarising sideshows that inspire ignorantly sentimentalised displays of passion.'

'Will she understand that?'

'Eventually. I'll simplify it for her. Anyway, how's Parliament?'

'Haven't had time to do much yet.'

'But you'll soon be rationalising the obscene into the palatable?'

'How come someone who is so... cynical can be so - '

'Attractive?'

'Ego as well, but justified. Although I think I was going to say 'beautiful.''

'You think? However, I have things to do, or rather we have. Eh, Izzy?'

'Yes, but whatever we do we must do them to the best of our ability,' the girl said before turning her head away shyly.

'Indeed.'

Her aunt stood up, beckoned to the girl and went towards the door.

Jordan, standing, asked her if she would like to do something with him one evening.

'We'll see, and don't forget the reason I came, will you.'

'Bye, bye, Mister Politician,' said Isobel, giving him a quick wave before following her aunt out of the room.

Before he could think about the last few minutes, there was a knock on the door and before he could say enter, a young wraith-like woman with slightly exophthalmic grey-green eyes which, despite their intensity managed at the same time to look surprised, came into the room. Her cheekbones were prominent in a pale, pinched face, the skin having a slight sheen as if perspiring.

'I could come after all. I want you to do something about - '

'Could you sit down first?

She did so and continued. 'I've been sexually harassed.'

'Where?'

'At work; my line manager. He just leered over me when the others had gone, he's been doing it for a while, I've told no one because people like him'

'What did he say to you?'

A Pause. 'Nothing, really.'

'Shouldn't you be telling this to someone senior to him?'

'Well, you are. You're an MP.'

'Have you not reported this at all?'

'No.'

'I suggest you do. I sympathise with you but this really isn't my territory. If you don't want to tell anyone at work then I guess you should see the police, I really don't know. Are you sure it's not just some clumsy, laddish thing from a man who, maybe, is pretty shy of women, perhaps scared. I'm no psychologist and I'm not making excuses for him, but I think you should, as said, go to someone senior in your firm. I'm sorry if you're upset, but it isn't my area of assistance, really.'

'You're our representative; you're supposed to help us.'

'Quite, but not in situations like this.'

He stood, his hand out, helping her rise from the chair before turning it into a handshake.

'All the best, Miss.'

'Thanks a lot, Mister Wilde.' She didn't bother to close the door after her.

'And that's why they say you should learn to ignore surgeries,' he said aloud.

He felt sorry for her, even if the claim had no real foundation, but others could deal with it. He was sure also that the last four adults he'd spoken to wouldn't, if he ever did stand for re-election in the future, vote for him. Perhaps Isobel would.

The next constituents to sit facing him were two women; one moaning about the East Europeans living in her road, the other telling of her misery caused by the flickering streetlight outside her bedroom window. Not only could he understand why he'd never been interested in being a councilor; but also the need to create believable reasons not to attend these things.

He could hear a radio nearby, maybe the house owner had turned it on, but he'd finished now, anyway. He thought he heard, 'About seventy years ago it was for men and women, both genders played darts.'

The voice should have said 'sexes,' of course. It seemed, he thought, that such was the increasing liberal distortion of language that words were gradually losing their meaning. Perhaps, in the future, if the equation 'two plus two equals four' caused offence because 'four' had come to be regarded as somehow offensive, then 'five' or perhaps 'three' would be seen as more acceptable.

The business he was in, however, wasn't to listen to neurotic people and their probably unsolvable difficulties but to immerse himself in his job, in institutional politics, and to use its mores, norms, behind-the-scenes unofficial negotiations, the deals - Archer's 'skulduggery' seemed to be a word that suited the venerability of his workplace - in the life of formal politics. But it seemed also, increasingly, about Claire Cluckrose and the desire to, maybe, somehow... humanise her, tame her perhaps. Maybe they weren't the right words, but they would do for now.

On the Tube shortly afterwards on his way to an informal party debate, he tried not to listen to the mundanities surrounding him like moles pushing up out of the ground: the wastefulness of someone's 'Well, I mean, you know, I mean, you know... ' and the poly decibels of an annoyed Eastern European telling their listener that they were on a train. Surely that should be a recorded message sent by a touch on a screen?

The political discussion was on the increasing number of violent crimes in the city. He was aware that the matter was becoming overtly political and that unless something was done, or rather seen to be done, votes would be lost. It was taking place in one of the smaller rooms with mostly long-serving members and a few newer ones.

It began with some rather pompous tub-thumping.

'The very safety of our citizens, particularly our younger ones, are at stake.' and from another, 'This is not Chicago, this is the great city of London. The forces of law must deal with this, and we must help them.'

It was the way they said it. Some people, Jordan thought, could strut sitting down.

After a discussion on whether increased funds should be made available to the Met and where they should come from, he stood slightly away from the disproportionately small table to gain attention and spoke, wondering briefly if he was allowing his dislike of neo-liberalism to outweigh party loyalty.

'At the risk of arousing anyone's ire, an important moment in the increase of London's recorded crime rate was a recent Home Secretary, running scared of what has become almost a normative orthodoxy of cries of 'racism,' and instructing the police to call a halt to stop and search because it was biased against black youths.'

He looked around him quickly.

'I met a young policeman recently who, when I mentioned the supposed bias, told me that it *was* mostly young blacks who carry knives. If that is the case, and I have no reason to doubt it, it should, as pointed out by the Met's Chief Commissioner at the time, be continued as a deterrent. His advice seems to have been ignored.'

There were a few audible murmurs from the other end of the table, someone saying 'This is a rather dodgy area here, we have to be careful.'

'But that's just part of it; got to look at the root causes and all that,' said someone opposite him.

'That's pretty easy,' said a man sitting next to the previous speaker. 'Most of 'em are from poor backgrounds and many live in soulless, alienating tower blocks.'

'Oh, it's the architecture's fault is it?' asked a previous speaker.

'Our designed environment does have an influence and it's a large one. What did Churchill say? 'We shape our environment, it then shapes us.' If people at the bottom of the economic index have a rather negative culture, their children are left with an urge to belong and to find a status. They can get plenty of that in gangs, with their apparently obligatory duty to carry some sort of weapon. it's all there.'

'And there's the drug-carrying of course,' someone else said.

'You're breaking my heart,' groaned an elderly man Jordan had occasionally seen around the place. 'Tears for the innocent under-privileged, it's never their fault. You'll be switching to the Opposition next.'

'We can be caring too,' Jordan said, reiterating an oft-repeated line, 'the Left doesn't have a monopoly on it.'

The man looked across at him, frowning. 'Didn't you make some sort of speech recently defending the digital companies?'

'Not really defending them, but the whole thing about data leakage et cetera could, I think, be dealt with reciprocally, it doesn't have to be heavy-handed. As somebody said, if you're not paying for the product, you *are* the product. Scraping people's personal data and using it to sell things isn't a sinister bug: it's surely the declared business model of almost the entire internet. I think the question really is, do we want free stuff or do we want control over our own data? Don't think you can't have it both ways. I think people have made the choice, anyway.'

But he felt neither caring nor really interested in either of the subjects discussed. He realised that he'd purposely criticised a once leading minister and had, perhaps, taken a bit of a gamble but, unless it suited him otherwise, he was determined not to be seen as a 'yes' man or as another new, bright-eyed, naïve MP.

He wanted to be noticed, and it seemed he had He wasn't sure where this would get him, if anywhere, but, if he could help it, he wouldn't be a consistently willing recipient of taken-for-granted, entrenched party lines.

CHAPTER NINETEEN

He wasn't sure why he went to the police station except that, thinking of the sheet of paper he'd given to the man who'd come down to the basement and who he'd shown the toilets to, he'd felt a growing apprehension. What if it was some kind of secret material and the man gave it to an intelligence agency or something - they must have them here, they did back in Poland - and told them where he'd got it? Of course, he could say that he had merely mentioned to the man that he'd found some sheets of paper that looked interesting and, after he'd looked at it, had asked if there were any more he could give him and then had virtually run out of the building. It was more or less true.

If he was asked why he'd shown the stuff to this particular person he would say, truthfully, that the other workers on the site wouldn't have understood why he thought it was interesting, their English wasn't as good as his. He'd just wanted someone to show them to, really.

The constable at the reception desk could speak six words of Polish, which he laughingly shared with the caller who, after explaining why he was there, sensed that he should really be talking to someone a little higher up. The officer confirmed the thought by telling him to wait while he got somebody to attend to him. He used his phone.

After a few silent minutes a man of a higher rank came to the desk and asked how he could help. The caller explained again his reason for being there.

'Well, Mister Cuch - have I pronounced that correctly?'

'No, but it doesn't matter.'

'Would you mind sitting in our waiting room while I find someone who can deal with this more comprehensively than I can? Would you like tea? Coffee?'

I do not want to be here long, I have work to do.'

'Sure, of course,' said the sergeant as he guided Cuch through swing doors into a short corridor then to the corner of a canteen where he brought the latter refreshment and sat down next to him, saying nothing. The constable at the desk soon came in and whispered in the sergeant's ear who then stood and, telling the builder to drink up, told him he'd take him upstairs to see his chief.

At the top of the building, Cuch was escorted into an office, asked to be seated by the clean-shaven man behind a desk introducing himself as Chief Superintendent Adams and asked how long ago he had given away the paper he'd told the sergeant about.

'About three weeks. Month.'

'You haven't seen the man since?'

'No. I think he was with some others, they wanted to support us; we were striking.'

'What for?'

'Better wages, we were being ripped off, *Cyganic*. We still are.'

'What others?'

'I don't know, there were two or three people with him.'

'Would your workmates know?'

'Should not think so.'

'Are the workers still there? The same ones?'

'Most of them.'

'He was asked to confirm the address of the building and also his own.

'Would you go through what you told he officer at the desk again, as thoroughly as you can, please.'

'‘Go through'?'

'Repeat.'

'There were sheets of paper, all yellow with some sort of writing or marks and things on, but the one at the top was for someone called D and there was a date on it, but I don't remember.' He paused. 'Maybe I shouldn't be here, maybe it's not important, it means nothing, I just thinking. '

'Continue, Mister Cuch.'

'It said something like, 'You know what to do, don't send this again.' It said that the person it was written to was supposed to tell the Government that the Russian Government had evidence of - I remember words - 'covert western infiltration into general armaments programme,' It said, 'to help ensure increase in armed preparedness."

The speaker stopped, looking rather pleased with himself.

'You did well, that was a mouthful. And there was no more that you could understand?'

'No.'

'See who it was from?'

'Just numbers and some letters at the bottom.'

'Which you don't remember.'

'Sorry.'

'It's alright. You've done well.'

Cuch put a hand inside his jacket and handed a few A4 sheets to his questioner.

'These are the bits you mentioned, yes?' The officer briefly looked through them. 'Afraid I don't understand them either. You have nothing else?'

'No. I can explain a bit what the man looked like, but no more.'

He did, giving a scanty picture of height and hair colour.

The Chief Superintendent stood.

'Well, Mister Cuch, thanks for bringing these and explaining why you came here. It could well be nothing of course; we will have to find out. If you can think of anything else to tell us, ring here or come in again. It will be appreciated. Meanwhile,' he rose from the desk, 'don't go far away.' He raised his voice. 'Sergeant, would you take Mister Cuch's details before he leaves.' He smiled his visitor out of the room.

On his way back to the site, Albin Cuch felt relieved that he'd gone where he had, though knowing he hadn't done anything really wrong, anyway, in not telling the authorities - *wtadze* - before he had done. In fact, it could be that nobody had done anything wrong. But he had done what he thought he should do. He could now forget it.

Ralph was in lecturing mode again, but this time was in a classroom and doing just that.

'It's a cultural norm for the middle classes that their children go to university; for the working class it's to learn a trade.'

He checked himself, aware of the projection of his own experience. Perhaps fathers didn't tell their offspring they should become artisans these days, but nevertheless the richer parents still had a different code and talked in abstractions, of ideas more then their manual-working counterparts who tended to speak in concrete terms and spoke in a more vernacular manner rather than, when appropriate, such as in education, in a more public, formal way.

All these things, this informal learning, along with the limiting experience of peers led the children of manual workers to become... manual workers. Formal education was, in effect, a system for the middle classes to reproduce themselves.

He cut short his near-proselytizing, beckoned a student to sit with him at his desk while he told him why he'd given his essay a low mark and how to improve it - he would re-mark it if he gave him the rewrite in next morning's seminar - and then met Paul in a café in the local High Street.

'What have you been teaching 'em today in your failed attempt to be objective?' his friend asked.

'Social inequality.'

'And it'll always be thus. Three people walking along chatting; two have dark eyes, the other blue. Guess who's gonna be deviant, unequal? And what if two of 'em are richer than the other or one's wearing a brown suit, the other's navy blue?'

'Of course, the concept depends on what the reference point is.'

'Like the old Tories 'You've never had it so good' stuff. They make the past the salient frame of reference.'

'And just like any view or fact opposing their policies, they mock the integrity of its source.'

'The media do that for them.'

'They also cement the idea of personality, not policy. Arguably it hasn't always been like it.'

'If you're gonna mention Attlee, who looked like a Chinese mandarin, and his reformist government of the Fifties, don't forget he was a Major and the populace was used to a militaristic ethos and being told what to do. They were, except for the BMA, glad of his voice.'

'And he had to bribe the docs to come in on the National Health Service.'

'Seen your woman lately? Or, rather, you wish she was.'

'Yes.'

'You didn't say.'

'Didn't see you. Why? Feeling a little jealous? Sorry, I shouldn't have said that, it was childish.'

"Childlike,' only children can be childish, and jealousy is a bourgeois, patriarchal concept, and in a new world there will be no jealousy, there'll be no need for it. Remember, Marx's communist utopia was set in a land of plenty, not in a grim paucity. All would be adequately - '

'Each according to his need.'

'Sure, but who or what created the needs, or are they really intense wants? Does she think a lot of you?'

'Shouldn't think so.'

'You'd like her to, though'

''Course.'

'Women, eh? Can't live with 'em, can't live... with 'em. Mister Myers, he's a Freudian, but admits there are other things than sex.'

'Really.'

'He was wondering whether he was, as a patient recently suggested, playing god. And he said, 'In the arbitrary mess of the human situation who am *I* to meddle in the compromise between an encultured self and an instinctual one in the egoistic battle between superego and id?'

'He might say that, but of course he does. You've got quite a memory, Paul, but you're also intellectualizing like mad. I'm sorry, but what of feelings? You can't run away forever from them, from you. Okay, you know this and it's really the province of Myers and yourself, but... '

'I don't see me in terms of the adult world. I'm not *real* for fuck sake.'

Ralph hesitated. 'Is this the real self or a fake one who's saying that? Who have I been talking to all these years, a fake person?'

'Oh, that's so neat and tidy. Who writes your scripts Ralph? My parents weren't real to me, therefore there was no relationship and no *me*. As a child I wanted recognition from them, It seemed I wanted it as a baby. Can you understand that? I blotted that out. I'm more aware of these things now because I've been told them. I don't know why I'm telling you.'

'D'you feel validated.'

'I had a secret intellect; it was hidden because I wasn't recognised. I invented a sort of secret, intellectual god, a super-being who knew *everything* and could judge my intelligence; be the only true judge of all intellect.'

'Human recognition would be no use then, only *He* would recognise you. Your creation comforted you, didn't it; perhaps still does. What d'you think his judgement would be?'

'According to an aunt, a hospital doctor said to my parents that when he saw me as a baby he said, 'Good god, mother, look how bright that child's eyes are.'

He paused for a while. They were the only customers. Ralph could hear the gurgling explosions of a Gaggia machine at the end of the counter.

He continued. 'I feel so alone with my intellect.' He looked quickly at Ralph. 'Well, I did till I met you; and Edward a bit now, I suppose. I like it when you, or anybody really, knows more than me about anything, I don't feel quite so on my own then. The feeling doesn't last long. I would love to be unlearned, knowing little.'

"Where ignorance is bliss 'tis folly to be wise?' Can you love anyone?'

'You sound just like Myers, he's always grinding away at that.'

'Is that a bad thing?'

'I realise that I can't really love anyone, only fall in love with love; I make them into a fantasy I suppose. When I had a girlfriend - '

'Aileen?'

'I forgot you knew about her. I panicked if she didn't look right.'

'Right?

'Yes, if she didn't have make-up on - '

'And didn't look like a film star, a fantasy maybe?'

'She wasn't... solid.'

'You mean you're not.'

'I know.'

Paul had been looking down at the table, his half-drunk coffee Ignored. He swung his head up and around. 'D'you know; I masturbated when I was ten; it was an escape, I know now.'

'Escape from what?

'And did you know that Cock Lane, near Holborn Viaduct, got its name because it was the only street in medieval times to be licensed for prostitution?'

'And?'

'A cock is a thing, an object that grows out of the body in a place where... it's a symbol, a representation, but it can't represent love. It's lust-making really isn't it. Sometimes I think it's - '

'Disgusting?'

'Suppose so. Only old people are supposed to think that.'

'How do you show love?'

'I don't *know,*' he shouted.'

A girl behind the counter momentarily glanced at him. He looked up at the ceiling then around the room and gazed into his lap. He looked up at his friend.

'I always have an image of myself,' he said quietly. 'I can see myself all of the time, the whole time. My intellect and analytical ability is separate from me.'

'The 'me' that doesn't exist?'

'If we talk about consciousness here it'll be an academic debate.'

'Which you'll escape into. Maybe you use yourself as a case study.'

'Yes. I don't look at people, really, I look at houses. I'm searching for peace I think.'

'A womb?'

''Course.'

'Do you feel that or know it because you've been told that it's so?'

'Both. Progress, eh?'

'Were you bullied at school?'

'You sound like an amateur shrink. Actually, I stopped it at the start. This boy, Tom Brand - great name for a bully - hit me when we were in the cloakroom and I smashed a fist into his face and he looked startled and in pain. I felt horrible that I'd hurt someone, so I went to him and apologised. Then he hit me again, but it didn't matter, I felt sorry for what I'd done and kept saying 'Sorry, sorry,' while he knocked me around the room. The other kids must have thought I was frightened of him and that's why I was saying it.

'Houses are wombs, I suppose, that's why I'm always looking at them, imagining the inside of them, to find one to give me something that's mine, just mine.'

'Something that gives you life.'

He looked briefly around him again.

'I'm not hungry mate, I'm gonna go to where I should have been an hour ago.'

'The Job Centre place.'

He got up quickly. 'See you,' he said, and went.

Ralph sat there feeing that he seemed to spend a lot of time sitting alone after being left in a café somewhere. At least his friend had told him something of his turmoil, it hadn't really happened before. Amateur maybe, but during the last half- hour he seemed to have taken on the role of an ersatz therapist.

Leaving, he walked past a row of small Edwardian villas. There was dark stone-dash and wisteria-hidden windows, and he tried to empathise with his friend gazing at the same homes, and wondering if he would have an urge to knock on a panelled-glass front door to be allowed in out of the sun, and to lie on a chaise longue in restful dark with shelves of quiet volumes full with botany and music, and maybe imagining a dream-like past and seeing a nanny, upright and strict, walking comfortingly past a half-open door.

There would, perhaps, be a maidservant with lemon tea, a conservatory, a young master in a straw boater, rose in hand, part-hidden behind a lone caryatid. Maybe Paul would see a series of waitresses as mothers: the French one at the local patisserie, the Russians in the greasy spoon in Leyton, the Lithuanians at a Soho bar, and with a lazy turn of his head perhaps could almost see them, *Bonjour! Zdravstvuyte! Labas!* gazing down at him, smiling, welcoming...

He was still thinking of Paul as he turned into his street and saw a policeman leaning against one of the brick piers holding his front gate. He was looking casually around him as Ralph approached and halted on the pavement in front of him. The constable turned his head towards a figure in a belted raincoat and trilby hat standing in the porch. The man looked at the homecomer.

'Is this your house, sir?'

'Why? Who are you?'

He briefly held up some sort of badge.

'If you would let me in I'll explain.'

Ralph reluctantly did so.

''D'you know how many words there are for luck? Fate, fortune, chance, kismet, nemesis. That's a lot, which means that it plays a large part in human affairs, Mister Wilde.'

'Destiny.'

'Maybe that'll be the one that fits you. I'm being facetious of course.'

The man who was speaking was sat behind an overlarge desk in, Jordan thought, considering his job, an undersized room. The secretary to the country's Business Secretary rated more than a grey-painted, pseudo-Adam interior with a few sparsely adorned bookshelves and some sheets of written-on paper blue-tacked to a wall. The window, which was Georgian and, Jordan noticed, had a decent view along Whitehall, didn't compensate for a rather austere lack of status.

'I brought you here because a vacancy's come up, that's why I mentioned luck, and my boss, Peter Weynard, Secretary of State for Business, Energy and Individual Strategy, to give him his full title - before that, the Department of Business Innovation and Skills. Anyway, you've been spotted; that is someone pointed you out to him, recommended you, if you like.

'Quite simply, he may want you to work for him. You have a successful business background it seems and he thinks you may be useful. Incidentally, your idea of self-regulation for these digital companies hasn't quite come about has it.'

'Well, the GDPR now requires any company holding data to 'better protect our privacy.' But what's 'better?' Who decides what it is? In essence, it smacks of a kind of self-regulation to me. I don't think that much will change.'

'Maybe. Anyhow, I liked your idea of a 'populism weaponised by digital technology."

'Where did you hear that?'

'Someone told me. He reckons our Leader, and this government, should tweet itself into popular dominance, which seems to be happening with the Grand Old Party in the U.S. However, how d'you feel about working for Weynard?'

'If my business expertise can be of use, sure. I've begun a new career; I wish it to amount to something.'

The bureaucrat looked briefly at his papers before continuing.

'Westminster, with its dark corridors and locked doors, actually and metaphorically, eh? You wish for your corridors to be brighter and the doors unlocked. Perhaps it'll happen. Afraid I'm busy now, though, as you can see. You'll be contacted soon. Cheerio, Mister Wilde.'

Having a more-or-less free day, Jordan walked against the crowd back to the station and caught the Tube to the City and sat in a station café, musing on the idea that what he had just been told could perhaps be the foundation of something worthwhile

Trying not to listen to the City-speak of margins, equities and the esoteric language of profit - he wasn't sure whether it was because it now seemed rather boring to him or whether he was missing his usual full-time involvement in that world - he watched two young waitresses laughing across the room to each other. He gazed up at the sun glowing through the station's roof struts onto the elaborate symmetry of Victorian Roman columns amd then glanced down to the trains and the Lowry-like figures on the nearest platform. One of them was Alfred Clinton.

He looked appreciably older that when Jordan had last seen him about ten years previously, a few months after Jordan had aborted a photography course they were both doing at an institute in Putney - Alfred wanting to do it as a living, Jordan, merely half-interested, as a hobby - though there had been the occasional Christmas cards from the former along with newspaper cuttings and indecipherable comments down the column sides.

As usual he was moving quickly, with long, firm strides as if he was going somewhere specific and had to be there at a certain time to get something done, never just wandering about to look at this, or that. He had, as always, a camera hanging from a strap around his shoulder. His lank hair was even longer than Jordan remembered and he was wearing a tweed jacket which could have been the same one he'd always seemed to wear. Jordan's hand was halfway to the window to knock on it when he realised that, as his old acquaintance was fifty yards away, it would be a pointless way of attempting to attract his attention.

When they'd first met, few of their fellow students seemed to like Alfred. He was outspoken, opinionated and occasionally uninformed, though there was always intellectual credibility. If he disagreed with anyone, as he often did, his response was accompanied by a sneer and, sometimes, a silent snarl. When listening to someone he'd exaggeratedly angle his head and frown as if the speaker was either slurring his speech or was linguistically challenged.

He was pedantic, often dogmatic and possibly the least spendthrift of anyone Jordan had known. In the cinematic haven of the Scala, which offered cakes and coffee in the foyer, he'd bring a thermos flask of tea, and while in the National Theatre cafe he'd order a tea and for the next few hours, holding court to a small batch of friends, would make swift journeys to the counter to have his cup filled with hot water into which he'd drop one of a large supply of tea bags he invariably carried with him.

For a brief period he'd taught English, but couldn't seem to find any work teaching film studies, his main pedagogic passion; he was completing a thesis on Tarkovsky at the time.

In his twenties he'd taken up photography, his work well-known enough for an exhibition of local landscapes in D.H. Lawrence's house in Nottinghamshire, the same county he, himself, was from. There was a London exhibition of his East European work, too.

He'd sent Jordan a shot of the barley sugar onions and lighthouse spires of Moscow's St. Basil's Cathedral against a pre-digital ultramarine sky and a photo taken at the back of Krakow's Glowny station where the prostitutes chalked their fees on the soles of their shoes and raised a foot to catch trade from passers-by; their commerce scratched away on a pavement should the police come clumsily grabbing. It showed an out-of-focus leather sole inches from the camera; in the background, a white face, red gash of a mouth, black-lined eyes and breasts like white eggs.

Jordan left the cafe quickly and went across to the platform Clinton was on. After greeting each other, the photographer mentioned that he wasn't gong anywhere special and that they should have a drink. They went to a pub off Kingsway, a favourite haunt of Clinton's where he testified that he'd found neither the job nor the woman he wanted, but had enough interests to keep him almost content. He asked Jordan little about himself, but the latter briefly informed him, anyway, that he'd become an MP and it looked as if he could be working for the Secretary of State for Business, though he hadn't met the man yet. Alfred congratulated him.

'That's Peter Weynard isn't it? I've done some stuff for him.'

'You know him?'

'Yes, but before whatever he is now. I had a local exhibition of pictures I took in the City, and he went to it and it impressed him.'

'From what i remember, you're pretty good at buildings.'

'I happened to be in the gallery when he came in and he bought a couple of prints. He commissioned me to take some shots in Isleworth somewhere.'

'What d'you know about him?'

'Nothing much. He was born in New York I believe; his parents were the usual wealthy upper-middle class English. He went to some European school, then, inevitably, Eton. I did some rural stuff for him, too; his cottage in the s Cotswolds. I liked doing stuff there, Middle England and all that.

'I didn't know him well, but he did mention that his pater wanted him to study classics at Balliol, perhaps a sort of artistic sojourn away from the business stuff for a while, but he went into the City and stayed there I suppose until, like you, he went into the politics game. All I know, really. Look, as we're pretty near the Freemasons headquarters and I've never photographed it, what about coming with me?' He briefly lifted the camera to his eye.

It was an imposing building and they had a brief look around the foyer which Clinton took some shots of. As they were leaving they heard a sudden swishing, humming sound which became louder and more intense as they went through the swing doors and onto the pavement.

To their left was a growing crowd of people at a street junction, some already holding up flashing phones as if they were at a festival, others stretching upwards to see the source of the sound.

They went towards it, getting as near as they could, catching glimpses, through a rush of paramedics, of a stretcher and an ambulance. The people not taking pictures were quietly looking on, perhaps part of them, Jordan thought, wanting to watch death.

Inside the circle of onlookers they could now see an overturned car with a red helicopter by its side hanging its blades over it like a huge, broken sycamore seed; it looked, for an insane instant, as if a visiting funfair had arrived. Then, from the huddle of medics, a thumbs-up; the signal for blades to stretch, rotate and rise, the sound alien in the narrow streets; an infinite regress of noise trapped in echoes.

Hanging onto the outside of the rising cockpit, feet on the ski, a uniformed figure looked down at a body in a grey blanket being winched up from the road, then across as he saw an open casement and yelled, 'Shut it! Shut it!' A hand slammed the window in, slivers of glass glistening as they fell. Jordan saw Arthur raising his camera towards the window and taking a shot in one seamless movement.

Rotors flailing, the machine hovered for a few seconds then rose; the swinging stretcher being pulled nearer its red belly. As it cleared the buildings and flew eastward, people slowly moved away, some still looking up as it vanished ever higher across the rooftops.

Glancing up at the window, Jordan thought he saw a face, and wondered if the man's thoughts had been smashed from his brain by the twelve-foot blades a fork's length from his dining table. He looked at Arthur. He was pale and seemed shaken, and said that he'd had to battle to be able to even move through the sound. Jordan guessed that taking the photo was a reflex action for him however he felt.

He turned to Jordan.

'I'm feeling crap. Look, I'm going. Was good to see you. I'm supposed to be going to Athens on holiday next week; I'll contact you when I'm back. Okay? Cheers.'

He almost scurried away; the striding persona had turned into a scuttle.

For an instant, Jordan wasn't sure what to do. He looked up at the window again. There was no face there this time. He briefly glanced at the dispersing crowd. Standing in the doorway of a small haute couture shop was Claire Cluckrose.

He felt bemused. His world was suddenly narrowing: to meet Arthur again and being told that he had worked for someone he himself hoped to work for, and very soon afterwards to see Claire once more, not at Westminster this time but here at a clattering scene of injury and shock.

The pleasing thought that, fortunately, her niece didn't seem to be with her was overtaken by the drawn face and the guarded, defensive look in her eyes which wasn't taking in the scene so much as looking inward, as if replaying her recent experience of a helicopter thrashing above a conjunction of city roads. She was as still as if she'd stopped breathing. He was unsure about comforting her, or how to.

He looked around him. A police car was still there and two officers were talking to a group of onlookers standing on a pavement. He walked towards her and touched her arm.

She appeared startled for a moment. She looked vulnerable.

'What are you doing here?' she asked.

'I could ask the same of you. Are you okay?'

'The question reminds me of films where someone's rolling around in agony after an accident and they're asked if they're 'alright.' 'Yeah, sure, my leg's broken but, hey, it's okay.''

She looked briefly down then up at him.

'Sorry. Yes, it was a bit of a surprise wasn't it. Did you see it all? The rescue; the noise. He must have been badly hurt.'

'Let's have coffee, eh? I saw a place a few yards away. Come on.'

He held her arm firmly and guided her there.

'Most people pronounce the name wrongly,' she said, looking around her after he'd put coffees on he table. 'Nero,' it's a short 'e' not a long one.'

'Drink it, you'll feel better.'

'Magic caffeine.'

She drank some. 'I do. Thanks. The noise is still in my head, though.'

'How's Isobel?'

'What you really want to say, I think, is that you're more attracted to me now that I appear vulnerable after that incident, which brings out your masculine, protective feelings for women,, but you haven't the nerve to say so because, really, you're frightened of rejection. Am I right? I'm sorry, I'm a little unbalanced from that thing hovering like some evil machine bringing death and destruction.'

'Sounds like a trailer for a movie.'

'Does it? Let's forget this conversation took place. How's politics?'

'Not sure, but I may be getting somewhere.'

'Does that mean there's something you're fighting for which can help people?'

'Not really, I meant for me.'

'You're a politician, who else would it be for?'

'That's unfair.'

'Is it? Maybe. But I was going to one of our offices nearby which I should, and will, go to now, I'm afraid.'

'The lady vanishes.'

'Yes.' She quickly drained her cup. 'Thanks for the coffee.'

She hesitated then held out her hand. He took it and gave it a slight squeeze.

'Cheerio then, and I've fully recovered now. Bye.'

As she turned away he looked at her perfectly-shaped calves and upright back; a part of her anatomy he was becoming familiar with.

Clinton contacted him three days afterwards and suggested they meet in a restaurant on the South Bank. He lived in a block of Fifties flats a mile or so south, an area that Jordan, because of his rather parochial territorial attitudes, found rather alien.

After a meal, and in answer to Jordan's question, Arthur, with a pleased grin, showed him the photograph. The face behind the window was hazy, the open mouth a reminder of Munch's The Scream, but the foreground fist gripping the window handle showed clearly the stretched veins and the white of the tightened skin.

Taking it back from him he said, 'I actually met this bloke the day after. I was going to a shop I often go to, this time to pick up a tripod, and walking on the opposite side of the road when he came out of his building. I was sure it was him. I went across and asked him, jokingly, if he'd seen any good choppers lately. I made a spiral sign. He looked alarmed.

'I told him I'd taken a snap of him closing the window. He stood there, trembling slightly. I asked him if he was okay, I felt sorry for him. Anyway, I chatted to him and we went to this café and he told me what had happened, though I don't think he really wanted to talk. It was hard work. Apparently, he'd been experiencing increasingly inimical dreams of long, steel blades smashing through glass and tearing his throat. They had obviously affected him.'

Jordan instantly saw the opening scenes of Apocalypse Now with its silhouetted helicopters rising from behind a hill and filling the screen, their clacking thunder vibrating the cinema. Arthur hadn't asked the man's name, referring to him as 'the window man,' yet while telling Jordan about him he seemed genuinely sorry, almost as if he was a friend he was concerned for, a trait Jordan hadn't really associated with him and certainly not visible to the students and would-be paparazzi they'd known at college.

He talked some more about his intended Aegean holiday and what he hoped to photograph. They then separated; the photographer to ply his trade at a studio somewhere.

Over the next few days Jordan occasionally thought of the man's trauma, his pain; and the shadowy, three-quarter profile in the photo, which wedged itself into his head unwanted.

But mostly he thought of Claire Cluckrose, seeing her again walking away from him. He didn't want to get used to it.

CHAPTER TWENTY ONE

The raincoat man made himself comfortable on the front room sofa without being invited to and, removing his hat, slowly, with what seemed exaggerated attention, sorted through some papers he'd brought with him in a rather old-fashioned briefcase. The policeman, entirely unnecessarily, was standing in the porch.

'Right,' said the man after a while. 'You were with some other people on the day in question outside a building site when some papers were given to you.' He looked up. 'Am I correct?'

'Is this what this is about? And you're not correct, I took one sheet.'

'Why would you be interested in them, in it?'

Ralph wasn't sure what his attitude should be; newspapers could, perhaps, have an interest in the 'Polish paper' as Paul had christened it, but he hadn't given much thought to an intelligence agency's curiosity being stirred.

He shrugged. 'Academically, I suppose.'

'Not politically?'

'Why would I?'

'You tell me.'

'Well, it - '

'You've just joined a local communist group.'

'How d'you know? Is it illegal?'

'What do you think this paper was about?'

'Well, it could have been from an armaments firm.'

'How do you know that?'

'I don't, but the initials could have represented those firms. The one I saw was to an MP; obviously the sender wanted him to let his PM or defence minister or somebody know what was happening. It seemed the sender had knowledge that the Russian government had evidence of Western meddling in their arms programme. I don't really see why Special Branch - you are from there aren't you? - would want to know about the firms or the MP involved.'

'Don't you? What else?'

'It appeared to be not so much firms' representative lobbying, but their turning an MP into a lobbyist. Look, this is all hypothetical really.'

'Continue.'

'Well, we wondered if - '

'We?'

'A couple of friends, just chatting about it.'

'From the party?'

'I suppose so. Does it matter?'

'Carry on.'

'It was idle speculation. We wondered if it was bribery or whether the writer had something on the man. Whatever, this seemed a blatant attempt to get more orders for more weapons. Look, this is just some blokes chatting. Is that banned now? Anyway, they could be fake couldn't they?'

'They won't be.' What was your conclusion on this?'

'Well, it didn't look that great for the Tory government of the time.'

The man, for the first time, smiled. 'That's the real interest isn't it.'

'The idea seemed pretty simple really: increase East-West tension, more weapons seen as needed, more profits for the manufacturers and investors, all good money-making stuff. It wouldn't look that great for the present government either. It's interesting, don't you think? You obviously do or you wouldn't be here.'

'This is not just academic for you though is it. Thinking of going to a newspaper with it? Morning Star? New Worker, or some such.?'

'You're a mind reader.'

'Don't be sarcastic Mister Kearns, it's the cheapest form of wit.'

'Humour.'

'I'm not interested in pedantry, but I am in what you were given and if it has any consequences. Okay, the inevitable question now: Have you still got the paper? I assume you have.'

'No, it got lost; or rather I think I threw it in the rubbish bag by mistake. Sorry.'

'Lost, or thrown away?'

'Does it matter? It's probably in a landfill site or whatever by now. Sorry, I'd have willingly given it to you. But I will look for it; it just may be here somewhere.'

'I'm not sure I believe you, Mister Kearns, but we'll leave it there, for now.'

The man got up and looked briefly around him.

'You can have any colours you like as long as they're white, grey and magnolia, eh?'

'Something like that.'

He went into the hall and turned.

'Look for it.'

'I shall.'

He went to the front door, then along with the uniformed officer got into a nondescript car parked across the road and drove off.

As Ralph went to a drawer in his bedside chest and looked at the sheet of paper, wondering why the man wished to look like George Raft in a Forties noir movie, he was somewhat surprised that he seemed, of late, to be able to lie so easily. But then, the interview would probably come to nothing and he could, perhaps, forget about it; after telling Paul and Edward, anyway.

He closed the drawer but not before glimpsing an old crossword he'd made up years before with the anagram clue, 'He works in the classroom. (12).' The answer was 'schoolmaster.' He'd been rather pleased with this one and began to think of one for 'Special Branch;' It didn't have to be an anagram of course, something to do with a tree perhaps. He was getting as bad as Paul. He took the sheet of paper out and flung it in the large drawer under his bed.

He mused on lying and the reason it was so frowned upon by society - because it disrupted order, created a sense of insecurity - then thought of Jada, someone he hadn't considered for a while, and who he'd never lied to; there would have been no point in doing so. She'd probably known he wasn't in love with her.

Whilst thinking of her, he had a glimpse of Doreen, head bowed, looking miserable, and felt a dulling sort of perception about both of them; of his rather fragmented, unsatisfying emotional journeys, seemingly random and only sporadically worthwhile. He'd wanted something more... genuine, but had, at least up till now, done little about getting it.

He took a while longer than usual to get to sleep, but doubted whether Mister Raincoat would bother him again, except perhaps to ask him if he'd found the papers in question.

After finishing an early afternoon lesson the next day, and resting against the whiteboard while the classroom emptied, he looked across to the empty chair on his left where Jada had always sat, until a year ago when her estranged husband's jealousy had finally won and she'd left the course. He'd known nothing of her and Ralph.

It was a common story amongst mature female students. Men, feeling inadequate and frightened that their partners or wives were stretching towards new horizons - and wondering who was helping them get there - would occasionally come to the college and demand to know where their women were. When he asked for ideas for research projects a third of the females would opt for something to do with domestic violence, which he would turn into a working hypothesis that they could test. Perpetua, on the protest march, had been such a one,

Jada used to sit there wearing a tracksuit, her braided extensions rising above a headband, gazing at him with Bambi eyes and a knowing mouth and occasionally sipping brandy from a plastic bottle. He'd thought it was mineral water.

It had been a frenetic time. He'd been to a gym with her, seen the frown under the dark nest of hair to ward off posing machos, the burnt umber skin, the occasional ear-to-ear grin; watched her puff out her pain in press-ups, drown her sadness in saunas and lift weights, followed by his ungainly attempts to keep time with her aerobics group.

He'd held her up in a nightclub, rushed to her bedside in a local hospital because she'd collapsed, gazed at the zigzagging, merging colours on the screen while her liver was being scanned and, after being dragged for a sunset ride on the 'Barracuda' at Southend, lying next to her on his bed like a contortionist dying in his own arms.

He had, he recalled, arranged the tables and chairs, as always, in a three-sided rectangle, for many mature students had known bad educative experiences when young and, especially at the beginning of an academic year, desks set out in well-remembered rows would trigger the same fears. Most of the people on the course had been from ethnic minorities, mainly African females, and nearly all had gone on to university.

He'd played devil's advocate. When he'd first met them he would explain that under the guise of an evangelical mission Europeans had introduced Christianity to Africa for the purposes of social and economic control of half a continent - the more politically aware would nod wisely - and that we had made god, not the other way around, the real question being, why?

The classroom would glow with outrage and anger and, occasionally, a kind of pity. He'd wanted to shock their mindset, to create a sliver of a chance that he just may be right, thus helping them to detach, to step back. They were then halfway to a sociological view of the world, and that's what he was teaching. There were always some female students who would say to him on their way out after the first lecture, lightly touching his shoulder as he sat at his desk, 'We'll pray for you, Ralph.' He was sure they had.

He had begun the sociology of deviance the previous year at the beginning of term two and started on the semiotics part the day before Jada had left. He'd suggested that the police worked within the class structure and held pre-existing concepts, 'pictures in their heads,' of what criminality was and 'criminals' were like. He'd asked them for the signs the Bill pounced on.

The two Dagenham lads, who always sat together, immediately and in concert had said, 'Workin' class, innit.'

'They're protecting the bourgeoisie from the proles,' a student had shouted, her Catholicism weakening after six months of Marx.

He'd asked for the signals that would suggest 'working class-ness.' Pam, an Afro-Caribbean, had suggested it was the walk; another subtly suggested that it was the way a cigarette was held. He'd then turned his back to them, bounced on his heels, squaring his shoulders and asked for 'Two lagers, John.'

He did this every year. He'd then ask if they thought he was mimicking the son of an Emeritus Professor of Literature at King's College, Cambridge, or a plasterer stopping for a drink on his way home from a building site. A cheap laugh, but it had made the point.

One of several Nigerians had said the type of car was an obvious clue, another, leisure activities and musical tastes. A usually silent Somali had suggested that accent and appearance were the obvious signals and, rather late, someone had mentioned race. And so they'd gone on, most of them saying something and in the end creating a comprehensive coverage of perceived clues.

Jada, as ever, had said nothing, merely looking at him steadily. He'd hinted strongly that there would be questions on this at the end of term and suggested a mnemonic to help them. Their answers had come back like drumbeats, and they'd made up a little chant:

'Dreadlocks, hip-hop, Beemer, mean - tattoos, skins, hard, obscene.' which was, rather enjoyably, a part send-up of stereotypes.

Some of them had left the classroom happily singing it, possibly because they were going home to change for a birthday party for the twin girls in the class. He'd reminded them, tongue-in-cheek, to turn up in English time, not African.

It had been decided they would go to a local east London pub for the party. He rarely drank, often being mocked by builders when he'd been working on sites during his signwriting apprenticeship years before. The class had settled in well in the time they'd been together and most had wanted to go. Jada he'd known outside the classroom since she had tearfully pleaded that her essay had been worth more than the grade he'd given it because she had worked so hard; perhaps he should have realised then that she had problems.

He'd mumbled about professional integrity and had encouraged her to work harder. He hadn't given in. He hadn't months before when a student who had done a lot of research on prostitution and, accompanied by her tough-looking CID husband and a pitiful, lame child - a three-pronged attack - had harangued him in front of other staff to give her the Distinction she thought her work was worth.

The next day Jada had rung him in the staff room and asked if he wanted to go to a bar with her and some friends that evening. He'd thanked her and declined. Later that night, with tears in her voice, she'd called and asked for his address. A little afterwards he'd seen her under the street lights walking up a garden path some houses away peering short-sightedly at the number on a front door, a manoeuvre she repeated on the next one. Going to her and taking her hand he'd gently guided her back to his home.

After this, for the following few days, she would occasionally slip into the staff room, unheard and unseen, and put a sandwich - and even an apple - on his desk, and not tell him.

They'd driven to the pub late and on the way he'd made the mistake of mentioning the class flirt whom, apparently, he'd spent more time talking to in class than the other students. The car had seemed to stiffen; he'd felt apprehensive. She had this effect on him. She'd left the car before it had quite stopped. Ignoring wondering classmates she'd pushed straight through to the bar and ordered a brandy.

There'd been a small stage to the side and on it, as well as music exploding from decibel-smashing speakers, was the girl who had organised the get-together and who'd been groining her miniskirted thighs around and pushing them out at everybody standing around. The swot whose name he could never remember had been next to her wearing a blond wig and rhythmically lifting up a kilt, showing his briefs. The two Ugandans, looking like bouncers, had chuckled deeply and the Nigerian women, gold bangles and ear rings glittering, had quietly smiled, their Victorian values safe and firm; not for them the two-inch band of flesh at their waists, tops of knickers showing.

He'd noticed the Ghanaian women were wearing traditional dress, which seemed to glow, as did their smooth skins, and also the Romford Marxist leaning against the flock-papered wall frowning disapprovingly. Most of them had looked very different from the way they did in class and seemed genuinely glad to see him.

Circulating, he'd drunk some wine - someone seemed to keep filling his glass - learnt more about Robert Gabriel Mugabe from an extrovert Zimbabwean student until one of the older women had come over to talk to him about her intended career in social work.

Then Jada had appeared by his side, eyes narrowed. She'd turned and minced to the stage, jumped up and begun dancing about in a clumsy, clattering way in front of a track-suited skinhead, repeatedly pressing herself against him. As she'd briefly pulled away she'd left a noticeable bulge in his crotch. Looking round at Ralph she'd given him a teasing grin. He'd stridden across and pulled her off the stage. He could hardly see through the noise.

'Get off, get off, get off!' she'd shouted. 'Let me go!'

She'd tried to pull her hand away; he'd gripped harder, almost dragged her across to the door and, in a tiny chip of cold detachment, saw them performing some exotic dance where the man strides smoothly across the dance floor dragging his sylph-like partner horizontally behind him. He'd been angry, and as he'd pulled the door open glimpsed one of the Dagenham students hiding under a table. She'd continued to shout at him to let her go as he'd hurried her to his car parked across the road.

He had held her against the passenger door for a few seconds then moved quickly to open the driver's side door. She'd kicked the side of the car and continued doing so as he'd got in. He'd leaned across to open the door for her and then seen two women run from the pub towards her.

'He's her tutor, he's abusing her,' one had shrilled. 'He's using his authority.'

Again, the distancing irrelevance as he'd thought that this could be a cue for a future lecture on perceptions of power. In the wing mirror he'd seen some men hastily cross towards him. He'd left the window down; the other woman had pushed her arm in and grabbed his hand as it turned the ignition.

'She's with me,' he'd said as calmly as he could.' I brought her here, she's - '

'I'm not!' Jada had screamed.' I'm not with him, I'm not, I'm not!' and had begun to cry.

He'd pushed the hand away and driven off.

After a hundred yards or so he'd stopped then went back to see if she was alright. He'd slowly passed the pub where a group of women had been comforting her. He could see her sobbing. He'd driven homewards.

A few minutes later he'd found himself driving the wrong way down a one-way street and realised he was drunk. He rarely touched alcohol and when he did it quickly affected him. He'd stopped the car, it just happened to be outside a small police station. A constable had appeared and told him to get out. He had done so and irrelevantly emptied his pockets, placing their contents on the roof of the car. He'd heard himself giggling as they'd slid slowly down. He was breathalysed.

She was leaning against the porch when he'd got back. Opening the door and closing it behind them, she'd followed him into the bedroom where he'd let out an angry explosion of the evening's emotions.

'You could have got me lynched,' he'd yelled. 'Why did you lie? Why?'

She'd suddenly slid down the wall and knelt on the floor. He'd picked her up and gently laid her on the bed. She'd slept instantly in his arms. He hadn't mentioned the breathalysing. He'd held her tightly throughout the night.

The car had been stored in the college's motor vehicle buildings - and probably used for teaching - for the length of his drink-driving ban, and he was wondering how it would feel when he drove it for the first time in a year. He'd finished an evening class and just to make sure that the motor vehicle lecturer had got his message he'd glanced out of the window to see if the car was outside the workshops. It was. He'd hurried down the stairs wondering why he felt such anticipation at driving again, something quite ordinary, mundane even. He'd got used to buses.

It had felt immediately familiar. Driving slowly out the gate he'd turned westward, overtook two lorries and accelerated towards a main junction a mile away. As he'd neared it he became gradually aware that what was irritatingly taking his attention was flashing blue lights hitting the driving mirror. Their significance escaped him - he'd even flicked the mirror up to dull the flashes - until he'd heard the siren and saw a police car suddenly behind him. The traffic lights in front were red. He'd slowed and stopped. Turning in his seat he'd seen two policemen step out from either side of their car, their movements almost synchronised.

He had taught for nine hours in a twelve-hour day and was tired; he'd assumed he'd been speeding. He'd remembered the last time police had approached his car; the unbelieving shake of the head from the older one, the embarrassed grin from the other as he'd picked up his wallet, small change and comb from the roadside, and thought of Jada with her bloodshot, beautiful eyes telling him the following morning that her husband was coming back and she wouldn't be able to see him again

He thought also of the last lesson she'd had with him, of what they'd all been discussing, the little chant, and her remarking facetiously that she'd seen a squirrel in the college earlier and wanted to know if it was deviant.

Quickly he'd pulled two paperbacks from the glove compartment, 'Sociology,' and 'Philosophical Theory,' and dropped them face upwards on the passenger seat. As the two uniformed figures looked in at him from both sides of the car he'd lowered the window and raised the volume on Classic FM.

Now, before introducing the topic of sexual divisions to his next class - knowing he would be stepping into a MeToo-provisioned minefield, and inevitably someone mentioning, accusingly, that the world was controlled by 'old white men' yet taking umbrage if he, purposely to illustrate a point, were to refer to 'old women' - he thought of Claire and realised he'd been waiting for a while for her to ring. It hadn't happened. He should have known that if he wanted to see her he would have to contact her. She wouldn't call him.

CHAPTER TWENTY TWO

He entered the House, took a seat and looked around him at the other MPs. The place wasn't full, a little surprising for PM's Question Time but he was more interested in his meeting with Peter Weynard - which he would be attending in half an hour - than being where he was. He recalled Archer telling him about these sessions.

'There they are, party leaders squaring up over the despatch box; it's history in the making, but way more hammy than any realistic staging of it. If you're goin' to speak, your sphincter tightens then the noise assails you, then the grandeur of the place. People around you will be bouncing up and down on their seats hoping the Speaker will ask them to address a question. They get seduced by being in the limelight. It's like a panto: all the hoisted emotions, affectations, priapic banter and silly punchlines. Problem is it's personalisation drowning out policy. The serious point of these questions is ballsed-up by gladiatorial point-scoring. In the end, of course, they nod along to their leader.'

He watched some examples of Archer's descriptions and analysis - assuming he had obtained them from various politicians and would-be ones he had helped over the years - while listening to some predictable questions being asked about European intransigence over confused, and confusing, demands by the government's inconsistent enthusiasm for leaving its aegis, and an obscure one about post-feminism and a woman novelist in the Ukraine.

He was struck by how many of the participants, buoyed to silliness by the limelight, wanted to impress their colleagues and the watching press. Listening to the baying and the schoolyard banter alternating with hurled insults, he felt briefly concerned that a female SNP member was going to vault across the Tory front bench and attack someone. It felt like there was nobody left in charge. Staying as long as he sensibly could without being late and hoping his noiseless exit went unnoticed, he made his way to he Minister's office.

It was only a little larger than the bureaucrat's, but painted, appropriately, in tints of blue, and it felt more personal, with a photo of, Jordan assumed, the occupant's wife and teenage son on an Ikea-looking desk. He was a rather corpulent man, with sandy-colour hair and fleshy face.

'Sit down, Wilde. This will be pretty short I'm afraid, busy busy, busy, things to do. Wasn't there a character in Alice who went around saying something like that, or was that the Disney version? Anyhow, business, commerce, finance, economics et cetera - Just your background, like me of course - and Brexit; companies fretting about what it all means, is going to mean, and what their bottom line's going to be.

'I'm not wanting your objective opinion, even a political one, but a money one; the future, investment and so on; your take. You're pretty up-to-date with the nitty-gritty on the ground, so to speak. Don't think our families have met have they, there's a lot of familial, or what people would call rather fatuously, nepotism, in the City, but ne'er mind. The state of the market, what's happening, what the financial leaders feel, the big boys, the corporations... that's what I want from you, stuff like that. Oh, and,' he smiled, 'I'd better ask if you want the job, such as it is.

'I think the position's called financial advisor to the business and strategy team, something like that. Bit of a part-time thing really, but there'll be an upgrade in salary of course, won't interfere with your ordinary MP's work much; surgeries, voting, and so forth. If you're happy with that I'll be contacting you occasionally for some info, opinions etcetera. Alright with you? Oh, incidentally, as you may know, there's been talk of a recession, sort of hypothetically, but it could happen again of course. Maybe we'll run to some academics, think tanks, you know the sort of thing. What would you suggest is done to head off any forthcoming one?'

'Three or four things.'

'Such as?'

'Well, there are triggers. One could be a trade war starting, which looks as if it has anyway, another could be a sharp, long-term rise in interest rates, bond yields, or investors could simply

become worried and pull funds out of perceived risky investment.'

'And?'

'Governments need to step up structural policies to make their
countries more efficient, like labour market policies to encourage
more people into work, curbing cartels. The more efficient your
economy can become the longer the expansion can continue
without hitting capacity barriers. Second... Do you want to hear
this or the City talk stuff?'

'I like what you're saying, and the way you're saying it. It's
wider, more politically viable, if you will. Continue.'

'Third, they should strengthen the financial sector, and they
need to work at reducing the public debt accumulated as a result
of the last recession.'

'That it?'

'Finally, they need to tighten monetary policy and get interest
rates up. They have to do this carefully of course. I don't think it
was a good idea to import a foreigner to run The Bank.'

'I was, I suppose, expecting some sort of vested, self-
interested, jargonised insider stuff , but... Yes, a wider view, a
pragmatic one, indeed.'

'Obvious things, really.'

'Our leader,' he bent forward and lowered his voice,' wouldn't
think that though, it may even quite impress.' He smiled. 'However, I'm sure you've noticed in the short while you've been here
that amongst the more gung-ho members of our Parliament,
there's an almost emotional antipathy to the power of international capital.

'You may also have noticed that firms which diverge from the
ideological purity of leaving Europe, and there are many of
course, are treated to private expletives or accused publicly.
That'll change. Ideology tends to melt in the face of reality.'

He stood, as did Jordan, and shook his interviewee's hand.

'As said, you'll be contacted. Good day. '

As Jordan left he wasn't quite sure what he'd let himself in for
but, so far, it was seeming pretty easy, really, and perhaps he had,
in a short time, become a little hardened, cynical even, but his
once-growing ambition of 'making a difference,' though still

alive, had settled somewhat. However, it seemed he was being noticed.

He had little to do, no need, for a change, to attend anything, but instead of the Commons bar or going into the City and a grey-painted gastro pub with its made-to-order Dalston grot, bare brick walls, industrial lighting and eclectic furniture - though he could have done with a smoked-mackerel pâté, fishcakes and scallops washed down with a bottle of Merlot - he made for the Overground and to Pippy's at Hampstead Heath.

With its Raj-like fans spinning on the anaglypta ceiling, a large model of a WW1 biplane hanging from it, Victorian pictures of Ming vases, framed bas-reliefs of country cottages, Victorian display cabinets and a rocking horse by the counter, it was a kind of comforting oddity.

He was finishing his scrambled eggs when an almost familiar figure ponderously entered and ordered a glass of wine. It was Luke Kenyon, who Jordan recognised just before he sat heavily down at the next table. He looked up at Jordan with deadened eyes, frowned and let his head droop over his vodka.

He didn't look quite the heir-to-everything being he seemed when Jordan had first met him; his confident blue eyes and affectively creased jacket now looking crumpled and inadequate. But this was a man who still appeared steeped in a privileged indulgence which, Jordan guessed, had been casually displayed in bars from Manhattan to Mumbai.

He felt a childlike urge to quietly take the drink from him and gently pour it over his lank hair to awaken him. There was no need, as Kenyon abruptly pushed his head up, blinked several times and said, in a slightly slurry voice, 'Good lord, I know you. We've met; what?'

'Guess we have. Surprised you remember.'

'May have had a few, but never forget a face, or a voice.'

He chuckled quietly, showing a flash of his almost luminescent teeth.

'S'ppose that helped me into the Service. Nearly said 'Circus' then, always been a Le Carre fan you know.'

'You're in? - '

'Forget it, shouldn't have said it.'

He gazed at the fan above him, his eyes trying to follow its spinning. He sat back in his chair.

'I'm enjoying this feeling you know, but must admit I was warned from the beginning not to drink, which wasn't so long ago, common sense really. What did Oscar Wilde say - no relation of course - 'Common sense isn't.'? Quite. It does seem rather to apply to me at this moment doesn't it. Been to that pub round the corner, opposite the Tube, on my own, heard it was good. Chatted to a few people; couple of queers in there, nice brown-haired lady, or thought so till she started talking politics, another damn Leftie, be the ruination of this country if we let 'em. Can't remember what I said to her now, but a good time, really. They serve a very nice port, unusual in pubs nowadays. Anyway, doesn't matter to you, unless you're some sort of spy too.'

He almost giggled, then instantly squared his shoulders, held his head up and said, 'Must stop this.' He then bent his head towards his listener, squinted exaggeratedly and said, 'You're okay; a man of principle I feel, though you didn't send me any hot tips so I could take over the stock exchange, or at least make some money.'

'Can't remember why I didn't.'

'You know, I sometimes wonder if people come into the Service - d'you think I'm soberin' up? - the Oxbridge grads, the Firsts, and they're not always from the upper-middle either, because they have some point to prove. Perhaps some want revenge on something, some nebulous entity, maybe fate or something. But anyhow, I'm beginning to doubt whether they want to do something for their country or whether they've seen too many Bond films. I know three of 'em, there's possibly more, that have Aston Martins.'

'Do they have blades on their hubcaps like Boudicca's?'

'Why are you being so face... '

'Facetious. I suggest you don't order any more to drink.'

'Sounds like one of Q's inventions; it was Q wasn't it? Ours is called RS, no idea why. Very few of us look like hipsters you know. How's Henry thingy these days? Not that I care.'

'Why did you join?'

'Country, of course. Hell, shouldn't be doing this, talking to you. Christ, why am I?'

'Drink?'

'Is that an invitation?'

'No. An answer.'

'Hell.' Kenyon took a large swig, stared at his glass then smacked his lips.

'I like the boss man; he's alright, the little I've seen of him, Just about more U than Non-U of course. I suppose the Mitford class-allocation is foreign to you.'

He flicked his hand away, an almost feminine gesture which reminded his listener of when they'd first met.

'But he gets these little obsessions sometimes, not so much a bee in his bonnet but a hive. I haven't been there long of course, but currently a few of us are supposed to be looking into something that seems pretty small. Not certain why they're bothering, but small things can become big things.'

He paused, his demeanour still a trifle unanchored.

'I suppose it could upset the party a little, but seems to me more of a very minor storm in a true blue teacup, too small to interest anyone really. It's not me that's on it, anyway, I'm just a... This chappie found some old stuff; bits o' paper that don't look good politically. I dunno.' He started hic-cuppng. 'Thing is, there's this increasing worry over demos and bits of political unrest, so this little bit appears bigger than it is.'

He took a large sip from his glass, emptying it.

'Anyway, what you doing these days, still helping the rich get richer in your up-market bingo world, your glamorous lottery of high finance?'

'Politics.'

'You're some sort of... I dunno, activist?'

'No. A politician.'

'A real one?'

'Yes'.

'Oh, congrats.'

He paused for a while, seeming a little more sober.

'Shouldn't have mentioned all this, should I.'

He stood, only a little unsteadily, and held out a dangling hand.

'Let's forget this conversation took place.'

'Already forgotten.'

Jordan watched through the glass front to see whether he would go to the nearby station - if he could remember where it was - or try to figure out where to get a taxi. On the pavement he looked to his left then right and, holding his back straight, moved slowly in the latter direction.

Jordan sat and thought of what the man had told him. Maybe he should care, at least in his role as an MP, but he didn't. His indifference began filling with images of Claire, but not in the forms he'd seen her in: on a suburban doorstep, in a pub, at a meeting, with her niece, shaken by a helicopter... But in her home sitting in front of a triple mirror on a dresser, bending forward, looking steadily at her lips as she coloured them with that dark, bright red she sometimes used and, like his mother would do, wipe the surplus quickly off her front teeth, maybe dropping the tissue into a lattice waste basket and quickly brushing a comb through her hair, then standing and placing her hands below her hips, briefly straightening her dress; she wouldn't take long on the process.

He then saw her pirouetting in a tight skirt on a stage, walking against the light into a restaurant somewhere, laughing with that generous mouth, even seeing her casually driving a bus, or piloting a 747 and looking imperiously down on the tops of clouds. He reproached himself for this fanciful, almost lovelorn teenager stuff. He then felt a rather inappropriate ennui.

He left the place, walking in the opposite direction to Kenyon. He fancied wandering along Keats Grove and stretching his legs around Belsize Park. At least, it was a man that had walked away from him this time, it wasn't Ms Cluckrose.

'Well, here we are, not long after the hundred-year anniversary of the revolution and living in a State that increasingly allows corporations not only to not pay their tax, but because of Byzantine payments to their branches in other countries, even to post losses.'

It was Eaton speaking on a Saturday afternoon in his usual position at the end of the Nissen hut.

'In one case I saw that, despite over six billion in sales, one phone company claimed a near-five hundred million loss. I won't mention that these corporate disrupters are, with their two-hundred-million-pound yachts, claiming that they don't earn enough to pay their taxes in full, because the Right will call it the politics of envy. To remind you; we're still widely food-banked and in austerity. The people are being held in contempt.'

He looked briefly around him at his listeners.

'When cuckoo businesses set up in our nest they put their hands round our throats; schools, hospitals, infrastructure are starved. But they're seen as the good guys, capitalism at its most successful, FTSE heroes.

'However, I didn't come here to state the obvious, but suggest maybe we should do something to boost our numbers. I'd like some recruitment ideas. If you have any, write 'em down and leave 'em on the table.'

He left his spot and walked to the other end of the hall to talk with some late entrants.

Ralph was present, but not Paul. He'd been at the former's home continuing his battle against contemporary clichés; especially those used by politicians.

'There is an assumption made by politicians,' he'd said, 'when using the term 'generation' - how long is one, anyway? - that it's, somehow, homogenous, that its members are of one social class, i.e. the middle one, a projection from the speakers of course. This implies that the values of WC adolescents, say, are nearer to those of their MC counterparts than they are to their parents, a so-called generation gap; as if the parents of *both* classes hold the same expectations of their kids' working lives. And what about the differences in leisure pursuits, say, ballet, opera and classical music versus goin' dahn the pub, Ladbrokes et cetera. Okay, a little stereotypical, but still generally valid.'

Ralph had noticed before with Paul that intellectual stimuli seemed to fill him, stimulate him disproportionately to any emotional one. When he had stopped talking his head had drooped.

'D'you know, if I'd told my mum that I'd just directed an Oscar-winning film or been awarded the Nobel Prize for Literature - Dylan getting one has devalued it - she'd have said, in her respectable WC way, 'Oh, that's nice,' hardly understanding what I'd said.'

'If you did win a prize like that would you really feel it, would you feel you had now been recognized?' Ralph had asked him, guessing that no matter how talented, creative, perceptive he was, he wouldn't, couldn't accept praise. He could win all the prizes in he world but his emotional impoverishment would swallow them up like a cloud.

He hadn't answered and had been silent for a while, then, 'I'm not coming this evening. Don't feel like it, but tell me if anything interesting happens. See you.' and had gone home.

Ralph, while listening to Eaton and looking around him to see if Claire would appear, went to the bar to join Edward. As he got there he heard a voice saying:

'Oh, come on, Hymie, Jews like to think of themselves as being an oppressed minority, you're like it yourself sometimes, but they don't really qualify for that in today's politics, do they? I mean, numerically, yes, but you could also categorise them as white, rich, over-nationalistic about Israel and unforgivably aligned with American imperialism.'

The voice, belonging to a middle-aged man, was directed at a white-haired, obviously Jewish one.

'That's derogatory, Billy.'

'But it's true.'

'No. You calling me Hymie just now.'

CHAPTER TWENTY THREE

'I was playing stereotypes. You know that, what's got into yer?'

'Take no notice,' Edward said quietly to Ralph. 'They're the best of muckers, known each other for years. I did hear that Billy has Jewish blood, but he denies it. Anyway, he can categorically say that some of his best friends are Jews, well, one of 'em. Don't get many people of that persuasion in the party, but Maurice is a good comrade.'

'You've this thing about Americans,' said Maurice to his companion. 'They're a rich country and we should perhaps be grateful for their - '

'They not only tell us how to speak but how to eat and drink. When was the last time you saw someone under the age of fifty eat with a knife in one hand and a fork in the other? As for drinking beer from a bottle... '

'Okay, so you can't get a proper mouthful.'

'Don't get me started. Did you hear the one about - I'm even talking like you now, what have you done to me?'

'Not enough, you'd be a better man if you had a religion, other than the party, to give you rules. I've told you before.'

'Rules? You take no notice of your religion; you flew on the Sabbath once and said that as your seat belt was fastened you were *wearing* the plane. Anyhow, how's the missus? I saw you the other day with her, couldn't stop; was on a bus. It was nice, you were holding hands.'

'I always do. If I let go she shops.'

'Jewish humour, eh?' Edward said in an aside to Ralph.

'I heard that. It goes back to the Torah,' said Maurice. 'It's a kind of a clandestine way of opposing Christianization.'

'What's the three words his wife never wants to hear when she's making love?' his friend asked, turning to the people at the bar. "Honey, I'm home."

A voice softly cut in.

'Goes back to the Haskalah, too, Maurice.'

'Hey, Cluckrose,' he said, turning to give Claire a hug.

'Nice to see you, Maurice. Excuse me,' she smiled, and went off to talk with a woman sitting at a corner of the front row.

'I'm going,' said Maurice. 'You coming?

He and Billy raised their hands in goodbye gestures and left.
Edward turned to Ralph.

'It's like watching a vaudeville act sometimes when they're here. I wish they'd come more. The older one's descendants were Russian Jews; the tsars didn't treat that race very kindly either, apparently. Paul not with you?'

'No, he said that he had neither the emotional nor cerebral energy to push against the rest of the world.'

'I feel the same sometimes. You?

Ralph was watching Claire. 'I suppose so.'

'Yeah, she's got great legs, ain't she.'

Just then some swing music came from a corner behind the bar.

'Nice, but why?' asked Ralph.

'Well, there's not many of us here, there rarely is at an afternoon meeting. There's no hurry. Relax.'

Claire was walking back towards the bar again. Ralph went towards her.

'Oh, hello,' she grinned, 'Have I missed anything, I've just got here.'

'No, but unless you dance with me you *will* have missed something.'

She raised an eyebrow. 'Sure of ourselves aren't we.'

'No, but will you? It's a while since I have.'

She hesitated. 'Alright. Jive, incidentally, has Latin roots and was taken up by the East Coast in the Thirties. This is Candy Man.'

They moved a few yards to the area at the back of the seats and began. She was wearing a Fifties skirt, slightly flaring, showing her slim waist, as if, thought Ralph later, she knew there would be music to dance to.

She was a little fast for him, but after a minute he felt comfortable with her, at the slightest touch of his hand on hers she was spinning away and back again as if they'd been doing it together for a while.

'You're pretty good. Come here often?' he asked.

'Only when there's an opportunity to debate this government's attempt to put religious hatred on the statute as a crime and to ignore aggressive religiosity.' She continued dancing. 'What of the dislike poured on atheism; cries of 'blasphemy,' 'sacrilege' et cetera? Religious hatred may be condemned and punishable, but it's okay to hate the secular.'

'Christ, you said all that without missing a step.'

'I think I may have. And you're not too bad yourself.'

She turned, his hand holding hers above her head, then spinning again.

When the tune had finished and in the gap before another being played, a few people clapped and another couple appeared ready to dance to the next one.

'Want a drink?'

'I'll have half a lager.'

He got their drinks, turned and looked for her. She was sitting on a front seat again facing the make-do stage. He sat down next to her.

'You look a lot different than on the protest march.'

'It's the clothes. You know, as morally right as it is to defend the right of little girls not to have their genitals cut into bits, it risks offending communities where the practice of it has been a tradition for hundreds of years.'

'Yet another liberal conundrum. Tough. D'you want to see a film or something with me?'

'The right to give offence is one of the very foundations of freedom of speech.'

'I'm glad you feel that..'

'Okay, but It seems we're gradually enshrining the right *not* to be offended, which means the end of liberty. Discourse is being calcified. Alright then, I'll let you know.'

' How?'

'I suppose you'll give me your number.'

He showed it on his phone. She put it on hers.

'You're going to say you must be going now, aren't you.'

'Not 'must', that's an excuse. But I am anyway.'

She swigged the last of her beer and, walking back along the side of the seats, gave a flippant wave without turning to him. It was a gesture he felt was one almost of dismissal.

Edward gave him a knowing grin when Ralph returned to him, then said, 'Heard any more from the secret policeman? No, you'd have mentioned it. Since you told me about him I keep thinking I'm being followed.'

'Shadows in the night, eh? Doubt it.'

'You've still got the paper haven't you? Bet you're tempted to show it to them. Have you told them that you still have 'it?'

'No.'

'Get the Tories in trouble, the cover-up and stuff. As we've said, the recriminations; It's a kind of a whistle-blowing thing, people will be angry.'

'Powerful people, too.'

'You could give it to Paul. It'd be safe then.'

'Haven't told him about trilby hat man. Don't want to worry him, he's a bit down.'

'What's the matter?'

'Usual, really. It's complex.'

'And deep?'

'It is.'

What Paul had said to him a few days previously was relevant in the context of his being with Edward.

He had told him that he liked Edward, but felt scared of his feelings. In answer to Ralph's 'why?' he'd replied that he was frightened of liking two people at the same time, of giving affection to them simultaneously. He was scared of hurting one of them.

'I can't. It comes from mum and dad. I feel it now,' he'd said. Ralph had asked what Myers response would have been.

'The usual: it's baby, child. If I gave love to mum then... I felt dad looked at me as if I'd done something wrong and I was scared, and if I felt anything for him then my mum would have picked up on it and it would have hurt her. It felt horrible hurting my mother. I hated it. It frightened me. I suppose I was scared of losing one of them, or even both. I'm projecting it onto you and Edward, I guess. I know it's stupid, so immature but, it's what I feel.'

Ralph had tried to reassure him that it was okay to like Edward. 'You won't lose me,' he'd told him. 'Can you picture losing me?'

Paul had looked at the ground, shaking his head, and suggested they go for a walk around the lake in Wansford Park; which they had done, though he had rarely spoken during their circumambulation of the water.

Edward was speaking to him. 'I thought Eaton was going to make a speech about his favourite public-private finance hate.'

'Perhaps he'll do it next time. What was he going to say?'

'I know what *I'd* say.'

'Tell me.'

'Well, I'd talk about the demise of large public projects because of the relentlessness of a liberal philosophy that puts balance sheet finance above paying for things openly, and lauding the private sector above the public one.'

'So lit isn't just about ludicrous contradictions and the distortion of the world then? Not just about truth-strangling, reality-distorting, fact-forfeiting anti-intellectual fascism then?'

'No. It's fostered the belief that there's no financial challenge that can't be solved by a deal, a sleight of hand, and a taste for creative accounting.'

'Think you'll find it was a Labour government that started that.'

'It wasn't a socialist one though.'

'They hid behind the language of socialism. Have you ever made a spiel here, on that raised bit at the end?'

'Eaton's stage. No.'

'You should.'

'You're probably right.'

'You've never told me what you do; your job.'

'IT. We'll talk about the rights and wrongs of that phenomenon another time. Talking of which, I need to do stuff at home for work. I'm doing more and more of that. A man's gotta do. Buy you a drink next time. Say hello to Paul, eh?'

Next day, disliking keeping home on Sunday and Paul doing some paid work helping a neighbour erect a garden fence, he travelled west of the City and enjoyed himself looking at some

Georgian facades, Regency town houses and early Victorian buildings which, although sometimes tucked away in side streets, were invariably grand.

He thought of Paul, who sometimes saw houses as kinds of anthropomorphic metaphors for his parents, though never explicitly stating he was talking of his own.

'Boughed leaves against a window are like a mother's hair touching an infant's face,' he'd say. 'A cupola is an offered breast, and eaves, the brim of a merry widow hat.' He'd spoken of a 'full-bosomed caryatide holding up a pediment, the folds of its long skirt being there for a child to hide its face in.

Ralph had asked him what a gable would be.

'Perhaps a raised eyebrow, and railings would be an upright thing, a father telling his son to hold his back up, and a chequer pattern flint wall would be... tough and hard. Something like, ''it a six, son, you can do it,' or 'Catch it, catch it!' A pitched roof could be a large body frowning down on a boy, scaring him.'

When he was like this he was, invariably, quiet for long moments afterwards. Maybe, Ralph thought, he was the frightened boy, his father's house, somehow, inside of him.

He continued walking; pleasantly remembering that London contained almost as many trees as it had residents. Fortunately, it had not quite been overbuilt into an amorphous mass, it was, just about, still a series of villages of Victorian and Edwardian streets, of London brick, of pavement trees and, further out, of Thirties avenues and orchard gardens.

Getting off a Tube train at his local station, a tiny part of his retinal awareness informed him that he had noticed the rather short, bald man not far behind him on a street two or three hours previously. He stopped on the platform and let him pass, watching him stand on the ascending escalator.

Christ, he was getting like Edward. Why would anyone want to traipse after either of them?

Turning into his road he thought of how good it had been to dance with Claire, touching her, holding her hand, her quick feet, skirt riding up intermittently and showing a flash of thigh. Maybe, just maybe, she would ring him.

CHAPTER TWENY FOUR

He had little to do after another surgery: a corpulent woman with six children, three of them present, complaining - as she tried to seat her sugar drink-fortified buttocks on a cane chair - that she needed a larger house and she didn't like the district she was living in anyway, a man moaning about the length of time it took his local council to clear up the social malaise of fly-tipping mattresses on the corner of his road, a woman saying she'd had to go to hospital because of the stress suffered from the noise of an extension being built on to an adjacent house, and an elderly woman sweetly asking how much his parliamentary salary was, because she'd had a wager with a friend on the amount. He told her, minus the expenses.

He'd had a drink with Archer beforehand. The agent had been commenting on the 'maleficent bauble' as he called the smartphone.

'Social media was set up to exploit a vulnerability in the human psyche by delivering a little dopamine once in a while. Every ping and flash from the phone has the addictive hallmarks of nicotine. Some very unpleasant forces are starting to exploit digital populism, mate. Populism is a style, a revolt against the dull, slow. institutionalised approach to modern politics.

'There's no time for the boring business of negotiation and compromise online. Could argue, I suppose, that the present incumbent of the White House is the perfect politician for the digital age. The tech can help though. Have you,' he'd asked, 'had to rush away from anywhere to get back to vote yet?' There's no need to ask people to do that. Walking through the divisions is a waste of time when electronic votes could be used.'

Jordan had things to do; mostly written work, including letters to constituents. The few MPs he knew employed secretaries of PAs to do them but, though expecting he would, in time, do the same, wrote them himself.

It was a pleasant day; he purposely held off from ringing Cluckrose, thinking that maybe he would interest her more if he didn't - though knowing it wouldn't. He vaguely thought about her cinema concern, which he'd done nothing about, and decided to walk up Parliament Hill and have a look over London. He'd not done it before, and maybe he'd be able to see the seat of Parliament and get a satisfying feeling knowing that he was now part of it.

On the way he watched pliant zombies using their phones and seemingly generating an aura of self-congratulation as if they'd invented the smartphone, as if Steve Jobs had cloned himself into infinitely receding copies before he died. They probably opened the weather app to see if it was a nice day rather than looking at the sky, and used sat nav for a journey they'd been doing for years.

He decided to have a bite to eat in Pippy's first, where he sat at the same table as when Luke Kenyon had flopped himself down in front of him. After a meal he felt more like a postprandial rest than a climb however mild the incline, and crossed the road to a pub.

It was the sort of Hampstead drinking house that local residents, their furniture and plant-laden gardens and dining rooms barely distinguishable from each other, would easily feel at home in. Feeling a tiny bit of an aversion to its rather precious atmosphere he bought a bitter and sat in a corner away from the counter.

There was a dividing wall behind him and an archway where there was obviously another table; he could smell sauerkraut and fish. As he supped he heard:

'Most of the dilemmas we wrestle with - the rise in the West of right-wing populism, the trauma of Brexit - have their roots in the pathologies of globalization and our collective confusion about what to do next.'

'Indeed,' spoke a rather exaggeratedly languorous voice. 'How to navigate this world of pulverising forces.'

He was almost sure it was Mister Kenyon. Perhaps this was his local, or he had made it so after Jordan had last seen him.

Other voices joined in. Jordan neither wanted to listen to nor talk politics. A jacket brushed past him, creased, almost rumpled; a linen one. He turned his head and saw Kenyon's back as he headed towards the toilets. He wasn't sure whether to move or not. As Kenyon came quickly away from his ablutions he spotted Jordan before the latter could bend his head down.

'Good lord, 'tis you again.'

He held out a limp hand. Jordan rather feebly shook it.

He gestured with his thumb. 'I'm around the corner with some people.' He lowered his voice. 'Truth is, they're rather boring me. Politics et cetera.' He frowned for a second. 'But then, you're a parliamentarian aren't you, you're used to it.'

He considered his listener for a while.

'Look, wait a mo and I'll excuse myself. I want to talk to you about something. D'you want to move over there?'

He gestured to an empty table in the opposite corner. Jordan rather reluctantly moved there.

Returning after a short while from what Jordan assumed was his excusing himself from the people he'd been sitting with, he joined him.

'Want another drink?'

'No thanks.'

'Look, there's some... paper evidence we're rather concerned about.'

'We?'

'I work for a government agency.''

'You told me both these things when I last saw you. I didn't really understand why you told me then, why are you repeating it?'

'Yes, unfortunately I do just about remember. You were going to keep mum. Hope you have.'

'I have.'

'Good, because you're going to have to be even more mum now. Why do we say 'mum'? However, this is quite a coincidence meeting you like this because I was going to contact you shortly.'

'Why?'

'Quite by accident I noticed a photograph of you attached to an LT7, doesn't matter what it is, but it suggests a low-level connection.'

"A low-level' what?'

'Threat.'

'I'm a threat?'

'Not you, a person who was aligned with you.'

'Aligned? Who?'

'A woman. You were seen with her in the Houses of Parliament. She is, though you may not be aware - '

'Cluckrose?'

'That's the name.'

'She had a child with her. What's she supposed to be, an infant suicide bomber?'

'You're being facetious. It's just that it's thought, an intelligent guess, really, that you have some sort of relationship with her.'

Jordan felt the phrase summed it up quite cogently.

'It's not so much her, rather someone she knows.'

'And?'

'I'm referring to the man who has something, could still have it; hidden it, though he says he's destroyed it. We've spotted a connection between you and this man.'

'A connection.'

'Yes.'

'Six degrees of separation, eh?'

'It's the Communist Party. Both this woman and this man are members.'

'Aren't we supposed to live in a democracy?'

He said this almost by rote, but it was a little surprising to him that she was a member. He knew it shouldn't have been.

'There are lots of people in it. Isn't this rather ridiculous? She may not even know him.'

'We believe that she does. She's seen him extracurricula, as it were.'

Jordan wasn't sure whether he was surprised or not at this. He knew he had no right not to like it. But he didn't. Was he a friend? A boyfriend? He felt a splinter of jealousy; they obviously had ideologies in common. Maybe other things.

'What has this to do with me?'

'Have another drink.'

'I don't know this man; she does. Shouldn't you be talking to her?'

'Maybe you'd warn her.'

'I'm not sure how to react to that.'

'Look, I can make this official you know. You're an MP.'

'We've established that.'

'There was silence for a while then Jordan sarcastically asked if he wanted him to spy on her.

'Not actually spy; just... see what she knows about him.'

'In case he's going to blow up Buck House? Lead a revolution?'

'What we'd like to know is whether he actually still has this potentially damaging document and, if so, what he intends to do with it, or whether he has actually destroyed it.'

'You do want me to spy on her. She's a friend; I don't want to do that. I couldn't.'

'Look, Jordan, may I call you that? I have to remind you that you are a Member of Parliament. It comes with responsibilities.'

'I'm not responsible to your Service or whoever.'

'We could pull rank and make you, though. Sorry to have to say that, but needs must.'

'That's not an apology, that's a rationalisation.'

'Jordan, we want you to help us. By 'us' I mean the State, if you like.'

'For the good of England's green and pleasant land?'

'Something like that. The balance of individual advancement in politics and loyalty to your party is often unstable, but you have a chance to, perhaps, combine both here.'

'And if I refuse?'

'Please don't, Mister Wilde. As I think I've said before, it may come to very little, but... ' He gave a resigned shrug.

'Not 'Jordan' any more then?'

Kenyon was silent, looking at his listener with an expression Jordan found difficult to decipher.

'Okay, I get information about this man, I don't know what sort I'm expected to get, and then what? Who do I tell it to?'

'Me of course. He just may have told this woman something about the document and she could perhaps tell you, that'd be useful. Failing that, maybe see if she'll tell you things about him.'

'What things?'

Those that may add up to someone who could, perhaps, be actively dangerous. You, of course, will tell me. I'll contact you. Easy. Now, how about that drink?'

Jordan stood. 'No, I've things to think about. Get my head around, as they say.'

'Be seeing you then.'

'Perhaps.'

He left without saying goodbye.

He wasn't sure what to do. He could, he supposed, ask her about the people she knew in the party - though she'd wonder how he knew she was a member - what sort of people they were, anyone in particular she knew. It was going to be difficult. The jealous teenager inside kicked in and maliciously thought it wouldn't be a bad thing for her friend to be out of the picture whether he was planning anything treasonable or not. He did have to make a decision, though.

The feeling of this unwanted, unjustified pressure from Kenyon seemed to increase a little as the days passed. Less than a week after the pub meeting her name appeared on his surgery list for six days hence.

He forced himself to adopt an attentive demeanour with the two people before her, virtually forgetting what they'd come about as soon as they'd left the room.

She was on her own this time and, without being invited, sat down immediately.

Often he didn't really notice what a person was wearing and if asked to describe it half an hour after meeting them, he struggled. But he did notice her high-necked sweater and tight skirt as he opened the door to the anteroom and beckoned her in. She sat slightly forward with her hands half-crossed between her knees.

'Hello again, Mister Wilde.'

'It's Jordan.'

'The cinema. Tried to do anything about it?'

'I've been busy.'

'You mean you've prioritised other things. At least you didn't say you haven't time.'

'I should have done something about it. I suppose you were expecting me too. Apologies, I will look into it. How's the do-gooding?'

'I hope we're doing some of that.'

'I wouldn't have thought you believed in the concept of those organisations. I assumed you thought they'd be stopping governments fulfilling their duties, that there should, ideally, be no need for organised charity.'

'Quite, but how much would the State do?'

'How's the party?'

She frowned.

'The local one. You're a member.'

'How d'you know that?'

'You mentioned it.'

The frown extended itself.

'Just curious is all.'

'Shouldn't think you had any interest whatsoever. And if you're saying it to make conversation, you can do, and have done, better.'

'How's Izzy?'

'Alright. For some reason she thinks she likes you. 'Are we going to see Mister Politician again?' she asks.'

'Give my regards. I was wondering, sort of, what kind of people you get at your meetings.'

'Leftie nuts, outcasts with chips on their shoulders, jealous of privilege, Morning Star and Marxist Weekly readers drunkenly singing The Red Fag in pubs.'

'The working class can kiss my arse, I've got the foreman's job at last'?'

'The inadequates, people living in the past, romantic idealists, and the posh ones pretending they're on the side of the workers because it's trendy to do so. I'm sure you can think of other stereotypes you've used.'

'I haven't used them. Wondered what was behind the ideology, the possible practicalities of it. Forgive my ignorance.'

'Is this a bit of sarcasm? By the people, for the people, brotherhood, liberty, each according to his need, the suffering of the many must not be the foundation of the wealth of the few...

You've heard most of it. I think, though, trying to sell it to a Tory would be like explaining social media to a ninety-five-year old.'

'From what I can tell, you'll end up with authoritarianism again, the electoral route to which is full of democracy's assassins using the very institutions of democracy to gradually kill it. It's a kind of tragic paradox.'

'You could say that's what Tory voters do, too. Anyway, what we have now is a system which rewards false debate and illogicality.'

Jordan watched her as she was speaking, her hands neatly interlocked on top of a leg. The phrase, used about a past film actress, 'sex with a teacup on her knee.' came to mind. He didn't want the conversation to take the turn it had, perhaps inevitably; he wanted, or rather needed, to elicit some things from her under the guise of a an amiable chat.

'He smiled. 'A few terrorists in the organisation then?'

'Wouldn't know; shouldn't think so.'

'Nobody doing anything covertly to bring the government crashing down?'

'Same answer.'

'Can't offer any tea. I'll have to get it organised. D'you get on with everybody there? Guess you're like-minded. Any special one?'

'No.'

'No boyfriend then?'

He grinned again, hoping it didn't look too false.

'That would be my business.'

''Course. Just chatting.'

'And I'm just going.'

As she stood, she said, 'Don't forget the cinema.' Then, opening her eyes wide as if slightly astonished, said, 'There were some members who went to some sort of building strike in town to stir up trouble.' Her eyes opened wider, 'How about that, eh?'

'Your sarcasm surprises me.'

'That's the only piece of practical, revolutionary activity I've heard of recently. Don't think they did much, if anything. Well-intentioned perhaps, but you need to organise yourselves before you can organise others. I'm all for strikes, of course.'

'As you would be.'

'It's a hundred and fifty years this year since the TUC was founded. Come to think of it, nobody's mentioned it yet. Should have a little celebration maybe.'

'Didn't the unions start out as conservative guilds merely to keep the wage differential between artisans and labourers?'

'In the beginning, yes. I shan't send you an invite.'

'How do you know I'd refuse it?'

'You'd have to be… very curious.'

'I am. I really would like to hear people's genuinely-held be-liefs; what they actually think about the establishment, capital-ism, over and above the well-travelled clichés.'

'Seriously?'

'Yes.'

Part of him at that moment felt he was being sincere.

'What are you going to do now?'

'Why?'

'Have you time for something to eat? I'm rather hungry. On me.'

'As ever, work to do. I'm leaving you again.'

She walked into the anteroom, he following.

'Look, If you're pushed you'll push back, won't you. Well, I'm going to be pushy. Let's make a… meeting, a connection.'

'You can say *the* word, you know.'

'Okay, I'll try again. Let's make a date.'

'There, it wasn't so difficult was it.'

'And?'

'I could, possibly, be free next Thursday afternoon. We'll see.'

'I'll make sure I'll be also.'

'Perhaps you'll have done something about the cinema busi-ness by then, eh?'

'I'll walk with you to your, I dunno, bus stop? Station? Car?'

'It's a bus stop. It's okay, you do what you've got to do'.

'I've finished here. I - '

'Bye then.'

She left the house, shutting the front door.

He watched her through the bay window walking smartly along the suburban street, thinking he could hear her high heels clicking on the neat, weed-free pavement.

As he cleared a few things off the desk, he knew she'd given him nothing that was useful. He lazily attempted to make a connection between Kenyon's man and a construction site. He saw none.

Paul was commenting on an article he'd read about Renaissance Man stating that we were 'all Renaissance Man now.'

'Ask a McDonalds worker, a labourer, plumbing apprentice, or an office cleaner if they think they are,' responded Ralph.

Perhaps he could bring this up in class when talking of social inequality, a subject which, when he'd begun teaching, had referred to social class, now it would refer to colour, sexual orientation and a seemingly endless list of differences and perceived inequalities - perhaps one could, he thought, in a neo-liberalist future if mentioning the colour or shape of a person's eyes, be 'eyeist.' He recalled mentioning a tyrannosaurus rex to someone, when a passing woman had interjected in an exaggerated whisper with, 'That's speciesist.' He'd hoped she was kidding.

'Maybe,' said Paul, 'only in a utopian future envisaged by Marx, where a man would 'hunt deer in the morning, catch fish in the afternoon and attend the theatre in the evening without *being* a hunter, fisherman or theatre critic' would such a being exist.'

'But, arguably, we have a dystopia: a socially atomised, corporate greed world of globalized capitalism where education still works for the good of the economic establishment. You get university flyers proclaiming, 'Get your three-year degree in just two years and start earning money sooner.'

I've seen 'em. I suppose though, outside their job, an individual can do many things; there are opportunities to express talents.'

'But they're not open to everyone; social class variables are in play. What about cultural expectations and formal education. We can't all achieve a Renaissance.'

'Perhaps we could define him in terms of making love to his partner, cooking breakfast and catching the train for work, without being a sexual predator, a cook or train driver.'

'Like it.'

They were walking along a street with an abundance of established trees in front gardens hanging over walls of London brick, with newly-planted pavement trees freshening the long, narrow road.

'I don't like long streets,' said Ralph. 'Don't think I'd like to live in one.'

'Probably 'cos you were delayed in the birth canal.'

'D'you think that's why we sometimes say, 'we're stuck'?'

'Could be.'

Ralph noticed Paul was getting restless, looking up and around him in quick movements like a wary bird.

'You know, Myers thinks that I won't face myself 'cos if I do I won't be loved. It's partly what I'm scared of; not being loved. The real me *can't* be loved, I suppose.'

'Do you feel that?'

'That's the fuckin' point, I'm escaping *from* me. I'm sorry, I shouldn't - '

'Carry on. Any time.'

'I've had a kind of recurring dream for a while now.'

'Does your bloke think that the unconscious wants to help, so by talking of your dreams to him he can help your unconscious get the conscious part better?'

'Assuming I've ever *been* better.'

'Also that the subconscious is benign? I don't think it is.'

'How's this: Freud discovered the instincts, the fears, the lusts, the hates; but if only he'd found some data, he could have been one of the greats.'

'Like it. What's the dream?'

'I'm in a city that I know, taking a route to somewhere I'm familiar with yet can't quite remember it. There are always wide streets, trees, slightly uphill, perhaps railway sidings in the distance, and with someone, but I don't know who they are. I talk to them. 'Come on, over here, this way. No, it's not this street, must be the next one.' But, it isn't and I can see the horizon and everything's flat and there's rarely anyone about, and I don't know where I am or what to do.'

'With someone?'

'Sometimes, I think, with you.'

CHAPTER TWENTY FIVE

'What does Myers make of it?

'I have to work it out myself, that's the point.' D'you know, my aunt used to tell my mum that when I was a baby I just pretended to be a baby.'

'She thought you were *that* bright?'

'D'you think my need for a god is a defence against facing myself? '

'Would that apply to everyone?'

''Course not.'

'Perhaps you want Myers to be your intellectual god.'

Paul stopped his restlessness.

'No, not anymore. He makes mistakes.'

'Such as?'

'He'll say 'undefinable' instead of 'indefinable' and he says 'bloody' sometimes.'

'Like your dad.'

'And sometimes he'll get out a notebook, hold up his pen, look at me expectantly and tell me to begin, as if he's playing at being an analyst.'

'Have you told him?'

'Haven't the courage.' He clenched his hands. 'I need to separate from him, he says.'

They came to a park entrance. Paul looked across at the City Of London sign.

'We had one of those in my park. I remember scratching a pair of bollocks on the edge of it when I was ten.'

'You said 'we'. There must be some belonging somewhere.'

'I fool Myers. I play games.'

'Isn't that counter-productive?'

'I talk about psychology with him and the little I know of Freud and others, and his response is to discuss, debate, argue with me as if I'm a friend or fellow therapist, not a patient. I kinda seduce him, I think. He shouldn't allow me to. I've been counting over the last week the number of people eating on trains and buses, station platforms, pavements et cetera - places that are not institutionalised as appropriate eating places, if you like - and out of forty adults, only seven were men.'

'Why do you think that was?'

'The old one: 'men do, women just want to be.' 'I have appetite, sate me.''

'Kind of fallopian tubes with teeth.'

'Bet you wouldn't say that to Lady Cluckrose.'

'Probably not; if I did I guess we'd discuss the nature of women, men's image of 'em, and more. Analyse it.'

'Like I do, but more… scary?'

'Maybe.'

'Have you noticed that the smell of passed-sell-by-date yoghurt is a perfect blend of vagina and faeces?'

'Can't say I have, but let's have a coffee or something.'

Paul began walking quicker.

'I've lived a false life since birth. I'm unrecognised, nothing has really been solid. The true part of me is buried, frightened to come out.'

'Be born.'

'Perhaps. Exams I've passed, drawings and stuff I've done and been praised for are only a kind of a symbolic recognition. *I'm* not recognised.'

'Seen as real?'

'Yes.'

'Perhaps, like he said, you're scared of separating. Do you see me as separate?'

'I need a plaque or something stuck on a wall stating that I've lived; an external recognition, an identity. I was the only one at school chosen to go to Art College. I was twelve.'

'I know.

'I knew I should have gone but nobody else was going, I'd have been on my own. You're going to say I'd have made friends. But I couldn't do it. The kids in my street would have ostracised me. I never told my parents about the college, they wouldn't have understood.'

He halted and stood looking down at the pavement for a while then caught up. They walked in silence then went into a corner cafe called Time for Tea.

It had tea cosies, quietly played Fifties pop music, floral table cloths matching the wallpaper, a photo of the young Queen, and occupied mostly by elderly females whose 'oohs,' 'aahs' and 'so

I saids,' Paul suggested quietly, indicated that they 'hadn't an idea in their bobbing, cackling heads.'

The women left. Paul bent forward a little towards Ralph and said, quickly looking towards the temporarily deserted counter, 'I sometimes live in a kind of third person; I'm continually watching myself; always, always, always.'

He sat up, looked around him then forward again.

'I don't stop analysing. Even as I'm saying this I'm aware of saying it and of analysing the awareness of saying I'm aware. I act a lot of the time, perhaps *all* of the time. I feel I'm telling the truth, feeling what I think, but I'm acting even now and even as I say 'I'm acting even now,' I'm aware there's a detached part that's watching me, listening to me and watching that which is watching me.

'It doesn't matter how quickly I'm thinking, moving, how occupied I am, it's there; a kind of infinite regress of observing. It rarely stops. Even now I see myself talking to you.' He paused. 'Perhaps at this moment I'm acting a man who needs a therapist.''

He looked away then back again.

'I know you think I'm so far out to sea I probably can't get back, but I am trying.'

'I know you are, and you will.'

'Thanks.'

'I'm glad you told me what you have.'

With Paul having more forms to complete for the Benefits Agency, and Ralph wanting to update some notes for class, they went silently to the station and returned to their respective homes. The latter had just begun work when his phone rang.

For a second or two he didn't recognise her voice. She used his name. He felt lifted. She was suggesting they see a noir film at a small cinema club near where she lived. He agreed readily. It was a matinee show the next day.

The following morning he cancelled his afternoon class, something he hadn't done for a long time. He didn't trust the stand-in to teach the students very much, but he'd make it up to them when he next saw them.

He met her outside an improvised cinema that looked as if it had once been a small warehouse. He was early but she arrived soon afterwards. They had a coffee at a modest bar, the walls of which were papered in old film posters; a true cineaste could have spent half a day looking at them.

'I took it as said that you like noir,' she said, 'I'd have been surprised if you didn't.'

'Of course, though it's hard to precisely define it.'

'How would you?

'Maybe strange, erotic, kinda poetic, ambiguous, cruel… Best I can do.'

'Could throw in cynical attitudes, sexual motivations. It's rooted in German Expressionism and hardboiled American crime fiction, I believe.'

'Don't forget the Deco.'

They watched the film - there were only five other customers, seated at the back - with men moving downhill through a forest and hopping across a stream still wearing their fedoras, ties and raincoats with collars pulled up.

Ten minutes after it started she leaned back, took her shoes off and rested her heels on top of the empty seat in front of her. He had an urge to lean forward, put his hand loosely around an ankle and trail it back along her calf, under her knee then further up. It was hard to concentrate on the movie.

When it had finished, she once again, but this time almost apologetically, indicated that she should be going home. They walked to the station talking about the film.

'The women,' said Ralph, 'are often portrayed in these films as secondary, as objects of sex.'

'What's new? Most films still do, and especially at that time. And are you pandering to the women's champion you see in me? Want brownie points?'

'No.'

'I'm a feminist, but - '

'Also a woman? Sorry, I pre-empted what I thought you were going to say.'

'I was. Why are you nervous?'

'You're perceptive. I'll stop being so.'

They passed a large, double-bayed, red brick Edwardian house with wide windows, black-and-white diamond pattern path leading to steps, a porch and the original front door painted jade green. Ralph lightly sneered.

'The Farrow & Ball marker of affluent, liberal middle class conventionality.'

'Does that last include me?'

'Anything but.'

'It needs trees in the front garden, though, to offset those windows.'

'Precisely. Put trees against a period house or planted along a street, or in an urban square, and they... '

'Illuminate?'

'Yeah, you see a building through or past a tree and it becomes part *of* the building, they become one.'

'And when they touch eaves and balconies - '

'And unkempt cemeteries with their large trees and wild bushes.'

'Hanging over eroded headstones and tombs.'

'A steeple rising above chestnut trees.'

'We're playing a sort of what-do-you-like game, aren't we,' she said, smiling. 'Here's another image: a tree at the side of a Regency window.'

'Okay; plane trees touching, above an Edwardian street.'

'Like bright fans behind Victorian chimneys.'

'Ah, England, their England.'

They stopped. Both laughed. He looked at her.

'You're so different now. So... '

'Are you rendered inarticulate?'

'I may be.'

'Let's get to the station.'

It was a short distance, begun with his 'What about the sun playing on leaves, glistening on window panes.'

'A bit corny. You're losing your creative spark.'

They were quiet on the train, he noticing, as ever, the dulled eyes of teenagers fixed on their phones. But it didn't annoy him this time; she'd created a momentary shield.

As they neared her stop, she said, as he began to stand, ''tis alright, I'll get home safely.' and stood.

'I shall ring you soon. Okay?'

She grinned. 'Yes.'

As the doors closed he could just see a remnant of that little wave, it was a friendly one this time. Perhaps, he thought, more than that. At least, it was she who had rung him..

Dusk was beginning. As he got off two stops further on, the station entrance was brightened by the LT roundel sticking proudly out above it, as was the pavement and a short, hairless man walking along it. The figure seemed familiar.

CHAPTER TWENY SIX

He'd just had a call from Archer asking him how he was getting on. He'd told him of the Weynard meeting, his strange response to which was to talk of party loyalty as an asset which once lost was hard to regain. Not that the Weynard thing meant anything like that, he couldn't really see himself thrusting against the political values he believed in for any personal advancement.

He remembered Archer saying, way back, that politics was the trade of the star rather than the compliant corps de ballet. Little chance of being a star; more likely some sort of cast-off if he didn't get some relevant information for Kenyon.

He was tempted to tell him of his dilemma so he could, perhaps, be informed of what Kenyon's employers could legally do, if they so wanted, to end his hardly-begun career. But he'd been elected by the public; he was, technically, representing his constituents, the people who'd got him his job. Could the secret services have any jurisdiction to make him do something he didn't want to, over something that was nothing to do with him?

The phone rang again. It was Kenyon. It began amiably enough with his, 'Hello old man, how's tricks? I thought of you recently when somebody asked me if I was ever interested in standing as an MP. I told him it was absurd. He said absurdity has never been a handicap in politics.'

'What did you want?'

'Well, just a chat, really, see how you were.' Then, as if an afterthought, 'What are you doing, or going to do about our friend the document man, Mister incriminating man. Anything?

'Not yet.'

'And how's the relationship game, eh? Getting on okay with the lady?'

'I've... an idea, it's a long shot and it'll be difficult but - '

'Doesn't matter if it gets us somewhere.

'Us?'

'Actually, yes. You're involved now.'

'Hardly. Only if - '

'Oh yes. As said, do your duty and all that, eh? And what's this idea then?'

'I'll tell you if I find out anything.'

'I think you mean 'when.' I'll be in touch.'

He made himself a drink. He knew he should do something - trying not to believe he had to - but she wouldn't, of course, invite him to any socialist anniversary at her party hall. He would have to go there uninvited, undoubtedly unwanted. And maybe she wouldn't even be there. Perhaps it would be more advantageous on a personal level if she was, he would look like a man of his word. Christ, this was going to be harder than being a politician. Cynically, some might say, it would require even more acting.

It wasn't difficult to discover where and when the local Communist Party held its meetings. There was one the evening after next.

He drove there, parked nearby, took a deep breath and went into a rather tatty building. There were about twenty people there; he'd purposely arrived a little early to get used to the feel of the place, and he made for the bar. A little of his favourite spirit would help.

As he turned to see if he'd missed spotting her, somebody asked if he was new there.

'Guess I am, but not a member, just sort of - '

'Seeing the lie of the land?'

'Yes, wondering what goes on. It interests me.'

'A sympathiser?'

'I just want to understand, I suppose.'

The man went off to sit on one of the seats.

More people came in, a few younger ones - his un-thought image had been of elderly stalwarts, rather grizzled and determined-looking, even bitter perhaps. One of them said good evening to him, he too asking if he was a new member or thinking of becoming so.

'Not sure, but I'm interested in the movement though, knowing not that much of it to be honest. I should know more of course.'

'You certainly should, Jordan Wilde,' said a voice by the side of him. 'What's a Tory doing here? Spying on us?' It was said with a grin.

Jordan forced a laugh. 'Yes, I've been sent here to ascertain whether there's any danger of a potential revolution beginning, the seeds of which have been sown here. Even, maybe, that the Houses of Parliament could be blown up.'

'Well, Guy Fawkes had a go, possibly the only honest intention ever to exist in that place. I'm Edward, by the way.'

'As said, I'd like to know more about the views here, what you do and what makes people join. I know we could ask that of any political affiliation, but I know little about this one.'

'As long as you don't believe the propaganda - which you probably do - that we're all envious of privilege, angry 'cos of a ballsed-up infancy, sociopaths and losers who hate the world and that we've never grown out of a rebellious adolescence.'

'Yes, you do come in for a bit of flak.'

'More a blitzkrieg, and mostly from the media of course. As Karl baby says: 'Those who own the means of material production control the means of mental production."

'Fair enough.'

'What we see as 'news' is also manufactured. However, you're my MP so I guess I should be nice to you, but... nothing personal you understand.'

Just then the tall, broad frame of Eaton stepped up in front of the row of seats.

'Good evening. I shan't be saying much but it has been suggested by a comrade,' he looked briefly at the half-full chairs, 'though I don't think she's here yet, that we celebrate the hundred-and-fiftieth year of the TUC. There's a proud history of unionism in this country that needs celebrating.

'You may not know, if you don't, you should, that the first TUC meeting was held in 1868 when the Manchester and Salford Trades Council convened the founding meeting in the Manchester Mechanics Institute at what was then 103 David Street. Most work and jobs then were useful, needed, often basic and primary; now it seems, as Orwell said, 'The instinct to perpetuate useless work is, at bottom, simply a fear of the mob. It's safer to keep them too busy to think.'

'However, the fact that the TUC was formed by Northern Trades Councils was not coincidental. One of the issues which prompted this initiative was the perception that the London Trades Council was taking a dominant role in speaking for the Trades Union Movement as a whole. Yes, another bloody sectarian problem. Never mind, they came together and have done many good things for the people. So, any suggestions, ideas, let me, or even Ms Cluckrose know.'

He walked away to the trestle table near the entrance and sat.

Edward grinned at Jordan. 'I don't think you should let him see you, he'll take issue with you on everything. You know I could mention this to the local rag.'

'I don't want them to know, but if they did I'd tell them the truth; I genuinely want to find out what people think, what they feel about your movement's philosophy.'

'It's a bit more than a 'movement' don't you think?'

'Of course, and it's not seen, let's say, as 'subversive' here as in the US perhaps, but bad enough by most people, and of course I'm not going to publicly, as it were, excuse it, legitimise it, but I do want to know about the people who support it, the believers, if you like. Let me buy you a drink.'

'It's okay.' Edward looked at him with a sceptical smile. 'I think you and your mob would like this country to be more like the States, actually. There, the rich, the corporations have fostered a hatred virtually since the civil war. To protest there about bad wages, living conditions, especially unionisation, has been skewed into being un-American, i.e. unpatriotic. Anything perceived as being remotely socialist is almost treason.'

'Supposedly you've done your bit with strikes and demos and stuff, eh?'

'Did quite a few protests at one time; though not as much as I should have. Haven't done anything for a while, until recently, when me and a couple of others were at a strike, but it was a pretty tame affair, no real co-ordinated action, not much ideology, really. Guess we should have done something more than we did, which was very little.'

CHAPTER TWENTY SIX

'What sort of strike?'

'Building site. Shouldn't think it lasted long, probably little more than a go-slow in its effect.'

Just then a man came up to Edward and said, 'Can't stay; just popped in to get out of the flat, starting a new topic tomorrow, one I haven't done before and it's taking longer to prepare than I thought.'

'I was wondering if you'd come. Have a drink, at least.'

'No, it's okay. It's tempting, but I'm going to have to force myself to go back now. I've had some fresh air, I shall dutifully return, mein herr. See you.'

He nodded to Jordan and left, with Edward calling after him, 'She's not here, mate.'

'A regular? Seems a bit familiar.'

'That's Ralph, he's fairly new, came with me on the strike thingy. Yeah, I would like a drink. Thanks.'

After getting it and handing it to him, Jordan asked why he had joined the party.

'What started it, I think, was reading The Ragged Trousered Philanthropist when I was about sixteen. It certainly wasn't the kind of book my dad would have read or commended to me. He was an accountant for HM Prisons and, I suppose, fitted the stereotype. You know; How do you tell an extrovert accountant? He looks at *your* feet when he's talking to you.

It got me interested in the workers, largely invisible to the rich except when they want their roofs fixed, boiler mended, house painted et cetera. Read a bit of Engels, and Thompson's The Making of the English Working Class: 'I am seeking to rescue the poor stockinger, the Luddite cropper, the utopian artisan et cetera from the enormous condescension of posterity.' And before you say it; class very much still exists.'

'Am I that obvious?'

'Well, you are a Tory.'

'I was going to suggest we don't talk politics, yet here I am - '

'Everything's political, chum. It's about power.'

'And *we* have it at the moment.'

'Your mates have got it; you support them and help them get more of it under the guise of it being 'good for the economy.' Think I'll have another.'

'At least you didn't say 'cronies.' It's alright, I'll get it.'

Jordan repeated his initial order.

'Are the other members as passionate as I feel you are? Do they come from a socialist background, or maybe some event made them choose an anti-status quo viewpoint? Perhaps they're just good people, so are determined to see some sort of social fairness, a justice, if you like.'

'Could be a combination of all those things. Difficult to say.'

'You did come then.'

It was Claire Cluckrose who had, obviously, just come in. She was standing a few feet to the side of the two men.

Edward looked from her to Jordan and back again. He frowned, mouth slightly open.

'You know each other?'

'We've met. He canvassed me.'

'Is *that* what they call it these days?' he grinned.

'Er, I didn't know whether you'd be here or not,' said Jordan.

'I didn't really think you'd come. You've surprised me.'

'I did say I wanted to come.'

'I'm still surprised.'

'Think I'd stick out like a sore thumb?'

'That's a fifth-rate analogy.'

'Yes, ma'am.'

'Are you going to let me in on this?' asked Edward.

'I do know him.' She briefly looked around her. 'Anyone recognised you yet?'

'Only this one.'

'It threw me too, and he's something in the city,' said Edward.

'So was cholera. Let me buy you both a drink, I can see what you've got, I think.'

As she did so, Jordan wished it was just the two of them there, or preferably somewhere else, like on a beach in the Maldives, of a taverna in Corfu, maybe a sauna in Karlskrona.

She gave them their drinks. He was about to ask her if she was going to stay when she said, looking at him with an amused glint in her eyes, 'I was listening on the radio to some MPs proving they were both culturally and actually illiterate, when I thought that maybe politicians are merely expensive optical illusions, simulacra of people glitching and repeating - creatures that look flashy but lack substance, merely a trick of the light. And as much as I'd like to hear your response to that, I shall speak to Eaton for a while then go.'

She went to join the man at the trestle table.

'Those legs again,' said Edward, looking after her. He took another gulp. 'Tell you what; he's got something that'll shit your party up.'

'Who's 'he'? And what's he got then?'

'Never you mind; but your lot have been more naughty than usual, mate,'

'Yes? When?'

'Way back. Important stuff, pal. Trying to turn the Cold War into a hot one. Lots o' big guns needing big bangs. I mean, what was the cost of a fifteen-inch shell then, eh? let alone three air-craft carriers, a flotilla of frigates, a brace of battleships and a sniper in a pear tree. Not bad, eh? Especially as I'm drinking on an empty stomach.'

'Have another, you can tell me about blowing my party away.'

Edward threw his arms in the air. 'Bang!'

'You're making a bit of a noise. Let's sit down somewhere on our own.'

'Cheers. Don't mind if I do, what? Love taking the mickey out of your lot. But, ta, anyway.'

Jordan led him to the front row of seats where he resumed drinking as soon as another glass had been put into his hand.

'How are you going to do it then?' Jordan asked.

'With what my friend's got up his sleeve or, rather, stashed away somewhere.'

'Where's 'somewhere?''

'Dunno, at home I suppose.'

'I'm not even sure who you're talking about.'

'Told you. Ralphy boy. He's my mucker.

'What's he going to do with it? Has he still got it?'

'That'd be telling, wouldn't it. Why are you this interested?'

'Am I?'

'You want to save your mob from a big embarrassment don't you.'

'How would this 'embarrassment' manifest itself? You haven't given me details.'

'I don't know that many myself, don't think there was much, but I'm not saying any more. To be honest, though, it may all be a nothing.'

'You've changed your mind.'

'It seemed genuine. I don't know.'

'What seemed genuine?'

'What I said.' He drained his glass. 'A tale about infiltration and winding up the Brits to... I wonder if Eaton's planning any more for the evening.'

The latter, talking to a few members sitting opposite him, raised a hand to Edward who returned the gesture.

'I've a mind to introduce you to boss man; he'd probably eat you up. But I'm going home to get some food and sleep this off. Cheers. Thanks for the drinks.'

As he walked away he stopped and turned.

'I was thinking. I wonder if Ralphy knows that Cluckrose knows you, eh? Cheers, man.'

Jordan turned his head towards the trestle table; Eaton was still there. She wasn't. He wondered if it was still okay for Thursday. Not wanting to engage with Eaton, he left soon afterwards, pondering on what Edward had said. It wasn't that much but he had, he supposed, something to tell Kenyon.

He had no way of contacting him but it didn't matter. He had been home barely an hour when the man rang him.

'Any jolly old news, Mister Jordan?'

'About what?'

'I think you're cognisant of what I mean.'

'I may have. I was speaking to somebody this evening who knows the person I think you and your... employers are interested in. I saw him for a minute myself.'

'Where?'

'At the local Communist Party place.'

'I see you're biting the ideological bullet then and putting yourself out a bit. All for a good cause, of course.'

Jordan gave him a summary of what he'd been told.

'Okay. Seems as if it could still be in his home. I'll run it up the flagpole, see if anyone salutes. Be good.'

He allowed Edward's farewell remark to sink in. Was this Ralph person the girl's boyfriend or something? He didn't like it. He didn't like the immaturity of his feelings either. And he still hadn't bothered to even attempt to save her cinema project.

CHAPTER TWENTY SEVEN

After refreshing himself in yet another up-and-coming east London 'events' café, he continued his afternoon walk in Hackney. On one side of him was a silver graffiti-covered pub, on the other a Victorian factory being converted to apartments trendily called The Leathercloth Factory. They were surrounded by Sixties flats and a run-down Nineteenth Century industrial estate. He would prefer to have been strolling past Georgian houses, magnolia gardens and magic mews and gazing at the steepled skylines of Hampstead and Highbury, Pimlico and Putney, or along the Thames to Henley, and the Lea Navigation from Limehouse Cut to Ware; walks, often with Paul, he'd done before.

A few hours previously he had been teaching sexual divisions to a class of mostly mature females and was telling them that male domination of the world was fostered by the anticipatory roles manifested in children's books. His research had not been that rigorous, relying mostly on what he could remember when young and from books saved from childhood; a few Peter and Janet ones in particular.

He'd spotted in several that the illustrations, apart from showing male fire fighters and doctors, invariably showed Peter in front of Janet when buying ice creams at the seaside or looking up at a Punch and Judy show on the beach, hurrying towards daddy or mummy, or running to the swings; as well as the 'Here is Janet helping mummy' and 'Peter helping daddy' pictures.

Although it held a mild academic interest, a small, interior voice was suggesting that the women in the class would think better of him. Certainly better than if they'd seen the A4 sheet which Paul, as a joke, had recently typed for him to hand out in class.

'Because men must not infringe upon women's traditional areas of authority, but under the name of 'Liberation' women can selectively encroach upon ours, and if we open a door for them we're male chauvinist pigs and if we don't we're ill-mannered louts and if we call them 'love' we are patronising yet are typically male if we don't address them in terms of endearment and if we want to make love on successive nights we're animals and if we don't we're useless and if we, even light-heartedly, suggest in the hearing of a feminist that we'd like 'to give her one' they accuse us of sexism - confusing it with 'sexuality' - and if we go out for an occasional drink with friends we're with our drinking cronies again and if we give love to our children we pander to them and if we raise our voices to them we're tyrants, and because hell hath no fury like a wife whose husband won't or cannot give her what she wants she can turn his children against him with little compunction and if she runs off with the milkman she gets the house, the kids and the alimony and it's your fault because you're a bastard and... for many other reasons we're f****d if we're gonna support the women's Liberation movement.'

Paul, though aware of the out-of-date 'Liberation' word, had seen no harm in it; it was merely a 'relatively mild piece of bitter, male exaggeration,' he'd explained.

He caught a bus travelling further east and looked out of a top deck window. He was seeing terraces of London bricks, ten-in-a-row chimney pots, and the ever-present hovering cranes, emblematic of the area's 'regeneration.' As somebody born and bred not far from this area he couldn't take it s new appellation of 'Village' seriously.

 He turned two fingers and thumbs into the rectangular frame of an imaginary lens. It wasn't a lush setting: the natural frame of the window was filled with a wasteland of rubble and bricks where tower blocks were going to be built, empty beer bottles, a remnant of a bonfire, a frame of a bicycle sticking up like an isosceles triangle, then pubs, cafes, a row of grey shops and a couple of youths playing footie under a lamp post with a bald tennis ball. This was, physically and emotionally, rather too close to his childhood.

Getting off at a Tube station he went back to his flat. As he entered the hall he noticed the kitchen door was shut. He opened it and did the same with the dining room one also. He rarely closed the doors; he liked them open, liked space, at least an illusion of it.

There was a plant in a glass wall holder that looked a little awry, as if something or someone had brushed against it. It was all slightly strange. He opened the cutlery drawer in the kitchen to make a coffee and there were two knives among the spoons. He had probably done that. The week before, when involved in thinking through a philosophical theory he wanted to explain clearly to students the following day, he'd absent-mindedly poured bran flakes into a tea pot and placed the salt in the fridge.

But the doors. This was more than his occasional domestic misplacement of things. He was reminded of a film he'd seen as a child in which a man hid things from his house or put them in different places from their institutionalized ones, or hung a painting upside down in order to make his wife feel that she was going mad. But this was more real. Wasn't it? He went to his bedside chest where sketches he'd made when in the Lake District with Paul; and of a naked girl when at a life drawing class were.

They weren't quite right, out of order somehow. He then remembered the small mat inside the front door. It had been askew; he hadn't left it like that. Someone had been here.

For a few seconds he wondered where he'd put the sheet of paper - the 'yellow piece' as he internally saw it - then went to the bedroom and pulled out the large drawer in the base of the bed and, on a track suit which he'd used for a short-lived interest in jogging and half-hidden under several pairs of pants and socks, was the paper, still.

Why didn't they think of looking there? Had years of finding fiendishly clever hiding places hindered there ability to look somewhere where a person not seriously hiding something would put it? He considered. He needed to share this with someone. Not Paul, he would worry. Better Edward. He probably wouldn't be in till the evening; he'd ring him then.

He couldn't quite understand the intrusion, the break-in; there were no signs of the latter, they'd been clever. How did they, or trilby man, know he hadn't made a copy? Maybe they thought he was, after all, too innocent, too unsophisticated to do so. Knowing there was little logic to it, he went to his study and quickly made copies. He perused them for a while then tore them into pieces and flushed them away in the bathroom.

He wasn't really sure of what they wanted this stuff for - he had immediately dismissed the idea of a common-or-garden burglary almost as soon as he'd realized someone had been in his home. Was it because it really did involve a secret, one that had been potentially dangerous for the country's citizens? If so, they were fulfilling their brief, their patriotic duty towards the country they served; or was it to protect the government of that time and, by political association, the current one? He thought he'd try Edward's number anyway.

He'd just retuned home and listened to Ralph's exposition of the last hour or so and who he felt might have been responsible.

'Are you sure there was a break-in?'

'Yes, too many little things for there not to have been; though I don't know how it was done. Nothing seemed forced.'

'Well, if you're sure. Are you worried?'

'Shouldn't think they'd come again.'

'Perhaps you should really hide it this time.'

'Or give it to somebody to keep.'

'I'll have it.'

'No, they could suspect you. I don't think they would Paul.'

'Wouldn't it bother him?'

'Not if I tell him something. It'll be alright.'

'I was speaking to a Tory MP last night when you came in, god forgive me. Don't think you recognised him. He's our local one. I got a bit drunk I think.'

'What was he there for?'

'Wanted to understand, he said, why we're not Conservative voters. Actually, I can't remember much of it. He bought the drinks.'

'I forgive you, just. See you at the next meeting then, or before. Bye.'

He read the page again and wondered if there could have been a war at the time. In any event, the rich, using the seductive force of patriotism as a national response to war, would have built a larger army which, in the end, would have meant workers dying to defend the property of the rich He thought that maybe he was being too simplistic to quote Marx and say that all war was class war, but, cynically, he could have added that by the system using the concept of objectifying people and turning them into consumers, into objects of profit, that in war they became objects of death.

He rang Paul who asked him to come round.

It wasn't far. He drove there and parked behind the Fifties block of flats he lived in. It was on the fourth floor: a narrow corridor, cramped rooms, a small kitchen with its door painted red - for Ralph, other than politically, an alienating colour - and a small balcony, the railings of which were covered with the leaves and flowers of potted plants that Paul seemed to give loving care to.

As he entered, Ralph casually gave its occupant the sheet of paper.

'Stick this somewhere for me. I was gonna throw it away, but you may as well have it. Just for interest. You know what it is.'

Paul took it 'Mind if I fold it?' He did so. 'I'm supposed to be seeing Myers later.'

'I forgot. It's his day, isn't it.'

'When I last saw him He was chatting to me - he tells me things about himself sometimes, not sure he's not infringing the rules of psychotherapeutic practice, but never mind - about a patient of his who admitted he was sadistic towards women. Anyway, it turns out that when he was a baby he had bitten his mum's nipple and she'd thrown him away from her, literally threw him across the bed. I don't know how he got back to that memory, but still.

Myers pointed out that maybe he was kind of testing women. That is, if he hurt them, mostly emotionally, occasionally physically, and they left him, it was really his mother throwing him away again, discarding him. If they stayed with him afterwards, then it meant that they loved him.

'I don't hurt women though. Not that I have any. Coincidence you bought that thing round 'cos there seems to be a few Cold War anti-Russian jokes going about.'

'Jokes are about rule-breaking.'

'And sick jokes are an escape from stark reality, yes?'

'Quite. Like the battle axe mother-in-law ones.'

'Also detracts from her being a sex object for the son-in-law perhaps. This bloke goes into a shop in Stalingrad and asks the counter lady, 'You don't have any meat?' She replies, 'We don't have any fish. It's the shop over the road that doesn't have any meat.' This babushka asks an official if communists or scientists invented communism. 'Communists of course,' said the official. 'Thought so,' she says.' 'If scientists had invented It they would have tested it on dogs first.'

'Don't let 'em bother you. They were justified at the time, but they're about Russian State capitalism, not Marxian socialism. You know that, anyway.'

'A man tries to call the KGB after a fire at its headquarters. An operator replies that he can't be connected as the KGB has just burnt down, and says the same when the man calls back a minute later. The third time, the operator recognises his voice. 'Why do you keep calling back? I just told you the KGB has burnt.' 'I know,' the man replies. 'I just like to hear it."

'Enough, Paul.'

'A man trying to buy a car in Moscow is told it'll be delivered in ten years time. 'Morning or afternoon?' asks the man. The garage man says, 'It'll be ten years, what difference does it make? ' and he says, 'Well, the plumber's coming in the morning.'

Ralph looked across at him sitting on his sofa.

'Enough.'

He'd noticed before that when his friend was telling jokes, even in some near-maniacal moments of shrill hyperbole, building, often from bland, everyday comments, a whole pyramid of ludicrous and often funny narratives and bizarre incidents, when he'd stopped, sometimes suddenly, there was an emptiness behind his eyes.

'Nervous about seeing Myers?'

'No. Yes, s'ppose so.'

'Do you know what you'll be talking about?'

'Whatever it is, it'll soon get round to childhood memories of my dad, images et cetera.'

'Like?'

'How long you got?'

'Up to you.'

'Like, when he'd be in a pub - mum was rarely with him - and he'd give me some crisps while I was outside. I'm not sure whether kids were allowed in or whether he wanted to be with his mates without me. He kinda bribed me with sweets and stuff. I didn't mind being outside. I peeped in sometimes; all loud laughs and smoking and men saying things like, 'I said to 'er, 'While you're down there, darlin'... 'and men laughing. I couldn't understand why they laughed about the things they did. There were few women in there then. 'Alienated,' 'brutalised,' are some of the words Myers uses.'

'Does he mean your da,d or you?'

'Mostly me.'

'Is he right?

''Course. I try to be... fair to him, my dad, in my mind, and can recognize he had to kow-tow to people 'cos he had no talents really, no skills; he was an unskilled labourer, after all, but... '

'You can't forgive him.'

Paul looked up sharply. 'Suppose not.' Another silence. Then, 'D'you know, when I'm thinking, talking, I'm aware that I'm thinking it, and I know that I know that I'm thinking I t, and I know that I know that I know that I'm thinking it. '

'You've mentioned this. I'm not playing Freud here, but is Myers your 'father'?'

'He says things like 'Every woman you meet is your mother, every man, your father.' Also, that for the lost child, the wish for a different father could be the beginning of homoeroticism, of something like that. Well, I'm oft to see him now.'

He stood. I know you're going to offer me a lift, but it's okay, I'll get a bus, doesn't cost much.'

Ralph followed him down the flights of stairs and crossed the road with him to the stop.

'When you gonna see the Ice Maiden again?'

'Do you really see her like that?'

The bus came.

'Keep trying,' said Paul as he got on then smiled through the closing doors.

Ralph walked to a nearby café that, at this time of day, he knew would possibly be empty, and ordered a rare fry-up. After a stodgy but satisfying cherry pie and custard he thought again of his friend.

It was obvious to him that at an early age his needs hadn't been met. In fact, he recalled Paul telling him what his therapist had said; that he was certain that he had been left to cry on his own and that when his mother did eventually come to him he had emotionally switched off, disassociated himself from her and, possibly, his father.

Myers had, he'd told him, little doubt that it went back to him needing the breast yet having his nappy changed, and being given the tit when he'd shit himself. That was the beginning, and it seemed to Ralph that however optimistic his analyst was, his friend's psyche would never fully compensate for his unmet, barely-born needs.

The analyst was also adamant that all religions, in some way or other, were to do with faeces and the physical and psychological cleansing of it. For him, people's initial sensations other than from the breast came with the wiping away of faeces, and their first internalisation of guilt came when they messed themselves, thus indicating they'd done something 'wrong.' Baptism, the pilgrimage of Hindus to The Ganges, the word 'salvation' arising from the Roman word for 'salt' used for cleansing, were some of his obvious examples. 'In the beginning was the body'seemed a foundation stone for Gordon Myers.

This would interest his patient, and Ralph could imagine Paul being intellectually excited by these hypotheses and airing his scant knowledge of them, though having his own thoughts on the subjects, and speaking to Myers as if they were fellow analysts.

He looked around him at the café's faded wall colours and at a fly-spotted fluorescent ceiling light. As he was the only occupant, he decided to ring her.

'I was thinking of you a moment ago,' she answered.

'A rare event?'

'Suppose so.'

'And what were the thoughts?'

'I was thinking about how we know things.'

'Yeah, what does it mean to 'know."

'It seems to me the only way we can know anything is 'see, hear, touch, taste, smell.''

'Quite, and no rationalist has yet come up with an a priori synthetic truth; something that tells us about the world independent of experience '

'So, I guess it's science then in the end.'

'No. Science, like magic and religion, is a self-contained belief system that cannot of itself be wrong, plus what a scientific truth is today will be heresy tomorrow, their paradigms shift, 'truth' shifts.'

'Maths doesn't.'

'Maths can only tell us something about the world when it's applied to the world, there's no numbers in nature, and everything behind the equals sign is another way of saying that which is before it. They're also analytic truths; that two chairs plus two chairs make four chairs is true regardless of whether the chairs exist or not.'

'So, everything's a kind of construct then?'

'Yes, language is the ultimate one. We can't get outside of it. let's talk about … movies or - '

'The 'favourite films' game?'

'There are worse ones. What's your favourite word?'

'Sarajevo.'

'I like Derrarra, though not sure what it means.'

'it's Italian.'

'I watched an Italian film the other evening: Two Women.'

'La Ciociara.'

'I can imagine you in that polka-dot dress when Loren was lying on - '

'Do you imagine me much? Little fantasies?'

'Sometimes.'

'What else am I wearing?'

'In the film, or in my fantasies?'

'Isn't the polka-dot one a fantasy?'

'Not really.'

'But the others?'

'This is dangerous territory. How's work?'

'A deflection. It's going okay; we're getting stronger links with African countries now. I was reading about Freud the other evening.'

'Ever wondered why he's so well-known?'

'I assume that's a rhetorical question.'

'The media, owned of course by a ruling class, pushes out theories to benefit its owners. His is one of them.'

'Benefit?'

'If the world perceives its troubles, its violence, its pathology et cetera as a result of the unconscious, attention is taken away from criticism of its major capitalist institutions.'

'What about Marx then? He's equally well-known.'

'Doubt whether you've heard of him much without a negative branding attached, except, of course, at the meetings. You rarely know him as an economist or philosopher either, he's just some almost-crazed, ruthless, evil Father Christmas, though you could argue that he was rather naive in that he thought people were somehow essentially good.'

She looked at him for a moment. 'You're not always like this, Mister Kearns.'

'You asked me a question.'

'Are you annoyed, angry at something or someone?'

'Maybe. But certainly not you.'

'Good to hear.'

'Knock, knock.'

'Er… who's there?'

'Little old lady.'

'Little old lady who?'

'Didn't know you could yodel.'

'Promise me you won't say that again.

'If you promise you'll have a meal with me, or theatre or something.'

'Alright.'

'Tomorrow or - '

'Can't; Thursday tomorrow. Ring me soon.' There was a brief pause. 'You know, I almost miss you.'

He felt pleased. This was progress. He felt like felling Paul, but thought better of it.

CHAPTER TWENTY EIGHT

His uncle's secretary had just called - Jordan hadn't recognised the name, perhaps the old boy had got a new one, Matilda had been with them for years - asking him to call her CEO boss. It was Friday; nothing had come of the previous day. He had rung Cluckrose in the late afternoon to be told that, unexpectedly, she had to work all day. He'd been disappointed.

He rang his uncle.

'Jordan, my boy, we haven't spoken for a while. How's everything?'

'That would take a long while to answer.'

'Yes, but you're alright I take it?'

'Getting by.'

'You're missed somewhat. I know we lent you out to the subsidiary for a different sort of experience, but the firm misses you.'

'Part of me misses it.'

'What part is that Jordan?'

'The family part I suppose.'

'The party not replacing it then? Your cronies in the House?''

'I have few of those.'

'I assume you miss finance.'

'I could be doing some of that any time soon.'

'Anything the firm can assist with?'

'Shouldn't think so, and this may be more prosaic perhaps than the firm's used to; I nearly said 'we' then.'

'You'll always be here, Jordan. Talking of which, let us know of any Government projects. I don't know what you're doing of course; infrastructure investment, funding, bureaucracy even, though most of that stuff's tied up, I suppose; but we could always help.'

'Could argue that sounds like a kind of political insider trading; could be perceived as a little immoral, uncle.'

'No, no, not at all, someone will always offer their expertise to government.'

'Financial acumen.'

'Yes.'

'Nice generic term; could mean a quasi legal catch-all.'

'I wouldn't ask you to do anything... what's the term, 'dodgy.''

'Of course not. How's aunt Sybil?'

'Well.'

'And my cousins?'

'The same. They'll both be coming into the firm shortly I hope.'

'Fine. We'll talk another time, uncle; things to do. Thanks for enquiring.'

'Of course, as befits a busy representative of the people. Cheerio then, Jordan.'

He had little to do for a while; he wanted to think through Claire's change of mind. He wasn't sure whether he believed her, but couldn't imagine her lying.

He wanted, felt he needed, to get things moving with her, something established; he pushed 'something' away, he meant a relationship, something real. She attracted him. A lot. Why did she have to be so Left, so damn revolutionary? She was doing good, her charity work should have satisfied her social conscience, shouldn't it? But then, her socialism wasn't just about community and helping others, she believed in it. He'd supposed, really, she would be more intelligent than that.

It was the grin, its surety, the ultra-confidence behind it and, seemingly, everything else; every nuance of her abilities, appearance, her perspective on the world. Reality was a two-way process, but it was as if - he knew it was fatuous as he thought it - she felt, knew, she was more real than the reality around her, as if reality wasn't relative at all, but a kind of absolute, *her* absolute.

What of this friend of hers; 'Ralphy' was it? Who was he? He remembered he'd seen the man for a few seconds, but could barely visualize him. He was hardly a muscle-bound superman; taller than himself, possibly, but not a classic cleft chin hero. He knew this wouldn't really matter though, what would, as a friend, a partner - he fought shy of 'lover' - would be the basic prerequisite of sharing a political *weltanschauung* that broached little contradiction.

He had just finished some work for a constituent; helping him draft a letter to his local council complaining about the length of time between dustbin days, and saying that he would contact them himself if things didn't improve, when Weynard's PA rang him and asked him to come to the House and see her boss. He went.

He began immediately.

'Sit down, Mister Wilde. Try not to keep you too long. PFI; rail, energy, water. When these were privatized three decades ago, ostensibly to increase efficiency, widen share ownership blah, blah, blah, we all thought it a good thing.'

'Perhaps not all.'

'No, and we know what happened, though we mustn't, of course, say it publicly, and let's face it, we have extended the grip of private companies and finance further into day-to-day life.'

'Including the Royal Mail at a fraction of its worth.'

'We know all this and also that almost three decades after water was sold-off, share ownership is now largely in the hands of a small group of international investors.'

'Many of them based in tax havens,'

'Yes. Meanwhile new investment has been financed by borrowing rather than by shareholders. I mean, when water was privatized, we generously took on the outstanding debts of the sector - almost five billion of them - leaving the new owners debt-free.'

'I'm aware of this.'

'Also, and you must know this, German banks, Chinese et cetera own more of our rail system than we do and use profits to subsidize cheaper fares in their own countries.'

'Quite.'

'Thing is, it seems the current thinking is, or will be, that we need to put our own banks and companies into these things.'

'Not the people's money.'

'That's the Opposition's intention of course.'

'Drive out the foreign ones, somehow?'

'Doubt that's possible; but reduce their impact, their invest-ment. Energy, and especially rail need more money ploughed in and they need to be more attractive to our own companies. The more people realize the amount of foreign money invested... ' He shrugged.

'In short, we're potentially losing voters.'

'Indeed. Also, although I mentioned debts just now, we have to be sensitive to concerns about excessive profits. We've recently proposed a cap, for example, to end rip-off energy prices.'

'Should gain a few votes there.'

'I called you in to pick your brains; perhaps there's ways of attracting more British money, if you like.'

'My family firm can't be - '

'Of course, not directly, anyway. There are obviously other people working on this, early days and all that. Just thought you may be able to help somewhat. The Opposition's manifes-to pledge to take back control of water, rail et cetera and fix the energy markets is seen by an increasing number to be radically exciting and transformative, though it'll never happen, of course. Think on it then. I'll be seeing you.'

There was a bit of a forced smile, Jordan thought, as he left. He could, though, he supposed, think of something, but somehow the government needed to virtually guarantee a profit with their privatization incentives, and how could they legally decrease, or attempt to get rid of foreign investment? Nevertheless, he'd see what he could do.

He went to another parliamentary meeting, attended rather sparsely and unenthusiastically about some minor welfare reform or other and decided to ring her later in the evening.

After a meal in one of his favourite City restaurants, he re-turned home and did so.

She answered immediately. 'Did I not say that I would contact you?'

'Think you did.'

'You know I did.'

'Look, I may be assuming too much, but it is a nice evening and - '

''Nice' should be discarded from the language.'

'A pleasant evening.'

'What do you propose to do on such a one?'

'Ideally, see you.'

'To do what?'

'Maybe a walk, a drink. A traditional London pub somewhere?'

A silence.

'Are you still there?

'Supposing I said no? Yes, there is one I know that's bearable.'

She told him its location and when she would be there.

He recognised it as soon as he got out of the station; The shrubs, ferns, the trendy grey, the sort of place that would suit her; casually, easily sure of itself. He hoped Kenyon wouldn't be about. He sat in the same corner, away from the bar.

She entered soon afterwards. She hadn't dressed up for this at all. He wondered briefly why she was wearing such... ordinary clothes, though she made them look anything but. He gestured to her and she sat down opposite him.

'Well, how's the 'House,' I think you call it.'

'Hard to answer, I'm still feeling my way. I may be able to use my expertise soon, though.'

'Financial?'

'Yes.'

'How?'

'To help a minister.'

'In his financial life?'

'No, political one. Is this suspicion born of cynicism?'

'Especially where your lot are concerned; yes. Going to help grow the economy are you by making it easier for companies to pay out larger dividends and increase share prices, and making cash out of betting on that? A controlled, upmarket bingo.'

'It's good for the economy in the end. '

'The economy: another name for a giant hoover sucking wealth from ordinary people.'

'We're talking shop. Look, it doesn't mean I'm a bad person because of my politics. I think I'm pretty kind and considerate, really. That does sound rather facile but - '

'Do you mean, considering what side you're on?'

'Does there have to be sides?'

'From my side, yes.'

'D'you ever ask questions about a person separate from their politics? Can't you strip that away? You don't seem curious about... me. You just don't ask questions.'

'If you're trying to plug into my so-called maternal instinct in order to receive some tender caring for the neglected little boy, I just hope your more important assumptions are less inaccurate.'

'I'm not sure what to say.'

'Say nothing then.'

She looked down for a few seconds. She was silent.

The sardonic tone had gone when she said, a little more slowly and looking slightly up at him, 'Strangely enough, I don't actually dislike being with you, though I don't know why. But yes, it is politics I'm afraid.'

'You only want to argue, to debate with me. Just that?'

'As you say, I don't think I have an interest in much else with you. That sounds rather harsh I suppose, but... '

He felt suddenly very apart from her.

'Nothing?'

'Not really.'

'I see.'

'I hope so.'

'Not even... sex then. We can talk about it, maybe.'

'"*Even* sex then'? That sounded so hollow and superficial.'

'Afraid that's exactly what I'm feeling at the moment.'

'We'll talk about it if you wish. What, as a man, is your generalisation of women's relationships with men, their partners?'

'Not sure about this.'

'That it's the latter that will most readily break the monogamy? That it's they who have the stronger sexual drive? And thus, of course, overtly justifying it? You're saying nothing. Okay, what if I were to say that it's often the opposite that occurs.'

'Really.'

She leaned towards him.

'Women's bodies are actually designed for sin because the clitoris is, if you like, a kind of superhighway of decadent sensation-for-the-sake-of it, a multi-orgasmic mouth of a simmering volcano which is more responsive and excitable than the tip of the penis. We not only have more erogenous zones, but more erotic self-focus. Women derive arousal from their very own sexiness as much as or more than their male partners. And don't forget the high-tech sex toys.'

She stopped and frowned a little.

'You're still saying nothing.'

'What d'you expect me to say after that?'

'I have an open mind.'

'For most people, 'open' means 'vacant,' but certainly not in your case.'

'Thing is... Jordan, that although you are quite an attractive man, I don't see the point in seeing much more of each other.'

'We don't, anyway.'

'I know, but my work's piling up, needs to be done, and... there is someone I've become interested in.'

Even as he felt it, he realised how corrosive an emotion jealousy was.

'You... Was that your intention? To excite me then dump me?'

'Glad you didn't say 'leading me on.' You sound like a teenager. But, I'm sorry.'

'You *can* say sorry, then. You don't get it right all the time.'

'As they say, you need to learn to lose in politics much more than learning to win.'

'This isn't politics.'

'And there's no justification for you to get annoyed, nothing's happened between you and me. I did think of telling you on the phone, but that would have been rather lazy and weak.'

He looked at her and tried to abstract her, attempt to make her an object of some sort of analysis, and wondered if she was, despite the external solidity, sureness, concealing herself and, perhaps by long practice, holding herself in, not letting something go. He wasn't sure.

He wished her to have so much giving and, when released by himself, to give it all to him. But he knew this wasn't an analysis, a discovery; it was fantasy. It seemed crude and inadequate to use lazy clumps of words to refer to her, but the phrase, 'What you see is what you get.' seemed utterly apposite.

He half-expected her to leave at that moment, but she sat looking at him with an expression he had little hope of deciphering. He couldn't quite meet her eyes. He was about to suggest that they could, perhaps, see each other occasionally as friends, when she said:

'I think I know what you're going to say. You don't *really* want that do you?'

Usually, his intuitive angst would visit him in a timely and justified manner, but it hadn't this time, it hadn't warned him. He had felt almost optimistic going into the pub.

There was no point in staying there. He got up quickly, nodded to her, knowing as he did that it must have looked like the gesture of a departing courtesan, turned and walked to the exit.

After a paradoxically numbed but restless travel home, he unfolded himself from his couch, reached out for an almost full whisky bottle and decided to get himself pissed. There were other drinking euphemisms that went through his mind: 'aled-up', 'rat-arsed,' 'maggoted' and another he'd heard recently, 'besotted. It seemed entirely in context.

And if this someone she'd mentioned really was this bloke, could he, perhaps, be the man Luke Kenyon was interested in, was out to get? If so, he'd certainly like to help him succeed. The thought came that she may have been the brown-haired 'Leftie' Kenyon had once tipsily referred to.

As he imbibed a hefty swipe of his favourite spirit he was aware that it was the first of the day; he'd bought neither of them a drink in the pub. As he tried recalling more slang terms for intoxication, he attempted to push away images of her and her niece standing outside an Art Deco cinema, smiling at him and waving goodbye.

CHAPTER TWENTY NINE

Ralph was on his way to the local town hall to hear some words of faux wisdom concerning pedagogy; perhaps some tactics, gimmicks on how to teach - 'edutainment' as he preferred to call them. The best advice he'd heard in his early training days was that teaching was about a particular group of people in a particular place at a particular time. He reflected a little on truisms he'd picked up over the years and intuitively reversed: 'Tell 'em the good things about their work before the bad.' He'd found that they usually felt better after his initial criticisms, and then the praise.

He usually did this at his desk where he mildly enjoyed calling up the African students to sit beside him and go through their essays or projects while silently appreciating the women's smooth, unblemished skin, especially the Somalis. He'd forgiven them long ago for their 'god is good, satan is bad' dichotomy.

He would have liked Claire in his class; she would have been both an academically in-tune partner and an awkward challenge. And he could have shown off; casually, effortlessly impressed her. But then it was difficult to think of many theoretical insights or intellectual achievements that would have left her feeling that.

The hall wasn't far from the college; a building, with its Ionic capitals, swags, tongue and dart, and ovulo and beading reeking of colonial masturbation. Inside was a pedagogic lady on the stage with too much make-up putting aitches in front of aitches while he sat and cynically awaited the buzz words of Edu-biz.

When he'd first attended these events, he would go for a quiet drink with his new colleagues further into Essex, when it had been Beefeater-Harvester-Land and tattoo-shouldered Essex man-girls cackled into mobiles, and skins with beemers chuntered on about the A12, their mini-heart and dolphin earrings jingling, and old men with 'Los Angeles Raiders' baseball caps bored on about their caravans.

Recollecting these things, he had a picture of Doreen once telling him to stop his observing and to see *her,* almost shouting it, or as near as she could get to that volume, and wondering if she meant anything at all to him.

He didn't want to think about it, nor, this time, did he feel like a drink with anyone, even Audrey, who he knew was in the hall, the girl who taught botany at an Eighteenth Century high-walled garden used by the college, who would occasionally gaze at him with long, lingering looks from her wistful dark eyes when they were both in the staffroom at the same time. He said goodbye to his fellow lecturers and returned home, worrying about Paul.

He'd noticed over the previous few weeks that his conditions - disliking the term for their almost absolute connotations, knowing that all humans are on a spectrum of feelings add behaviours at some point at some time - were becoming more evident.

Ralph would ask him what he thought about something or other and he would snap back, 'I can't concentrate on questions, I'm looking at the park keeper's house.' and other instances when only a minimum of effort was required to focus on two simple things. And a day or so later, when again asked a simple question, 'When you talk to me begin your statement with my name.' He had. 'No. You didn't leave enough time between my name and what you said; make it at least three seconds.' And when they'd had dinner at Ralph's place; Paul taking a bath without asking and breaking the tangled plug chain by yanking it.

He had seen before how rigidly deliberate his friend's movements were getting: when he washed up and clatteringly piled the dishes, turned off a tap, moved a chair, placed plates on a table, or put a plug in a socket. Ralph had guessed that it was another function of his paranoia, that the world was hostile, inimical, and therefore it had to be managed, controlled.

This fear sometimes seemed to include himself. Recently they had been in a supermarket together, and seeing that his friend had more bags than himself, Ralph had casually reached for one, whereupon the holder had pulled abruptly away from his would-be helper, eyes looking almost maniacal. Later, when asked why he'd reacted as he had, he'd answered that he thought Ralph was gong to steal them. And the next evening as Ralph had caught up with him after a sudden haste as they were walking to a party meeting, he had moved away suddenly and said loudly, obviously scared, 'Keep away from me, you're too near me.'

He made himself a meal, ate it and rang Claire. She had just got in. He expected her to say she was going to eat or do something first and she'd ring him back, he doubting that she would.

'I was thinking of you a moment ago,' she said.

'Good.'

'Strangely enough, it may be.'

'You give little away.'

'What d'you think there is to give away?'

'I don't know. There's a lot. Anyway, did you know that there's a total absence of white working class boys in so-called 'top' universities.?'

'Yes, the issues are deep and enduring.'

'Including political invisibility, low aspiration and poor State schooling outside of London.'

'Quite. And did you say that without any preamble because you're feeling a little nervous?'

'Maybe.'

'The landlord's selling this flat. I have first choice; he said he'd like me to have it.'

'Going to?'

'Maybe; an English woman's home is her castle. Be nice to have this one.'

He felt briefly that concepts like 'possession' and 'ownership' didn't seem to suit her; though he would like to be involved in them, with her as the owned. But he couldn't visualize anyone, or anything doing that.

'How's the job?'

'Fine, maybe a promotion, but I'd rather do than oversee, though if the former's being done adequately maybe I'll do the latter.'

'It's more money?'

'Yes.'

'Strange, but I have this picture of you - '

'Only one?'

'You're joking. Of being not *of* money, as it were.'

'A rigged means of exchange, but we all need it.'

'You seem quite the antithesis of the sort of person to get promoted in this liberal world.'

'What sort of person gets it then?'

'Best one would be a vertically challenged, one-eyed, Jewish lesbian negress.'

'With a limp?'

'Ideally. It's such a conceit isn't it, that whites should be seen as kind of post-ethnic cosmopolitans. It's like the embourgeoisement thesis of the Sixties, that 'we are all middle class now' - currently it's, 'we are all ethnics now.''

'Unfortunately, the belief in multiculturalism seems to have broken down everywhere, except perhaps amongst mayors of diverse cities.'

''tis a pity.'

'Is this why you rang? Theory... social observations ?'

'I had another picture of you then; the way you looked at that speaker the other evening, Moorcroft.'

'Would you like me to look at you like that?'

'Man hears a knock on his door. There's a snail on the step which the man throws as far as he can. Three years later, another knock. He opens the door, looks down at a snail. It says, 'What'd' you do that for?'

She laughed. 'What prompted you to tell me that?'

'I like the sound of your laugh.'

'You didn't want to give yourself away and answer my question though, did you. And I can see you're not going to reply. Okay. When's Eaton going to arrange the TUC anniversary celebration, any idea?'

'No. I even like the way you disregard somebody saying what they like about you.'

'Somebody?'

'Okay, me.'

'You don't really like it.'

'No. it's interesting though.'

'Interesting?'

'Alright, fascinating.'

'In a kind of detached way?'

'I suppose.'

'What do you *feel*?'

'I think you know the answer.'

'A little hurt?'

'Guess so.'

There was a pause, then, 'I suppose what we could do, if you like, is - '

His mobile began to ring. He took it from his pocket.

'Answer it.'

'Sorry, I thought I'd switched it off.'

'It's okay, I'll wait.'

It was a male voice, rather low-pitched and slow, asking if its owner was speaking to a Ralph Kearns.

'This is Selwyn Road police station, sir. I'm afraid there's been a bad accident, concerning a Paul Goode.'

Ralph paused a moment, trying to reformulate the words to make precise sense of them.

'It's rather tragic sir, I'm afraid'

He still couldn't, though the man's last statement did seem more meaningful. He heard himself asking whether he should come to the police station or go to a hospital.

'Someone will come to you sir. Are you at home?'

After Ralph had confirmed he was, the officer told him that they would be with him 'very shortly.'

He slowly returned the phone to his pocket

'Did you hear any of that?'

I think I heard you mention the police.'

'Look, something bad has happened to Paul. A friend.'

'I've seen him with you and Edward.'

'They're coming any minute now. I don't know what's happened, but it sounds bad.'

'I'm sorry. Do you want to continue talking to me till they come?'

'I want to, but - '

'You want to let it sink in, prepare yourself. I understand. Call me afterwards. Please.'

'Thanks. Bye.'

He stood for a while, holding the phone above the receiver, not wanting to put it back, partly because he wanted her to be still there, her voice, her presence. He replayed what the policeman had said. He felt his hands clench. It wasn't true. Was it? A potent emotion of constrained panic filled him.

He sat. What had Ralph done? Had done to him? The word 'tragic' again. What did that mean? Surely he wasn't... No. That frightened man was his friend. 'He's my friend,' he almost shouted aloud.

He began pacing around the room, went to the hall, opened the front door, shut it again; returned. He heard a car and went to the door before they knocked. He gestured them in; a policeman and a policewoman. He wasn't sure whether to invite them to sit.

The woman suggested that he sit down. He did. He didn't want to speak. It was the man who spoke.

'I believe my colleague at the station informed you that Mister Goode had a dreadful accident. I'm afraid I have to tell you that he's dead.'

'You mean, gone?'

Even as he asked the question he wasn't sure why he had. Perhaps he was seeking confirmation that his friend had disappeared, vanished, wasn't here anymore.

'Afraid so, sir.'

'We really are sorry.' It was the woman this time.

'What... happened?'

'Somebody was walking past your friend's apartment block when he heard someone shout. He gave quite a graphic description. All I'll repeat to you is that he saw a man in front of him point upwards and looked to where he was indicating and saw a man kneeling on a sill, the window open. He fell forward. Down. It happened about three hours ago. The man turned away. He never saw any more.'

Ralph's first thought was rather calm: that the red-tiled sill must have been hurting his knees, the bottom of the metal window frame, his shins. He wondered detachedly whether Paul had held his arms out when he fell as if he was an aircraft, or perhaps held them rigidly at his sides.

He pondered on what remnants of actions and images had welled up in Paul's mind as he'd let himself go. Perhaps, when kneeling on the sill, an image of a patch of worn carpet he'd raised himself from, or his looking down at a shoe he hadn't tied properly, or maybe a flicker of concern for someone who saw him fall or came across him, legs akimbo, sprawled across the pavement. Perhaps it was the casual ease with which his body would be carried into an ambulance, or the sound of a sweeper's brushes tidying his debris away. Or the impenetrable dark; the despair.

Ralph also wondered whether he knew, when he'd shut the window the night before, that it would be the last time he'd do it, and maybe even a dull awareness that he wouldn't need his door key any more. And then his own question: could he have made more time for him before he… ?

The policewoman stepped towards him and put a hand on his shoulder.

'We are informing you, Mister Kearns, because Mister Goode had a note in his jacket stating that you were his next of kin. We'll leave you now, but we'll be in touch. If you wish for any more information or there's anything we can do for you, ring or come to the station. We are both very sorry.'

Her colleague nodded towards him and they left.

He forced himself to sit. Slow motion images of a body descending filled the space behind his eyes, not his fiend's, somebody else's, anyone's; he didn't want to speed them up. His friend had smashed himself onto the road. God, why was he so desperate?

A week previously, Paul had mentioned casually that Myers may shortly be moving to Miami permanently, and not just to holiday there for a few weeks during the winters as he'd been doing for years. Over this time they'd become kind of unethical friends; perhaps he was more dependent on the man than Ralph realised, or wanted to; it wasn't easy to acknowledge that his best friend was more dependant on an analyst than himself.

But then, maybe Paul wanted Claire, and felt that because Ralph wanted her, he didn't want him. Perhaps, although spending more time with Edward than he did, he was jealous of him with Edward. Was this Ronnie all over again, without the motor bike?

He had once told Ralph that sometimes he wanted to throw himself out of the womb, to be really born, psychologically born. Perhaps to propel himself to the ground was a distorted attempt to do this, or even, because he was aware he couldn't actually be reborn however huge the urge, he had desperately ended any attempt to be so.

Ralph knew there was fear. Paul had tried to tell him how frightened he was. He remembered him saying, 'I feel so frightened, I'm terrified really.' He'd paused then, frowning, and said, 'My 'me' is a tiny creature living inside the body watching the 'I,' the constructed 'I' all the time, watching the face, limbs, flesh age. Sometimes, I feel that when my body's too old, I'll find another vehicle for myself - or rather, for 'me' as there is no self - and carry on.'

It was, Ralph knew, another example of him forever escaping from whatever he was so frightened of. He recalled him saying once that he became his pain, and drawing a circle with a smaller one attached. In the larger he'd written 'self,' in the smaller 'pain.' He'd then reversed them; he *was* the pain. Not any more.

Had Myer's old sepia photo of the effigy of a woman swinging on a rope by her neck at a Cambridge college all those years ago had any relevance? Perhaps the image had become his mother, and that he was glad she was hanging there, high above the ground, or maybe it wasn't her that was being destroyed, but the *absence* of her, her indifference that the figure had reminded him of.

But then, it could be that it was triggered by a single incident. Perhaps the Service, the secret people - he wasn't sure how to refer to them - had got into his flat, guessing maybe that Ralph had given the 'Polish paper' to him or Edward, and Paul was certain that, as Ralph had experienced previously in his own home, someone had entered his flat.

He could imagine Paul coming home and finding little things awry; maybe a bedroom drawer not quite shut, a curtain pulled back, perhaps shirts and jeans disarranged in the wardrobe. It could have been simpler: he could have spotted the bald man following him; all feeding his paranoia. But who *could* know why?

Ralph couldn't keep inside, he had to get out; walk, run jump, punch a wall, kick a lamp post; anything to get rid of his anger, this loss. He went out to his car and sat in it before deciding he didn't want to sit; a quick insight warning him that he would drive dangerously anyway.

He walked to his station and got on a train not caring where it went. He wasn't working today; he couldn't have gone in, anyway. He forced himself to sit; at least there was a moving, outside world he could occasionally see and try to interest himself in. He got off randomly at several stations and stepped on other trains until he saw that Turnham Green wasn't far away and alighted there.

Walking around a familiar Edwardian estate near the station, he recalled Paul naming period houses 'Georgie,' 'Vicky,' 'Eddie,' and, on their walks, his occasional touching of the back of Ralph's hand to draw attention to something, an architectural detail perhaps: an ogee arch, a pilaster, a Roman capital. He missed that touch. Where was Paul? He didn't want to see his body. He wished to see *him.*

He thought again of their London walks. The next one, chosen by Paul, would have followed the Overground from Stratford to Richmond along the roads that were nearest to the line. Ralph had moaned about having to virtually zigzag all the way. 'Hold on to the idea,' Paul would say dramatically when an area looked particularly awkward or dismal, 'that there'll be a café somewhere.' It was the laughs, the banter; the hyperbole.

He took a bus for a few stops, looking out at the terraced houses, pavement trees, a distant crane, a glimpse of water - a stream or canal perhaps - and instantly the place seemed an amalgam, a condensed version of their perambulations symbolising all of them. He felt tears moisten his cheeks. Again; images, loss, associations reprising themselves. He walked some more, the area was unfamiliar. He passed a 'Star of Jesus' church with African women outside handing out religious pamphlets with evangelising zeal, and wished he could rid himself of his own intellectualized disbelief in faith.

Walking by a ladder against an old Burtons building where a window cleaner was leathering a suntrap window, he fancifully thought that, maybe, through the grime, he was seeing reflections of pantile roofs, white render, stylized shells, perhaps imagining foyers of chrome and black, walnut and jade, the glistening spire of the Chrysler... though he was, Ralph suspected, probably just thinking about cleaning a window. It was a pointless thought. Pointless.

CHAPTER THIRTY

'When we came down from the trees and learned to speak, we over-hunted our animal prey and invented farming - I think it was the Roman general Agricola who introduced it here - developed better tools and produced more than we could eat, like a surplus of grain which we kept in shared silos, hence the need for writing to keep track of who owned how much grain. We wrote on shells, apparently, which became tokens representing grain, i.e. debt. I think I've got this right.'

Archer had been doing some reading and was relaying it to Jordan as they sat in a Wansford pub on a Saturday morning; the agent arranging the meeting because he wanted to know how his client was getting along.

'Sounds as if debt wasn't a good thing, but it's good for - '

'The economy, banks et cetera, guessed you'd say that. 'Course, the people in charge hogged it, so they created religions, telling the masses they were the 'true representatives of god.''

'Nice one.'

'Maybe. So, this culture spread across most of the world, except in Africa and South America because of the deserts and jungles. When we invented ships trade flourished and merchants got rich. The biggy is that landowners now had to compete with merchants.

'So they ended the feudal system, threw the serfs off their land and lent them money to come back and pay their debts by squeezing as much value out of the land as possible. So now everybody, from the landowner to the lowest serf, had dollar signs in their eyes. Profit was everything. Enter modern finance.'

'At last.'

'Bankers hawk the future at a rate of interest, everybody is in debt, and the only outcome is the industrial revolution, followed, perhaps inevitably, by the ruin of the planet. Some of this is my own thinking of course.'

'You haven't 'gone over to the other side have you?'

'Nah, it just interested me is all. What interests me more though, is what you're gonna do re Weynard. Anything?'

'I'm thinking on it.'

'You don't seem quite as interested as you usually are.'

'In what?'

'Well, what I'm saying, what's around you, not even your conversation with Weynard. I'd have thought that someone with, at least, moderate ambitions for self-advancement would have been a little more enthusiastic.'

'Er, let's talk about something else for a while, eh? Did you read about the new woman CEO of an ad agency who said she wanted to get rid of the 'stale, pale, white males' in the firm. Imagine 'female' in place of 'male' there. The uproar.'

'You bet. Talking of females; how's Cluckrose? Seen her lately?'

'Don't want to talk about that one.'

'Like that is it?'

'Guess so.'

'You have seen her then.'

'Yes, Mister Archer.'

'You sound irritated.'

'I am. We weren't going to talk about it.'

'You mean *you* weren't. I think you want to really.'

'Well, surprisingly, I don't seem to have anyone else to tell it to and you're - '

'A pretty understanding bloke?'

'Something like that.'

'Have another drink and continue.'

Archer went to the bar and returned with proseccos.

'It sounds ridiculous, but she's chucked me.'

'You mean it's unbelievable that she did?'

'No, we were never... but it's as if we were and I've been - '

'Spurned?'

'Yes.'

'Why?'

'There's another bloke she's interested in. I think I met him once.'

'The way you looked then... as if you want to do something about this geezer.'

'Does it show? Well, I wouldn't mind doubling the trouble he's in.'

'Trouble?'

'You're a discreet man I feel, so I'll tell you what I'm pretty sure I shouldn't. Okay. I've been contacted by our well-known secret services - there's a contradiction in terms - to find out more about a chap in the Communist Party, who, I think, is the one I've just mentioned. He's got some sort of evidence that could somehow incriminate a previous Tory government.'

'No, you shouldn't have told me. Ne'er mind. I guess you're talking of a potential scandal of a past government that wouldn't do the current one, of which you're a member, much good either.'

'What I can actually do, I don't know. I should think they've tried to get hold of this evidence by now. I mean, I'm not going to infiltrate his party, become his pal and encourage him to tell me what he's got, am I.'

'If she knows him then you could ask her... No, you can't.'

'That was what was suggested. I feel if I don't do something it'll kick back on me, and ... '

'Bollocks up your career?'

'Correct.'

'A minister or two, eventually the PM - having a rough time at the moment of course - will be told, I guess. The dark arts of Westminster, eh? Who said that politics are deserts of abstraction, leaving little more than systems of opinions and formulas that hide reality from us.'

'Perhaps that's what we do; disguise what's real in some sort of acceptable phantasm of diktats, controls and policies couched in mostly self-deluding egoistic rhetoric supposedly for the public good, whatever that is.'

'Not bad. I don't think you do that, but it happens, even in our vaunted pluralist system where the two main tribes hammer and bay at each other from opposite sides of the track.'

'I think you mean 'honourable opposite opinions respectably held.''

'If you like. We digress.'

'What am I supposed to do? They won't like it that - '

'They?'

'The man who sees me - that I won't see the girl any more. I can imagine him attempting to make me keep trying with her, but she may know nothing about the whole thing.'

'I assume this isn't quite how you expected things to go when you started out, eh? Certainly not when I first met you.'

'I'm supposed to be doing... '

'Things for the greater good?'

'Something like that; away from the corporate world I was raised in but still using some of what I've learnt from it.'

'I don't think Weynard's gonna be a kindly patron to you if, when, he hears about this.'

'No, but he won't miss me, there's other people working on what he wants; economists et cetera.'

'Economists are put on the earth to make astrologers look good.'

'I think I wish I was back in it now, though; I miss the firm.'

Archer looked at his watch.

'Can understand that, but have to go.'

He stood. 'Pity about crazy girl; sorry, didn't mean the 'crazy' bit.'

'What's crazy is that I feel like this, yet nothing happened between us.'

'Cheer you up. Man sticks a gun in the ribs of rather affluent-looking geezer in the street. 'Give us your money,' he demands. 'But, I'm a politician,' says the man. 'Then give me *my* money,' the man says. We'll have a longer drink next time. Move on, Jordan, life's too short to skin a tomato. And remember, don't lie, don't cheat, don't steal.'

'I know; the government hates competition. Cheerio.'

Archer moved quickly through the door and as Jordan watched it close, his phone beeped.

'Speak of the devil.' came to mind as he recognised Luke Kenyon's voice. He wanted them to meet on the second floor of a pub in Amersham four hours hence. Jordan had nothing urgent to do, knowing that even if he had he would have said yes.

Later, walking down the side of the sloping cornfield from the station to the suburban High Street, he wished a good afternoon to someone coming the opposite way, knowing he wouldn't have said it to anyone if moving through the concourse of Waterloo Station; manners being largely a function of space, time and the amount of people.

It was a Fifties mock-Georgian building next to a railway bridge where the sound of trains and the vibrations they caused were clearly discerned in an inhospitable, long, narrow room with grimy windows in an establishment that looked a certain candidate to be on the list of rapidly disappearing suburban drinking houses.

He was there a little before Kenyon, who came striding in, his previous languor seemingly gone, and asked if he could get him a drink. Other than bar staff and a man and his dog they were the only ones there.

'Thanks. I feel like a whisky.'

After it had been brought to the table, its carrier, taking a sip of his own before sitting down opposite Jordan, began:

'It would seem that our man may have given what we're looking for to a friend. A guess, really. The place was searched but nothing found. We need to know for certain. We had him tailed, though didn't see the point of that actually. However, something seemed to upset him, poor sod's taken his own life, apparently. Pressure's on us now. We've been getting nudges from HM Government.'

He bent forwards towards his listener; to the latter he was no longer the spoilt, privileged almost-fop he appeared to be when he'd first encountered him.

'And this one's particularly unpopular at the moment, so what he has needs to be no more.'

Jordan drained his glass. 'Does the responsibility of people's deaths not bother you?'

'Of course, but I have a job to do.'

'Let me buy you one,' said Jordan. He did so and sat again.

'Why do you do it? he asked. 'Love of your country?'

'*Our* country.'

'What *is* a country? All the people? Some of them? the earth, the trees? Have you searched yourself for *really* why you do it? Is it a feeling of superiority you get working for a perceived glamorous, mysterious organisation? Though, of course, you were born into a taken-for-granted feeling of superiority, I suppose.'

'It's a much-respected one, as you know.'

'Is it the smugness you enjoy? How am I doing? Not bad for someone who's half-pissed, eh?'

He knew he wasn't, but thought it a good idea to hide his lack of courage behind half-pretending to be.

'Or perhaps you were overly influenced by Bond films and spy books, eh? Gonna be dead-letter boxes next? Am I speaking out of turn? Sorry, old man. *Regnum Defende,* defence of the realm.' He lifted his glass towards Kenyon. 'Good old Box 500, I believe that's what you call it.'

'I'll remind you that it's also a powerful organisation and that you're treading on dangerous ground, Jordan Wilde.'

'And you're supposed to protect British parliamentary democracy. Hardly democratic, the way you're treating me.'

Kenyon leant forward again.

'I asked you to do a relatively simple thing. And yes, to help your party, perhaps your country one could argue. It seems you haven't attempted to do so. It's not directly your fault that a potential source of information has been lost, but your lack of commitment doesn't bode well for you I can assure you.'

He stood up, and looked down at Jordan with an expression the latter interpreted as a mixture of disappointment, annoyance and, almost, pity.

'Be safe, Mister Wilde,' he said as he left the now even more empty building.

Again, the feeling of being left; but it was okay with this one, he never wanted to see Luke Kenyon again. But Claire... 'crazy girl,' 'the girl,' these appelations had a resonance as he realised he'd never settled on a particular one to refer to when having an internal conversation about her. 'Cluckrose' was the nearest. He should, needed, to forget her. And this detective-informer business he also wanted to wipe away.

The following day he happened to be talking to Weynard's secretary in the House canteen when the man's phone rang. It was his boss asking him to get hold of Jordan.

'He's here with me now, actually.'

'Send him up to me would you,' Jordan heard.

The bureaucrat raised an eyebrow.

'I heard,' said Jordan. 'May as well go now, I suppose.'

'I believe he's asked you to do some finance stuff for him. Good. See you, then.'

He knew there'd be little good about it.

He wasn't asked to sit this time. As he closed the office door, Weynard looked at him with little warmth in his eyes.

'Briefly, Mister Wilde, I don't think your expertise - is there a plural for that? - is needed now. I have an idea you're not that surprised. This is, of course, off the record. Apparently, you haven't been, let us say, trying hard enough in certain directions; the phrase 'not loyal' was mentioned somewhere I think. You know what this is about. Apparently, you need to do something. This meeting never took place. You may go.'

As Jordan turned to leave, Weynard said, with hearty sarcasm, 'Anyway, good fortune with your career.' and as he closed the door, heard, as if spoken under the man's breath; 'Though I don't think it will be a particularly long and productive one.'

He left the House and made his way home, knowing he'd probably missed the chance to get his own back, to punish Ralphy boy. But it didn't really matter, he'd been punished enough; his friend had died. What was it Sartre had said? 'The only question is suicide.' His friend had, perhaps, both asked it and answered it.

Maybe it was Kenyon's mob that was the cause. Either way, it had happened, as, it seemed, had the ending of any hope of the progression of his ambitions. He felt disappointed and also, despite Archer's efforts, rather naive and uninformed about the tough, intransigent world he had entered.

CHAPTER THIRTY ONE

Ralph had just been to a church where he'd discussed Paul's funeral with the vicar, emphasising that his friend wouldn't have wanted a conventional, religious funeral, and had requested a humanitarian one. The cleric agreed and Ralph gave him some information on his deceased friend. He hadn't teased his brain with what to say, hadn't dredged up and examined what he knew of his soon-to-be cremated pal, how tortured, how manic depressive he could be, how anxious, how fearful, yet how capable of short-lived joys he was. It was of little import. The people who knew him, or thought they did, would have memories of him; at least they'd know something of the person he was. It would be a short commemoration.

He hadn't informed Myers yet; the analyst would, he supposed, comply with whatever rules governing relationships between therapists and patents were, though he would surely wish to be present at the ceremony.

It was a late spring day; bright green leaves, daffodils, the grass around the blackened headstones and eroded tombs recently mown; a place for some peace when he needed quiet. He liked churches and saw no contradiction between this and his atheism.

Sometimes feeling in alien territory when seeing residential streets brooded over by priapic distortions of architectural triumphalism, he gained an immediate sense of quiet and comfort when sighting a church spire; it was 'England, their England.' He wandered around the graveyard. Somehow, even the trees seemed more at rest here than elsewhere. He thought of the last few funerals he'd been to. They were some time ago, but he remembered them.

The last had been for an aunt who'd died at 103. He could still see the copy of 'Saga' on a sill in the chapel, the plate-glass views of pylons, his greying cousins, her Benfleet bungalow and the pampas grass she would pick to spray with lacquer for the vase. And the surprises; cousin Ernie suddenly seeming likeable, a shop steward uncle's reluctant Marxism, a granddaughter's mini skirt and high heels and the 'Luv'ly buffet, Gwen,' 'Good innin's she 'ad.' 'Smashin' service.'

An elderly couple had given him a lift to the post-funeral get-together and as the husband slowed outside the pub the woman had turned her head and said, seemingly pointing at him, 'Look at that awful hat.' 'All he needs,' Ralph had said, 'is a dead deer slung on the roof.' She had, instead, been pointing out of the side window at a vividly coloured piece of headwear belonging to a female friend of the deceased. There'd been food laid on, but he didn't eat; the smell of garlic and the appearance of the cold quiche seemed to represent death.

The one before that, causing him to alight from a train at Turkey Street station and its adjacent beer can-strewn puddle of a canal and sauerkraut-smelling nearby pub, was one he'd been invited to by a widowed aunt. He'd sat at the back and once more listened to a vicar creating an empty, meaningless gospel of fiction for a weeping widow and friends. Leaving a fading 'Let's Make Memories.' and 'I'm Forever Blowing Bubbles.' he'd walked out and into the graveyard to silently admire the church tower's embattlements and the squat steeple rising from them.

Over a drink in a bowling pavilion afterwards he'd quietly joined the others and listened to their fake jocularity and superficial memories. Liked a good drink, did Reg,' ''member 'im once sayin', 'Let's get to 'eaven and shag the angels.' And asked himself whether any of it hid the reality of their pain. How many there actually felt it, how many a quiet relief?

The funeral a week later was, as he'd intended, a rather brief affair, Ralph attempting to push away a montage of memories by focusing on where he would scatter the ashes; perhaps around a tree by a Georgian window in London somewhere. He remembered a particular building having the requisite features near the banks of the Thames in Mortlake. He would take them there.

There were rather more people present than he had expected, mostly members of the local party that Eaton, who was there himself, had encouraged to attend. Claire, who he had spoken to only once since informing her of the time and place, when she'd asked him how he was feeling and could she do anything to help - he obstinately refusing her offer, wanting her, and himself, to think he could get through it alone - was present and, as sombre as he felt, he couldn't but notice how lovely she looked in black. She'd briefly kissed his cheek when she saw him and then had quiet word with a few of the gathering afterwards.

Edward made a rather touching speech from the lectern about his short but sweet association with Paul. Myers was also there. Ralph didn't wish to say anything formally; his relationship with his friend had little to do with the wider populace. It was between them.

Ralph formed his mouth into a closed-lip rueful smile and thanked the mourners as they left, shaking hands with some of them and reminding them where they were to go for the get-together afterwards; it was his own flat, where one of his students, a part-time caterer, had organised the repast.

In the short time they were in his home, people did the usual thing after a funeral of talking of the deceased for a while then about what they had in common with them, mostly the party in this case, then about themselves - Ralph rather miserably thinking of Wilde's definition of a bore, 'Someone who will talk about themselves when you want to talk about *your*self' - and laughing, telling a few jokes then looking meaningfully at their watches.

He thanked them as they left; Edward and Eaton especially, and asked Myers, who had been sitting thoughtfully, hardly speaking to anyone, to stay behind for a while. Claire, who had been talking mostly with Eaton, was the last of the others to leave.

'I hope you didn't come out of pity,' he said to her.

'No, and I think you know that. I like this flat, did you do the paintings?'

'Yes.'

'I guessed as much.'

'Have a closer look some time, eh?'

'I will. I really can't stay now though, my neighbour's looking after my niece and she can only be there for so long.'

'Didn't know you had a niece.'

'I have; maybe you'd like to meet her.'

'Maybe you'll bring her here.'

'Yes.' She moved lightly towards him to kiss his cheek again, but he turned his head slightly so that they brushed lips. She looked a little surprised.

'I'll see you, Claire.'

It felt strangely formal to use her name.

'You will. Bye.'

He turned to Myers.

'Er, I don't know the rules governing an occasion like his when a psychologist's client has' - he couldn't say it - 'but I'd like you to talk to me, if you would.'

'A little, yes. He spoke of you quite frequently, you were a mainstay for him; he would have been even more insecure without it.'

'I'm sure you did all you could. There's vacant chairs, do sit.'

Myers relaxed on the nearest.

'Had he ever talked of... you know.'

'No, though he occasionally told me he felt like doing it. He said he had enough Nitrazepam to kill a horse, but I doubted whether he would take them. This was something else, this awful end. As I told you on the phone, I read about it. I know no more than that. How are you coping?'

'I'm getting by. It's okay.'

'He used to tell me about your walks and your interest in period houses et cetera.'

'Indeed.'

'Well, it seemed for him that it began as a child, a baby even. Life wasn't real to him, his home especially, and when he saw buildings, houses other than in his own cramped street, he, as he said recently, almost became them. A house had an atmosphere - he was talking of the exterior - something that represented another him, a different him from the sick one he was and was used to; a side door, windows, colour of the bricks, whatever. A house was a kind of inner identity for him, an alternative one.

He told me that he would dream of a house and then a week, a month, a year later he would see it for real in a street somewhere. Another time he would see a house add would then dream about it. He wasn't always sure what came first, he said, the house or the dream.'

'I think I can understand that. Are you allowed, as it were, to tell me anything more… significant? Do you wish to?'

'Okay. My opinion is that something over and above his condition forced him to do what he did. Of course I don't know what it was. He would, I think, have gone on for ever as he was, but improving slightly.'

'Only slightly? Have you ever had someone as… bad as him, in *his* pain?'

'Yes. As an example, I remember being excited about one of my early patients who I'd seen monthly for over four years and who had, during this time, just sat perfectly still, looking down between his knees and only glancing at me for a second just before he left at the end of his sessions. During the final minute of his last one he suddenly looked up and smiled. I don't think I'd seen his teeth before. I'd wanted him to smile next time and, maybe, one day to speak. I didn't see him again.'

Myers was silent for a while, then 'There was something he'd started to speak of recently, something he'd never mentioned before that intrigued me.'

He looked up at Ralph who was still standing.

'This isn't just a detached thing, your friend wasn't just an object of study and dissection to me, but in what I'm going to say now he was, If you like, an artefact of theory. He told me he'd been on a flat roof recently, he didn't say where, and could see the chimneys of the terraced houses opposite stretching out into perspective.

'He stood by a chimneystack and said that it was bigger than he thought it would be and wanted to hug one of the chimneys. It seemed huge to him. He reached up, but felt 'frightened, horrible,' and couldn't do it.'

Myers shook his head and gave a resigned smile.

'There won't be many of my colleagues who would agree with what I'm about to say, they'd say it was too Freudian or maybe beyond it, but I would argue that chimneys are the father's penis. As a young boy he was terrified of loving his father; he looked into his eyes and couldn't, just couldn't love him, it was wrong.

'The intriguing, fascinating thing about chimneys for him was that from a sunlit, tree-framed distance they were, if you like, perhaps soft penises, things that wouldn't hurt him, but close up they were hostile, brutal, nightmarish. And yes, before you say it, this is before culture gets in with its taboos of incest and homosexuality. This is primal.

'I'm coming to the conclusion that, perhaps, the id, that ineradicable bundle of animal instincts within the child, the baby, wants to be taken over by the father; at an unconscious level wants to be fucked by him.

'Sorry if this sounds outrageous, but try not to put value judgements on it. A baby can't think, it feels. So much can go wrong for a baby, even before that, in the womb. Freud didn't go back far enough. Actually, I'm surprised there's not more people messed up, more queues outside places where people like me work.'

'So Sigmund wasn't just a charismatic bearer of a paradigm then. I'm trying to remember Laing's definition of schizophrenia: 'A separation of thought from feeling, fragmentation of self, the creation of a false self.' There was another.'

"Emotional impoverishment.' Yes. Why do you mention it?'

'Paul.'

'Yes, that certainly encompassed him.'

'I guess this is all largely a deflection from me facing what's happened, eh?'

The analyst rose from his seat.

'Denial's underrated, Mister Kearns.'

'Ralph.'

'Sure. I am sad that he's gone, not just for your sake and others, but my own. I shall miss him. And, of course, wonder for a while if I really could have done more.'

'Don't beat yourself up, as they say. He respected you I assure you.'

'If you do wish to talk to me some more, call me. Goodbye.'

They shook hands.

On his own now, Ralph thought of the kind of unconscious, reverse paedophilia his guest had mentioned, guessing that his students would, unfortunately, have been offended by it. Those who had learnt from his insistence that the crux of the subject he was teaching them was the attempt to be value-free in its observations would have understood, but most people he'd worked and grown up with and had taught, couldn't seem to rid themselves of morality even for a second, couldn't step back from conditioned reactions and try to discuss something without immediately placing value judgments upon it.

What Myers had said hadn't been a social fact but a psychological one. It would be interesting if he could get Myers to give a talk to his class. But it would have been another reminder that he would never see Paul again.

CHAPTER THIRTY TWO

Prime Minister's Question Time was over, leaving Jordan thinking of how difficult the role of PM really was; the least its involvement in a hundred daily decisions. It wasn't a theological post or an ideological sinecure; it was a battlefield of praxis. Jordan hadn't asked a question and was on his way out of the Chamber when he saw Alan watts coming towards him, eyes straight ahead. Jordan said hello to him and slowed his pace. Watts seemed to turn his head to him a little reluctantly. He nodded, smiled and walked on past. So much for his 'something about me,' comment mused Jordan. He'd obviously heard about his meeting with Weynard, probably from the man himself.

He left the building and sat down in a local restaurant trying to work out how his current evaluation could be re-valued. Maybe he could get something, just something, from Cluckrose; at least let Kenyon know he was trying even though there wasn't much, if anything, he could possibly do. Perhaps he could meet her again, bump into her accidentally, as it were. It felt cheaply cunning and adolescent.

Despite this, he found out when the next meeting of her party - he was beginning to use the familiarity of the shortened name to himself now - was taking place and decided to attend. He assumed she would be there and he needed to get her on her own; he didn't intend to beg, and certainly not in public.

It was in three days time, a period which he part-filled by going to a parliamentary meeting involving a debate on some general rules regarding local councils' assets, to which he hadn't been formally invited, and a rather busy surgery day attempting to solve the social dissatisfactions of a dozen people. He'd found himself having some healthy, domestic shots of whisky till late in the evenings.

He drove to the corrugated cardboard hut, as he'd named it, quite early. The four other people there looked at him rather quizzically, perhaps recognising who he was. They didn't speak to him. As more people entered he noticed the bunting around the frieze as well as that draped in front of the bar. A barman appeared and Jordan got himself a drink.

'Hundred and fifty years of showin' 'em, eh?' the barman said to him.

Before Jordan could ask what he meant, one of the men ordered drinks and said to the man behind the counter, 'Show 'em what, eh? Show 'em how weak and accepting the working class of this country can be?'

'Come on, if it weren't for unions you wouldn't be earning the money you are.'

'Could be more, conditions could be better for everyone if the masses had joined in without generally being forced to 'cos of poverty.'

'That's hardly fair, you're gonna get divisions when you oppose the people who create the values we live by.'

'Hegemony, Sid, quite, but… '

Jordan wandered away, not really sure what the time period mentioned signified. He sat at one end of the back row, picking up a leaflet as he did so, noticing every chair had one. He read quickly and realised it was an anniversary of the trades union movement. Part of him asked what he was doing here, another, more pragmatic part, told him. But she wasn't here. Surely she would come, it seemed quite an important date for socialists; would she not wish to celebrate it?

The man he'd seen previously, the head man, entered with Edward behind him. The former went to the front of the now fast-filling seats, held up his hands and said, 'Good evening. I'm not here to give you a history lesson but to remind you of things like the Merthyr rising, the Chartists and leaders like Robert Owen, Ben Tillett, Scargill, Ken Gill and others. You should know of these people and the union movement generally, of course. And while you're thinking of them,' he pointed to the bar, 'enjoy yourselves. Toast them, eh? Toast them. Cheers.'

As people clapped enthusiastically and made for the bar, Eaton stepped toward the front seats where their occupants warmly shook his hand.

Jordan looked around him again. She had just come in and was taking off a casual corduroy jacket showing a t-shirt with something printed on it which he couldn't quite read. As she went towards the cloakroom she spotted him and frowned. He read what it said as she came out of the room, he now waiting outside of it.

He read it aloud. 'No amount of cajolery can eradicate from my heart a deep, burning hatred of the Tory Party. As far as I am concerned they are lower than vermin.' He knew it was a quote, but couldn't remember whose.

'Hardly nuanced is it,' he said to her. 'Did I bring that on?'

'It's not meant to be, and you don't mean enough for that, I'm afraid. It's merely a reminder.'

'Surprised you needed one. But I didn't come here to - '

'What *are* you doing here? I'm sure it's not to see me.'

'It is, I wanted to say that perhaps we could - '

'Start again?'

'Maybe.'

'Excuse me.'

She went towards the bar where Edward warmly greeted her while Jordan stood where he was, gazing at the cloakroom door till someone exited it and looked at him rather strangely. He turned away and sat on the back row feeling incompetent and embarrassed. He was tempted to leave, but reminded himself that, as far as Kenyon was concerned, it would be better if he at least attempted to find out from the man himself where he had hidden the prized evidence. But why didn't Kenyon's cronies just threaten him, or even torture him to get the damned stuff? Or were they too old-school British to stoop to the level of the CIA or the old KGB?

The member he was thinking of then came in, hesitated briefly, went to the bar, kissed Cluckrose on the mouth and began speaking to Edward. She looked a little surprised, but neither angry nor resentful.

Jordan couldn't help himself. He went slowly towards her and whispered, 'Oh, but that 'twas me.'

She replied quietly. 'Am I supposed to be familiar with that line? Some sort of faux Shakespeare is it? I think you should leave. Really.'

'I will, but not until I've spoken to your friend.'

He decided to take a chance. He tapped Ralph on the shoulder.

'I'd like a word if I may.'

'Er… Okay.'

'Let's go outside, it's getting hot in here.'

Jordan led the way and as soon as they were breathing in the dusk air, began.

'You may or may not remember me. We've met only once. Here. Not too long ago.'

'Yeah, I think I do.'

'I heard that a friend of yours died recently. Is that correct?'

'It is.'

'I'm sorry. That's all I wanted to say, really. Rather pointless I know, but there it is.'

'Well, thank you.'

'I did hear that… it was suicide. That's even worse for you of course. I'll stop now. As long as you're coming to terms with it, as they say.'

'I am. Just. I keep thinking that I should know you. Should I?'

'I suppose so, if you're interested in politics that is.'

They both briefly laughed.

'I'm your local MP.'

'Of course. I saw you at a party meeting. I also exchanged a few words with you at your campaign thing. I didn't recognise you. So what are you doing here?'

'Difficult to explain.'

'Come to spy on us? Is that why you were here before?'

'Hardly. A believer are you, in your party?'

'Of course. I wouldn't be here otherwise.'

'Don't know whether I'm quoting someone here, but ideological tunnel vision is never going to survive contact with real-world economics.'

'Probably the same bloke that said, 'Revolutionaries are impossiblists.'

'Who do you think runs this country? You'd like it to be The Boilermakers Union, or UNITE, or ASLEF wouldn't you, but they don't.'

'Neither does your government. A political and economic system is in charge. Of the world. You know its name.'

'Would you like LGBTQs or some such to be in charge?'

'You're stretching the sarcasm now, but it may imply that you're against the 'Oh, please me, offend me, I'm dying for it' mob, along, perhaps, with an underlying, but not admitted, fear of them.'

'Actually, I am against.'

'Perhaps that's something we have in common.'

'Unusual for a party member to push against neo-liberalism, the Left practically invented it.'

'I'm different. I don't look through the lens of liberal prejudice.'

'The whole glut of 'ists', 'phobics,' 'isms'... '

'They're defences, ways of dealing with perceived attacks on their increasingly dominant ideology.'

'Quite. But this country has been given so much by conservatism; better education, better standards of living. The man in the street now has a better quality of - '

"Quality' can't be measured. You sound as if you're giving a speech again. And why did the establishment give workers - albeit reluctantly for fear of potential social revolution when made aware of the causes of their condition - a basic education as industrialisation grew?'

'Is that a rhetorical question?'

'You're a politician, you should know. Do you think it was an altruistic urge to help them 'fulfil' themselves through learning, through creativity? No, it was to help further profit for the owners of production by assisting the proles to understand their machines better, to read the instructions, to work out problems, to specialise.'

'Someone's been spitting in your mouth. I suspect you have a Dickensian view of class. It's not like that now.'

'No, it's relatively worse; a mere ten percent of the population owns ninety percent of the wealth of this country.'

'They say, if you're not a socialist at sixteen you have no heart, if you are one at forty you're a fool.'

'Better a fool than belonging to a rump of Conservative tubthumpers.'

'Rather a cliché. I've heard people in your mob described as freaks and uniques.'

'You sound as if you're practising for questions in the House. What did you do before you started thumping tubs then?'

'Merchant banking.'

'To quote Steinbeck: 'The bank is something else than man. It happens that every man in a bank hates what a man does. And yet the bank does it. The bank is something more than men. It's the monster.''

'And where would we be without it?'

They were silent for a short while, as if attempting to refresh their critical faculties. Jordan continued.

'Bet you'd love to do some damage to my party, eh?'

'Well, it would seem that I could easily do so.'

'In what way?'

'Why should I tell you?'

'Why not? Can't see how little old you could hurt it.'

'Let's say that I have certain documentation that could really embarrass it.'

'What does it say?'

'I'm obviously not telling you, but, again, let's say that there are people - who though they should be neutral obviously support the establishment, they are part of it - who've been interested in it for quite a while.'

'So, you're threatening to use some sort of past secret to hurt the enemy.'

'Well done.'

'Why don't people like you hone their ideology to help formulate realistic principles of governing and workable ideas and policies instead of bruising a government in power by using past secrets? You may be highly academicized, but you're undereducated.'

'How d'you know it's a 'past' secret?'

'You know what I mean, finding some sort of dodgy evidence for something, a conspiracy or whatever. Where is it, anyway? You sure you're not making this up?'

'What do you want to know for?'

The man paused. For Jordan, it was an almost transformative look that darkened his face.

'I remember now. You were talking to Edward at the meeting the day before my place was searched.'

'Searched?'

'You got him drunk didn't you. I remember. Was it you that told someone about me having incriminating stuff?'

'Don't know what you mean.'

'You've actually spoken to him.'

'Who?'

'My *friend*.' He was shouting now. He was at one of your meetings. He spoke. You've heard his voice. You could have been responsible for his death.'

'Responsible?'

'Yes; indirectly. If it wasn't for you, perhaps, I wouldn't have given him the damned thing. They probably searched his place. Nothing to do with you then?'

Jordan felt his shirt collar grabbed. He was instantly pulled closer to the man.

'My friend's dead. He's *dead*.'

As Jordan tried to push him away, the door of the hall opened and she was standing there.

'What are t you *doing?* You're grown men, aren't you? *Stop* it.'

Trying to look calm and unruffled as he pulled the man's fist away from his neck, Jordan turned his head towards her.

'Is this your latest paramour or is it just platonic?' He felt anger. 'You're like identical political twins living in some sort of ideological plasma.'

He was aware as he said it that it was churlish, the emotional charge behind it childlike.

He had to leave. He had never wanted so much to get away from a situation, a collection of circumstances that he couldn't really define. He walked quickly to his car. As he drove away into the beginning of a drizzly, windy night, he felt he was living in a hostile vacuum.

He didn't feel he'd got even with her, or gained any satisfaction from revenge. She wouldn't care anyway; why would she? As for Leftie man; he was in enough pain because of his friend's death. And projecting it onto him.

He felt that so much of himself that he couldn't even emotionally categorise seemed to have conjoined in a short, peculiarly volatile moment of time outside of an old Nissen hut in east London. It was a building, he felt, could have symbolised his own interior hollowness.

Jordan was alone in his flat, drinking. It had been three inconsequential, nothing-days since his encounter with his foe; another old-fashioned term he realised he'd used. He'd stopped bothering to think of Luke Kenyon. Let him do what he will. He had tried; at least he could say that, with both the man and the girl. He wouldn't again. He couldn't think of what he would try *for* any more.

He had gone into politics wanting enough power to affect people, to make decisions and, hopefully, help build policies that, maybe, improved their lot; mostly to earn, or to make more money. Why not? It was, fortunately, the world we lived in. What was the phrase he'd often used in his hustings speeches? 'Make a difference.' It wasn't going to happen.

Was it worth him continuing in the House? What would be his official reason if he dropped out? 'The secret services put pressure on me to infiltrate the Communist Party and recover evidence that would have highly embarrassed our party'? But if it came to it, he'd think of something convincing and acceptable.

There was little he would miss. He hadn't developed the evening drinking habit with his party colleagues, he'd said nothing in the Chamber after his maiden speech, he hadn't made any friends and he certainly wouldn't miss the surgeries. But, all his good intentions would then become… futile, nothing.

If he did resign, Weynard would be quite pleased, probably Luke Kenyon also; though he'd probably counted him out of having any significant meaning to anything now. He could go back to the firm, other than what he'd attempted this was all he had really known. But it now seemed rather narrow and insular. He hoped he could still see Archer and listen to his trenchant observations - he'd arranged to see him recently but had to let him down. 'Just like a politician, can't resist making promises you can't keep,' was his typical response.

And Henry; was he still going through his political menopause, had he now firmly settled into the fixed ideation of his never-to-be attained communistic world? Or, as Archer would have put it: 'Bogus, gestural politics born of desperation.'

Whatever, he wouldn't contact him again. He needed to get through this darkness, this long winter evening, and know that light wasn't far away. He would get beyond it. He would find something. There must be something for him. Wasn't there?

CHAPTER THIRTY THREE

Because his car was being serviced, Ralph had gone to the meeting that evening by Tube, where mobiles were being indulgently shouted into and the staccato sibilance of other tech devices formed a penetrative accompaniment. Perhaps a solipsistic social atomism was now the norm. Maybe a question for the students: 'Is the concept of deferred gratification dying?'

He wondered if she would be there. He thought it may be the trade unions anniversary celebration, he wasn't sure. Leaving the station, he began walking, looking around him reluctantly, unable to turn it into his habitual escapism of noting things like the sun hitting a slowly-turning chimney cowl, a darkened doorway at the end of an alley, or the squeak of a park swing as a laughing child deserted it for the next excitement.

He didn't want to arrive quite yet, didn't wish to spend his time having further commiserations laid upon him or for people to give him pitying looks or comforting arm-squeezes. He wished to be treated as a regular member who liked to chat with them about the party, political ideas, and to slag off 'Militant Unions Destroying The Country' headlines. He thought lightly that 'Sun readers' was almost an oxymoron. 'Military intelligence,' and 'Oldham Athletic' were others, perhaps.

He also didn't want her not to be there, and feeling rather tense because he'd be looking out for her most of the time. Realising he was in one of Wansford's conservation areas, he walked more purposely.

They were mostly Thirties chalet bungalows with long gardens, the streets laid out in grid fashion; an unusual and welcome place and so relatively near central London. The properties were well-kept, but he couldn't understand the choice of dark brown plastic windows on an increasing number of them; windows were there to let in light. There were other examples of Asianification: the gold-tipped railings, the inlaid silver designs in the glass doors and sashes. He knew his annoyance came from a dislike of another country's aesthetic supplanting his own, his purist streak further bruised by the knowledge that the council employee responsible for maintaining the original architectural integrity of the place knew as much about Art Deco as Ralph did about space travel.

An idea came that he should start visiting all the conservation areas in the borough and then, over time, those in the other London boroughs. He would, when he went to them, talk quietly to his departed friend, maybe a running, architectural commentary as he walked and looked. He would miss that touch on the back of his hand. He wouldn't feel it again. He must get used to the finality.

Once in the hut he saw Edward at the bar. Then her. He went over to her and kissed her lips, not thinking of what her reaction would be and, somehow, not really caring. He turned to Edward and asked if it was the union celebration this evening. Before he could answer, Ralph was aware of someone whispering into Claire's ear. She didn't seem to like it. The speaker, who seemed familiar, then turned towards him and asked if he could talk to him outside. Ralph followed him out, turning his head towards her and shrugging his shoulders questioningly.

He hadn't intended to argue with the man; he'd no idea what he wanted to speak to him about, but when, after a while, he was confronted with what he felt was almost an affirmation of his thoughts on the final cause of his friend's demise, he felt a rage run through him. He wanted to punish its perpetrator; smash him.

His fist was tightening on the man's collar when suddenly she was there. He reluctantly relaxed his grip as the man's hands tried to push him off. He couldn't quite remember what she'd said; something about them needing to grow up, and then the Wilde man shouting sarcastic innuendos at her before marching quickly across the road and disappearing into the deepening dusk.

They'd both stopped because, Ralph was disinterestedly aware later, the child's instant reflex action when hearing a woman shout, was fear and obeisance. She turned to Ralph, saying nothing. He couldn't interpret the look, but it would seem that she knew the departing man. He asked her if she did. Then realised she'd mentioned the name before.

'Yes. A little.'

'How little?'

'Just that. What's going on?' she asked quietly.

'I could well ask *you* that. How well do you know him?' Okay, I've got no right to ask, but I am.'

She was silent

'Fancy him do you? He's your class isn't he, a man who probably denies it exists, but you've fallen for it. Was he to be a kind of intellectual conquest? Turn him around to your, our, way of thinking? Mould him; batter him into seeing things as they are? Been mother have you; feeding him healthy, nourishing ideals, the utopia stuff? 'There, there Jordy, you're quite the little Marxist now aren't you. There, good boy. ''

'Stop it,' she shouted again. 'You've got it so wrong.' She paused. 'I've seen him a few times. Seen him; talked with him. That's it. He can be interesting company and he's not an unattractive man, but - '

'That's a double negative.'

'Again, stop it. Sometimes you're all... words, you - '

'No, There's more than that.'

'Let it out then. Show it.'

He grabbed hold of her upper arms, pulled her hard towards him and kissed her, even harder. He held her there then slowly eased her away.

'Should I apologise?'

'No. Don't.' She took a deep breath. 'What was it really about?'

'Let's go somewhere. I'll explain.'

She went back in to get her jacket.

He looked at the silver birch near the hut entrance lit from the naked bulb above the door and willed her to return quickly. It had begun to rain.

She came back to him.

'Let's go to mine,' he said. 'I'll explain there. I don't have the car I'm afraid.'

'For a change, I have mine.'

They didn't speak until they were in his flat. She took off her jacket and sat on the settee. He pulled a chair across and, facing her, attempted to explain, to justify the incident with the politician; mentioning Kenyon and who he worked for, the construction site, the police, the search, or searches, and what he suspected was Wilde's part in it, particularly regarding Paul.

She listened with a questioning frown throughout, and was silent for a while afterwards before responding.

'I won't ask you if you regret giving it to your friend. Sorry, I'm being cruel aren't I.'

'Whether I gave it to him or not is irrelevant, if these people thought I had, it's purely a function of them. I want to show you something.'

He beckoned to a door at the end of the large living room. She walked towards it. He reached over her shoulder and pushed it open. It was the bedroom. He pointed to the wall beside the bed. It had Klimt-like figures painted across the whole area: two women at opposite ends of what looked like a large bed, a man who could have been a satyr, and stylised shapes of stars and leaves surrounding them.

'Not sure whether I like it even now. But it's there and it's staying.'

'I like it,' she said, and walked further into the room.

'You paint it?'

'Yes.'

He turned gently towards her and firmly held her shoulders.

'Look, what about letting *your*self go, eh?'

She did. They both did. They made love; came together, coalesced in a way that Ralph had never experienced before and, in between it all, laughed; they seemed to laugh throughout the night. He was surprised; and pleased, that she was almost laddish in her humour; gone the sarcasm, the sharpness, in their place, coarseness, the risqué, belly laughs.

As dawn started to break, neither of them having slept, she said with a smile that she would be walking around her office like a cowboy at the end of a long ride. For a second it was hard to believe the woman he had known - however little of her that was - had said it.

'You did say you'd come back here, but I never thought it would be like this.'

'Neither did I,' she said.

They hen slept.

When he awoke she was sitting, half-dressed, on the end of the bed watching him. She seemed to fill the room.

'There's something I should tell you.'

He rubbed his eyes.

'They want me to manage an office in Africa.'

'They?'

'The charity. They need me to head up a section. There are a few people coming with me, some locals will make up the rest.'

He was awake now, but not quite comprehending.

'You've said yes?'

'I have.'

He still couldn't quite understand. Didn't want to.

'Africa?'

'Yes, Gambia; Serekunda, it's the second largest city. It's possibly the poorest country in the continent. Forty percent live in poverty.'

'You're definitely going?'

'Guess so.'

'What about the flat?'

'Doesn't matter, I've been waiting for an opportunity like this for some while.'

'How long are you going for?'

'Don't know. At least six months, maybe a year.'

He tried to dilute what she'd said by asking her pragmatic questions, as if she was someone he'd just met.

'What sort of living conditions will you have? What's the climate like?'

'Tropical. There's a long rainy season. Hot and wet.'

'Do they speak English?

'Yes, there are ten languages spoken there I think, but English is the official one, though not for much longer, its increasingly seen as a relic of empire, apparently.'

She paused, took a breath. 'Do you really think that this intelligence agency stuff is still going on and they'll continue watching you, ramp it up till they find what they want? I can see why it's important to both them and the government, but they're not going to come all the way out there to find it are they.'

'What d'you mean? Out where?'

He wasn't quite sure what was being said.

'Couldn't you come with me? You'd fit in. You could teach. Alright, so you probably won't get the stimulus you seem to get now, but you could do such a lot.'

She moved nearer to him and gently kissed his mouth. 'You could change things, Ralph. You teach a lot of Africans here; let the mountain come to Mohammed this time.'

It felt odd when she used his name. It was, possibly, only the second time she had. He felt affection from her and yet, hearing it somehow separated her from him. As if she was a stranger.

He glanced into his brain for facts about Africa: The second most populous continent and, at over eleven million square miles, covering six percent of the world's total surface area. A Joseph Conrad line trailed behind it. 'A certain enormous buck nigger fixed my conception of blind, furious, unreasoning rage, as manifested in the human animal to the end of my days. Of the nigger I used to dream for years afterwards.'

He could have used this with his students, could have discussed the racism, white supremacy, the context, the time in which it was written, perhaps the author's seeming fascination with darkness.

'I shall talk to you soon.'

She was getting dressed. He couldn't seem to speak.

She finished quickly and came back to him. She kissed him on the lips as he lay there then went to the door.

'I will see you.'

The room was empty once more, though it had never felt as empty as this. He lay there, not having the energy to raise himself.

Maybe she was right about Kenyon's employers; they wouldn't go all that way for him. But they could certainly keep tabs on him here. If he left he would be safe, and be with her.

But his students. What he did with them was an identity for him, a sometimes frustrating one, perhaps a not-very-honest one, for in essence he was using them to satisfy a need for constant intellectual stimulus - which, in turn, was, maybe, to help him run away from himself, and if that was what he'd been doing he had done it pretty successfully so far.

And there they were, year after academic year, in front of him, with him. He needed them. And if the intelligence agencies wanted him and felt the urge to break down his classroom door, then let them.

He got up and began making breakfast. There were Paul's ashes to scatter. He knew exactly where he would do it, and the precise tree under which they would lie. As he was eating he thought of Frank. He wondered what he would have made of his decision.

Would he have been pleased that he was going to stick with his pupils, help them to step back and look, analyse, to question everything. Perhaps he would have been more pleased if he took a leap in the dark and tried to help the poor and deprived in another continent and, maybe more subtly than he usually did, spread the party word.

Maybe, Ralph thought with a shaft of guilt, he would, looking at him with those keen eyes, have spotted his fear. He didn't really question why the opinion of a long-dead man he'd hardly known, mattered or, more significantly, what he represented. No. First, he must open his wardrobe, reach down for a ceramic urn, wrap it and catch a train.

www.ingramcontent.com/pod-product-compliance
Lightning Source LLC
Chambersburg PA
CBHW070215030726

47505CB00006B/1694

* 9 7 8 1 9 1 3 1 4 4 0 5 0 *